THE
YELLOW FAIRY
BOOK

COMPLETE AND UNABRIDGED

EDITED BY ANDREW LANG

ILLUSTRATIONS BY HENRY J. FORD

FOR YOUNG READERS

First published in 1894 by Longmans, Green, and Co.

First Racehorse for Young Readers Edition 2020.

All rights to any and all materials in copyright owned by the publisher are strictly reserved by the publisher.

Racehorse for Young Readers books may be purchased in bulk at special discounts for sales promotion, corporate gifts, fund-raising, or educational purposes. Special editions can also be created to specifications. For details, contact the Special Sales Department, Skyhorse Publishing, 307 West 36th Street, 11th Floor, New York, NY 10018 or info@ skyhorsepublishing.com.

Racehorse for Young Readers™ is a pending trademark of Skyhorse Publishing, Inc.®, a Delaware corporation.

Visit our website at www.skyhorsepublishing.com.

10 9 8 7 6 5 4 3 2 1

Library of Congress Control Number: 2019948683

Print ISBN: 978-1-63158-565-4
Ebook ISBN: 978-1-63158-566-1

Cover series design by Michael Short
Interior artwork by Henry J. Ford

Printed in China

DEDICATION
TO JOAN, TODDLES, AND TINY

Books Yellow, Red, and Green and Blue,
All true, or just as good as true,
And here's the Yellow Book for you!

Hard is the path from A to Zed,
And puzzling to a curly head,
Yet leads to Books—Green, Blue, and Red.

For every child should understand
That letters from the first were planned
To guide us into Fairy Land.

So labour at your Alphabet,
For by that learning shall you get
To lands where Fairies may be met.

And going where this pathway goes,
You too, at last, may find, who knows?
The Garden of the Singing Rose.

THE SWINEHERD TAKES THE TEN KISSES

IV

CONTENTS

PREFACE

HE Editor thinks that children will readily
forgive him for publishing another Fairy Book. We have had
the Blue, the Red, the Green, and here is the Yellow. If children
are pleased, and they are so kind as to say that they *are* pleased,
the Editor does not care very much for what other people may say. Now, there
is one gentleman who seems to think that it is not quite right to print so many
fairy tales, with pictures, and to publish them in red and blue covers. He is
named Mr. G. Laurence Gomme, and he is president of a learned body called
the Folklore Society. Once a year he makes his address to his subjects, of
whom the Editor is one, and Mr. Joseph Jacobs (who has published many delightful fairy tales with pretty pictures)[1] is another. Fancy, then, the dismay of
Mr. Jacobs, and of the Editor, when they heard their president say that he did
not think it very nice in them to publish fairy books, above all, red, green, and
blue fairy books! They said that they did not see any harm in it, and they were

---

1   You may buy them from Mr. Nutt, in the Strand.

ready to "put themselves on their country," and be tried by a jury of children. And, indeed, they still see no harm in what they have done; nay, like Father William in the poem, they are ready "to do it again and again."

Where is the harm? The truth is that the Folklore Society—made up of the most clever, learned, and beautiful men and women of the country—is fond of studying the history and geography of Fairy Land. This is contained in very old tales, such as country people.

These people are thought to know most about Fairy Land and its inhabitants. But, in the Yellow Fairy Book, and the rest, are many tales by persons who are neither savages nor rustics, such as Madame D'Aulnoy and Herr Hans Christian Andersen. The Folk lore Society, or its president, say that *their* tales are not so true as the rest, and should not be published with the rest. But *we* say that all the stories which are pleasant to read are quite true enough for us; so here they are, with pictures by Mr. Ford, and we do not think that either the pictures or the stories are likely to mislead children.

As to whether there are really any fairies or not, that is a difficult question. Professor Huxley thinks there are none. The Editor never saw any himself, but he knows several people who have seen them—in the Highlands—and heard their music. If ever you are in Nether Lochaber, go to the Fairy Hill, and you may hear the music yourself, as grown-up people have done, but you must go on a fine day. Again, if there are really no fairies, why do people believe in them, all over the world? The ancient Greeks believed, so did the old Egyptians, and the Hindus, and the Indians, and is it likely, if there are no fairies, that so many different peoples would have seen and heard them? The Rev. Mr. Baring-Gould saw several fairies when he was a boy, and was travelling in the land of the Troubadours. For these reasons, the Editor thinks that there are certainly fairies, but they never do anyone any harm; and, in England, they have been frightened away by smoke and schoolmasters. As to Giants, they have died out, but real Dwarfs are common in the forests of Africa. Probably a good many stories not perfectly true have been told about fairies, but such stories have also been told about Napoleon, Claverhouse, Julius Caesar, and Joan of Arc, all of whom certainly existed. A wise child will, therefore, remember that, if he grows up and becomes a member of the Folk lore Society, *all* the tales in this book were not offered to him as absolutely truthful, but were printed merely for his entertainment. The exact facts he can learn later, or he can leave them alone.

There are Russian, German, French, Icelandic, American Indian, and other stories here. They were translated by Miss Cheape, Miss Alma, and Miss Thyra Alleyne, Miss Sellar, Mr. Craigie (he did the Icelandic tales), Miss Blackley, Mrs. Dent, and Mrs. Lang, but the American Indian stories are copied from English versions published by the Smithsonian Bureau of Ethnology, in America. Mr. Ford did the pictures, and it is hoped that children will find the book not less pleasing than those which have already been submitted to their consideration. The Editor cannot say "good-bye" without advising them, as they pursue their studies, to read *The Rose and the Ring,* by the late Mr. Thackeray, with pictures by the author. This book he thinks quite indispensable in every child's library, and parents should be urged to purchase it at the first opportunity, as without it no education is complete.

—A. LANG.

THE CAT AND THE MOUSE
IN PARTNERSHIP

CAT HAD MADE ACQUAINTANCE WITH A MOUSE, AND HAD spoken so much of the great love and friendship she felt for her, that at last the Mouse consented to live in the same house with her, and to share in the housekeeping. "But we must provide for the winter or else we shall suffer hunger," said the Cat. "You, little Mouse, cannot venture everywhere in case you run at last into a trap." This good counsel was followed, and a little pot of fat was bought. But they did not know where to put it. At length, after long consultation, the Cat said, "I know of no place where it could be better put than in the church. No one will trouble to take it away from there. We will hide it in a corner, and we won't touch it till we are in want." So the little pot was placed in safety; but it was not long before the Cat had a great longing for it, and said to the Mouse, "I wanted to tell you, little Mouse, that my cousin has a little son, white with brown spots, and she wants me to be godmother to it. Let me go out to-day, and you can take care of the house alone."

"Yes, go certainly," replied the Mouse, "and when you eat anything good, think of me; I should very much like a drop of the red christening wine."

But it was all untrue. The Cat had no cousin, and had not been asked to be godmother. She went straight to the church, slunk to the little pot of fat, began to lick it, and licked the top off. Then she took a walk on the roofs of the town, looked at the view, stretched herself out in the sun, and licked her lips whenever she thought of the little pot of fat. As soon as it was evening, she went home again.

"Ah, here you are again!" said the Mouse; "you must certainly have had an enjoyable day."

"It went off very well," answered the Cat.

"What was the child's name?" asked the Mouse.

"Top Off," said the Cat drily.

"Topoff!" echoed the Mouse, "it is indeed a wonderful and curious name. Is it in your family?"

"What is odd about it?" said the Cat. "It is not worse than Breadthief, as your godchild is called."

Not long after this another great longing came over the Cat. She said to the Mouse, "You must again be kind enough to look after the house alone, for

I have been asked a second time to stand godmother, and as this child has a white ring round its neck, I cannot refuse."

The kind Mouse agreed, but the Cat slunk under the town wall to the church, and ate up half of the pot of fat. "Nothing tastes better," said she, "than what one eats by oneself," and she was very much pleased with her day's work. When she came home the Mouse asked, "What was this child called?"

"Half Gone," answered the Cat.

"Halfgone! what a name! I have never heard it in my life. I don't believe it is in the calendar."

Soon the Cat's mouth began to water once more after her licking business. "All good things in threes," she said to the Mouse; "I have again to stand god-mother. The child is quite black, and has very white paws, but not a single white hair on its body. This only happens once in two years, so you will let me go out?"

"Topoff! Halfgone!" repeated the Mouse, "they are such curious names; they make me very thoughtful."

"Oh, you sit at home in your dark grey coat and your long tail," said the Cat, "and you get fanciful. That comes of not going out in the day."

The Mouse had a good cleaning out while the Cat was gone, and made the house tidy; but the greedy Cat ate the fat every bit up. "When it is all gone one can be at rest," she said to herself, and at night she came home sleek and satisfied. The Mouse asked at once after the third child's name.

"It won't please you any better," said the Cat, "he was called Clean Gone."

"Cleangone!" repeated the Mouse. "I do not believe that name has been printed any more than the others. Cleangone! What can it mean?" She shook her head, curled herself up, and went to sleep.

From this time on no one asked the Cat to stand godmother; but when the winter came and there was nothing to be got outside, the Mouse remembered their provision and said, "Come, Cat, we will go to our pot of fat which we have stored away; it will taste very good."

"Yes, indeed," answered the Cat; "it will taste as good to you as if you stretched your thin tongue out of the window."

They started off, and when they reached it they found the pot in its place, but quite empty!

"Ah," said the Mouse, "now I know what has happened! It has all come out! You are a true friend to me! You have eaten it all when you stood god-mother; first the top off, then half of it gone, then—"

"Will you be quiet!" screamed the Cat. "Another word and I will eat you up."

"Cleangone" was already on the poor Mouse's tongue, and scarcely was it out than the Cat made a spring at her, seized and swallowed her.

You see, that is the way of the world.

THE SIX SWANS

 KING WAS ONCE HUNTING IN A GREAT WOOD, AND HE hunted the game so eagerly that none of his courtiers could follow him. When evening came on he stood still and looked round him, and he saw that he had quite lost himself. He sought a way out, but could find none. Then he saw an old woman with a shaking head coming toward him; but she was a witch.

"Good woman," he said to her, "can you not show me the way out of the wood?"

"Oh, certainly, Sir King," she replied, "I can quite well do that, but on one condition, which if you do not fulfil you will never get out of the wood, and will die of hunger."

"What is the condition?" asked the King.

"I have a daughter," said the old woman, "who is so beautiful that she has not her equal in the world, and is well fitted to be your wife; if you will make her Queen I will show you the way out of the wood."

The King in his anguish of mind consented, and the old woman led him to her little house where her daughter was sitting by the fire. She received the King as if she were expecting him, and he saw that she was certainly very beautiful; but she did not please him, and he could not look at her without a secret feeling of horror. As soon as he had lifted the maiden on to his horse the old woman showed him the way, and the King reached his palace, where the wedding was celebrated.

The King had already been married once, and had by his first wife seven children, six boys and one girl, whom he loved more than anything in the world. And now, because he was afraid that their step-mother might not treat them well and might do them harm, he put them in a lonely castle that stood in the middle of a wood. It lay so hidden, and the way to it was so hard to find, that he himself could not have found it out had not a wise-woman given him a reel of thread which possessed a marvellous property: when he threw it before him it unwound itself and showed him the way. But the King went so often to his dear children that the Queen was offended at his absence. She grew curious, and wanted to know what he had to do quite alone in the wood. She gave his servants a great deal of money, and they betrayed the secret to her, and also told her of the reel which alone could point out the way. She had no rest now till she had found out where the King guarded the reel, and then she made some little white shirts, and, as she had learnt from her witch-mother, sewed an enchantment in each of them.

And when the King had ridden off she took the little shirts and went into the wood, and the reel showed her the way. The children, who saw someone coming in the distance, thought it was their dear father coming to them, and sprang to meet him very joyfully. Then she threw over each one a little shirt, which when it had touched their bodies changed them into swans, and they flew away over the forest. The Queen went home quite satisfied, and thought she had got rid of her step-children; but the girl had not run to meet her with her brothers, and she knew nothing of her.

The next day the King came to visit his children, but he found no one but the girl.

"Where are your brothers?" asked the King.

"Alas! dear father," she answered, "they have gone away and left me all alone." And she told him that looking out of her little window she had seen her brothers flying over the wood in the shape of swans, and she showed him the feathers which they had let fall in the yard, and which she had collected. The King mourned, but he did not think that the Queen had done the wicked deed, and as he was afraid the maiden would also be taken from him, he wanted to take her with him. But she was afraid of the step-mother, and begged the King to let her stay just one night more in the castle in the wood. The poor maiden thought, "My home is no longer here; I will go and seek my brothers." And when night came she fled away into the forest. She ran all through the night and the next day, till she could go no farther for weariness. Then she saw a little hut, went in, and found a room with six little beds. She was afraid to lie down on one, so she crept under one of them, lay on the hard floor, and was going to spend the night there. But when the sun had set she heard a noise, and saw six swans flying in at the window. They stood on the floor and blew at one another, and blew all their feathers off, and their swan skin came off like a shirt. Then the maiden recognised her brothers, and overjoyed she crept out from under the bed. Her brothers were not less delighted than she to see their little sister again, but their joy did not last long.

"You cannot stay here," they said to her. "This is a den of robbers; if they were to come here and find you they would kill you."

"Could you not protect me?" asked the little sister.

"No," they answered, "for we can only lay aside our swan skins for a quarter of an hour every evening. For this time we regain our human forms, but then we are changed into swans again."

Then the little sister cried and said, "Can you not be freed?"

"Oh, no," they said, "the conditions are too hard. You must not speak or laugh for six years, and must make in that time six shirts for us out of star-flowers. If a single word comes out of your mouth, all your labour is vain." And when the brothers had said this the quarter of an hour came to an end, and they flew away out of the window as swans.

But the maiden had determined to free her brothers even if it should cost her her life. She left the hut, went into the forest, climbed a tree, and spent the night there. The next morning she went out, collected star-flowers, and began to sew. She could speak to no one, and she had no wish to laugh, so she sat there, looking only at her work.

When she had lived there some time, it happened that the King of the country was hunting in the forest, and his

"AND THEN HER DRESS"

hunters came to the tree on which the maiden sat. They called to her and said "Who are you?"

But she gave no answer.

"Come down to us," they said. "We will do you no harm."

But she shook her head silently. As they pressed her further with questions, she threw them the golden chain from her neck. But they did not leave off, and she threw them her girdle, and when this was no use, her garters, and then her dress. The hunts-men would not leave her alone, but climbed the tree, lifted the maiden down, and led her to the King. The King asked, "Who are you? What are you doing up that tree?"

But she answered nothing.

He asked her in all the languages he knew, but she remained as dumb as a fish. Because she was so beautiful, however, the King's heart was touched, and he was seized with a great love for her. He wrapped her up in his cloak, placed her before him on his horse, and brought her to his castle. There he had her dressed in rich clothes, and her beauty shone out as bright as day, but not a word could be drawn from her. He set her at table by his side, and her modest ways and behaviour pleased him so much that he said, "I will marry this maiden and none other in the world," and after some days he married her. But the King had a wicked mother who was displeased with the marriage, and said wicked things of the young Queen. "Who knows who this girl is?" she said; "she cannot speak, and is not worthy of a king."

After a year, when the Queen had her first child, the old mother took it away from her. Then she went to the King and said that the Queen had killed it. The King would not believe it, and would not allow any harm to be done her. But she sat quietly sewing at the shirts and troubling herself about nothing. The next time she had a child, the wicked mother did the same thing, but the King could not make up his mind to believe her. He said, "She is too sweet and good to do such a thing as that. If she were not dumb and could defend

The Six Brothers Changed Into Swans By Their Stepmother.

herself, her innocence would be proved." But when the third child was taken away, and the Queen was again accused, and could not utter a word in her own defence, the King was obliged to give her over to the law, which decreed that she must be burnt to death. When the day came on which the sentence was to be executed, it was the last day of the six years in which she must not speak or laugh, and now she had freed her dear brothers from the power of the enchantment. The six shirts were done; there was only the left sleeve missing from the last shirt.

When she was led to the stake, she laid the shirts on her arm, and as she stood on the pile and the fire was about to be lighted, she looked around her and saw six swans flying through the air. Then she knew that her release was at hand and her heart danced for joy. The swans fluttered round her, and hovered low so that she could throw the shirts over them. When they had touched them the swan skins fell off, and her brothers stood before her living, well, and beautiful. Only the youngest had a swan's wing instead of his left arm. They embraced and kissed each other, and the Queen went to the King, who was standing by in great astonishment, and began to speak to him, saying, "Dearest husband, now I can speak and tell you openly that I am innocent and have been falsely accused."

She told him of the old woman's deceit, and how she had taken the three children away and hidden them. Then they were fetched, to the great joy of the King, and the wicked mother came to no good end.

But the King and the Queen with their six brothers lived many years in happiness and peace.

THE DRAGON OF THE NORTH[2]

ERY LONG AGO, AS OLD PEOPLE HAVE TOLD ME, THERE lived a terrible monster, who came out of the North, and laid waste whole tracts of country, devouring both men and beasts; and this monster was so destructive that it was feared that unless help came no living creature would be left on the face of the earth. It had a body like an ox, and legs like a frog, two short fore-legs, and two long ones behind, and besides that it had a tail like a serpent, ten fathoms in length. When it moved it jumped like a frog, and with every spring it covered half a mile of ground. Fortunately, its habit was to remain for several years in the same place, and not to move on till the whole neighbourhood was eaten up. Nothing could hunt it, because its whole body was covered with scales, which were harder than stone or metal; its two great eyes shone by night, and even by day, like

---

2   'Der Norlands Drache,' from *Esthnische Mährchen*. Kreutzwald.

the brightest lamps, and anyone who had the ill luck to look into those eyes became bewitched, and was obliged to rush of his own accord into the monster's jaws. In this way, the Dragon was able to feed upon both men and beasts without the least trouble to itself, as it needed not to move from the spot where it was lying. All the neighbouring kings had offered rich rewards to anyone who should be able to destroy the monster, either by force or enchantment, and many had tried their luck, but all had miserably failed. Once, a great forest in which the Dragon lay had been set on fire; the forest was burnt down, but the fire did not do the monster the least harm. However, there was a tradition amongst the wise men of the country that the Dragon might be overcome by one who possessed King Solomon's signet ring, upon which a secret writing was engraved. This inscription would enable anyone who was wise enough to interpret it to find out how the Dragon could be destroyed. Only, no one knew where the ring was hidden, nor was there any sorcerer or learned man to be found who would be able to explain the inscription.

At last a young man, with a good heart and plenty of courage, set out to search for the ring. He took his way toward the rising sun, because he knew that all the wisdom of old time comes from the East. After some years he met with a famous Eastern magician, and asked for his advice in the matter. The magician answered:

"Mortal men have but little wisdom, and can give you no help, but the birds of the air would be better guides to you if you could learn their language. I can help you to understand it if you will stay with me a few days."

The youth thankfully accepted the magician's offer, and said, "I cannot now offer you any reward for your kindness, but should my undertaking succeed your trouble shall be richly repaid."

Then the magician brewed a powerful potion out of nine sorts of herbs which he had gathered himself all alone by moonlight, and he gave the youth nine spoonfuls of it daily for three days, which made him able to understand the language of birds.

Upon parting the magician said to him, "If you ever find Solomon's ring and get possession of it, then come back to me, that I may explain the inscription on the ring to you, for there is no one else in the world who can do this."

From that time the youth never felt lonely as he walked along; he always had company, because he understood the language of birds; and in this way he learned many things which mere human knowledge could never have taught him. But time went on, and he heard nothing about the ring. It happened one evening, when he was hot and tired with walking, and had sat down under a tree in a forest to eat his supper, that he saw two gaily plumaged birds, that were strange to him, sitting at the top of the tree talking to one another about him. The first bird said:

"I know that wandering fool under the tree there, who has come so far without finding what he seeks. He is trying to find King Solomon's lost ring."

The other bird answered, "He will have to seek help from the *Witch-maiden*,[3] who will doubtless be able to put him on the right track. If she has not got the ring herself, she knows well enough who has it."

"But where is he to find the Witch-maiden?" said the first bird. "She has no settled dwelling, but is here to-day and gone to-morrow. He might as well try to catch the wind."

The other replied, "I do not know, certainly, where she is at present, but in three nights from now she will come to the spring to wash her face, as she does every month when the moon is full, in order that she may never grow old nor wrinkled, but may always keep the bloom of youth."

"Well," said the first bird, "the spring is not far from here. Shall we go and see how it is she does it?"

"Willingly, if you like," said the other.

The youth immediately resolved to follow the birds to the spring, only two

---

3   Höllenmädchen.

things made him uneasy: first, lest he might be asleep when the birds went, and secondly, lest he might lose sight of them, since he had not wings to carry him along so swiftly. He was too tired to keep awake all night, yet his anxiety prevented him from sleeping soundly, and when with the earliest dawn he looked up to the tree-top, he was glad to see his feathered companions still asleep with their heads under their wings. He ate his breakfast, and waited until the birds should start, but they did not leave the place all day. They hopped about from one tree to another looking for food, all day long until the evening, when they went back to their old perch to sleep. The next day the same thing happened, but on the third morning one bird said to the other, "To-day we must go to the spring to see the Witch-maiden wash her face." They remained on the tree till noon; then they flew away and went toward the south. The young man's heart beat with anxiety lest he should lose sight of his guides, but he managed to keep the birds in view until they again perched upon a tree. The young man ran after them until he was quite exhausted and out of breath, and after three short rests the birds at length reached a small open space in the forest, on the edge of which they placed themselves on the top of a high tree. When the youth had overtaken them, he saw that there was a clear spring in the middle of the space. He sat down at the foot of the tree upon which the birds were perched, and listened attentively to what they were saying to each other.

"The sun is not down yet," said the first bird; "we must wait yet awhile till the moon rises and the maiden comes to the spring. Do you think she will see that young man sitting under the tree?"

"Nothing is likely to escape her eyes, certainly not a young man," said the other bird. "Will the youth have the sense not to let himself be caught in her toils?"

"We will wait," said the first bird, "and see how they get on together."

The evening light had quite faded, and the full moon was already shining down upon the forest, when the young man heard a slight rustling sound.

After a few moments there came out of the forest a maiden, gliding over the grass so lightly that her feet seemed scarcely to touch the ground, and stood beside the spring. The youth could not turn away his eyes from the maiden, for he had never in his life seen a woman so beautiful. Without seeming to notice anything, she went to the spring, looked up to the full moon, then knelt down and bathed her face nine times, then looked up to the moon again and walked nine times round the well, and as she walked she sang this song:

> *"Full-faced moon with light unshaded,*
> *Let my beauty ne'er be faded.*
> *Never let my cheek grow pale!*
> *While the moon is waning nightly,*
> *May the maiden bloom more brightly,*
> *May her freshness never fail!"*

Then she dried her face with her long hair, and was about to go away, when her eye suddenly fell upon the spot where the young man was sitting, and she turned toward the tree. The youth rose and stood waiting. Then the maiden said, "You ought to have a heavy punishment because you have presumed to watch my secret doings in the moonlight. But I will forgive you this time, because you are a stranger and knew no better. But you must tell me truly who you are and how you came to this place, where no mortal has ever set foot before."

The youth answered humbly: "Forgive me, beautiful maiden, if I have unintentionally offended you. I chanced to come here after long wandering, and found a good place to sleep under this tree. At your coming I did not know what to do, but stayed where I was, because I thought my silent watching could not offend you."

The maiden answered kindly, "Come and spend this night with us. You will sleep better on a pillow than on damp moss."

THE WITCH-MAIDEN SEES THE YOUNG MAN UNDER A TREE

The youth hesitated for a little, but presently he heard the birds saying from the top of the tree, "Go where she calls you, but take care to give no blood, or you will sell your soul." So the youth went with her, and soon they reached a beautiful garden, where stood a splendid house, which glittered in the moonlight as if it was all built out of gold and silver. When the youth entered he found many splendid chambers, each one finer than the last. Hundreds of tapers burnt upon golden candlesticks, and shed a light like the brightest day. At length they reached a chamber where a table was spread with the most costly dishes. At the table were placed two chairs, one of silver, the other of gold. The maiden seated herself upon the golden chair, and offered the silver one to her companion. They were served by maidens dressed in white, whose feet made no sound as they moved about, and not a word was spoken during the meal. Afterward, the youth and the Witch-maiden conversed pleasantly together, until a woman, dressed in red, came in to remind them that it was bedtime. The youth was now shown into another room, containing a silken bed with down cushions, where he slept delightfully, yet he seemed to hear a voice near his bed which repeated to him, "Remember to give no blood!"

The next morning the maiden asked him whether he would not like to stay with her always in this beautiful place, and as he did not answer immediately, she continued: "You see how I always remain young and beautiful, and I am under no one's orders, but can do just what I like, so that I have never thought of marrying before. But from the moment I saw you I took a fancy to you, so if you agree, we might be married and might live together like princes, because I have great riches."

The youth could not help but be tempted with the beautiful maiden's offer, but he remembered how the birds had called her the witch, and their warning always sounded in his ears. Therefore he answered cautiously, "Do not be angry, dear maiden, if I do not decide immediately on this important matter. Give me a few days to consider before we come to an understanding."

"Why not?" answered the maiden. "Take some weeks to consider if you like, and take counsel with your own heart." And to make the time pass pleasantly, she took the youth over every part of her beautiful dwelling, and showed him all her splendid treasures. But these treasures were all produced by enchantment, for the maiden could make anything she wished appear by the help of King Solomon's signet ring; only none of these things remained fixed; they passed away like the wind without leaving a trace behind. But the youth did not know this; he thought they were all real.

One day the maiden took him into a secret chamber, where a little gold box was standing on a silver table. Pointing to the box, she said, "Here is my greatest treasure, whose like is not to be found in the whole world. It is a precious gold ring. When you marry me, I will give you this ring as a marriage gift, and it will make you the happiest of mortal men. But in order that our love may last forever, you must give me for the ring three drops of blood from the little finger of your left hand."

When the youth heard these words a cold shudder ran over him, for he remembered that his soul was at stake. He was cunning enough, however, to conceal his feelings and to make no direct answer, but he only asked the maiden, as if carelessly, what was remarkable about the ring?

She answered, "No mortal is able entirely to understand the power of this ring, because no one thoroughly understands the secret signs engraved upon it. But even with my half-knowledge I can work great wonders. If I put the ring upon the little finger of my left hand, then I can fly like a bird through the air wherever I wish to go. If I put it on the third finger of my left hand I am invisible, and I can see everything that passes around me, though no one can see me. If I put the ring upon the middle finger of my left hand, then neither fire nor water nor any sharp weapon can hurt me. If I put it on the forefinger of my left hand, then I can with its help produce whatever I wish. I can in a single moment build houses or anything I desire. Finally, as long as I wear the ring on the thumb of my left hand, that hand is so strong that it can break down rocks and walls. Besides these, the ring has other secret signs which, as I said, no one can understand. No doubt it contains secrets of great importance. The ring formerly belonged to King Solomon, the wisest of kings, during whose reign the wisest men lived. But it is not known whether this ring was ever made by mortal hands: it is supposed that an angel gave it to the wise King."

When the youth heard all this he determined to try and get possession of the ring, though he did not quite believe in all its wonderful gifts. He wished the maiden would let him have it in his hand, but he did dare to ask her to do so, and after a while she put it back into the box. A few days after they were again speaking of the magic ring, and the youth said, "I do not think it possible that the ring can have all the power you say it has."

Then the maiden opened the box and took the ring out, and it glittered as she held it like the clearest sunbeam. She put it on the middle finger of her left hand, and told the youth to take a knife and try as hard as he could to cut her with it, for he would not be able to hurt her. He was unwilling at first, but the maiden insisted. Then he tried, at first only in play, and then seriously, to strike her with the knife, but an invisible wall of iron seemed to be between them, and the maiden stood before him laughing and unhurt. Then she put the ring on her third finger, and in an instant she had vanished from his eyes. Presently she was beside him again laughing, and holding the ring between her fingers.

"Do let me try," said the youth, "whether I can do these wonderful things."

The maiden, suspecting no treachery, gave him the magic ring.

The youth pretended to have forgotten what to do, and asked what finger he must put the ring on so that no sharp weapon could hurt him?

"Oh, the middle finger of your left hand," the maiden answered, laughing.

She took the knife and tried to strike the youth, and he even tried to cut himself with it, but found it impossible. Then he asked the maiden to show him how to split stones and rocks with the help of the ring. So she led him into a courtyard where stood a great boulder. "Now," she said, "put the ring upon the thumb of your left hand, and you will see how strong that hand has become. The youth did so, and found to his astonishment that with a single blow of his fist the stone flew into a thousand pieces. Then the youth bethought him that he who does not use his luck when he has it is a fool, and that this was a chance which once lost might never return. So while they stood laughing at the shattered stone he placed the ring, as if in play, upon the third finger of his left hand.

"Now," said the maiden, "you are invisible to me until you take the ring off again."

But the youth had no mind to do that; on the contrary, he went farther off, then put the ring on the little finger of his left hand, and soared into the air like a bird.

When the maiden saw him flying away she thought at first that he was still in play, and cried, "Come back, friend, for now you see I have told you the truth." But the young man never came back.

Then the maiden saw she was deceived, and bitterly repented that she had ever trusted him with the ring.

The young man never halted in his flight until he reached the dwelling of the wise magician who had taught him the speech of birds. The magician was delighted to find that his search had been successful, and at once set to work to interpret the secret signs engraved upon the ring, but it took him seven weeks to make them out clearly. Then he gave the youth the following instructions how to overcome the Dragon of the North: "You must have an iron horse cast, which must have little wheels under each foot. You must also be armed with a spear two fathoms long, which you will be able to wield by means of the magic ring upon your left thumb. The spear must be as thick in the middle as a large tree, and both its ends must be sharp. In the middle of the spear you must have two strong chains ten fathoms in length. As soon as the Dragon has made himself fast to the spear, which you must thrust through his jaws, you must spring quickly from the iron horse and fasten the ends of the chains firmly to the ground with iron stakes, so that he cannot get away from them. After two or three days the monster's strength will be so far exhausted that you will be able to come near him. Then you can put Solomon's ring upon your left thumb and give him the finishing stroke, but keep the ring on your third finger until you have come close to him, so that the monster cannot see you, else he might strike you dead with his long tail. But when all is done, take care you do not lose the ring, and that no one takes it from you by cunning."

The young man thanked the magician for his directions, and promised, should they succeed, to reward him. But the magician answered, "I have profited so much by the wisdom the ring has taught me that I desire no other reward." Then they parted, and the youth quickly flew home through the air. After remaining in his own home for some weeks, he heard people say that the terrible Dragon of the North was not far off, and might shortly be expected in the country. The King announced publicly that he would give his daughter in marriage, as well as a large part of his kingdom, to whosoever should free the country from the monster. The youth then went to the King and told him that he had good hopes of subduing the Dragon, if the King would grant him all he desired for the purpose. The King willingly agreed, and the iron horse, the great spear, and the chains were all prepared as the youth requested. When all was ready, it was found that the iron horse was so heavy that a hundred men could not move it from the spot, so the youth found there was nothing to do but move it with his own strength by means of the magic ring. The Dragon was now so near that in a couple of springs he would be over the frontier. The youth now began to consider how he should act, for if he had to push the iron horse from behind he could not ride upon it as the sorcerer had said he must. But a raven unexpectedly gave him this advice: "Ride upon the horse, and push the spear against the ground, as if you were pushing off a boat from the land." The youth did so, and found that in this way he could easily move forward. The Dragon had his monstrous jaws wide open, all ready for his expected prey. A few paces nearer, and man and horse would have been swallowed up by them! The youth trembled with horror, and his blood ran cold, yet he did not lose his courage; but, holding the iron spear upright in his hand, he brought it down with all his might right through the monster's lower jaw. Then quick as lightning he sprang from his horse before the Dragon had time to shut his mouth. A fearful clap like thunder, which could be heard for miles around, now warned him that the Dragon's jaws had closed upon the spear. When the youth turned round he saw the point of the spear sticking up high above the Dragon's upper jaw, and knew that the other end must be fastened firmly to the ground; but the Dragon had got his teeth fixed in the iron horse, which was now useless. The youth now hastened to fasten down the chains to the ground by means of the enormous iron pegs which he had provided. The death struggle of the monster lasted three days and three nights; in his writhing he beat his tail so violently against the ground, that at ten miles' distance the earth trembled as if with an earthquake. When he at length lost power to move his tail, the youth with the help of the ring took up a stone which twenty ordinary men could not have moved, and beat the Dragon so hard about the head with it that very soon the monster lay lifeless before him.

You can fancy how great was the rejoicing when the news was spread abroad that the terrible monster was dead. His conqueror was received into the city with as much pomp as if he had been the mightiest of kings. The old King did not need to urge his daughter to marry the slayer of the Dragon; he found her already willing to bestow her hand upon this hero, who had done all alone what whole armies had tried in vain to do. In a few days a magnificent wedding was celebrated, at which the rejoicings lasted four whole weeks, for all the neighbouring kings had met together to thank the man who had freed the world from their common enemy. But everyone forgot amid the general joy that they ought to have buried the Dragon's monstrous body, for it began now to have such a bad

THE YOUTH SECURES THE DRAGON

smell that no one could live in the neighbourhood, and before long the whole air was poisoned, and a pestilence broke out which destroyed many hundreds of people. In this distress, the King's son-in-law resolved to seek help once more from the Eastern magician, to whom he at once travelled through the air like a bird by the help of the ring. But there is a proverb which says that ill-gotten gains never prosper, and the Prince found that the stolen ring brought him ill-luck after all. The Witch-maiden had never rested night nor day until she had found out where the ring was. As soon as she had discovered by means of magical arts that the Prince in the form of a bird was on his way to the Eastern magician, she changed herself into an eagle and watched in the air until the bird she was waiting for came in sight, for she knew him at once by the ring which was hung round his neck by a ribbon. Then the eagle pounced upon the bird, and the moment she seized him in her talons she tore the ring from his neck before the man in bird's shape had time to prevent her. Then the eagle flew down to the earth with her prey, and the two stood face to face once more in human form.

"Now, villain, you are in my power!" cried the Witch-maiden. "I favoured you with my love, and you repaid me with treachery and theft. You stole my most precious jewel from me, and do you expect to live happily as the King's son-in-law? Now the tables are turned; you are in my power, and I will be revenged on you for your crimes."

"Forgive me! forgive me!" cried the Prince; "I know too well how deeply I have wronged you, and most heartily do I repent it."

The maiden answered, "Your prayers and your repentance come too late, and if I were to spare you everyone would think me a fool. You have doubly wronged me; first you scorned my love, and then you stole my ring, and you must bear the punishment."

With these words she put the ring upon her left thumb, lifted the young man with one hand, and walked away with him under her arm. This time she did not take him to a splendid palace, but to a deep cave in a rock, where there were chains hanging from the wall. The maiden now chained the young man's hands and feet so that he could not escape; then she said in an angry voice, "Here you shall remain chained up until you die. I will bring you every day

"HERE YOU SHALL REMAIN CHAINED UP UNTIL YOU DIE."

enough food to prevent you dying of hunger, but you need never hope for freedom anymore." With these words she left him.

The old King and his daughter waited anxiously for many weeks for the Prince's return, but no news of him arrived. The King's daughter often dreamed that her husband was going through some great suffering; she therefore begged her father to summon all the enchanters and magicians, that they might try to find out where the Prince was and how he could be set free. But the magicians, with all their arts, could find out nothing, except that he was still living and undergoing great suffering; but none could tell where he was to be found. At last a celebrated magician from Finland was brought before the King, who had found out that the King's son-in-law was imprisoned in the East, not by men, but by some more powerful being. The King now sent messengers to the East to look for his son-in-law, and they by good luck met with the old magician who had interpreted the signs on King Solomon's ring, and thus was possessed of more wisdom than anyone else in the world. The magician soon found out what he wished to know, and pointed out the place where the Prince was imprisoned, but said: "He is kept there by enchantment, and cannot be set free without my help. I will therefore go with you myself."

So they all set out, guided by birds, and after some days came to the cave where the unfortunate Prince had been chained up for nearly seven years. He recognised the magician immediately, but the old man did not know him, he had grown so thin. However, he undid the chains by the help of magic, and took care of the Prince until he recovered and became strong enough to travel. When he reached home he found that the old King had died that morning, so that he was now raised to the throne. And now after his long suffering came prosperity, which lasted to the end of his life; but he never got back the magic ring, nor has it ever again been seen by mortal eyes.

Now, if *you* had been the Prince, would you not rather have stayed with the pretty witch-maiden?

THE STORY OF THE EMPEROR'S NEW CLOTHES[4]

ANY YEARS AGO THERE LIVED AN EMPEROR WHO was so fond of new clothes that he spent all his money on them in order to be beautifully dressed. He did not care about his soldiers, he did not care about the theatre; he only liked to go out walking to show off his new clothes. He had a coat for every hour of the day; and just as they say of a king, "He is in the council chamber," they always said here, "The Emperor is in the wardrobe."

In the great city in which he lived there was always something going on; every day many strangers came there. One day, two impostors arrived who gave themselves out as weavers, and said that they knew how to manufacture the most beautiful cloth imaginable. Not only were the texture and pattern uncommonly beautiful, but the clothes which were made of the stuff possessed this wonderful property that they were invisible to anyone who was not fit for his office, or who was unpardonably stupid.

"Those must indeed be splendid clothes," thought the Emperor. "If I had them on I could find out which men in my kingdom are unfit for the offices they hold; I could distinguish the wise from the stupid! Yes, this cloth must be woven for me at once." And he gave both the impostors much money, so that they might begin their work.

They placed two weaving-looms, and began to do as if they were working, but they had not the least thing on the looms. They also demanded the finest silk and the best gold, which they put in their pockets, and worked at the empty looms till late into the night.

"I should like very much to know how far they have got on with the cloth," thought the Emperor. But he remembered when he thought about it that whoever was stupid or not fit for his office would not be able to see it. Now he certainly believed that he had nothing to fear for himself, but he wanted first to send somebody else in order to see how he stood with regard to his office. Everybody in the whole town knew what a wonderful power the cloth had, and they were all curious to see how bad or how stupid their neighbour was.

"I will send my old and honoured minister to the weavers," thought the Emperor. "He can judge best what the cloth is like, for he has intellect, and no one understands his office better than he."

Now the good old minister went into the hall where the two impostors sat working at the empty weaving-looms. "Dear me!" thought the old minister, opening his eyes wide, "I can see nothing!" But he did not say so.

Both the impostors begged him to be so kind as to step closer, and asked him if it were not a beautiful texture and lovely colours. They pointed to the empty loom, and the poor old minister went forward rubbing his eyes; but he could see nothing, for there was nothing there.

"Dear, dear!" thought he, "can I be stupid? I have never thought that, and nobody must know it! Can I be not fit for my office? No, I must certainly not say that I cannot see the cloth!"

"Have you nothing to say about it?" asked one of the men who was weaving.

"Oh, it is lovely, most lovely!" answered the old minister, looking through his spectacles. "What a texture! What colours! Yes, I will tell the Emperor that it pleases me very much."

"Now we are delighted at that," said both the weavers, and thereupon they named the colours and explained the make of the texture.

The old minister paid great attention, so that he could tell the same to the Emperor when he came back to him, which he did.

The impostors now wanted more money, more silk, and more gold to use in their weaving. They put it all in their own pockets, and there came no threads on the loom, but they went on as they had done before, working at the empty loom. The Emperor soon sent another worthy statesman to see how the weaving was getting on, and whether the cloth would soon be finished. It was the same with him as the first one; he looked and looked, but because there was nothing on the empty loom he could see nothing.

"Is it not a beautiful piece of cloth?" asked the two impostors, and they pointed to and described the splendid material which was not there.

"Stupid I am not!" thought the man, "so it must be my good office for which I am not fitted. It is strange, certainly, but no one must be allowed to notice it." And so he praised the cloth which he did not see, and expressed to them his delight at the beautiful colours and the splendid texture. "Yes, it is quite beautiful," he said to the Emperor.

Everybody in the town was talking of the magnificent cloth.

Now the Emperor wanted to see it himself while it was still on the loom. With a great crowd of select followers, amongst whom were both the worthy statesmen who had already been there before, he went to the cunning impostors, who were now weaving with all their might, but without fibre or thread.

"Is it not splendid!" said both the old statesmen who had already been there. "See, your Majesty, what a texture! What colours!" And then they pointed to the empty loom, for they believed that the others could see the cloth quite well.

"What!" thought the Emperor, "I can see nothing! This is indeed horrible! Am I stupid? Am I not fit to be Emperor? That would be the most dreadful thing that could happen to me."

"Oh, it is very beautiful," he said. "It has my gracious approval." And then he nodded pleasantly, and examined the empty loom, for he would not say that he could see nothing.

His whole Court round him looked and looked, and saw no more than the others; but they said like the Emperor, "Oh! it is beautiful!" And they advised him to wear these new and magnificent clothes for the first time at the great procession which was soon to take place. "Splendid! Lovely! Most beautiful!" went from mouth to mouth; everyone seemed delighted over them, and the Emperor gave to the impostors the title of Court Weavers to the Emperor.

Throughout the whole of the night before the morning on which the procession was to take place, the impostors were up and were working by the light of over sixteen candles. The people could see that they were very busy making the Emperor's new clothes ready. They pretended they were taking the cloth from the loom, cut with huge scissors in the air, sewed with needles without thread, and then said at last, "Now the clothes are finished!"

The Emperor came himself with his most distinguished knights, and each impostor held up his arm just as if he were holding something, and said, "See! here are the breeches! Here is the coat! Here the cloak!" and so on.

"Spun clothes are so comfortable that one would imagine one had nothing on at all; but that is the beauty of it!"

"Yes," said all the knights, but they could see nothing, for there was nothing there.

THE EMPEROR COMES TO SEE HIS NEW CLOTHES

"Will it please your Majesty graciously to take off your clothes," said the impostors, "then we will put on the new clothes, here before the mirror."

The Emperor took off all his clothes, and the impostors placed themselves before him as if they were putting on each part of his new clothes which was ready, and the Emperor turned and bent himself in front of the mirror.

"How beautifully they fit! How well they sit!" said everybody. "What material! What colours! It is a gorgeous suit!"

"They are waiting outside with the canopy which your Majesty is wont to have borne over you in the procession," announced the Master of the Ceremonies.

"Look, I am ready," said the Emperor. "Doesn't it sit well!" And he turned himself again to the mirror to see if his finery was on all right.

The chamberlains who were used to carry the train put their hands near the floor as if they were lifting up the train; then they did as if they were holding something in the air. They would not have it noticed that they could see nothing.

So the Emperor went along in the procession under the splendid canopy, and all the people in the streets and at the windows said, "How matchless are the Emperor's new clothes! That train fastened to his dress, how beautifully it hangs!"

No one wished it to be noticed that he could see nothing, for then he would have been unfit for his office, or else very stupid. None of the Emperor's clothes had met with such approval as these had.

"But he has nothing on!" said a little child at last.

"Just listen to the innocent child!" said the father, and each one whispered to his neighbour what the child had said.

"But he has nothing on!" the whole of the people called out at last.

This struck the Emperor, for it seemed to him as if they were right; but he thought to himself, "I must go on with the procession now." And the chamberlains walked along still more uprightly, holding up the train which was not there at all.

THE GOLDEN CRAB[5]

NCE UPON A TIME THERE WAS A FISHERMAN WHO HAD A wife and three children. Every morning he used to go out fishing, and whatever fish he caught he sold to the King. One day, among the other fishes, he caught a golden crab. When he came home he put all the fishes together into a great dish, but he kept the Crab separate because it shone so beautifully, and placed it upon a high shelf in the cupboard. Now while the old woman, his wife, was cleaning the fish, and had tucked up her gown so that her feet were visible, she suddenly heard a voice, which said:

"Let down, let down thy petticoat
That lets thy feet be seen."

She turned round in surprise, and then she saw the little creature, the Golden Crab.

---

5   'Prinz Krebs,' from *Griechische Mährchen*. Schmidt.

"What! You can speak, can you, you ridiculous crab?" she said, for she was not quite pleased at the Crab's remarks. Then she took him up and placed him on a dish.

When her husband came home and they sat down to dinner, they presently heard the Crab's little voice saying, "Give me some too." They were all very much surprised, but they gave him something to eat. When the old man came to take away the plate which had contained the Crab's dinner, he found it full of gold, and as the same thing happened every day he soon became very fond of the Crab.

One day the Crab said to the fisherman's wife, "Go to the King and tell him I wish to marry his younger daughter."

The old woman went accordingly, and laid the matter before the King, who laughed a little at the notion of his daughter marrying a crab, but did not decline the proposal altogether, because he was a prudent monarch, and knew that the Crab was likely to be a prince in disguise. He said, therefore, to the fisherman's wife, "Go, old woman, and tell the Crab I will give him my daughter if by to-morrow morning he can build a wall in front of my castle much higher than my tower, upon which all the flowers of the world must grow and bloom."

The fisherman's wife went home and gave this message.

Then the Crab gave her a golden rod, and said, "Go and strike with this rod three times upon the ground on the place which the King showed you, and to-morrow morning the wall will be there."

The old woman did so and went away again.

The next morning, when the King awoke, what do you think he saw? The wall stood there before his eyes, exactly as he had bespoken it!

Then the old woman went back to the King and said to him, "Your Majesty's orders have been fulfilled."

"That is all very well," said the King, "but I cannot give away my daughter until there stands in front of my palace a garden in which there are three fountains, of which the first must play gold, the second diamonds, and the third brilliants."

So the old woman had to strike again three times upon the ground with the rod, and the next morning the garden was there. The King now gave his consent, and the wedding was fixed for the very next day.

*THE FISHERMAN BRINGS THE CRAB
ON THE GOLDEN CUSHION*

Then the Crab said to the old fisherman, "Now take this rod; go and knock with it on a certain mountain; then a man[6] will come out and ask you what you wish for. Answer him thus: 'Your master, the King, has sent me to tell you that you must send him his golden garment that is like the sun.' Make him give you, besides, the queenly robes of gold and precious stones which are like the flowery meadows, and bring them both to me. And bring me also the golden cushion."

The old man went and did his errand. When he had brought the precious robes, the Crab put on the golden garment and then crept upon the golden cushion, and in this way the fisherman carried him to the castle, where the Crab presented the other garment to his bride. Now the ceremony took place, and when the married pair were alone together the Crab made himself known to his young wife, and told her how he was the son of the greatest king in the world, and how he was enchanted, so that he became a crab by day and was a man only at night; and he could also change himself into an eagle as

6   Ein Mohr.

often as he wished. No sooner had he said this than he shook himself, and immediately became a handsome youth, but the next morning he was forced to creep back again into his crab-shell. And the same thing happened every day. But the Princess's affection for the Crab, and the polite attention with which she behaved to him, surprised the royal family very much. They suspected some secret, but though they spied and spied, they could not discover it. Thus a year passed away, and the Princess had a son, whom she called Benjamin. But her mother still thought the whole matter very strange. At last she said to the King that he ought to ask his daughter whether she would not like to have another husband instead of the Crab? But when the daughter was questioned, she only answered:

"I am married to the Crab, and him only will I have."

Then the King said to her, "I will appoint a tournament in your honour, and I will invite all the princes in the world to it, and if any one of them pleases you, you shall marry him."

In the evening the Princess told this to the Crab, who said to her, "Take this rod, go to the garden gate and knock with it, then a man will come out and say to you, 'Why have you called me, and what do you require of me?' Answer him thus: 'Your master the King has sent me hither to tell you to send him his golden armour and his steed and the silver apple.' And bring them to me."

The Princess did so, and brought him what he desired.

The following evening the Prince dressed himself for the tournament. Before he went he said to his wife, "Now mind you do not say when you see me that I am the Crab. For if you do this, evil will come of it. Place yourself at the window with your sisters; I will ride by and throw you the silver apple. Take it in your hand, but if they ask you who I am, say that you do not know." So saying, he kissed her, repeated his warning once more, and went away.

The Princess went with her sisters to the window and looked on at the tournament. Presently her husband rode by and threw the apple up to her. She caught it in her hand and went with it to her room, and by-and-by her husband came back to her. But her father was much surprised that she did not seem to care about any of the Princes; he therefore appointed a second tournament.

The Crab then gave his wife the same directions as before, only this time the apple which she received from the man was of gold. But before the Prince went to the tournament he said to his wife, "Now I know you will betray me to-day."

But she swore to him that she would not tell who he was. He then repeated his warning and went away.

In the evening, while the Princess, with her mother and sisters, was standing at the window, the Prince suddenly galloped past on his steed and threw her the golden apple.

Then her mother flew into a passion, gave her a box on the ear, and cried out, "Does not even that prince please you, you fool?"

The Princess in her fright exclaimed, "That is the Crab himself!"

Her mother was still more angry because she had not been told sooner, ran into her daughter's room where the crab-shell was still lying, took it up and threw it into the fire. Then the poor Princess cried bitterly, but it was of no use; her husband did not come back.

Now we must leave the Princess and turn to the other persons in the story. One day, an old man went to a stream to dip in a crust of bread which he was going to eat, when a dog came out of the water, snatched the bread from his hand, and ran away. The old man ran after him, but the dog reached a door, pushed it open, and ran in, the old man following him. He did not overtake the dog, but found himself above a staircase, which he descended. Then he saw before him a stately palace, and, entering, he found in a large hall a table set for twelve persons. He hid himself in the hall behind a great picture, that he might see what would happen. At noon he heard a great noise, so that he trembled with fear. When he took courage to look out from behind the picture, he saw twelve eagles flying in. At this sight his fear became still greater. The eagles flew to the basin of a fountain that was there and bathed themselves, when suddenly they were changed into twelve handsome youths. Now they seated themselves at the table, and one of them took up a goblet filled with wine, and said, "A health to my father!" And another said, "A health to my mother!" and so the healths went round. Then one of them said:

> "A health to my dearest lady,
> Long may she live and well!
> But a curse on the cruel mother
> That burnt my golden shell!"

And so saying he wept bitterly. Then the youths rose from the table, went back to the great stone fountain, turned themselves into eagles again, and flew away.

Then the old man went away too, returned to the light of day, and went home. Soon after he heard that the Princess was ill, and that the only thing that did her good was having stories told to her. He therefore went to the royal castle, obtained an audience of the Princess, and told her about the strange things he had seen in the underground palace. No sooner had he finished than the Princess asked him whether he could find the way to that palace.

"Yes," he answered, "certainly."

And now she desired him to guide her there at once. The old man did so, and wh hey came to the palace he hid her behind the great picture and advise.   r to keep quite still, and he placed himself behind the picture also. Presently the eagles came flying in, and changed themselves into young men, and in a moment the Princess recognised her husband amongst them all, and tried to come out of her hiding-place; but the old man held her back. The youths seated themselves at the table; and now the Prince said again, while he took up the cup of wine:

"A health to my dearest lady,
Long may she live and well!
But a curse on the cruel mother
That burnt my golden shell!"

Then the Princess could restrain herself no longer, but ran forward and threw her arms round her husband. And immediately he knew her again, and said:

"Do you remember how I told you that day that you would betray me? Now you see that I spoke the truth. But all that bad time is past. Now listen to me: I must still remain enchanted for three months. Will you stay here with me till that time is over?"

So the Princess stayed with him, and said to the old man, "Go back to the castle and tell my parents that I am staying here."

Her parents were very much vexed when the old man came back and told them this, but as soon as the three months of the Prince's enchantment were over, he ceased to be an eagle and became once more a man, and they returned home together. And then they lived happily, and we who hear the story are happier still.

THE IRON STOVE[7]

NCE UPON A TIME WHEN WISHES CAME TRUE THERE WAS a king's son who was enchanted by an old witch, so that he was obliged to sit in a large iron stove in a wood. There he lived for many years, and no one could free him. At last a king's daughter came into the wood; she had lost her way, and could not find her father's kingdom again. She had been wandering round and round for nine days, and she came at last to the iron stove. A voice came from within and asked her, "Where do you come from, and where do you want to go?"

She answered, "I have lost my way to my father's kingdom, and I shall never get home again."

Then the voice from the iron stove said, "I will help you to find your home again, and that in a very short time, if you will promise to do what I ask you. I am a greater prince than you are a princess, and I will marry you."

Then she grew frightened, and thought, "What can a young lassie do with

7   Grimm.

an iron stove?" But as she wanted very much to go home to her father, she promised to do what he wished.

He said, "You must come again, and bring a knife with you to scrape a hole in the iron."

Then he gave her someone for a guide, who walked near her and said nothing, but he brought her in two hours to her house. There was great joy in the castle when the Princess came back, and the old King fell on her neck and kissed her. But she was very much troubled, and said, "Dear father, listen to what has befallen me! I should never have come home again out of the great wild wood if I had not come to an iron stove, to whom I have had to promise that I will go back to free him and marry him!" The old King was so frightened that he nearly fainted, for she was his only daughter. So they consulted together, and determined that the miller's daughter, who was very beautiful, should take her place. They took her there, gave her a knife, and said she must scrape at the iron stove. She scraped for twenty-four hours, but did not make the least impression.

When the day broke, a voice called from the iron stove, "It seems to me that it is day outside."

Then she answered, "It seems so to me; I think I hear my father's mill rattling."

"So you are a miller's daughter! Then go away at once, and tell the King's daughter to come."

Then she went away, and told the old King that the thing inside the iron stove would not have her, but wanted the Princess. The old King was frightened, and his daughter wept. But they had a swineherd's daughter who was even more beautiful than the miller's daughter, and they gave her a piece of gold to go to the iron stove instead of the Princess. Then she was taken out, and had to scrape for four-and-twenty hours, but she could make no impression. As soon as the day broke the voice from the stove called out, "It seems to be daylight outside."

Then she answered, "It seems so to me too; I think I hear my father blowing his horn."

"So you are a swineherd's daughter! Go away at once, and let the King's daughter come. And say to her that what I foretell shall come to pass, and if she does not come, everything in the kingdom shall fall into ruin, and not one stone shall be left upon another." When the Princess heard this she began to cry, but it was no good; she had to keep her word. She took leave of her father, put a knife in her belt, and went to the iron stove in the wood. As soon as she reached it she began to scrape, and the iron gave way and before two hours had passed she had made a little hole. Then she peeped in and saw such a beautiful youth all shining with gold and precious stones that she fell in love with him on the spot. So she scraped away harder than ever, and made the hole so large that he could get out. Then he said, "You are mine, and I am thine; you are my bride and have set me free!" He wanted to take her with him to his kingdom, but she begged him just to let her go once more to her father; and the Prince let her go, but told her not to say more than three words to her father, then to come back again. So she went home, but alas! she said *more than three words*; and immediately the iron stove vanished and went away over a mountain of glass and sharp swords. But the Prince was free, and was no longer shut up in it. Then she said good-bye to her father, and took a little money with her, and went again into the great wood to look for the iron stove; but she could not find it. She sought it for nine days, and then her hunger became so great that she did not know how she could live any longer. And when it was evening she climbed a little tree and wished that the night would not come, because she was afraid of the wild beasts. When midnight came she saw afar off a little light, and thought, "Ah! if only I could reach that!" Then she got down from the tree and went toward the light. She came to a little old house with a great deal of grass growing round, and stood in front of a little heap of wood. She thought,

"Alas! what am I coming to?" and peeped through the window; but she saw nothing inside except big and little toads, and a table beautifully spread with roast meats and wine, and all the dishes and drinking cups were of silver. Then she took heart and knocked. Then a fat toad called out:

> *"Little green toad with leg like crook,*
> *Open wide the door, and look*
> *Who it was the latch that shook."*

And a little toad came forward and let her in. When she entered they all bid her welcome, and made her sit down. They asked her how she came there and what she wanted. Then she told everything that had happened to her, and how, because she had exceeded her permission only to speak three words, the stove had disappeared with the Prince; and how she had searched a very long time, and must wander over mountain and valley till she found him.

Then the old toad said:

> *"Little green toad whose leg doth twist,*
> *Go to the corner of which you wist,*
> *And bring to me the large old kist."*

And the little toad went and brought out a great chest. Then they gave her food and drink, and led her to a beautifully made bed of silk and samite, on which she lay down and slept soundly. When the day dawned she arose, and the old toad gave her three things out of the huge chest to take with her. She would have need of them, for she had to cross a high glass mountain, three cutting swords, and a great lake. When she had passed these she would find her lover again. So she was given three large needles, a plough-wheel, and three nuts, which she was to take great care of. She set out with these things,

*"THEN SHE REACHED THE THREE CUTTING SWORDS, AND GOT ON
HER PLOUGH-WHEEL AND ROLLED OVER THEM."*

and when she came to the glass mountain which was so slippery, she stuck the three needles behind her feet and then in front, and so got over it, and when she was on the other side put them carefully away.

Then she reached the three cutting swords, and got on her plough-wheel and rolled over them. At last she came to a great lake, and, when she had crossed that, arrived at a beautiful castle. She went in and gave herself out as a servant, a poor maid who would gladly be engaged. But she knew that the Prince whom she had freed from the iron stove in the great wood was in the castle. So she was taken on as a kitchenmaid for very small wages. Now the Prince was about to marry another princess, for he thought she was dead long ago.

In the evening, when she had washed up and was ready, she felt in her pocket and found the three nuts which the old toad had given her. She cracked one and was going to eat the kernel, when behold! there was a beautiful royal dress inside it! When the bride heard of this, she came and begged for the dress, and wanted to buy it, saying that it was not a dress for a serving maid. Then she said she would not sell it unless she was granted one favour—namely, to sleep by the Prince's door. The bride granted her this, because the dress was so beautiful and she had so few like it. When it was evening she said to her bridegroom, "That stupid maid wants to sleep by your door."

"If you are contented, I am," he said. But she gave him a glass of wine in which she had poured a sleeping-draught. Then they both went to his room, but he slept so soundly that she could not wake him.

The maid wept all night long, and said, "I freed you in the wild wood out of the iron stove; I have sought you, and have crossed a glassy mountain, three sharp swords, and a great lake before I found you, and will you not hear me now?" The servants outside heard how she cried the whole night, and they told their master in the morning.

When she had washed up the next evening she bit the second nut, and there was a still more beautiful dress inside. When the bride saw it she wanted to buy it also. But the maid did not want money, and asked that she should sleep again by the Prince's door. The bride, however, gave him a sleeping-draught, and he slept so soundly that he heard nothing. But the kitchenmaid wept the whole night long, and said, "I have freed you in a wood and from an iron stove; I sought you and have crossed a glassy mountain, three sharp swords, and a great lake to find you, and now you will not hear me!" The servants outside heard how she cried the whole night, and in the morning they told their master. And when she had washed up on the third night she bit the third nut, and there was a still more beautiful dress inside that was made of pure gold. When the bride saw it she wanted to have it, but the maid would only give it her on condition that she should sleep for the third time by the Prince's door. But the Prince took care not to drink the sleeping-draught. When she began to weep and to say, "Dearest sweetheart, I freed you in the horrible wild wood, and from an iron stove," he jumped up and said, "You are right. You are mine, and I am thine." Though it was still night, he got into a carriage with her, and they took the false bride's clothes away, so that she could not follow them. When they came to the great lake they rowed across, and when they reached the three sharp swords they sat on the plough-wheel, and on the glassy mountain they stuck the three needles in. So they arrived at last at the little old house, but when they stepped inside it turned into a large castle. The toads were all freed, and were beautiful King's children, running about for joy. There they were married, and they remained in the castle, which was much larger than that of the Princess's father's. But because the old man did not like being left alone, they went and fetched him. So they had two kingdoms and lived in great wealth.

A mouse has run,
My story's done.

THE DRAGON AND HIS GRANDMOTHER

HERE WAS ONCE A GREAT WAR, AND THE KING HAD A great many soldiers, but he gave them so little pay that they could not live on it. Then three of them took counsel together and determined to desert.

One of them said to the others, "If we are caught, we shall be hanged on the gallows; how shall we set about it?"

The other said, "Do you see that large cornfield there? If we were to hide ourselves in that, no one could find us. The army cannot come into it, and to-morrow it is to march on."

They crept into the corn, but the army did not march on, but remained encamped close around them. They sat for two days and two nights in the corn, and grew so hungry that they nearly died; but if they were to venture out, it was certain death.

They said at last, "What use was it our deserting? We must perish here miserably."

Whilst they were speaking a fiery dragon came flying through the air. It hovered near them, and asked why they were hidden there. They answered, "We are three soldiers, and have deserted because our pay was so small. Now if we remain here we shall die of hunger, and if we move out we shall be strung up on the gallows."

"If you will serve me for seven years," said the Dragon, I will lead you through the midst of the army so that no one shall catch you."

"We have no choice, and must take your offer," said they. Then the Dragon seized them in his claws, took them through the air over the army, and set them down on the earth a long way from it.

THE DRAGON CARRIES OFF THE THREE SOLDIERS

He gave them a little whip, saying, "Whip and slash with this, and as much money as you want will jump up before you. You can then live as great lords, keep horses, and drive about in carriages. But after seven years you are mine." Then he put a book before them, which he made all three of them sign. "I will then give you a riddle," he said; "if you guess it, you shall be free and out of my power." The Dragon then flew away, and they journeyed on with their little whip. They had as much money as they wanted, wore grand clothes, and made their way into the world. Wherever they went they lived in merrymaking and splendour, drove about with horses and carriages, ate and drank, but did nothing wrong.

The time passed quickly away, and when the seven years were nearly ended two of them grew terribly anxious and frightened, but the third made light of it, saying, "Don't be afraid, brothers, I wasn't born yesterday; I will guess the riddle."

They went into a field, sat down, and the two pulled long faces. An old woman passed by, and asked them why they were so sad. "Alas! what have you to do with it? You cannot help us."

"Who knows?" she answered. "Only confide your trouble in me."

Then they told her that they had become the servants of the Dragon for seven long years, and how he had given them money as plentifully as blackberries; but as they had signed their names they were his, unless when the seven years had passed they could guess a riddle. The old woman said, "If you would help yourselves, one of you must go into the wood, and there he will come upon a tumble-down building of rocks which looks like a little house. He must go in, and there he will find help."

The two melancholy ones thought, "That won't save us!" and they remained where they were. But the third and merry one jumped up and went into the wood till he found the rock hut. In the hut sat a very old woman, who was the Dragon's grandmother. She asked him how he came, and what was his business there. He told her all that happened, and because she was pleased with him she took compassion on him, and said she would help him.

She lifted up a large stone which lay over the cellar, saying, "Hide yourself there; you can hear all that is spoken in this room. Only sit still and don't stir. When the Dragon comes, I will ask him what the riddle is, for he tells me everything; then listen carefully what he answers."

At midnight the Dragon flew in, and asked for his supper. His grandmother laid the table, and brought out food and drink till he was satisfied, and they ate and drank together. Then in the course of the conversation she asked him what he had done in the day, and how many souls he had conquered.

"I haven't had much luck to-day," he said, "but I have a tight hold on three soldiers."

"Indeed! three soldiers!" said she. "Who cannot escape you?"

"They are mine," answered the Dragon scornfully, "for I shall only give them one riddle which they will never be able to guess."

"What sort of a riddle is it?" she asked.

"I will tell you this. In the North Sea lies a dead sea-cat—that shall be their roast meat; and the rib of a whale—that shall be their silver spoon; and the hollow foot of a dead horse—that shall be their wineglass."

When the Dragon had gone to bed, his old grandmother pulled up the stone and let out the soldier.

"Did you pay attention to everything?"

"Yes," he replied, "I know enough, and can help myself splendidly."

Then he went by another way through the window secretly, and in all haste back to his comrades. He told them how the Dragon had been outwitted by his grandmother, and how he had heard from his own lips the answer to the riddle.

Then they were all delighted and in high spirits, took out their whip, and cracked so much money that it came jumping up from the ground. When the seven years had quite gone, the Dragon came with his book, and, pointing at the signatures, said, "I will take you underground with me; you shall have a meal there. If you can tell me what you will get for your roast meat, you shall be free, and shall also keep the whip."

Then said the first soldier, "In the North Sea lies a dead sea-cat; that shall be the roast meat."

The Dragon was much annoyed, and hummed and hawed a good deal, and asked the second, "But what shall be your spoon?"

"The rib of a whale shall be our silver spoon."

The Dragon made a face, and growled again three times, "Hum, hum, hum," and said to the third, "Do you know what your wineglass shall be?"

"A dead horse's hoof shall be our wineglass."

Then the Dragon flew away with a loud shriek, and had no more power over them. But the three soldiers took the little whip, whipped as much money as they wanted, and lived happily to their lives' end.

THE DRAGON DEFEATED

THE DONKEY CABBAGE

HERE WAS ONCE A YOUNG HUNTER WHO WENT BOLDLY into the forest. He had a merry and light heart, and as he went whistling along there came an ugly old woman, who said to him, "Good-day, dear hunter! You are very merry and contented, but I suffer hunger and thirst, so give me a trifle." The Hunter was sorry for the poor old woman, and he felt in his pocket and gave her all he could spare. He was going on then, but the old woman stopped him and said, "Listen, dear hunter, to what I say. Because of your kind heart I will make you a present. Go on your way, and in a short time you will come to a tree on which sit nine birds who have a cloak in their claws and are quarrelling over it. Then take aim with your gun and shoot in the middle of them; they will let the cloak fall, but one of the birds will be hit and will drop down dead. Take the cloak with you; it is a wishing-cloak, and when you throw it on your shoulders you have only to wish yourself at a certain place, and in the twinkling of an eye you are there. Take the heart out of the dead bird and swallow it whole, and early every morning when you get up you will find a gold piece under your pillow."

The Hunter thanked the wise woman, and thought to himself "These are splendid things she has promised me, if only they come to pass!" So he walked on about a hundred yards, and then he heard above him in the branches such a screaming and chirping that he looked up, and there he saw a heap of birds tearing a cloth with their beaks and feet, shrieking, tugging, and fighting, as if each wanted it for himself. "Well," said the Hunter, "this is wonderful! It is just as the old woman said'; and he took his gun on his shoulder, pulled the trigger, and shot into the midst of them, so that their feathers flew about. Then the flock took flight with much screaming, but one fell dead, and the cloak fluttered down. Then the Hunter did as the old woman had told him: he cut open the bird, found its heart, swallowed it, and took the cloak home with him. The next morning when he awoke he remembered the promise, and wanted to see if it had come true. But when he lifted up his pillow, there sparkled the gold piece, and the next morning he found another, and so on every time he got up. He collected a heap of gold, but at last he thought to himself, "What good is all my gold to me if I stay at home? I will travel and look a bit about me in the world." So he took leave of his parents, slung his hunting knapsack and his gun round him, and journeyed into the world.

It happened that one day he went through a thick wood, and when he came to the end of it there lay in the plain before him a large castle. At one of the windows in it stood an old woman with a most beautiful maiden by her side, looking out. But the old woman was a witch, and she said to the girl, "There comes one out of the wood who has a wonderful treasure in his body which we must manage to possess ourselves of, darling daughter; we have more right to it than he. He has a bird's heart in him, and so every morning there lies a gold piece under his pillow."

She told her how they could get hold of it, and how she was to coax it from him, and at last threatened her angrily, saying, "And if you do not obey me, you shall repent it!"

When the Hunter came nearer he saw the maiden, and said to himself, "I have travelled so far now that I will rest, and turn into this beautiful castle; money I have in plenty." But the real reason was that he had caught sight of the maiden's lovely face.

He went into the house, and was kindly received and hospitably entertained. It was not long before he was so much in love with the maiden that he thought of nothing else, and only looked in her eyes, and whatever she wanted, that he gladly did. Then the old witch said, "Now we must have the bird-heart; he will not feel when it is gone." She prepared a drink, and when it was ready she poured it in a goblet and gave it to the maiden, who had to hand it to the hunter.

"Drink to me now, my dearest," she said. Then he took the goblet, and when he had swallowed the drink the bird-heart came out of his mouth. The maiden had to get hold of it secretly and then swallow it herself, for the old witch wanted to have it. Thenceforward he found no more gold under his pillow, and it lay under the maiden's; but he was so much in love and so much bewitched that he thought of nothing except spending all his time with the maiden.

Then the old witch said, "We have the bird-heart, but we must also get the wishing-cloak from him."

The maiden answered, "We will leave him that; he has already lost his wealth!"

The old witch grew angry, and said, "Such a cloak is a wonderful thing, it is seldom to be had in the world, and have it I must and will." She beat the maiden, and said that if she did not obey it would go ill with her.

So she did her mother's bidding, and, standing one day by the window, she looked away into the far distance as if she were very sad.

"Why are you standing there looking so sad?" asked the Hunter.

"Alas, my love," she replied, "over there lies the granite mountain where the costly precious stones grow. I have a great longing to go there, so that

THE MAIDEN OBTAINS THE BIRD-HEART.

when I think of it I am very sad. For who can fetch them? Only the birds who fly; a man, never."

"If you have no other trouble," said the Hunter, "that one I can easily remove from your heart."

So he wrapped her round in his cloak and wished themselves to the granite mountain, and in an instant there they were, sitting on it! The precious stones sparkled so brightly on all sides that it was a pleasure to see them, and they collected the most beautiful and costly together. But now the old witch had through her witchcraft caused the Hunter's eyes to become heavy.

He said to the maiden, "We will sit down for a little while and rest; I am so tired that I can hardly stand on my feet."

So they sat down, and he laid his head on her lap and fell asleep. As soon as he was sound asleep she unfastened the cloak from his shoulders, threw it on her own, left the granite and stones, and wished herself home again.

But when the Hunter had finished his sleep and awoke, he found that his love had betrayed him and left him alone on the wild mountain. "Oh," said he, "why is faithlessness so great in the world?" and he sat down in sorrow and trouble, not knowing what to do.

But the mountain belonged to fierce and huge giants, who lived on it and traded there, and he had not sat long before he saw three of them striding toward him. So he lay down as if he had fallen into a deep sleep.

The giants came up, and the first pushed him with his foot, and said, "What sort of an earthworm is that?"

The second said, "Crush him dead."

But the third said contemptuously, "It is not worth the trouble! Let him live; he cannot remain here, and if he goes higher up the mountain the clouds will take him and carry him off."

Talking thus they went away. But the Hunter had listened to their talk, and as soon as they had gone he rose and climbed to the summit. When he had sat there a little while a cloud swept by, and, seizing him, carried him away. It travelled for a time in the sky, and then it sank down and hovered over a large vegetable garden surrounded by walls, so that he came safely to the ground amidst cabbages and vegetables. The Hunter then looked about him, saying, "If only I had something to eat! I am so hungry, and it will go badly with me in the future, for I see here not an apple or pear or fruit of any kind—nothing but vegetables everywhere." At last he thought, "At a pinch I can eat a salad; it does not taste

THE HUNTER IS TRANSFORMED INTO A DONKEY

particularly nice, but it will refresh me." So he looked about for a good head of cabbage and ate it, but no sooner had he swallowed a couple of mouthfuls than he felt very strange, and found himself wonderfully changed. Four legs began to grow on him, a thick head, and two long ears, and he saw with horror that he had changed into a donkey. But as he was still very hungry and this juicy salad tasted very good to his present nature, he went on eating with a still greater appetite. At last he got hold of another kind of cabbage, but scarcely had swallowed it when he felt another change, and he once more regained his human form.

The Hunter now lay down and slept off his weariness. When he awoke the next morning he broke off a head of the bad and a head of the good cabbage, thinking, "This will help me to regain my own, and to punish faithlessness." Then he put the heads in his pockets, climbed the wall, and started off to seek the castle of his love. When he had wandered about for a couple of days he found it quite easily. He then dirtied his face quickly, so that his own mother would not have known him, and went into the castle, where he begged for a lodging.

"I am so tired," he said, "I can go no farther."

The witch asked, "Countryman, who are you, and what is your business?"

He answered, "I am a messenger of the King, and have been sent to seek the finest salad that grows under the sun. I have been so lucky as to find it, and am bringing it with me; but the heat of the sun is so great that the tender cabbage threatens to grow soft, and I do not know if I shall be able to bring it any farther."

When the old witch heard of the fine salad she wanted to eat it, and said, "Dear countryman, just let me taste the wonderful salad."

"Why not?" he answered; "I have brought two heads with me, and will give you one."

So saying, he opened his sack and gave her the bad one. The witch suspected no evil, and her mouth watered to taste the new dish, so that she went into the kitchen to prepare it herself. When it was ready she could not wait till it was served at the table, but she immediately took a couple of leaves and put them in her mouth. No sooner, however, had she swallowed them than she lost human form, and ran into the courtyard in the shape of a donkey.

Now the servant came into the kitchen, and when she saw the salad standing there ready cooked she was about to carry it up, but on the way, according to her old habit, she tasted it and ate a couple of leaves. Immediately the charm worked, and she became a donkey, and ran out to join the old witch, and the dish with the salad in it fell to the ground. In the meantime, the messenger was sitting with the lovely maiden, and as no one came with the salad, and she wanted very much to taste it, she said, "I don't know where the salad is."

THE YOUNG MAN GIVES THE DONKEYS TO THE MILLER

Then thought the Hunter, "The cabbage must have already begun to work." And he said, "I will go to the kitchen and fetch it myself."

When he came there he saw the two donkeys running about in the court-yard, but the salad was lying on the ground.

"That's all right," said he; "two have had their share!" And lifting the re-maining leaves up, he laid them on the dish and brought them to the maiden.

"I am bringing you the delicious food my own self," he said, "so that you need not wait any longer."

Then she ate, and, as the others had done, she at once lost her human form, and ran as a donkey into the yard.

When the Hunter had washed his face, so that the changed ones might know him, he went into the yard, saying, "Now you shall receive a reward for your faithlessness."

He tied them all three with a rope, and drove them away till he came to a mill. He knocked at the window, and the miller put his head out and asked what he wanted.

"I have three tiresome animals," he answered, "which I don't want to keep any longer. If you will take them, give them food and stabling, and do as I tell you with them, I will pay you as much as you want."

The miller replied, "Why not? What shall I do with them?"

Then the Hunter said that to the old donkey, which was the witch, three beatings and one meal; to the younger one, which was the servant, one beating and three meals; and to the youngest one, which was the maiden, no beating and three meals; for he could not find it in his heart to let the maiden be beaten.

Then he went back into the castle, and he found there all that he wanted. After a couple of days the miller came and said that he must tell him that the old donkey which was to have three beatings and only one meal had died. "The two others," he added, "are certainly not dead, and get their three meals every day, but they are so sad that they cannot last much longer."

Then the Hunter took pity on them, laid aside his anger, and told the miller to drive them back again. And when they came he gave them some of the good cabbage to eat, so that they became human again. Then the beautiful maiden fell on her knees before him, saying, "Oh, my dearest, forgive me the ill I have done you! My mother compelled me to do it; it was against my will, for I love you dearly. Your wishing-cloak is hanging in a cupboard, and as for the bird-heart I will make a drink and give it back to you."

But he changed his mind, and said, "Keep it; it makes no difference, for I will take you to be my own dear true wife."

And the wedding was celebrated, and they lived happy together till death.

THE LITTLE GREEN FROG[8]

IN A PART OF THE WORLD WHOSE NAME I FORGET LIVED once upon a time two kings, called Peridor and Diamantino. They were cousins as well as neighbours, and both were under the protection of the fairies; though it is only fair to say that the fairies did not love them half so well as their wives did.

Now it often happens that as princes can generally manage to get their own way, it is harder for them to be good than it is for common people. So it was with Peridor and Diamantino; but of the two, the fairies declared that Diamantino was much the worst; indeed, he behaved so badly to his wife Aglantine, that the fairies would not allow him to live any longer; and he died, leaving behind him a little daughter. As she was an only child, of course this little girl was the heiress of the kingdom, but, being still only a baby, her mother, the widow of Diamantino, was proclaimed regent. The Dowager Queen was wise and good, and tried her best to make her people happy. The only

---

thing she had to vex her was the absence of her daughter; for the fairies, for reasons of their own, determined to bring up the little Princess Serpentine among themselves.

As to the other King, he was really fond of his wife, Queen Constance, but he often grieved her by his thoughtless ways, and in order to punish him for his carelessness, the fairies caused her to die quite suddenly. When she was gone the King felt how much he had loved her, and his grief was so great (though he never neglected his duties) that his subjects called him Peridor the Sorrowful. It seems hardly possible that any man should live like Peridor for fifteen years plunged in such depth of grief, and most likely he would have died too if it had not been for the fairies.

The one comfort the poor King had was his son, Prince Saphir, who was only three years old at the time of his mother's death, and great care was given to his education. By the time he was fifteen Saphir had learnt everything that a prince should know, and he was, besides, charming and agreeable.

It was about this time that the fairies suddenly took fright lest his love for his father should interfere with the plans they had made for the young prince. So, to prevent this, they placed in a pretty little room, of which Saphir was very fond, a little mirror in a black frame, such as were often brought from Venice. The Prince did not notice for some days that there was anything new in the room, but at last he perceived it, and went up to look at it more closely. What was his surprise to see reflected in the mirror, not his own face, but that of a young girl as lovely as the morning! And, better still, every movement of the girl, just growing out of childhood, was also reflected in the wonderful glass.

As might have been expected, the young Prince lost his heart completely to the beautiful image, and it was impossible to get him out of the room, so busy was he in watching the lovely unknown. Certainly it was very delightful to be able to see her whom he loved at any moment he chose, but his spirits sometimes sank when he wondered what was to be the end of this adventure.

THE PRINCE LOOKS INTO THE MAGIC MIRROR

The magic mirror had been for about a year in the Prince's possession, when one day a new subject of disquiet seized upon him. As usual, he was engaged in looking at the girl, when suddenly he thought he saw a second mirror reflected in the first, exactly like his own, and with the same power. And in this he was perfectly right. The young girl had only possessed it for a short time, and neglected all her duties for the sake of the mirror. Now it was not difficult for Saphir to guess the reason of the change in her, nor why the new mirror was consulted so often; but try as he would he could never see the face of the person who was reflected in it, for the young girl's figure always came between. All he knew was that the face was that of a man, and this was quite enough to make him madly jealous. This was the doing of the fairies, and we must suppose that they had their reasons for acting as they did.

When these things happened, Saphir was about eighteen years old, and fifteen years had passed away since the death of his mother. King Peridor had grown more and more unhappy as time went on, and at last he fell so ill that it seemed as if his days were numbered. He was so much beloved by his subjects that this sad news was heard with despair by the nation, and more than any by the Prince.

During his whole illness the King never spoke of anything but the Queen, his sorrow at having grieved her, and his hope of one day seeing her again. All the doctors and all the water cures in the kingdom had been tried, and nothing would do him any good. At last he persuaded them to let him lie quietly in his room, where no one came to trouble him.

Perhaps the worst pain he had to bear was a sort of weight on his chest, which made it very hard for him to breathe. So he commanded his servants to leave the windows open in order that he might get more air. One day, when he had been left alone for a few minutes, a bird with brilliant plumage came and fluttered round the window, and finally rested on the sill. His feathers were sky blue and gold, his feet and his beak of such glittering rubies that no one could bear to look at them, his eyes made the brightest diamonds look dull, and on his head he wore a crown. I cannot tell you what the crown was made of, but I am quite certain that it was still more splendid than all the rest. As to his voice, I can say nothing about that, for the bird never sang at all. In fact, he did nothing but gaze steadily at the King, and as he gazed, the King felt his strength come back to him. In a little while the bird flew into the room, still with his eyes fixed on the King, and at every glance the strength of the sick man became greater, till he was once more as well as he used to be before the Queen died. Filled with joy at his cure, he tried to seize the bird to whom he owed it all, but, swifter than a swallow, it managed to avoid him. In vain he described the bird to his attendants, who rushed at his first call; in vain they sought the wonderful creature both on horse and foot, and summoned the fowlers to their aid: the bird could nowhere be found. The love the people bore King Peridor was so strong, and the reward he promised was so large, that in the twinkling of an eye every man, woman, and child had fled into the fields, and the towns were quite empty.

All this bustle, however, ended in nothing but confusion, and, what was worse, the King soon fell back into the same condition as he was in before. Prince Saphir, who loved his father very dearly, was so unhappy at this that he persuaded himself that he might succeed where the others had failed, and at once prepared himself for a more distant search. In spite of the opposition he met with, he rode away, followed by his household, trusting to chance to help him. He had formed no plan, and there was no reason that he should choose one path more than another. His only idea was to make straight for those spots which were the favourite haunts of birds. But in vain he examined all the hedges and all the thickets; in vain he questioned everyone he met along the road. The more he sought the less he found.

At last he came to one of the largest forests in all the world, composed entirely of cedars. But in spite of the deep shadows cast by the wide-spreading branches of the trees, the grass underneath was soft and green, and covered with the rarest flowers. It seemed to Saphir that this was exactly the place where the birds would choose to live, and he determined not to quit the wood until he had examined it from end to end. And he did more. He ordered some nets to be prepared and painted of the same colours as the bird's plumage, thinking that we are all easily caught by what is like ourselves. In this he had to help him not only the fowlers by profession, but also his attendants, who excelled in this art. For a man is not a courtier unless he can do everything.

After searching as usual for nearly a whole day Prince Saphir began to feel overcome with thirst. He was too tired to go any farther, when happily he discovered a little way off a bubbling fountain of the clearest water. Being an experienced traveller, he drew from his pocket a little cup (without which no one should ever take a journey), and was just about to dip it in the water, when a lovely little green frog, much prettier than frogs generally are, jumped into the cup. Far from admiring its beauty, Saphir shook it impatiently off; but it was no good, for quick as lightning the frog jumped back again. Saphir, who was raging with thirst, was just about to shake it off anew, when the little creature fixed upon him the most beautiful eyes in the world, and said, "I am a friend of the bird you are seeking, and when you have quenched your thirst listen to me."

So the Prince drank his fill, and then, by the command of the Little Green Frog, he lay down on the grass to rest himself.

"Now," she began, "be sure you do exactly in every respect what I tell you. First you must call together your attendants, and order them to remain in a little hamlet close by until you want them. Then go, quite alone, down a road that you will find on your right hand, looking southwards. This road is planted all the way with cedars of Lebanon; and after going down it a long way you will come at last to a magnificent castle. "And now," she went on, "attend carefully to what I am going to say. Take this tiny grain of sand, and put it into the ground as close as you can to the gate of the castle. It has the virtue both of opening the gate and also of sending to sleep all the inhabitants. Then go at once to the stable, and pay no heed to anything except what I tell you. Choose the handsomest of all the horses, leap quickly on its back, and come to me as fast as you can. Farewell, Prince; I wish you good luck," and with these words the Little Frog plunged into the water and disappeared.

The Prince, who felt more hopeful than he had done since he left home, did precisely as he had been ordered. He left his attendants in the hamlet, found the road the frog had described to him, and followed it all alone, and at last he arrived at the gate of the castle, which was even more splendid than he had expected, for it was built of crystal, and all its ornaments were of massive gold. However, he had no thoughts to spare for its beauty, and quickly buried his grain of sand in the earth. In one instant the gates flew open, and all the dwellers inside fell sound asleep. Saphir flew straight to the stable, and already had his hand on the finest horse it contained, when his eye was caught by a suit of magnificent harness hanging up close by. It occurred to him directly that the harness belonged to the horse, and without ever thinking of harm (for indeed he who steals a horse can hardly be blamed for taking his sad-dle), he hastily placed it on the animal's back. Suddenly the people in the cas-tle became broad awake, and rushed to the stable. They flung themselves on the Prince, seized him, and dragged him before their lord; but, luckily for the Prince, who could only find very lame excuses for his conduct, the lord of the castle took a fancy to his face, and let him depart without further questions.

Very sad, and very much ashamed of himself poor Saphir crept back to the fountain, where the Frog was awaiting him with a good scolding.

"Whom do you take me for?" she exclaimed angrily. "Do you really be-lieve that it was just for the pleasure of talking that I gave you the advice you have neglected so abominably?"

But the Prince was so deeply grieved, and apologised so very humbly, that after some time the heart of the good Little Frog was softened, and she gave

PRINCE SAPHIR STEALS THE HORSE AND HARNESS

him another tiny little grain, but instead of being sand it was now a grain of gold. She directed him to do just as he had done before, with only this difference, that instead of going to the stable which had been the ruin of his hopes, he was to enter right into the castle itself, and to glide as fast as he could down the passages till he came to a room filled with perfume, where he would find a beautiful maiden asleep on a bed. He was to wake the maiden instantly and carry her off, and to be sure not to pay any heed to whatever resistance she might make.

The Prince obeyed the Frog's orders one by one, and all went well for this second time also. The gate opened, the inhabitants fell sound asleep, and he walked down the passage till he found the girl on her bed, exactly as he had been told he would. He woke her, and begged her firmly, but politely, to follow him quickly. After a little persuasion the maiden consented, but only on condition that she was allowed first to put on her dress. This sounded so reasonable and natural that it did not enter the Prince's head to refuse her request.

But the maiden's hand had hardly touched the dress when the palace suddenly awoke from its sleep, and the Prince was seized and bound. He was so vexed with his own folly, and so taken aback at the disaster, that he did not attempt to explain his conduct, and things would have gone badly with him if his friends the fairies had not softened the hearts of his captors, so that they once more allowed him to leave quietly. However, what troubled him most was the idea of having to meet the Frog who had been his benefactress. How was he ever to appear before her with this tale? Still, after a long struggle with himself, he made up his mind that there was nothing else to be done, and that he deserved whatever she might say to him. And she said a great deal, for she had worked herself into a terrible passion; but the Prince humbly implored her pardon, and ventured to point out that it would have been very hard to refuse the young lady's reasonable request. "You must learn to do as you are told," was all the Frog would reply.

But poor Saphir was so unhappy, and begged so hard for forgiveness, that at last the Frog's anger gave way, and she held up to him a tiny diamond stone. "Go back," she said, "to the castle, and bury this little diamond close to the door. But be careful not to return to the stable or to the bedroom; they have proved too fatal to you. Walk straight to the garden and enter through a portico, into a small green wood, in the midst of which is a tree with a trunk of gold and leaves of emeralds. Perched on this tree you will see the beautiful bird you have been seeking so long. You must cut the branch on which it is sitting, and bring it back to me without delay. But I warn you solemnly that if you disobey my directions, as you have done twice before, you have nothing more to expect either of me or anyone else."

With these words she jumped into the water, and the Prince, who had taken her threats much to heart, took his departure, firmly resolved not to deserve them. He found it all just as he had been told: the portico, the wood, the magnificent tree, and the beautiful bird, which was sleeping soundly on one of the branches. He speedily lopped off the branch, and though he noticed a splendid golden cage hanging close by, which would have been very useful for the bird to travel in, he left it alone, and came back to the fountain, holding his breath and walking on tip-toe all the way, for fear lest he should awake his prize. But what was his surprise, when instead of finding the fountain in the spot where he had left it, he saw in its place a little rustic palace built in the best taste, and standing in the doorway a charming maiden, at whose sight his mind seemed to give way.

"What! Madam!" he cried, hardly knowing what he said. "What! Is it you?"

The maiden blushed and answered: "Ah, my lord, it is long since I first beheld your face, but I did not think you had ever seen mine."

"Oh, madam," replied he, "you can never guess the days and the hours I have passed lost in admiration of you." And after these words they each related all the strange things that had happened, and the more they talked the more they felt convinced of the truth of the images they had seen in their mirrors. After some time spent in the most tender conversation, the Prince could not restrain himself from asking the lovely unknown by what lucky chance she was wandering in the forest; where the fountain had gone; and if she knew anything of the Frog to whom he owed all his happiness, and to whom he must give up the bird, which, somehow or other, was still sound asleep.

"Ah, my lord," she replied, with rather an awkward air, "as to the Frog, she stands before you. Let me tell you my story; it is not a long one. I know

"...AND STANDING IN THE DOORWAY A CHARMING MAIDEN,
AT WHOSE SIGHT HIS MIND SEEMED TO GIVE WAY."

neither my country nor my parents, and the only thing I can say for certain is that I am called Serpentine. The fairies, who have taken care of me ever since I was born, wished me to be in ignorance as to my family, but they have looked after my education, and have bestowed on me endless kindness. I have always lived in seclusion, and for the last two years I have wished for nothing better. I had a mirror'—here shyness and embarrassment choked her words—but regaining her self-control, she added, "You know that fairies insist on being obeyed without questioning. It was they who changed the little house you saw before you into the fountain for which you are now asking, and, having turned me into a frog, they ordered me to say to the first person who came to the fountain exactly what I repeated to you. But, my lord, when you stood before me, it was agony to my heart, filled as it was with thoughts of you, to appear to your eyes under so monstrous a form. However, there was no help for it, and, painful as it was, I had to submit. I desired your success with all my soul, not only for your own sake, but also for my own, because I could not get back my proper shape till you had become master of the beautiful bird, though I am quite ignorant as to your reason for seeking it."

On this Saphir explained about the state of his father's health, and all that has been told before.

On hearing this story Serpentine grew very sad, and her lovely eyes filled with tears.

"Ah, my lord," she said, "you know nothing of me but what you have seen in the mirror; and I, who cannot even name my parents, learn that you are a king's son."

In vain Saphir declared that love made them equal; Serpentine would only reply: "I love you too much to allow you to marry beneath your rank. I shall be very unhappy, of course, but I shall never alter my mind. If I do not find from the fairies that my birth is worthy of you, then, whatever be my feelings, I will never accept your hand."

The conversation was at this point, and bid fair to last some time longer, when one of the fairies appeared in her ivory chariot, accompanied by a beautiful woman past her early youth. At this moment the bird suddenly awakened, and, flying on to Saphir's shoulder (which it never afterward left), began fondling him as well as a bird can do. The fairy told Serpentine that she was quite satisfied with her conduct, and made herself very agreeable to Saphir, whom she presented to the lady she had brought with her, explaining that the lady was no other than his Aunt Aglantine, widow of Diamantino.

Then they all fell into each other's arms, till the fairy mounted her chariot, placed Aglantine by her side, and Saphir and Serpentine on the front seat. She also sent a message to the Prince's attendants that they might travel slowly back to the Court of King Peridor, and that the beautiful bird had really been found. This matter being comfortably arranged, she started off her chariot. But in spite of the swiftness with which they flew through the air, the time passed even quicker for Saphir and Serpentine, who had so much to think about.

They were still quite confused with the pleasure of seeing each other, when the chariot arrived at King Peridor's palace. He had had himself carried to a room on the roof, where his nurses thought that he would die at any moment. As the chariot drew within sight of the castle, the beautiful bird took flight, and, making straight for the dying King, at once cured him of his sickness. Then she resumed her natural shape, and he found that the bird was no other than the Queen Constance, whom he had long believed to be dead. Peridor was rejoiced to embrace his wife and his son once more, and with the help of the fairies began to make preparations for the marriage of Saphir and Serpentine, who turned out to be the daughter of Aglantine and Diamantino, and as much a princess as he was a prince. The people of the kingdom were delighted, and everybody lived happy and contented to the end of their lives.

THE SEVEN-HEADED SERPENT[9]

ONCE UPON A TIME THERE WAS A KING WHO DETERMINED to take a long voyage. He assembled his fleet and all the seamen, and set out. They went straight on night and day, until they came to an island which was covered with large trees, and under every tree lay a lion. As soon as the King had landed his men, the lions all rose up together and tried to devour them. After a long battle they managed to overcome the wild beasts, but the greater number of the men were killed. Those who remained alive now went on through the forest and found on the other side of it a beautiful garden, in which all the plants of the world flourished together. There were also in the garden three springs: the first flowed with silver, the second with gold, and the third with pearls. The men unbuckled their knapsacks and filled them with those precious things. In the middle of the garden they found a large lake, and when they reached the edge of it the Lake began to speak, and said to them, "What men are you, and what brings

9   'Die Siebenköpfige Schlange,' from Schmidt's *Griechische Mährchen*.

you here? Are you come to visit our king?" But they were too much frightened to answer.

Then the Lake said, "You do well to be afraid, for it is at your peril that you are come hither. Our king, who has seven heads, is now asleep, but in a few minutes he will wake up and come to me to take his bath! Woe to anyone who meets him in the garden, for it is impossible to escape from him. This is what you must do if you wish to save your lives. Take off your clothes and spread them on the path which leads from here to the castle. The King will then glide over something soft, which he likes very much, and he will be so pleased with that that he will not devour you. He will give you some punishment, but then he will let you go."

The men did as the Lake advised them, and waited for a time. At noon the earth began to quake, and opened in many places, and out of the openings appeared lions, tigers, and other wild beasts, which surrounded the castle, and thousands and thousands of beasts came out of the castle following their king, the Seven-headed Serpent. The Serpent glided over the clothes which were spread for him, came to the Lake, and asked it who had strewed those soft things on the path? The Lake answered that it had been done by people who had come to do him homage. The King commanded that the men should be brought before him. They came humbly on their knees, and in a few words told him their story. Then he spoke to them with a mighty and terrible voice, and said, "Because you have dared to come here, I lay upon you the punishment. Every year you must bring me from among your people twelve youths and twelve maidens, that I may devour them. If you do not do this, I will destroy your whole nation."

Then he desired one of his beasts to show the men the way out of the garden, and dismissed them. They then left the island and went back to their own country, where they related what had happened to them. Soon the time came round when the king of the beasts would expect the youths and maidens to

The Seven-headed Serpent

be brought to him. The King therefore issued a proclamation inviting twelve youths and twelve maidens to offer themselves up to save their country; and immediately many young people, far more than enough, hastened to do so. A new ship was built, and set with black sails, and in it the youths and maidens who were appointed for the king of the beasts embarked and set out for his country. When they arrived there they went at once to the Lake, and this time the lions did not stir, nor did the springs flow, and neither did the Lake speak. So they waited then, and it was not long before the earth quaked even more terribly than the first time. The Seven-headed Serpent came without his train of beasts, saw his prey waiting for him, and devoured it at one mouthful. Then the ship's crew returned home, and the same thing happened yearly until many years had passed.

Now the King of this unhappy country was growing old, and so was the Queen, and they had no children. One day the Queen was sitting at the window weeping bitterly because she was childless, and knew that the crown would therefore pass to strangers after the King's death. Suddenly a little old woman appeared before her, holding an apple in her hand, and said, "Why do you weep, my Queen, and what makes you so unhappy?"

"Alas, good mother," answered the Queen, "I am unhappy because I have no children."

"Is that what vexes you?" said the old woman. "Listen to me. I am a nun from the *Spinning Convent*[10] and my mother when she died left me this apple. Whoever eats this apple shall have a child."

The Queen gave money to the old woman, and bought the apple from her. Then she peeled it, ate it, and threw the rind out of the window, and it so happened that a mare that was running loose in the court below ate up the rind. After a time the Queen had a little boy, and the mare also had a male foal.

---

10   Convent Gnothi.

The boy and the foal grew up together and loved each other like brothers. In course of time the King died, and so did the Queen, and their son, who was now nineteen years old, was left alone. One day, when he and his horse were talking together, the Horse said to him, "Listen to me, for I love you and wish for your good and that of the country. If you go on every year sending twelve youths and twelve maidens to the King of the Beasts, your country will very soon be ruined. Mount upon my back: I will take you to a woman who can direct you how to kill the Seven-headed Serpent."

Then the youth mounted his horse, who carried him far away to a mountain which was hollow, for in its side was a great underground cavern. In the cavern sat an old woman spinning. This was the cloister of the nuns, and the old woman was the Abbess. They all spent their time in spinning, and that is why the convent has this name. All round the walls of the cavern there were beds cut out of the solid rock, upon which the nuns slept, and in the middle a light was burning. It was the duty of the nuns to watch the light in turns, that it might never go out, and if anyone of them let it go out the others put her to death.

As soon as the King's son saw the old Abbess spinning he threw himself at her feet and entreated her to tell him how he could kill the Seven-headed Serpent.

She made the youth rise, embraced him, and said, "Know, my son, that it is I who sent the nun to your mother and caused you to be born, and with you the horse, with whose help you will be able to free the world from the monster. I will tell you what you have to do. Load your horse with cotton, and go by a secret passage which I will show you, which is hidden from the wild beasts, to the Serpent's palace. You will find the King asleep upon his bed, which is all hung round with bells, and over his bed you will see a sword hanging. With this sword only it is possible to kill the Serpent, because even if its blade breaks a new one will grow again for every head the monster has. Thus you will be able to cut off all his seven heads. And this you must also do in order to deceive the King: you must slip into his bed-chamber very softly, and stop up all the bells which are round his bed with cotton. Then take down the sword gently, and quickly give the monster a blow on his tail with it. This will make him wake up, and if he catches sight of you he will seize you. But you must quickly cut off his first head, and then wait till the next one comes up. Then strike it off also, and so go on till you have cut off all his seven heads."

The old Abbess then gave the Prince her blessing, and he set out upon his enterprise, arrived at the Serpent's castle by following the secret passage which she had shown him, and by carefully attending to all her directions he happily succeeded in killing the monster. As soon as the wild beasts heard of their king's death, they all hastened to the castle, but the youth had long since mounted his horse and was already far out of their reach. They pursued him as fast as they could, but they found it impossible to overtake him, and he reached home in safety. Thus he freed his country from this terrible oppression.

THE GRATEFUL BEASTS[11]

HERE WAS ONCE UPON A TIME A MAN AND WOMAN WHO
had three fine-looking sons, but they were so poor that they
had hardly enough food for themselves, let alone their children. So the sons determined to set out into the world and to
try their luck. Before starting their mother gave them each a loaf of bread and
her blessing, and having taken a tender farewell of her and their father the
three set forth on their travels.

The youngest of the three brothers, whose name was Ferko, was a beautiful youth, with a splendid figure, blue eyes, fair hair, and a complexion like
milk and roses. His two brothers were as jealous of him as they could be, for
they thought that with his good looks he would be sure to be more fortunate
than they would ever be.

One day all the three were sitting resting under a tree, for the sun was
hot and they were tired of walking. Ferko fell fast asleep, but the other two

---

11   From the Hungarian. Kletke.

remained awake, and the eldest said to the second brother, "What do you say to doing our brother Ferko some harm? He is so beautiful that everyone takes a fancy to him, which is more than they do to us. If we could only get him out of the way we might succeed better."

"I quite agree with you," answered the second brother, "and my advice is to eat up his loaf of bread, and then to refuse to give him a bit of ours until he has promised to let us put out his eyes or break his legs."

His eldest brother was delighted with this proposal, and the two wicked wretches seized Ferko's loaf and ate it all up, while the poor boy was still asleep.

When he did awake he felt very hungry and turned to eat his bread, but his brothers cried out, "You ate your loaf in your sleep, you glutton, and you may starve as long as you like, but you won't get a scrap of ours."

Ferko was at a loss to understand how he could have eaten in his sleep, but he said nothing, and fasted all that day and the next night. But on the following morning he was so hungry that he burst into tears, and implored his brothers to give him a little bit of their bread. Then the cruel creatures laughed, and repeated what they had said the day before; but when Ferko continued to beg and beseech them, the eldest said at last, "If you will let us put out one of your eyes and break one of your legs, then we will give you a bit of our bread."

At these words poor Ferko wept more bitterly than before, and bore the torments of hunger till the sun was high in the heavens; then he could stand it no longer, and he consented to allow his left eye to be put out and his left leg to be broken. When this was done he stretched out his hand eagerly for the piece of bread, but his brothers gave him such a tiny scrap that the starving youth finished it in a moment and besought them for a second bit.

But the more Ferko wept and told his brothers that he was dying of hunger, the more they laughed and scolded him for his greed. So he endured the pangs of starvation all that day, but when night came his endurance gave way, and he let his right eye be put out and his right leg broken for a second piece of bread.

After his brothers had thus successfully maimed and disfigured him for life, they left him groaning on the ground and continued their journey without him.

Poor Ferko ate up the scrap of bread they had left him and wept bitterly, but no one heard him or came to his help. Night came on, and the poor blind youth had no eyes to close, and could only crawl along the ground, not knowing in the least where he was going. But when the sun was once more high in the heavens, Ferko felt the blazing heat scorch him, and sought for some cool shady place to rest his aching limbs. He climbed to the top of a hill and lay down in the grass, and as he thought under the shadow of a big tree. But it was no tree he leant against, but a gallows on which two ravens were seated. The one was saying to the other as the weary youth lay down, "Is there anything the least wonderful or remarkable about this neighbourhood?"

"I should just think there was," replied the other; "many things that don't exist anywhere else in the world. There is a lake down there below us, and anyone who bathes in it, though he were at death's door, becomes sound and well on the spot, and those who wash their eyes with the dew on this hill become as sharp-sighted as the eagle, even if they have been blind from their youth."

"Well," answered the first raven, "my eyes are in no want of this healing bath, for, Heaven be praised, they are as good as ever they were; but my wing has been very feeble and weak ever since it was shot by an arrow many years ago, so let us fly at once to the lake that I may be restored to health and strength again." And so they flew away.

Their words rejoiced Ferko's heart, and he waited impatiently till evening should come and he could rub the precious dew on his sightless eyes.

At last it began to grow dusk, and the sun sank behind the mountains; gradually it became cooler on the hill, and the grass grew wet with dew. Then Ferko buried his face in the ground till his eyes were damp with dew-drops, and in a moment he saw clearer than he had ever done in his life before. The moon was shining brightly, and lighted him to the lake where he could bathe his poor broken legs.

Then Ferko crawled to the edge of the lake and dipped his limbs in the water. No sooner had he done so than his legs felt as sound and strong as they had been before, and Ferko thanked the kind fate that had led him to the hill where he had overheard the ravens' conversation. He filled a bottle with the healing water, and then continued his journey in the best of spirits.

He had not gone far before he met a wolf, who was limping disconsolately along on three legs, and who on perceiving Ferko began to howl dismally.

"My good friend," said the youth, "be of good cheer, for I can soon heal your leg," and with these words he poured some of the precious water over the wolf's paw, and in a minute the animal was springing about sound and well on all fours. The grateful creature thanked his benefactor warmly, and promised Ferko to do him a good turn if he should ever need it.

Ferko continued his way till he came to a ploughed field. Here he noticed a little mouse creeping wearily along on its hind paws, for its front paws had both been broken in a trap.

Ferko felt so sorry for the little beast that he spoke to it in the most friendly manner, and washed its small paws with the healing water. In a moment the mouse was sound and whole, and after thanking the kind physician it scampered away over the ploughed furrows.

Ferko again proceeded on his journey, but he hadn't gone far before a queen bee flew against him, trailing one wing behind her, which had been cruelly torn in two by a big bird. Ferko was no less willing to help her than he had been to help the wolf and the mouse, so he poured some healing drops over the wounded wing. On the spot the queen bee was cured, and turning to Ferko she said, "I am most grateful for your kindness, and shall reward you some day." And with these words she flew away humming gaily.

Then Ferko wandered on for many a long day, and at length reached a strange kingdom. Here, he thought to himself, he might as well go straight to the palace and offer his services to the King of the country, for he had heard that the King's daughter was as beautiful as the day.

So he went to the royal palace, and as he entered the door the first people he saw were his two brothers who had so shamefully ill-treated him. They had managed to obtain places in the King's service, and when they recognised Ferko with his eyes and legs sound and well they were frightened to death, for they feared he would tell the King of their conduct, and that they would be hung.

No sooner had Ferko entered the palace than all eyes were turned on the handsome youth, and the King's daughter herself was lost in admiration, for she had never seen anyone so handsome in her life before. His brothers noticed this, and envy and jealousy were added to their fear, so much so that they determined once more to destroy him. They went to the King and told him that Ferko was a wicked magician, who had come to the palace with the intention of carrying off the Princess.

Then the King had Ferko brought before him, and said, "You are accused of being a magician who wishes to rob me of my daughter, and I condemn you

THE YELLOW FAIRY BOOK

to death; but if you can fulfil three tasks which I shall set you to do your life shall be spared, on condition you leave the country; but if you cannot perform what I demand you shall be hung on the nearest tree."

And turning to the two wicked brothers he said, "Suggest something for him to do; no matter how difficult, he must succeed in it or die."

They did not think long, but replied, "Let him build your Majesty in one day a more beautiful palace than this, and if he fails in the attempt let him be hung."

The King was pleased with this proposal, and commanded Ferko to set to work on the following day. The two brothers were delighted, for they thought they had now got rid of Ferko forever. The poor youth himself was heartbroken, and cursed the hour he had crossed the boundary of the King's domain. As he was wandering disconsolately about the meadows round the palace, wondering how he could escape being put to death, a little bee flew past, and settling on his shoulder whispered in his ear, "What is troubling you, my kind benefactor? Can I be of any help to you? I am the bee whose wing you healed, and would like to show my gratitude in some way."

Ferko recognised the queen bee, and said, "Alas! how could you help me? for I have been set to do a task which no one in the whole world could do, let him be ever such a genius! To-morrow I must build a palace more beautiful than the King's, and it must be finished before evening."

"Is that all?" answered the bee, "then you may comfort yourself; for before the sun goes down to-morrow night a palace shall be built unlike any that King has dwelt in before. Just stay here till I come again and tell you that it is finished." Having said this she flew merrily away, and Ferko, reassured by her words, lay down on the grass and slept peacefully till the next morning.

Early on the following day the whole town was on its feet, and everyone wondered how and where the stranger would build the wonderful palace. The Princess alone was silent and sorrowful, and had cried all night till her pillow was wet, so much did she take the fate of the beautiful youth to heart.

Ferko spent the whole day in the meadows waiting the return of the bee. And when evening was come the queen bee flew by, and perching on his shoulder she said, "The wonderful palace is ready. Be of good cheer, and lead the King to the hill just outside the city walls." And humming gaily she flew away again.

Ferko went at once to the King and told him the palace was finished. The whole court went out to see the wonder, and their astonishment was great at the sight which met their eyes. A splendid palace reared itself on the hill just outside the walls of the city, made of the most exquisite flowers that ever grew in a mortal garden. The roof was all of crimson roses, the windows of lilies, the walls of white carnations, the floors of glowing auriculas and violets, the doors of gorgeous tulips and narcissi with sunflowers for knockers, and all round hyacinths and other sweet-smelling flowers bloomed in masses, so that the air was perfumed far and near and enchanted all who were present.

This splendid palace had been built by the grateful queen bee, who had summoned all the other bees in the kingdom to help her.

The King's amazement knew no bounds, and the Princess's eyes beamed with delight as she turned them from the wonderful building on the delighted Ferko. But the two brothers had grown quite green with envy, and only declared the more that Ferko was nothing but a wicked magician.

The King, although he had been surprised and astonished at the way his commands had been carried out, was very vexed that the stranger should escape with his life, and turning to the two brothers he said, "He has certainly accomplished the first task, with the aid no doubt of his diabolical magic; but what shall we give him to do now? Let us make it as difficult as possible, and if he fails he shall die."

Then the eldest brother replied, "The corn has all been cut, but it has not yet been put into barns; let the knave collect all the grain in the kingdom into one big heap before to-morrow night, and if as much as a stalk of corn is left let him be put to death."

The Princess grew white with terror when she heard these words; but Ferko felt much more cheerful than he had done the first time, and wandered out into the meadows again, wondering how he was to get out of the difficulty. But he could think of no way of escape. The sun sank to rest and night came on, when a little mouse started out of the grass at Ferko's feet, and said to him, "I'm delighted to see you, my kind benefactor; but why are you looking so sad? Can I be of any help to you, and thus repay your great kindness to me?"

Then Ferko recognised the mouse whose front paws he had healed, and replied, "Alas! how can you help me in a matter that is beyond any human power! Before to-morrow night all the grain in the kingdom has to be gathered into one big heap, and if as much as a stalk of corn is wanting I must pay for it with my life."

"Is that all?" answered the mouse; "that needn't distress you much. Just trust in me, and before the sun sets again you shall hear that your task is done." And with these words the little creature scampered away into the fields.

Ferko, who never doubted that the mouse would be as good as its word, lay down comforted on the soft grass and slept soundly till the next morning. The day passed slowly, and with the evening came the little mouse and said, "Now there is not a single stalk of corn left in any field; they are all collected in one big heap on the hill out there."

Then Ferko went joyfully to the King and told him that all he demanded had been done. And the whole Court went out to see the wonder, and were no less astonished than they had been the first time. For in a heap higher than the King's palace lay all the grain of the country, and not a single stalk of corn had been left behind in any of the fields. And how had all this been done? The little mouse had summoned every other mouse in the land to its help, and together they had collected all the grain in the kingdom.

The King could not hide his amazement, but at the same time his wrath increased, and he was more ready than ever to believe the two brothers, who kept on repeating that Ferko was nothing more nor less than a wicked magician.

Only the beautiful Princess rejoiced over Ferko's success, and looked on him with friendly glances, which the youth returned.

The more the cruel King gazed on the wonder before him, the more angry he became, for he could not, in the face of his promise, put the stranger to death. He turned once more to the two brothers and said, "His diabolical magic has helped him again, but now what third task shall we set him to do? No matter how impossible it is, he must do it or die."

The eldest answered quickly, "Let him drive all the wolves of the kingdom on to this hill before to-morrow night. If he does this he may go free; if not he shall be hung as you have said."

At these words the Princess burst into tears, and when the King saw this he ordered her to be shut up in a high tower and carefully guarded till the dangerous magician should either have left the kingdom or been hung on the nearest tree.

Ferko wandered out into the fields again, and sat down on the stump of a tree wondering what he should do next. Suddenly a big wolf ran up to him, and standing still said, "I'm very glad to see you again, my kind benefactor. What are you thinking about all alone by yourself? If I can help you in any way only say the word, for I would like to give you proof of my gratitude."

Ferko at once recognised the wolf whose broken leg he had healed, and told him what he had to do the following day if he wished to escape with his life. "But how in the world," he added, "am I to collect all the wolves of the kingdom on to that hill over there?"

"If that's all you want done," answered the wolf, "you needn't worry yourself. I'll undertake the task, and you'll hear from me again before sunset to-morrow. Keep your spirits up." And with these words he trotted quickly away.

Then the youth rejoiced greatly, for now he felt that his life was safe; but he grew very sad when he thought of the beautiful Princess, and that he would never see her again if he left the country. He lay down once more on the grass and soon fell fast asleep.

All the next day he spent wandering about the fields, and toward evening the wolf came running to him in a great hurry and said, "I have collected together all the wolves in the kingdom, and they are waiting for you in the wood. Go quickly to the King, and tell him to go to the hill that he may see the wonder you have done with his own eyes. Then return at once to me and get on my back, and I will help you to drive all the wolves together."

Then Ferko went straight to the palace and told the King that he was ready to perform the third task if he would come to the hill and see it done. Ferko himself returned to the fields, and mounting on the wolf's back he rode to the wood close by.

Quick as lightning the wolf flew round the wood, and in a minute many hundred wolves rose up before him, increasing in number every moment, till they could be counted by thousands. He drove them all before him on to the hill, where the King and his whole Court and Ferko's two brothers were standing. Only the lovely Princess was not present, for she was shut up in her tower weeping bitterly.

The wicked brothers stamped and foamed with rage when they saw the failure of their wicked designs. But the King was overcome by a sudden terror when he saw the enormous pack of wolves approaching nearer and nearer, and calling out to Ferko he said, "Enough, enough, we don't want any more."

But the wolf on whose back Ferko sat, said to its rider, "Go on! go on!" and at the same moment many more wolves ran up the hill, howling horribly and showing their white teeth.

The King in his terror called out, "Stop a moment; I will give you half my kingdom if you will drive all the wolves away." But Ferko pretended not to hear, and drove some more thousands before him, so that everyone quaked with horror and fear.

Then the King raised his voice again and called out, "Stop! you shall have my whole kingdom, if you will only drive these wolves back to the places they came from."

FERKO LEADS THE WOLVES ON

But the wolf kept on encouraging Ferko, and said, "Go on! go on!" So he led the wolves on, till at last they fell on the King and on the wicked brothers, and ate them and the whole Court up in a moment.

Then Ferko went straight to the palace and set the Princess free, and on the same day he married her and was crowned King of the country. And the wolves all went peacefully back to their own homes, and Ferko and his bride lived for many years in peace and happiness together, and were much beloved by great and small in the land.

THE GIANTS AND THE HERD-BOY[12]

HERE WAS ONCE UPON A TIME A POOR BOY WHO HAD neither father nor mother. In order to gain a living he looked after the sheep of a great Lord. Day and night he spent out in the open fields, and only when it was very wet and stormy did he take refuge in a little hut on the edge of a big forest. Now one night, when he was sitting on the grass beside his flocks, he heard not very far from him the sound as if someone were crying. He rose up and followed the direction of the noise. To his dismay and astonishment he found a Giant lying at the entrance of the wood; he was about to run off as fast as his legs could carry him, when the Giant called out: "Don't be afraid, I won't harm you. On the contrary, I will reward you handsomely if you will bind up my foot. I hurt it when I was trying to root up an oak-tree." The Herd-boy took off his shirt, and

12   From the *Bukowniaer*. Von Wliolocki.

bound up the Giant's wounded foot with it. Then the Giant rose up and said, "Now come and I will reward you. We are going to celebrate a marriage to-day, and I promise you we shall have plenty of fun. Come and enjoy yourself, but in order that my brothers mayn't see you, put this band round your waist and then you'll be invisible." With these words he handed the Herd-boy a belt, and walking on in front he led him to a fountain where hundreds of Giants and Giantesses were assembled preparing to hold a wedding. They danced and played different games till midnight; then one of the Giants tore up a plant by its roots, and all the Giants and Giantesses made themselves so thin that they disappeared into the earth through the hole made by the uprooting of the plant. The wounded Giant remained behind to the last and called out, "Herd-boy, where are you?" "Here I am, close to you," was the reply. "Touch me," said the Giant, "so that you too may come with us underground." The Herd-boy did as he was told, and before he could have believed it possible he found himself in a big hall, where even the walls were made of pure gold. Then to his astonishment he saw that the hall was furnished with the tables and chairs that belonged to his master. In a few minutes the company began to eat and drink. The banquet was a very gorgeous one, and the poor youth fell to and ate and drank lustily. When he had eaten and drunk as much as he could he thought to himself, "Why shouldn't I put a loaf of bread in my pocket? I shall be glad of it to-morrow." So he seized a loaf when no one was looking and stowed it away under his tunic. No sooner had he done so than the wounded Giant limped up to him and whispered softly, "Herd-boy, where are you?" "Here I am," replied the youth. "Then hold on to me," said the Giant, "so that I may lead you up above again." So the Herd-boy held on to the Giant, and in a few moments he found himself on the earth once more, but the Giant had vanished. The Herd-boy returned to his sheep, and took off the invisible belt which he hid carefully in his bag.

The next morning the lad felt hungry, and thought he would cut off a piece

THE HERD-BOY BINDS UP THE GIANT'S FOOT

of the loaf he had carried away from the Giants' wedding feast, and eat it. But although he tried with all his might, he couldn't cut off the smallest piece. Then in despair he bit the loaf, and what was his astonishment when a piece of gold fell out of his mouth and rolled at his feet. He bit the bread a second and third time, and each time a piece of gold fell out of his mouth; but the bread remained untouched. The Herd-boy was very much delighted over his stroke of good fortune, and, hiding the magic loaf in his bag, he hurried off to the nearest village to buy himself something to eat, and then returned to his sheep.

Now the Lord whose sheep the Herd-boy looked after had a very lovely daughter, who always smiled and nodded to the youth when she walked with her father in his fields. For a long time the Herd-boy had made up his mind to prepare a surprise for this beautiful creature on her birthday. So when the day approached he put on his invisible belt, took a sack of gold pieces with him, and slipping into her room in the middle of the night, he placed the bag of gold beside her bed and returned to his sheep. The girl's joy was great, and so was her parents' the next day when they found the sack full of gold pieces. The Herd-boy was so pleased to think what pleasure he had given that the next night he placed another bag of gold beside the girl's bed. And this he continued to do for seven nights, and the girl and her parents made up their minds that it must be a good Fairy who brought the gold every night. But one night they determined to watch, and see from their hiding-place who the bringer of the sack of gold really was.

On the eighth night a fearful storm of wind and rain came on while the Herd-boy was on his way to bring the beautiful girl another bag of gold. Then for the first time he noticed, just as he reached his master's house, that he had forgotten the belt which made him invisible. He didn't like the idea of going back to his hut in the wind and wet, so he just stepped as he was into the girl's room, laid the sack of gold beside her, and was turning to leave the room, when his master confronted him and said, "You young rogue, so you were going to steal the gold that a good Fairy brings every night, were you?" The Herd-boy was so taken aback by his words, that he stood trembling before him, and did not dare to explain his presence. Then his master spoke. "As you have hitherto always behaved well in my service I will not send you to prison; but leave your place instantly and never let me see your face again." So the Herd-boy went back to his hut, and taking his loaf and belt with him, he went to the nearest town. There he bought himself some fine clothes, and a beautiful coach with four horses, hired two servants, and drove back to his master. You may imagine how astonished he was to see his Herd-boy returning to him in this manner! Then the youth told him of the piece of good luck that had befallen him, and asked him for the hand of his beautiful daughter. This was readily granted, and the two lived in peace and happiness to the end of their lives.

THE INVISIBLE PRINCE

NCE UPON A TIME THERE LIVED A FAIRY WHO HAD POW-
er over the earth, the sea, fire, and the air; and this Fairy had four
sons. The eldest, who was quick and lively, with a vivid imagi-
nation, she made Lord of Fire, which was in her opinion the
noblest of all the elements. To the second son, whose wisdom and prudence
made amends for his being rather dull, she gave the government of the earth.
The third was wild and savage, and of monstrous stature; and the Fairy, his
mother, who was ashamed of his defects, hoped to hide them by creating him
King of the Seas. The youngest, who was the slave of his passions and of a very
uncertain temper, became Prince of the Air.

Being the youngest, he was naturally his mother's favourite; but this did
not blind her to his weaknesses, and she foresaw that some day he would
suffer much pain through falling in love. So she thought the best thing she
could do was to bring him up with a horror of women; and, to her great delight, she saw this dislike only increased as he grew older. From his earliest
childhood he heard nothing but stories of princes who had fallen into all
sorts of troubles through love; and she drew such terrible pictures of poor

little Cupid that the young man had no difficulty in believing that he was the root of all evil.

All the time that this wise mother could spare from filling her son with hatred for all womenkind she passed in giving him a love of the pleasures of the chase, which henceforth became his chief joy. For his amusement she had made a new forest, planted with the most splendid trees, and turned loose in it every animal that could be found in any of the four quarters of the globe. In the midst of this forest she built a palace which had not its equal for beauty in the whole world, and then she considered that she had done enough to make any prince happy.

Now it is all very well to abuse the God of Love, but a man cannot struggle against his fate. In his secret heart the Prince got tired of his mother's constant talk on this subject; and when one day she quitted the palace to attend to some business, begging him never to go beyond the grounds, he at once jumped at the chance of disobeying her.

Left to himself the Prince soon forgot the wise counsels of his mother, and feeling very much bored with his own company, he ordered some of the spirits of the air to carry him to the court of a neighbouring sovereign. This kingdom was situated in the Island of Roses, where the climate is so delicious that the grass is always green and the flowers always sweet. The waves, instead of beating on the rocks, seemed to die gently on the shore; clusters of golden bushes covered the land, and the vines were bent low with grapes.

The King of this island had a daughter named Rosalie, who was more lovely than any girl in the whole world. No sooner had the eyes of the Prince of the Air rested on her than he forgot all the terrible woes which had been prophesied to him ever since he was born, for in one single moment the plans of years are often upset. He instantly began to think how best to make himself happy, and the shortest way that occurred to him was to have Rosalie carried off by his attendant spirits.

It is easy to imagine the feelings of the King when he found that his daughter had vanished. He wept her loss night and day, and his only comfort was to talk over it with a young and unknown prince, who had just arrived at the Court. Alas! he did not know what a deep interest the stranger had in Rosalie, for he too had seen her, and had fallen a victim to her charms.

One day the King, more sorrowful than usual, was walking sadly along the seashore, when after a long silence the unknown Prince, who was his only companion, suddenly spoke. "There is no evil without a remedy," he said to the unhappy father; "and if you will promise me your daughter in marriage, I will undertake to bring her back to you."

"You are trying to soothe me by vain promises," answered the King. "Did I not see her caught up into the air, in spite of cries which would have softened the heart of any one but the barbarian who has robbed me of her? The unfortunate girl is pining away in some unknown land, where perhaps no foot of man has ever trod, and I shall see her no more. But go, generous stranger; bring back Rosalie if you can, and live happy with her ever after in this country, of which I now declare you heir."

Although the stranger's name and rank were unknown to Rosalie's father, he was really the son of the King of the Golden Isle, which had for capital a city that extended from one sea to another. The walls, washed by the quiet waters, were covered with gold, which made one think of the yellow sands. Above them was a rampart of orange and lemon trees, and all the streets were paved with gold.

The King of this beautiful island had one son, for whom a life of adventure had been foretold at his birth. This so frightened his father and mother that in order to comfort them a Fairy, who happened to be present at the time, produced a little pebble which she told them to keep for the Prince till he grew up, as by putting it in his mouth he would become invisible, as long as he did not try to speak, for if he did the stone would lose all its virtue. In this way the good fairy hoped that the Prince would be protected against all dangers.

No sooner did the Prince begin to grow out of boyhood than he longed to see if the other countries of the world were as splendid as the one in which he lived. So, under pretence of visiting some small islands that belonged to his father, he set out. But a frightful storm drove his ship on to unknown shores, where most of his followers were put to death by the savages, and the Prince himself only managed to escape by making use of his magic pebble. By this means he passed through the midst of them unseen, and wandered on till he reached the coast, where he re-embarked on board his ship.

The first land he sighted was the Island of Roses, and he went at once to the court of the King, Rosalie's father. The moment his eyes beheld the Princess, he fell in love with her like everyone else.

He had already spent several months in this condition when the Prince of the Air whirled her away, to the grief and despair of every man on the island. But sad though everybody was, the Prince of the Golden Isle was perfectly inconsolable, and he passed both days and nights in bemoaning his loss.

"Alas!" he cried; "shall I never see my lovely Princess again? Who knows where she may be, and what fairy may have her in his keeping? I am only a man, but I am strong in my love, and I will seek the whole world through till I find her."

So saying, he left the court, and made ready for his journey.

He travelled many weary days without hearing a single word of the lost Princess, till one morning, as he was walking through a thick forest, he suddenly perceived a magnificent palace standing at the end of a pine avenue, and his heart bounded to think that he might be gazing on Rosalie's prison. He hastened his steps, and quickly arrived at the gate of the palace, which was formed of a single agate. The gate swung open to let him through, and he next passed successively three courts, surrounded by deep ditches filled with running water, with birds of brilliant plumage flying about the banks. Everything around was rare and beautiful, but the Prince scarcely raised his eyes to all these wonders.

He thought only of the Princess and where he should find her, but in vain he opened every door and searched in every corner; he neither saw Rosalie nor anyone else. At last there was no place left for him to search but a little wood, which contained in the centre a sort of hall built entirely of orange-trees, with four small rooms opening out of the corners. Three of these were empty except for statues and wonderful things, but in the fourth the Invisible Prince caught sight of Rosalie. His joy at beholding her again was, however, somewhat lessened by seeing that the Prince of the Air was kneeling at her feet, and pleading his own cause. But it was in vain that he implored her to listen; she only shook her head. "No," was all she would say; "you snatched me from my father whom I loved, and all the splendour in the world can never console me. Go! I can never feel anything toward you but hate and contempt." With these words she turned away and entered her own apartments.

Unknown to herself the Invisible Prince had followed her, but fearing to be discovered by the Princess in the presence of others, he made up his mind to wait quietly till dark; and employed the long hours in writing a poem to the Princess, which he laid on the bed beside her. This done, he thought of nothing but how best to deliver Rosalie, and he resolved to take advantage of a visit which the Prince of the Air paid every year to his mother and brothers in order to strike the blow.

One day, Rosalie was sitting alone in her room thinking of her troubles when she suddenly saw a pen get up from off the desk and begin to write all by itself on a sheet of white paper. As she did not know that it was guided by an invisible hand she was very much astonished, and the moment that the pen had ceased to move she instantly went over to the table, where she found some lovely verses, telling her that another shared her distresses, whatever they might be, and loved her with all his heart; and that he would never rest until he had delivered her from the hands of the man she hated. Thus encouraged, she told him all her story, and of the arrival of a young stranger in her

The Pen Got Up And Wrote All By Itself

ROSALIE

father's palace, whose looks had so charmed her that since that day she had thought of no one else. At these words the Prince could contain himself no longer. He took the pebble from his mouth, and flung himself at Rosalie's feet.

When they had got over the first rapture of meeting they began to make plans to escape from the power of the Prince of the Air. But this did not prove easy, for the magic stone would only serve for one person at a time, and in order to save Rosalie the Prince of the Golden Isle would have to expose himself to the fury of his enemy. But Rosalie would not hear of this.

"No, Prince," she said; "since you are here this island no longer feels a prison. Besides, you are under the protection of a Fairy, who always visits your father's court at this season. Go instantly and seek her, and when she is found implore the gift of another stone with similar powers. Once you have that, there will be no further difficulty in the way of escape."

The Prince of the Air returned a few days later from his mother's palace, but the Invisible Prince had already set out. He had, however, entirely forgotten the road by which he had come, and lost himself for so long in the forest, that when at last he reached home, the Fairy had already left, and, in spite of all his grief, there was nothing for it but to wait till the Fairy's next visit, and allow Rosalie to suffer three months longer. This thought drove him to despair, and he had almost made up his mind to return to the place of her captivity, when one day, as he was strolling along an alley in the woods, he saw a huge oak open its trunk, and out of it step two Princes in earnest conversation. As our hero had the magic stone in his mouth they imagined themselves alone, and did not lower their voices.

"What!" said one, "are you always going to allow yourself to be tormented by a passion which can never end happily, and in your whole kingdom can you find nothing else to satisfy you?"

"What is the use," replied the other, "of being Prince of the Gnomes, and having a mother who is queen over all the four elements, if I cannot win the love of the Princess Argentine? From the moment that I first saw her, sitting in the forest surrounded by flowers, I have never ceased to think of her night and day, and, although I love her, I am quite convinced that she will never care for me. You know that I have in my palace the cabinets of the years. In the first, great mirrors reflect the past; in the second, we contemplate the present; in the third, the future can be read. It was here that I fled after I had gazed on the Princess Argentine, but instead of love I only saw scorn and contempt. Think how great must be my devotion, when, in spite of my fate, I still love on!"

Now the Prince of the Golden Isle was enchanted with this conversation, for the Princess Argentine was his sister, and he hoped, by means of her influence over the Prince of the Gnomes, to obtain from his brother the release of Rosalie. So he joyfully returned to his father's palace, where he found his friend the Fairy, who at once presented him with a magic pebble like his own. As may be imagined, he lost no time in setting out to deliver Rosalie, and travelled so fast that he soon arrived at the forest, in the midst of which she lay a captive. But though he found the palace he did not find Rosalie. He hunted high and low, but there was no sign of her, and his despair was so great that he was ready, a thousand times over, to take his own life. At last he remembered the conversation of the two Princes about the cabinets of the years, and that if he could manage to reach the oak-tree, he would be certain to discover what had become of Rosalie. Happily, he soon found out the secret of the passage and entered the cabinet of the present, where he saw reflected in the mirrors the unfortunate Rosalie sitting on the floor weeping bitterly, and surrounded with genii, who never left her night or day.

This sight only increased the misery of the Prince, for he did not know where the castle was, nor how to set about finding it. However, he resolved to seek the whole world through till he came to the right place. He began by setting sail in a favourable wind, but his bad luck followed him even on the sea. He had scarcely lost sight of the land when a violent storm arose, and

Rosalie Guarded by the Genie

The Mirror of the Present

after several hours of beating about, the vessel was driven on to some rocks, on which it dashed itself to bits. The Prince was fortunate enough to be able to lay hold of a floating spar, and contrived to keep himself afloat; and, after a long struggle with the winds and waves, he was cast upon a strange island. But what was his surprise, on reaching the shore, to hear sounds of the most heart-rending distress, mingled with the sweetest songs which had ever charmed him! His curiosity was instantly roused, and he advanced cautiously till he saw two huge dragons guarding the gate of a wood. They were terrible indeed to look upon. Their bodies were covered with glittering scales; their curly tails extended far over the land; flames darted from their mouths and noses, and their eyes would have made the bravest shudder; but as the Prince was invisible and they did not see him, he slipped past them into the wood. He found himself at once in a labyrinth, and wandered about for a long time without meeting anyone; in fact, the only sight he saw was a circle of human hands, sticking out of the ground above the wrist, each with a bracelet of gold, on which a name was written. The farther he advanced in the labyrinth the more curious he became, till he was stopped by two corpses lying in the midst of a cypress alley, each with a scarlet cord round his neck and a bracelet on his arm on which were engraved their own names, and those of two Princesses.

The invisible Prince recognised these dead men as Kings of two large islands near his own home, but the names of the Princesses were unknown to him. He grieved for their unhappy fate, and at once proceeded to bury them; but no sooner had he laid them in their graves, than their hands started up through the earth and remained sticking up like those of their fellows.

The Prince went on his way, thinking about this strange adventure, when suddenly at the turn of the walk he perceived a tall man whose face was the picture of misery, holding in his hands a silken cord of the exact colour of those round the necks of the dead men. A few steps further this man came up with another as miserable to the full as he himself; they silently embraced, and

In the Labyrinth of Despair

then without a word passed the cords round their throats, and fell dead side by side. In vain the Prince rushed to their assistance and strove to undo the cord. He could not loosen it; so he buried them like the others and continued his path.

He felt, however, that great prudence was necessary, or he himself might become the victim of some enchantment; and he was thankful to slip past the dragons, and enter a beautiful park, with clear streams and sweet flowers, and a crowd of men and maidens. But he could not forget the terrible things he had seen, and hoped eagerly for a clue to the mystery. Noticing two young people talking together, he drew near thinking that he might get some explanation of what puzzled him. And so he did.

"You swear," said the Prince, "that you will love me till you die, but I fear your faithless heart, and I feel that I shall soon have to seek the Fairy Despair, ruler of half this island. She carries off the lovers who have been cast away by their mistresses, and wish to have done with life. She places them in a labyrinth where they are condemned to walk forever, with a bracelet on their arms and a cord round their necks, unless they meet another as miserable as themselves. Then the cord is pulled and they lie where they fall, till they are buried by the first passerby. Terrible as this death would be," added the Prince, "it would be sweeter than life if I had lost your love."

The sight of all these happy lovers only made the Prince grieve the more, and he wandered along the seashore spending his days; but one day he was sitting on a rock bewailing his fate, and the impossibility of leaving the island, when all in a moment the sea appeared to raise itself nearly to the skies, and the caves echoed with hideous screams. As he looked a woman rose from the depths of the sea, flying madly before a furious giant. The cries she uttered softened the heart of the Prince; he took the stone from his mouth, and drawing his sword he rushed after the giant, so as to give the lady time to escape. But hardly had he come within reach of the enemy, than the giant touched him with a ring that he held in his hand, and the Prince remained immovable where he stood. The giant then hastily rejoined his prey, and, seizing her in his arms, he plunged her into the sea. Then he sent some tritons to bind chains about the Prince of the Golden Isle, and he too felt himself borne to the depths of the ocean, and without the hope of ever again seeing the Princess.

Now the giant whom the Invisible Prince had so rashly attacked was the Lord of the Sea, and the third son of the Queen of the Elements, and he had touched the youth with a magic ring which enabled a mortal to live underwater. So the Prince of the Golden Isle found, when bound in chains by the tritons, he was carried through the homes of strange monsters and past immense seaweed forests, till he reached a vast sandy space, surrounded by huge rocks. On the tallest of the rocks sat the giant as on a throne.

"Rash mortal," said he, when the Prince was dragged before him, "you have deserved death, but you shall live only to suffer more cruelly. Go, and add to the number of those whom it is my pleasure to torture."

At these words the unhappy Prince found himself tied to a rock; but he was not alone in his misfortunes, for all round him were chained Princes and Princesses, whom the giant had led captive. Indeed, it was his chief delight to create a storm, in order to add to the list of his prisoners.

As his hands were fastened, it was impossible for the Prince of the Golden Isle to make use of his magic stone, and he passed his nights and days dreaming of Rosalie. But at last the time came when the giant took it into his head to amuse himself by arranging fights between some of his captives. Lots were drawn, and one fell upon our Prince, whose chains were immediately loosened. The moment he was set free, he snatched up his stone, and became invisible.

The astonishment of the giant at the sudden disappearance of the Prince may well be imagined. He ordered all the passages to be watched, but it was too late, for the Prince had already glided between two rocks. He wandered for a long while through the forests, where he met nothing but fearful monsters;

he climbed rock after rock, steered his way from tree to tree, till at length he arrived at the edge of the sea, at the foot of a mountain that he remembered to have seen in the cabinet of the present, where Rosalie was held captive.

Filled with joy, he made his way to the top of the mountain which pierced the clouds, and there he found a palace. He entered, and in the middle of a long gallery he discovered a crystal room, in the midst of which sat Rosalie, guarded night and day by genii. There was no door anywhere, nor any window. At this sight the Prince became more puzzled than ever, for he did not know how he was to warn Rosalie of his return. Yet it broke his heart to see her weeping from dawn till dark.

One day, as Rosalie was walking up and down her room, she was surprised to see that the crystal which served for a wall had grown cloudy, as if someone had breathed on it, and, what was more, wherever she moved the brightness of the crystal always became clouded. This was enough to cause the Princess to suspect that her lover had returned. In order to set the Prince of the Air's mind at rest she began by being very gracious to him, so that when she begged that her captivity might be a little lightened she should not be refused. At first the only favour she asked was to be allowed to walk for one hour every day up and down the long gallery. This was granted, and the Invisible Prince speedily took the opportunity of handing her the stone, which she at once slipped into her mouth. No words can paint the fury of her captor at her disappearance. He ordered the spirits of the air to fly through all space, and to bring back Rosalie wherever she might be. They instantly flew off to obey his commands, and spread themselves over the whole earth.

Meantime Rosalie and the Invisible Prince had reached, hand in hand, a door of the gallery which led through a terrace into the gardens. In silence they glided along, and thought themselves already safe, when a furious monster dashed itself by accident against Rosalie and the Invisible Prince, and in her fright she let go his hand. No one can speak as long as he is invisible, and besides, they knew that the spirits were all around them, and at the slightest sound they would be recognised; so all they could do was to feel about in the hope that their hands might once more meet.

But, alas! the joy of liberty lasted but a short time. The Princess, having wandered in vain up and down the forest, stopped at last on the edge of a fountain. As she walked she wrote on the trees: "If ever the Prince, my lover, comes this way, let him know that it is here I dwell, and that I sit daily on the edge of this fountain, mingling my tears with its waters."

These words were read by one of the genii, who repeated them to his master. The Prince of the Air, in his turn making himself invisible, was led to the fountain, and waited for Rosalie. When she drew near he held out his hand, which she grasped eagerly, taking it for that of her lover; and, seizing his opportunity, the Prince passed a cord round her arms, and throwing off his invisibility cried to his spirits to drag her into the lowest pit.

It was at this moment that the Invisible Prince appeared, and at the sight of the Prince of the Genii mounting into the air, holding a silken cord, he guessed instantly that he was carrying off Rosalie.

He felt so overwhelmed by despair that he thought for an instant of putting an end to his life. "Can I survive my misfortunes?" he cried. "I fancied I had come to an end of my troubles, and now they are worse than ever. What will become of me? Never can I discover the place where this monster will hide Rosalie."

The unhappy youth had determined to let himself die, and indeed his sorrow alone was enough to kill him, when the thought that by means of the cabinets of the years he might find out where the Princess was imprisoned, gave him a little ray of comfort. So he continued to walk on through the forest, and after some hours he arrived at the gate of a temple, guarded by two huge lions. Being invisible, he was able to enter unharmed. In the middle of the temple was an altar, on which lay a book, and behind the altar hung a great curtain.

The Prince approached the altar and opened the book, which contained the names of all the lovers in the world; and in it he read that Rosalie had been carried off by the Prince of the Air to an abyss which had no entrance except the one that lay by way of the Fountain of Gold.

Now, as the Prince had not the smallest idea where this fountain was to be found, it might be thought that he was not much nearer to Rosalie than before. This was not, however, the view taken by the Prince.

"Though every step that I take may perhaps lead me further from her," he said to himself, "I am still thankful to know that she is alive somewhere."

On leaving the temple the Invisible Prince saw six paths lying before him, each of which led through the wood. He was hesitating which to choose, when he suddenly beheld two people coming toward him, down the track which lay most to his right. They turned out to be the Prince Gnome and his friend, and the sudden desire to get some news of his sister, Princess Argentine, caused the Invisible Prince to follow them and to listen to their conversation.

"Do you think," the Prince Gnome was saying, "do you think that I would not break my chains if I could? I know that the Princess Argentine will never love me, yet each day I feel her dearer still. And as if this were not enough, I have the horror of feeling that she probably loves another. So I have resolved to put myself out of my pain by means of the Golden Fountain. A single drop of its water falling on the sand around will trace the name of my rival in her heart. I dread the test, and yet this very dread convinces me of my misfortune."

It may be imagined that after listening to these words the Invisible Prince followed Prince Gnome like his shadow, and after walking some time they arrived at the Golden Fountain. The unhappy lover stooped down with a sigh, and dipping his finger in the water let fall a drop on the sand. It instantly wrote the name of Prince Flame, his brother. The shock of this discovery was so real, that Prince Gnome sank fainting into the arms of his friend.

Meanwhile the Invisible Prince was turning over in his mind how he could

PRINCE GNOME LEARNS THE NAME OF HIS RIVAL AT THE GOLDEN FOUNTAIN

best deliver Rosalie. As, since he had been touched by the Giant's ring, he had the power to live in the water as well as on land, he at once dived into the fountain. He perceived in one corner a door leading into the mountain, and at the foot of the mountain was a high rock on which was fixed an iron ring with a cord attached. The Prince promptly guessed that the cord was used to chain the Princess, and drew his sword and cut it. In a moment he felt the Princess's hand in his, for she had always kept her magic pebble in her mouth, in spite of the prayers and entreaties of the Prince of the Air to make herself visible.

So hand in hand the invisible Prince and Rosalie crossed the mountain; but as the Princess had no power of living underwater, she could not pass the Golden Fountain. Speechless and invisible they clung together on the brink, trembling at the frightful tempest the Prince of the Air had raised in his fury. The storm had already lasted many days when tremendous heat began to make itself felt. The lightning flashed, the thunder rattled, fire bolts fell from heaven, burning up the forests and even the fields of corn. In one instant the very streams were dried up, and the Prince, seizing his opportunity, carried the Princess over the Golden Fountain.

It took them a long time still to reach the Golden Isle, but at last they got there, and we may be quite sure they never wanted to leave it anymore.

THE CROW[13]

NCE UPON A TIME THERE WERE THREE PRINCESSES WHO were all three young and beautiful; but the youngest, although she was not fairer than the other two, was the most loveable of them all.

About half a mile from the palace in which they lived there stood a castle, which was uninhabited and almost a ruin, but the garden which surrounded it was a mass of blooming flowers, and in this garden the youngest Princess used often to walk.

One day when she was pacing to and fro under the lime trees, a black crow hopped out of a rose-bush in front of her. The poor beast was all torn and bleeding, and the kind little Princess was quite unhappy about it. When the crow saw this, it turned to her and said:

"I am not really a black crow, but an enchanted Prince, who has been doomed to spend his youth in misery. If you only liked, Princess, you could

---

13   From the Polish. Kletke.

THE EVIL SPIRITS DRAG THE GIRL TO THE CAULDRON

save me. But you would have to say good-bye to all your own people, and come and be my constant companion in this ruined castle. There is one habitable room in it, in which there is a golden bed; there you will have to live all by yourself, and don't forget that whatever you may see or hear in the night you must not scream out, for if you give as much as a single cry my sufferings will be doubled."

The good-natured Princess at once left her home and her family and hurried to the ruined castle, and took possession of the room with the golden bed.

When night approached she lay down, but though she shut her eyes tight sleep would not come. At midnight she heard to her great horror someone coming along the passage, and in a minute her door was flung wide open and a troop of strange beings entered the room. They at once proceeded to light a fire in the huge fire-place; then they placed a great cauldron of boiling water on it. When they had done this, they approached the bed on which the trembling girl lay, and, screaming and yelling all the time, they dragged her toward the cauldron. She nearly died with fright, but she never uttered a sound. Then all of a sudden the cock crowed, and all the evil spirits vanished.

At the same moment the crow appeared and hopped all round the room with joy. It thanked the Princess most heartily for her goodness, and said that its sufferings had already been greatly lessened.

Now one of the Princess's elder sisters, who was very inquisitive, had found out about everything, and went to pay her youngest sister a visit in the ruined castle. She implored her so urgently to let her spend the night with her in the golden bed, that at last the good-natured little Princess consented. But at midnight, when the odd folk appeared, the elder sister screamed with terror, and from this time on the youngest Princess insisted always on keeping watch alone.

So she lived in solitude all the day-time, and at night she would have been frightened, had she not been so brave; but every day the crow came and thanked her for her endurance, and assured her that his sufferings were far less than they had been.

And so two years passed away, when one day the crow came to the Princess and said: "In another year I shall be freed from the spell I am under at present, because then the seven years will be over. But before I can resume my natural form, and take possession of the belongings of my forefathers, you must go out into the world and take service as a maidservant."

The young Princess consented at once, and for a whole year she served as a maid; but in spite of her youth and beauty she was very badly treated, and suffered many things. One evening, when she was spinning flax, and had worked her little white hands weary, she heard a rustling beside her and a cry of joy. Then she saw a handsome youth standing beside her; who knelt down at her feet and kissed the little weary white hands.

"I am the Prince," he said, "who you in your goodness, when I was wandering about in the shape of a black crow, freed from the most awful torments. Come now to my castle with me, and let us live there happily together."

So they went to the castle where they had both endured so much. But when they reached it, it was difficult to believe that it was the same, for it had all been rebuilt and done up again. And there they lived for a hundred years, a hundred years of joy and happiness.

HOW SIX MEN TRAVELLED THROUGH THE WIDE WORLD

HERE WAS ONCE UPON A TIME A MAN WHO UNDERSTOOD all sorts of arts; he served in the war, and bore himself bravely and well; but when the war was over, he got his discharge, and set out on his travels with three farthings of his pay in his pocket. "Wait," he said; "that does not please me; only let me find the right people, and the King shall yet give me all the treasures of his kingdom." He strode angrily into the forest, and there he saw a man standing who had uprooted six trees as if they were straws. He said to him, "Will you be my servant and travel with me?"

"Yes," he answered; "but first of all I will take this little bundle of sticks home to my mother," and he took one of the trees and wound it round the other five, raised the bundle on his shoulders and bore it off. Then he came back and went with his master, who said, "We two ought to be able to travel through the wide world!" And when they had gone a little way they came upon a hunter, who was on his knees, his gun on his shoulder, aiming at something. The master said to him, "Hunter, what are you aiming at?"

He answered, "Two miles from this place sits a fly on a branch of an oak; I want to shoot out its left eye."

"Oh, go with me," said the man; "if we three are together we shall easily travel through the wide world."

The hunter agreed and went with him, and they came to seven windmills whose sails were going round quite fast, and yet there was not a breath of wind, nor was a leaf moving. The man said, "I don't know what is turning those windmills; there is not the slightest breeze blowing." So he walked on with his servants, and when they had gone two miles they saw a man sitting on a tree, holding one of his nostrils and blowing out of the other.

"Fellow, what are you puffing at up there?" asked the man.

He replied, "Two miles from this place are standing seven windmills; see, I am blowing to drive them round."

"Oh, go with me," said the man; "if we four are together we shall easily travel through the wide world."

So the blower got down and went with him, and after a time they saw a man who was standing on one leg, and had unstrapped the other and laid it near him. Then said the master, "You have made yourself very comfortable to rest!"

"I am a runner," answered he; "and so that I shall not go too quickly, I have unstrapped one leg; when I run with two legs, I go faster than a bird flies."

"Oh, go with me; if we five are together, we shall easily travel through the wide world." So he went with him, and, not long afterward, they met a man who wore a little hat, but he had it slouched over one ear.

"Manners, manners!" said the master to him; "don't hang your hat over one ear; you look like a madman!"

"I dare not," said the other, "for if I were to put my hat on straight, there would come such a frost that the birds in the sky would freeze and fall dead on the earth."

"Oh, go with me," said the master; "if we six are together, we shall easily travel through the wide world."

THE YELLOW FAIRY BOOK

Now the Six came to a town in which the King had proclaimed that whoever should run with his daughter in a race, and win, should become her husband; but if he lost, he must lose his head. This was reported to the man who declared he would compete, "but," he said, "I shall let my servant run for me."

The King replied, "Then both your heads must be staked, and your head and his must be guaranteed for the winner."

When this was agreed upon and settled, the man strapped on the runner's other leg, saying to him, "Now be nimble, and see that we win!" It was arranged that whoever should first bring water out of a stream a long way off, should be the victor. Then the runner got a pitcher, and the King's daughter another, and they began to run at the same time; but in a moment, when the King's daughter was only just a little way off, no spectator could see the runner, and it seemed as if the wind had whistled past. In a short time he reached the stream, filled his pitcher with water, and turned round again. But, half way home, a great drowsiness came over him; he put down his pitcher, lay down, and fell asleep. He had, however, put a horse's skull which was lying on the ground, for his pillow, so that he should not be too comfortable and might soon wake up.

In the meantime the King's daughter, who could also run well, as well as an ordinary man could, reached the stream, and hastened back with her pitcher full of water. When she saw the runner lying there asleep, she was delighted, and said, "My enemy is given into my hands!" She emptied his pitcher and ran on.

Everything now would have been lost, if by good luck the hunter had not been standing on the castle tower and had seen everything with his sharp eyes.

"Ah," said he, "the King's daughter shall not overreach us;" and, loading his gun, he shot so cleverly, that he shot away the horse's skull from under the runner's head, without its hurting him. Then the runner awoke, jumped up, and saw that his pitcher was empty and the King's daughter far ahead. But he did not lose courage, and ran back to the stream with his pitcher, filled it once more with water, and was home ten minutes before the King's daughter arrived.

·MY·ENEMY·IS·GIVEN·INTO·MY·HANDS·

"Look," said he, "I have only just exercised my legs; that was nothing of a run."

But the King was angry, and his daughter even more so, that she should be carried away by a common, discharged soldier. They consulted together how they could destroy both him and his companions.

"Then," said the King to her, "I have found a way. Don't be frightened; they shall not come home again." He said to them, "You must now make merry together, and eat and drink," and he led them into a room which had a floor of iron; the doors were also of iron, and the windows were barred with iron. In the room was a table spread with delicious food. The King said to them, "Go in and enjoy yourselves," and as soon as they were inside he had the doors shut and bolted. Then he made the cook come, and ordered him to keep up a large fire under the room until the iron was red-hot. The cook did so, and the Six sitting round the table felt it grow very warm, and they thought this was because of their good fare; but when the heat became still greater and they wanted to go out, but found the doors and windows fastened, then they knew that the King meant them harm and was trying to suffocate them.

"But he shall not succeed," cried he of the little hat, "I will make a frost come which shall make the fire ashamed and die out!" So he put his hat on straight, and at once there came such a frost that all the heat disappeared and the food on the dishes began to freeze. When a couple of hours had passed, and the King thought they must be quite dead from the heat, he had the doors opened and went in himself to see.

But when the doors were opened, there stood all Six, alive and well, saying they were glad they could come out to warm themselves, for the great cold in the room had frozen all the food hard in the dishes. Then the King went angrily to the cook, and scolded him, and asked him why he had not done what he was told.

But the cook answered, "There is heat enough there; see for yourself." Then the King saw a huge fire burning under the iron room, and understood that he could do no harm to the Six in this way. The King now began again to think how he could free himself from his unwelcome guests. He commanded the master to come before him, and said, "If you will take gold, and give up your right to my daughter, you shall have as much as you like."

"Oh, yes, your Majesty," answered he, "give me as much as my servant can carry, and I will give up your daughter."

The King was delighted, and the man said, "I will come and fetch it in fourteen days."

Then he called all the tailors in the kingdom together, and made them sit down for fourteen days sewing at a sack. When it was finished, he made the strong man who had uprooted the trees take the sack on his shoulder and go with him to the King. Then the King said, "What a powerful fellow that is, carrying that bale of linen as large as a house on his shoulder!" and he was much frightened, and thought, "What a lot of gold he will make away with!" Then he had a ton of gold brought,

"AND HE HELD ONE NOSTRIL AND BLEW WITH THE OTHER
AT THE TWO REGIMENTS"

which sixteen of the strongest men had to carry; but the strong man seized it with one hand, put it in the sack, saying, "Why don't you bring me more? That scarcely covers the bottom!" Then the King had to send again and again to fetch his treasures, which the strong man shoved into the sack, and the sack was only half full.

"Bring more," he cried, "these crumbs don't fill it." So seven thousand waggons of the gold of the whole kingdom were driven up; these the strong man shoved into the sack, oxen and all.

"I will no longer be particular," he said, "and will take what comes, so that the sack shall be full."

When everything was put in and there was not yet enough, he said, "I will make an end of this; it is easy to fasten a sack when it is not full." Then he threw it on his back and went with his companions.

Now, when the King saw how a single man was carrying away the wealth of the whole country he was very angry, and made his cavalry mount and pursue the Six, and bring back the strong man with the sack. Two regiments soon overtook them, and called to them, "You are prisoners! lay down the sack of gold or you shall be cut down."

"What do you say?" said the blower, "we are prisoners? Before that, you shall dance in the air!" And he held one nostril and blew with the other at the two regiments; they were separated and blown away in the blue sky over the mountains, one this way, and the other that. A sergeant-major cried for mercy, saying he had nine wounds, and was a brave fellow, and did not deserve this disgrace. So the blower let him off, and he came down without hurt. Then he said to him, "Now go home to the King, and say that if he sends any more cavalry I will blow them all into the air."

When the King received the message, he said, "Let the fellows go; they are bewitched." Then the Six brought the treasure home, shared it among themselves, and lived contentedly till the end of their days.

THE WIZARD KING[14]

IN VERY ANCIENT TIMES THERE LIVED A KING, WHOSE power lay not only in the vast extent of his dominions, but also in the magic secrets of which he was master. After spending the greater part of his early youth in pleasure, he met a Princess of such remarkable beauty that he at once asked her hand in marriage, and, having obtained it, considered himself the happiest of men.

After a year's time a son was born, worthy in every way of such distinguished parents, and much admired by the whole Court. As soon as the Queen thought him strong enough for a journey she set out with him secretly to visit her Fairy godmother. I said *secretly*, because the Fairy had warned the Queen that the King was a magician; and as from time immemorial there had been a standing feud between the Fairies and the Wizards, he might not have approved of his wife's visit.

The Fairy godmother, who took the deepest interest in all the Queen's concerns, and who was much pleased with the little Prince, endowed him with the

14   From *Les Fées illustres*.

power of pleasing everybody from his cradle, as well as with a wonderful ease in learning everything which could help to make him a perfectly accomplished Prince. Accordingly, to the delight of his teachers, he made the most rapid progress in his education, constantly surpassing everyone's expectations. Before he was many years old, however, he had the great sorrow of losing his mother, whose last words were to advise him never to undertake anything of importance without consulting the Fairy under whose protection she had placed him.

The Prince's grief at the death of his mother was great, but it was nothing compared to that of the King, his father, who was quite inconsolable for the loss of his dear wife. Neither time nor reason seemed to lighten his sorrow, and the sight of all the familiar faces and things about him only served to remind him of his loss.

He therefore resolved to travel for change, and by means of his magic art was able to visit every country he came to see under different shapes, returning every few weeks to the place where he had left a few followers.

Having travelled from land to land in this fashion without finding anything to rivet his attention, it occurred to him to take the form of an eagle, and in this shape he flew across many countries and arrived at length in a new and lovely spot, where the air seemed filled with the scent of jessamine and orange flowers with which the ground was thickly planted. Attracted by the sweet perfume he flew lower, and perceived some large and beautiful gardens filled with the rarest flowers, and with fountains throwing up their clear waters into the air in a hundred different shapes. A wide stream flowed through the garden, and on it floated richly ornamented barges and gondolas filled with people dressed in the most elegant manner and covered with jewels.

In one of these barges sat the Queen of that country with her only daughter, a maiden more beautiful than the Day Star, and attended by the ladies of the Court. No more exquisitely lovely mortal was ever seen than this Princess, and it needed all an eagle's strength of sight to prevent the King being

THE PRINCESS AND THE EAGLE IN THE FLOWERY MEADOW

hopelessly dazzled. He perched on the top of a large orange tree, whence he was able to survey the scene and to gaze at pleasure on the Princess's charms.

Now, an eagle with a King's heart in his breast is apt to be bold, and accordingly he instantly made up his mind to carry off the lovely damsel, feeling sure that having once seen her he could not live without her.

He waited till he saw her in the act of stepping ashore, when, suddenly swooping down, he carried her off before her equerry in attendance had advanced to offer her his hand. The Princess, on finding herself in an eagle's talons, uttered the most heartbreaking shrieks and cries; but her captor, though touched by her distress, would not abandon his lovely prey, and continued to fly through the air too fast to allow of his saying anything to comfort her.

At length, when he thought they had reached a safe distance, he began to lower his flight, and gradually descending to earth, deposited his burden in a flowery meadow. He then entreated her pardon for his violence, and told her that he was about to carry her to a great kingdom over which he ruled, and where he desired she should rule with him, adding many tender and consoling expressions.

For some time the Princess remained speechless; but recovering herself a little, she burst into a flood of tears. The King, much moved, said, "Adorable Princess, dry your tears. I implore you. My only wish is to make you the happiest person in the world."

"If you speak truth, my lord," replied the Princess, "restore to me the liberty you have deprived me of. Otherwise I can only look on you as my worst enemy."

The King retorted that her opposition filled him with despair, but that he hoped to carry her to a place where all around would respect her, and where every pleasure would surround her. So saying, he seized her once more, and in spite of all her cries he rapidly bore her off to the neighbourhood of his capital. Here he gently placed her on a lawn, and as he did so she saw a magnificent palace spring up at her feet. The architecture was imposing, and in the interior the rooms were handsome and furnished in the best possible taste.

The Princess, who expected to be quite alone, was pleased at finding herself surrounded by a number of pretty girls, all anxious to wait on her, whilst a brilliantly-coloured parrot said the most agreeable things in the world.

On arriving at this palace the King had resumed his own form, and though no longer young, he might well have pleased any other than this Princess, who had been so prejudiced against him by his violence that she could only regard him with feelings of hatred, which she was at no pains to conceal. The King hoped, however, that time might not only soften her anger, but accustom her to his sight. He took the precaution of surrounding the palace with a dense cloud, and then hastened to his Court, where his prolonged absence was causing much anxiety.

The Prince and all the courtiers were delighted to see their beloved King again, but they had to submit themselves to more frequent absences than ever on his part. He made business a pretext for shutting himself up in his study, but it was really in order to spend the time with the Princess, who remained inflexible.

Not being able to imagine what could be the cause of so much obstinacy the King began to fear, lest, in spite of all his precautions, she might have heard of the charms of the Prince his son, whose goodness, youth, and beauty, made him adored at Court. This idea made him horribly uneasy, and he resolved to remove the cause of his fears by sending the Prince on his travels escorted by a magnificent retinue.

The Prince, after visiting several Courts, arrived at the one where the lost Princess was still deeply mourned. The King and Queen received him most graciously, and some festivities were revived to do him honour.

One day when the Prince was visiting the Queen in her own apartments he was much struck by a most beautiful portrait. He eagerly inquired whose it was, and the Queen, with many tears, told him it was all that was left her of her beloved daughter, who had suddenly been carried off, she knew neither where nor how.

The Prince was deeply moved, and vowed that he would search the world for the Princess, and take no rest till he had found and restored her to her mother's arms. The Queen assured him of her eternal gratitude, and promised, should he succeed, to give him her daughter in marriage, together with all the estates she herself owned.

The Prince, far more attracted by the thoughts of possessing the Princess than her promised dower, set forth in his quest after taking leave of the King and Queen, the latter giving him a miniature of her daughter which she was in the habit of wearing. His first act was to seek the Fairy under whose protection he had been placed, and he implored her to give him all the assistance of her art and counsel in this important matter.

After listening attentively to the whole adventure, the Fairy asked for time to consult her books. After due consideration she informed the Prince that the object of his search was not far distant, but that it was too difficult for him to attempt to enter the enchanted palace where she was, as the King his father had surrounded it with a thick cloud, and that the only expedient she could think of would be to gain possession of the Princess's parrot. This, she added, did not appear impossible, as it often flew about to some distance in the neighbourhood.

Having told the Prince all this, the Fairy went out in hopes of seeing the parrot, and soon returned with the bird in her hand. She promptly shut it up in a cage, and, touching the Prince with her wand, transformed him into an exactly similar parrot; after which, she instructed him how to reach the Princess.

The Prince reached the palace in safety, but was so dazzled at first by the Princess's beauty, which far surpassed his expectations, that he was quite dumb for a time. The Princess was surprised and anxious, and fearing the parrot, who was her greatest comfort, had fallen ill, she took him in her hand and caressed him. This soon reassured the Prince, and encouraged him to play his part well, and he began to say a thousand agreeable things which charmed the Princess.

Presently the King appeared, and the parrot noticed with joy how much he was disliked. As soon as the King left, the Princess retired to her dressing-room, the parrot flew after her and overheard her lamentations at the continued persecutions of the King, who had pressed her to consent to their marriage. The parrot said so many clever and tender things to comfort her that she began to doubt whether this could indeed be her own parrot.

When he saw her well-disposed toward him, he exclaimed: "Madam, I have a most important secret to confide to you, and I beg you not to be alarmed by what I am about to say. I am here on behalf of the Queen your mother, with the object of delivering your Highness; to prove which, behold this portrait which she gave me herself." So saying he drew forth the miniature from under

THE WIZARD KING PAYS A VISIT TO THE PRINCESS

his wing. The Princess's surprise was great, but after what she had seen and heard it was impossible not to indulge in hope, for she had recognised the likeness of herself which her mother always wore.

The parrot, finding she was not much alarmed, told her who he was, all that her mother had promised him and the help he had already received from a Fairy who had assured him that she would give him means to transport the Princess to her mother's arms.

When he found her listening attentively to him, he implored the Princess to allow him to resume his natural shape. She did not speak, so he drew a feather from his wing, and she beheld before her a Prince of such surpassing beauty that it was impossible not to hope that she might owe her liberty to so charming a person.

Meantime the Fairy had prepared a chariot, to which she harnessed two powerful eagles; then placing the cage, with the parrot in it, she charged the bird to conduct it to the window of the Princess's dressing-room. This was done in a few minutes, and the Princess, stepping into the chariot with the Prince, was delighted to find her parrot again.

As they rose through the air the Princess remarked a figure mounted on an eagle's back flying in front of the chariot. She was rather alarmed, but the Prince reassured her, telling her it was the good Fairy to whom she owed so much, and who was now conducting her in safety to her mother.

That same morning the King woke suddenly from a troubled sleep. He had dreamt that the Princess was being carried off from him, and, transforming himself into an eagle, he flew to the palace. When he failed to find her he flew into a terrible rage, and hastened home to consult his books, by which means he discovered that it was his son who had deprived him of this precious treasure. Immediately he took the shape of a harpy, and, filled with rage, was determined to devour his son, and even the Princess too, if only he could overtake them.

He set out at full speed; but he started too late, and was further delayed by a strong wind which the Fairy raised behind the young couple so as to baffle any pursuit.

You may imagine the rapture with which the Queen received the daughter she had given up for lost, as well as the amiable Prince who had rescued her. The Fairy entered with them, and warned the Queen that the Wizard King would shortly arrive, infuriated by his loss, and that nothing could preserve the Prince and Princess from his rage and magic unless they were actually married.

The Queen hastened to inform the King her husband, and the wedding took place on the spot.

As the ceremony was completed the Wizard King arrived. His despair at being so late bewildered him so entirely that he appeared in his natural form and attempted to sprinkle some black liquid over the bride and bridegroom, which was intended to kill them, but the Fairy stretched out her wand and the liquid dropped on the Magician himself. He fell down senseless, and the Princess's father, deeply offended at the cruel revenge which had been attempted, ordered him to be removed and locked up in prison.

Now as magicians lose all their power as soon as they are in prison, the King felt himself much embarrassed at being thus at the mercy of those he had so greatly offended. The Prince implored and obtained his father's pardon, and the prison doors were opened.

No sooner was this done than the Wizard King was seen in the air under the form of some unknown bird, exclaiming as he flew off that he would never forgive either his son or the Fairy the cruel wrong they had done him.

Everyone entreated the Fairy to settle in the kingdom where she now was, to which she consented. She built herself a magnificent palace, to which she transported her books and Fairy secrets, and where she enjoyed the sight of the perfect happiness she had helped to bestow on the entire royal family.

THE NIXY[15]

HERE WAS ONCE UPON A TIME A MILLER WHO WAS VERY well off, and had as much money and as many goods as he knew what to do with. But sorrow comes in the night, and the miller all of a sudden became so poor that at last he could hardly call the mill in which he sat his own. He wandered about all day full of despair and misery, and when he lay down at night he could get no rest, but lay awake all night sunk in sorrowful thoughts.

One morning he rose up before dawn and went outside, for he thought his heart would be lighter in the open air. As he wandered up and down on the banks of the mill-pond he heard a rustling in the water, and when he looked near he saw a white woman rising up from the waves.

He realised at once that this could be none other than the nixy of the mill-pond, and in his terror he didn't know if he should fly away or remain where he was. While he hesitated the nixy spoke, called him by his name, and asked him why he was so sad.

---

15   From the German. Kletke.

THE MILLER SEES THE NIXY OF THE MILL-POND

When the miller heard how friendly her tone was, he plucked up heart and told her how rich and prosperous he had been all his life up till now, when he didn't know what he was to do for want and misery.

Then the nixy spoke comforting words to him, and promised that she would make him richer and more prosperous than he had ever been in his life before, if he would give her in return the youngest thing in his house.

The miller thought she must mean one of his puppies or kittens, so promised the nixy at once what she asked, and returned to his mill full of hope. On the threshold he was greeted by a servant with the news that his wife had just given birth to a boy.

The poor miller was much horrified by these tidings, and went in to his wife with a heavy heart to tell her and his relations of the fatal bargain he had just struck with the nixy. "I would gladly give up all the good fortune she promised me," he said, "if I could only save my child." But no one could think of any advice to give him, beyond taking care that the child never went near the mill-pond.

So the boy thrived and grew big, and in the meantime all prospered with the miller, and in a few years he was richer than he had ever been before. But all the same he did not enjoy his good fortune, for he could not forget his compact with the nixy, and he knew that sooner or later she would demand his fulfilment of it. But year after year went by, and the boy grew up and became a great hunter, and the lord of the land took him into his service, for he was as smart and bold a hunter as you would wish to see. In a short time he married a pretty young wife, and lived with her in great peace and happiness.

One day when he was out hunting a hare sprang up at his feet, and ran for some way in front of him in the open field. The hunter pursued it hotly for some time, and at last shot it dead. Then he proceeded to skin it, never noticing that he was close to the mill-pond, which since childhood he had been taught to avoid. He soon finished the skinning, and went to the water to wash the blood off his hands. He had hardly dipped them in the pond when the nixy rose up in the water, and seizing him in her wet arms she dragged him down with her under the waves.

When the hunter did not come home in the evening his wife grew very anxious, and when his game bag was found close to the mill-pond she guessed at once what had befallen him. She was nearly beside herself with grief, and roamed round and round the pond calling on her husband without ceasing. At last, worn out with sorrow and fatigue, she fell asleep and dreamt that she was wandering along a flowery meadow, when she came to a hut where she found an old witch, who promised to restore her husband to her.

When she awoke the next morning she determined to set out and find the witch; so she wandered on for many a day, and at last she reached the flowery meadow and found the hut where the old witch lived. The poor wife told her all that had happened and how she had been told in a dream of the witch's power to help her.

The witch counselled her to go to the pond the first time there was a full moon, and to comb her black hair with a golden comb, and then to place the comb on the bank. The hunter's wife gave the witch a handsome present, thanked her heartily, and returned home.

Time dragged heavily till the time of the full moon, but it passed at last, and as soon as it rose the young wife went to the pond, combed her black hair with a golden comb, and when she had finished, placed the comb on the bank; then she watched the water impatiently. Soon she heard a rushing sound, and a big wave rose suddenly and swept the comb off the bank, and a minute after the head of her husband rose from the pond and gazed sadly at her. But immediately another wave came, and the head sank back into the water without having said a word. The pond lay still and motionless, glittering in the moonshine, and the hunter's wife was not a bit better off than she had been before.

In despair she wandered about for days and nights, and at last, worn out by fatigue, she sank once more into a deep sleep, and dreamt exactly the same dream about the old witch. So the next morning she went again to the flowery meadow and sought the witch in her hut, and told her of her grief. The old woman counselled her to go to the mill-pond the next full moon and play upon a golden flute, and then to lay the flute on the bank.

As soon as the next moon was full the hunter's wife went to the mill-pond, played on a golden flute, and, when she had finished, placed it on the bank. Then a rushing sound was heard, and a wave swept the flute off the bank, and soon the head of the hunter appeared and rose up higher and higher till he was half out of the water. Then he gazed sadly at his wife and stretched out his arms toward her. But another rushing wave arose and dragged him under once more. The hunter's wife, who had stood on the bank full of joy and hope, sank into despair when she saw her husband snatched away again before her eyes.

But for her comfort she dreamt the same dream a third time, and betook herself once more to the old witch's hut in the flowery meadow. This time the old woman told her to go the next full moon to the mill-pond, and to spin there with a golden spinning-wheel, and then to leave the spinning-wheel on the bank.

The hunter's wife did as she was advised, and the first night the moon was full she sat and spun with a golden spinning-wheel, and then left the wheel on the bank. In a few minutes a rushing sound was heard in the waters, and a wave swept the spinning-wheel from the bank. Immediately the head of the hunter rose up from the pond, getting higher and higher each moment, till at length he stepped on to the bank and fell on his wife's neck.

But the waters of the pond rose up suddenly, overflowed the bank where the couple stood, and dragged them under the flood. In her despair, the young wife called on the old witch to help her, and in a moment the hunter was turned into a frog and his wife into a toad. But they were not able to remain

'A WAVE SWEPT THE SPINNING-WHEEL FROM THE BANK.'

together, for the water tore them apart, and when the flood was over they both resumed their own shapes again, but the hunter and the hunter's wife found themselves each in a strange country, and neither knew what had become of the other.

The hunter determined to become a shepherd, and his wife too became a shepherdess. So they herded their sheep for many years in solitude and sadness.

Now it happened once that the shepherd came to the country where the shepherdess lived. The neighbourhood pleased him, and he saw that the pasture was rich and suitable for his flocks. So he brought his sheep there, and herded them as before. The shepherd and shepherdess became great friends, but they did not recognise each other in the least.

But one evening when the moon was full they sat together watching their flocks, and the shepherd played upon his flute. Then the shepherdess thought of that evening when she had sat at the full moon by the mill-pond and had played on the golden flute; the recollection was too much for her, and she burst into tears. The shepherd asked her why she was crying, and left her no peace till she told him all her story. Then the scales fell from the shepherd's eyes, and he recognised his wife, and she him. So they returned joyfully to their own home, and lived in peace and happiness ever after.

THE GLASS MOUNTAIN[16]

NCE UPON A TIME THERE WAS A GLASS MOUNTAIN AT the top of which stood a castle made of pure gold, and in front of the castle there grew an apple-tree on which there were golden apples.

Anyone who picked an apple gained admittance into the golden castle, and there in a silver room sat an enchanted Princess of surpassing fairness and beauty. She was as rich too as she was beautiful, for the cellars of the castle were full of precious stones, and great chests of the finest gold stood round the walls of all the rooms.

Many knights had come from afar to try their luck, but it was in vain they attempted to climb the mountain. In spite of having their horses shod with sharp nails, no one managed to get more than halfway up, and then they all fell back right down to the bottom of the steep slippery hill. Sometimes they broke an arm, sometimes a leg, and many a brave man had even broken his neck.

---

16   From the Polish. Kletke.

The beautiful Princess sat at her window and watched the bold knights trying to reach her on their splendid horses. The sight of her always gave men fresh courage, and they flocked from the four quarters of the globe to attempt the work of rescuing her. But all in vain, and for seven years the Princess had sat now and waited for someone to scale the Glass Mountain.

A heap of corpses, both of riders and horses, lay round the mountain, and many dying men lay groaning there unable to go any farther with their wounded limbs. The whole neighbourhood had the appearance of a vast churchyard. In three more days the seven years would be at an end, when a knight in golden armour and mounted on a spirited steed was seen making his way toward the fatal hill.

Sticking his spurs into his horse he made a rush at the mountain, and got up halfway, then he calmly turned his horse's head and came down again without a slip or stumble. The following day he started in the same way; the horse trod on the glass as if it had been level earth, and sparks of fire flew from its hoofs. All the other knights gazed in astonishment, for he had almost gained the summit, and in another moment he would have reached the apple-tree; but all of a sudden a huge eagle rose up and spread its mighty wings, hitting as it did so the knight's horse in the eye. The beast shied, opened its wide nostrils and tossed its mane, then rearing high up in the air, its hind feet slipped and it fell with its rider down the steep mountain side. Nothing was left of either of them except their bones, which rattled in the battered golden armour like dry peas in a pod.

And now there was only one more day before the close of the seven years. Then there arrived on the scene a mere schoolboy—a merry, happy-hearted youth, but at the same time strong and well-grown. He saw how many knights had broken their necks in vain, but undaunted he approached the steep mountain on foot and began the ascent.

For long he had heard his parents speak of the beautiful Princess who sat in the golden castle at the top of the Glass Mountain. He listened to all he heard, and determined that he too would try his luck. But first he went to the forest and caught a lynx, and cutting off the creature's sharp claws, he fastened them on to his own hands and feet.

Armed with these weapons he boldly started up the Glass Mountain. The sun was nearly going down, and the youth had not got more than halfway up. He could hardly draw breath he was so worn out, and his mouth was parched by thirst. A huge black cloud passed over his head, but in vain did he beg and beseech her to let a drop of water fall on him. He opened his mouth, but the black cloud sailed past and not as much as a drop of dew moistened his dry lips.

His feet were torn and bleeding, and he could only hold on now with his hands. Evening closed in, and he strained his eyes to see if he could behold the top of the mountain. Then he gazed beneath him, and what a sight met his eyes! A yawning abyss, with certain and terrible death at the bottom, reeking with half-decayed bodies of horses and riders! And this had been the end of all the other brave men who like himself had attempted the ascent.

It was almost pitch dark now, and only the stars lit up the Glass Mountain. The poor boy still clung on as if glued to the glass by his bloodstained hands. He made no struggle to get higher, for all his strength had left him, and seeing no hope he calmly awaited death. Then all of a sudden he fell into a deep sleep, and forgetful of his dangerous position, he slumbered sweetly. But all the same, although he slept, he had stuck his sharp claws so firmly into the glass that he was quite safe not to fall.

Now the golden apple-tree was guarded by the eagle which had overthrown the golden knight and his horse. Every night it flew round the Glass Mountain keeping a careful look-out, and no sooner had the moon emerged from the clouds than the bird rose up from the apple-tree, and circling round in the air, caught sight of the sleeping youth.

Greedy for carrion, and sure that this must be a fresh corpse, the bird

THE BOY IS ATTACKED BY THE EAGLE ON THE GLASS MOUNTAIN

swooped down upon the boy. But he was awake now, and perceiving the eagle, he determined by its help to save himself.

The eagle dug its sharp claws into the tender flesh of the youth, but he bore the pain without a sound, and seized the bird's two feet with his hands. The creature in terror lifted him high up into the air and began to circle round the tower of the castle. The youth held on bravely. He saw the glittering palace, which by the pale rays of the moon looked like a dim lamp; and he saw the high windows, and round one of them a balcony in which the beautiful Princess sat lost in sad thoughts. Then the boy saw that he was close to the apple-tree, and drawing a small knife from his belt, he cut off both the eagle's feet. The bird rose up in the air in its agony and vanished into the clouds, and the youth fell on to the broad branches of the apple-tree.

Then he drew out the claws of the eagle's feet that had remained in his flesh, and put the peel of one of the golden apples on the wound, and in one moment it was healed and well again. He pulled several of the beautiful apples and put them in his pocket; then he entered the castle. The door was guarded by a great dragon, but as soon as he threw an apple at it, the beast vanished.

At the same moment a gate opened, and the youth perceived a courtyard full of flowers and beautiful trees, and on a balcony sat the lovely enchanted Princess with her retinue.

As soon as she saw the youth, she ran toward him and greeted him as her husband and master. She gave him all her treasures, and the youth became a rich and mighty ruler. But he never returned to the earth, for only the mighty eagle, who had been the guardian of the Princess and of the castle, could have carried on his wings the enormous treasure down to the world. But as the eagle had lost its feet, it died, and its body was found in a wood on the Glass Mountain.

One day when the youth was strolling about in the palace garden with the Princess, his wife, he looked down over the edge of the Glass Mountain and saw to his astonishment a great number of people gathered there. He blew his silver whistle, and the swallow who acted as messenger in the golden castle flew past.

"Fly down and ask what the matter is," he said to the little bird, who sped off like lightning and soon returned saying:

"The blood of the eagle has restored all the people below to life. All those who have perished on this mountain are awakening up to-day, as it were from a sleep, and are mounting their horses, and the whole population are gazing on this unheard-of wonder with joy and amazement."

ALPHEGE, OR
THE GREEN MONKEY

 ANY YEARS AGO THERE LIVED A KING, WHO WAS
twice married. His first wife, a good and beautiful woman,
died at the birth of her little son, and the King her husband
was so overwhelmed with grief at her loss that his only
comfort was in the sight of his heir.

When the time for the young Prince's christening came the King chose as
godmother a neighbouring Princess, so celebrated for her wisdom and goodness that she was commonly called "the Good Queen." She named the baby
Alphege, and from that moment took him to her heart.

Time wipes away the greatest griefs, and after two or three years the King
married again. His second wife was a Princess of undeniable beauty, but had
not so amiable a disposition as the first Queen. In due time a second Prince
was born, and the Queen was devoured with rage at the thought that Prince
Alphege came between her son and the throne. She took care however to conceal her jealous feelings from the King.

At length she could control herself no longer, so she sent a trusty servant to her old and faithful friend the Fairy of the Mountain, to beg her to devise some means by which she might get rid of her stepson.

The Fairy replied that, much as she desired to be agreeable to the Queen in every way, it was impossible for her to attempt anything against the young Prince, who was under the protection of some greater Power than her own.

The Good Queen on her side watched carefully over her godson. She was obliged to do so from a distance, her own country being a remote one, but she was well informed of all that went on and knew all about the Queen's wicked designs. She therefore sent the Prince a large and splendid ruby, with injunctions to wear it night and day as it would protect him from all attacks, but added that the talisman only retained its power as long as the Prince remained within his father's dominions. The Wicked Queen, knowing this, made every attempt to get the Prince out of the country, but her efforts failed, till one day an accident did what she was unable to accomplish.

The King had an only sister who was deeply attached to him, and who was married to the sovereign of a distant country. She had always kept up a close correspondence with her brother, and the accounts she heard of Prince Alphege made her long to become acquainted with so charming a nephew. She entreated the King to allow the Prince to visit her, and after some hesitation which was overruled by his wife, he finally consented.

Prince Alphege was at this time fourteen years old, and the handsomest and most engaging youth imaginable. In his infancy he had been placed in the charge of one of the great ladies of the Court, who, according to the prevailing custom, acted first as his head nurse and then as his governess. When he outgrew her care her husband was appointed as his tutor and governor, so that he had never been separated from this excellent couple, who loved him as tenderly as they did their only daughter Zayda, and were warmly loved by him in return.

When the Prince set forth on his travels it was but natural that this devoted couple should accompany him, and accordingly he started with them and attended by a numerous retinue.

For some time he travelled through his father's dominions and all went well; but soon after passing the frontier they had to cross a desert plain under a burning sun. They were glad to take shelter under a group of trees nearby, and here the Prince complained of burning thirst. Luckily a tiny stream ran close by and some water was soon procured, but no sooner had he tasted it than he sprang from his carriage and disappeared in a moment. In vain did his anxious followers seek for him, he was nowhere to be found.

As they were hunting and shouting through the trees, a great black monkey suddenly appeared on a point of rock and said: "Poor sorrowing people, you are seeking your Prince in vain. Return to your own country and know that he will not be restored to you till you have for some time failed to recognise him."

With these words he vanished, leaving the courtiers sadly perplexed; but as all their efforts to find the Prince were useless they had no choice but to go home, bringing with them the sad news, which so greatly distressed the King that he fell ill and died not long after.

The Queen, whose ambition was boundless, was delighted to see the crown on her son's head and to have the power in her own hands. Her hard rule made her very unpopular, and it was commonly believed that she had made away with Prince Alphege. Indeed, had the King her son not been deservedly beloved a revolution would certainly have arisen.

Meantime the former governess of the unfortunate Alphege, who had lost her husband soon after the King's death, retired to her own house with her daughter, who grew up a lovely and most loveable girl, and both continued to mourn the loss of their dear Prince.

The young King was devoted to hunting, and often indulged in his

THE KING MAKES FRIENDS WITH THE GREEN MONKEY

favourite pastime, attended by the noblest youths in his kingdom. One day, after a long morning's chase he stopped to rest near a brook in the shade of a little wood, where a splendid tent had been prepared for him. Whilst at luncheon he suddenly spied a little monkey of the brightest green sitting on a tree and gazing so tenderly at him that he felt quite moved. He forbade his courtiers to frighten it, and the monkey, noticing how much attention was being paid him, sprang from bough to bough, and at length gradually approached the King, who offered him some food. The monkey took it very daintily and finally came to the table. The King took him on his knees, and, delighted with his capture, brought him home with him. He would trust no one else with its care, and the whole Court soon talked of nothing but the pretty green monkey.

One morning, as Prince Alphege's governess and her daughter were alone together, the little monkey sprang in through an open window. He had escaped from the palace, and his manners were so gentle and caressing that Zayda and her mother soon got over the first fright he had given them. He had spent some time with them and quite won their hearts by his insinuating ways, when the King discovered where he was and sent to fetch him back. But the monkey made such piteous cries, and seemed so unhappy when anyone attempted to catch him, that the two ladies begged the King to leave him a little longer with them, to which he consented.

One evening, as they sat by the fountain in the garden, the little monkey kept gazing at Zayda with such sad and loving eyes that she and her mother could not think what to make of it, and they were still more surprised when they saw big tears rolling down his cheeks.

The next day both mother and daughter were sitting in a jessamine bower in the garden, and they began to talk of the green monkey and his strange ways. The mother said, "My dear child, I can no longer hide my feelings from you. I cannot get the thought out of my mind that the green monkey is no other than our beloved Prince Alphege, transformed in this strange fashion. I know the idea sounds wild, but I cannot get it out of my heart, and it leaves me no peace."

As she spoke she glanced up, and there sat the little monkey, whose tears and gestures seemed to confirm her words.

The following night, the elder lady dreamt that she saw the Good Queen, who said, "Do not weep any longer but follow my directions. Go into your garden and lift up the little marble slab at the foot of the great myrtle tree. You will find beneath it a crystal vase filled with a bright green liquid. Take it with you and place the thing which is at present most in your thoughts into a bath filled with roses and rub it well with the green liquid."

The Green Monkey in the Bath.

At these words the sleeper awoke, and lost no time in rising and hurrying to the garden, where she found all as the Good Queen had described. Then she hastened to rouse her daughter and together they prepared the bath, for they would not let their women know what they were about. Zayda gathered quantities of roses, and when all was ready they put the monkey into a large jasper bath, where the mother rubbed him all over with the green liquid.

Their suspense was not long, for suddenly the monkey skin dropped off, and there stood Prince Alphege, the handsomest and most charming of men. The joy of such a meeting was beyond words. After a time the ladies begged the Prince to relate his adventures, and he told them of all his sufferings in the desert when he was first transformed. His only comfort had been in visits from the Good Queen, who had at length put him in the way of meeting his brother.

Several days were spent in these interesting conversations, but at length Zayda's mother began to think of the best means for placing the Prince on the throne, which was his by right.

The Queen on her side was feeling very anxious. She had felt sure from the first that her son's pet monkey was no other than Prince Alphege, and she longed to put an end to him. Her suspicions were confirmed by the Fairy of the Mountain, and she hastened in tears to the King, her son.

"I am informed," she cried, "that some ill-disposed people have raised up an impostor in the hopes of dethroning you. You must at once have him put to death."

The King, who was very brave, assured the Queen that he would soon punish the conspirators. He made careful inquiries into the matter, and thought it hardly probable that a quiet widow and a young girl would think of attempting anything of the nature of a revolution.

He determined to go and see them, and to find out the truth for himself; so one night, without saying anything to the Queen or his ministers, he set out for the palace where the two ladies lived, attended only by a small band of followers.

The two ladies were at the moment deep in conversation with Prince Alphege, and hearing a knocking so late at night begged him to keep out of sight for a time. What was their surprise when the door was opened to see the King and his suite.

"I know," said the King, "that you are plotting against my crown and person, and I have come to have an explanation with you."

As she was about to answer Prince Alphege, who had heard all, came forward and said, "It is from me you must ask an explanation, brother." He spoke with such grace and dignity that everyone gazed at him with mute surprise.

At length the King, recovering from his astonishment at recognising the brother who had been lost some years before, exclaimed, "Yes, you are indeed my brother, and now that I have found you, take the throne to which I have no longer a right." So saying, he respectfully kissed the Prince's hand.

Alphege threw himself into his arms, and the brothers hastened to the royal palace, where in the presence of the entire court he received the crown from his brother's hand. To clear away any possible doubt, he showed the ruby which the Good Queen had given him in his childhood. As they were gazing at it, it suddenly split with a loud noise, and at the same moment the Wicked Queen expired.

King Alphege lost no time in marrying his dear and lovely Zayda, and his joy was complete when the Good Queen appeared at his wedding. She assured him that the Fairy of the Mountain had henceforth lost all power over him, and after spending some time with the young couple, and bestowing the most costly presents on them, she retired to her own country.

King Alphege insisted on his brother sharing his throne, and they all lived to a good old age, universally beloved and admired.

FAIRER-THAN-A-FAIRY

NCE THERE LIVED A KING WHO HAD NO CHILDREN FOR
many years after his marriage. At length heaven granted him a
daughter of such remarkable beauty that he could think of no
name so appropriate for her as "Fairer-than-a-Fairy."

It never occurred to the good-natured monarch that such a name was certain to call down the hatred and jealousy of the fairies on the child, but this was what happened. No sooner had they heard of this presumptuous name than they resolved to gain possession of her who bore it, and either to torment her cruelly, or at least to conceal her from the eyes of all men.

The eldest of their tribe was entrusted to carry out their revenge. This Fairy was named Lagree; she was so old that she only had one eye and one tooth left, and even these poor remains she had to keep all night in a strengthening liquid. She was also so spiteful that she gladly devoted all her time to carrying out all the mean or ill-natured tricks of the whole body of fairies.

With her large experience, added to her native spite, she found but little difficulty in carrying off Fairer-than-a-Fairy. The poor child, who was only seven years old, nearly died of fear on finding herself in the power of this hideous

LAGREE GIVES THE TWO BOTTLES TO FAIRER-THAN-A-FAIRY

creature. However, when after an hour's journey underground she found herself in a splendid palace with lovely gardens, she felt a little reassured, and was further cheered when she discovered that her pet cat and dog had followed her.

The old Fairy led her to a pretty room which she said should be hers, at the same time giving her the strictest orders never to let out the fire which was burning brightly in the grate. She then gave two glass bottles into the Princess's charge, desiring her to take the greatest care of them, and having enforced her orders with the most awful threats in case of disobedience, she vanished, leaving the little girl at liberty to explore the palace and grounds and a good deal relieved at having only two apparently easy tasks set her.

Several years passed, during which time the Princess grew accustomed to her lonely life, obeyed the Fairy's orders, and by degrees forgot all about the court of the King her father.

One day, whilst passing near a fountain in the garden, she noticed that the sun's rays fell on the water in such a manner as to produce a brilliant rainbow. She stood still to admire it, when, to her great surprise, she heard a voice addressing her which seemed to come from the centre of its rays. The voice was that of a young man, and its sweetness of tone and the agreeable things it uttered, led one to infer that its owner must be equally charming; but this had to be a mere matter of fancy, for no one was visible.

The beautiful Rainbow informed Fairer-than-a-Fairy that he was young, the son of a powerful king, and that the Fairy, Lagree, who owed his parents a grudge, had revenged herself by depriving him of his natural shape for some years; that she had imprisoned him in the palace, where he had found his confinement hard to bear for some time, but now, he owned, he no longer sighed for freedom since he had seen and learned to love Fairer-than-a-Fairy.

He added many other tender speeches to this declaration, and the Princess, to whom such remarks were a new experience, could not help feeling pleased and touched by his attentions.

The Prince could only appear or speak under the form of a Rainbow, and it was therefore necessary that the sun should shine on water so as to enable the rays to form themselves.

Fairer-than-a-Fairy lost no moment in which she could meet her lover, and they enjoyed many long and interesting interviews. One day, however, their conversation became so absorbing and time passed so quickly that the Princess forgot to attend to the fire, and it went out. Lagree, on her return, soon found out the neglect, and seemed only too pleased to have the opportunity of showing her spite to her lovely prisoner. She ordered Fairer-than-a-Fairy to start the next day at dawn to ask Locrinos for fire with which to relight the one she had allowed to go out.

Now this Locrinos was a cruel monster who devoured everyone he came across, and especially enjoyed a chance of catching and eating any young girls. Our heroine obeyed with great sweetness, and without having been able to take leave of her lover she set off to go to Locrinos as to certain death. As she was crossing a wood a bird sang to her to pick up a shining pebble which she would find in a fountain close by, and to use it when needed. She took the bird's advice, and in due time arrived at the house of Locrinos. Luckily she only found his wife at home, who was much struck by the Princess's youth and beauty and sweet gentle manners, and still further impressed by the present of the shining pebble.

She readily let Fairer-than-a-Fairy have the fire, and in return for the stone she gave her another, which, she said, might prove useful some day. Then she sent her away without doing her any harm.

Lagree was as much surprised as displeased at the happy result of this expedition, and Fairer-than-a-Fairy waited anxiously for an opportunity of meeting Prince Rainbow and telling him her adventures. She found, however, that he had already been told all about them by a Fairy who protected him, and to whom he was related.

The dread of fresh dangers to his beloved Princess made him devise some more convenient way of meeting than by the garden fountain, and Fairer-than-a-Fairy carried out his plan daily with entire success. Every morning she placed a large basin full of water on her windowsill, and as soon as the sun's rays fell on the water the Rainbow appeared as clearly as it had ever done in the fountain. By this means they were able to meet without losing sight of the fire or of the two bottles in which the old Fairy kept her eye and her tooth at night, and for some time the lovers enjoyed every hour of sunshine together.

One day Prince Rainbow appeared in the depths of woe. He had just heard that he was to be banished from this lovely spot, but he had no idea where he was to go. The poor young couple were in despair, and only parted

Fairer than a fairy summons the Rainbows.

with the last ray of sunshine, and in hopes of meeting the next morning. Alas! the next day was dark and gloomy, and it was only late in the afternoon that the sun broke through the clouds for a few minutes.

Fairer-than-a-Fairy eagerly ran to the window, but in her haste she upset the basin, and spilt all the water with which she had carefully filled it overnight. No other water was at hand except that in the two bottles. It was the only chance of seeing her lover before they were separated, and she did not hesitate to break the bottle and pour their contents into the basin, when the Rainbow appeared at once. Their farewells were full of tenderness; the Prince made the most ardent and sincere protestations, and promised to neglect nothing which might help to deliver his dear Fairer-than-a-Fairy from her captivity, and implored her to consent to their marriage as soon as they should both be free. The Princess, on her side, vowed to have no other husband, and declared herself willing to brave death itself in order to rejoin him.

They were not allowed much time for their adieus; the Rainbow vanished, and the Princess, resolved to run all risks, started off at once, taking nothing with her but her dog, her cat, a sprig of myrtle, and the stone which the wife of Locrinos gave her.

When Lagree became aware of her prisoner's flight she was furious, and set off at full speed in pursuit. She overtook her just as the poor girl, overcome by fatigue, had lain down to rest in a cave which the stone had formed itself into to shelter her. The little dog who was watching her mistress promptly flew at Lagree and bit her so severely that she stumbled against a corner of the cave and broke off her only tooth. Before she had recovered from the pain and rage this caused her, the Princess had time to escape, and was some way on her road. Fear gave her strength for some time, but at last she could go no further, and sank down to rest. As she did so, the sprig of myrtle she carried touched the ground, and immediately a green and shady bower sprang up round her, in which she hoped to sleep in peace.

But Lagree had not given up her pursuit, and arrived just as Fairer-than-a-Fairy had fallen fast asleep. This time she made sure of catching her victim, but the cat spied her out, and, springing from one of the boughs of the arbour she flew at Lagree's face and tore out her only eye, thus delivering the Princess forever from her persecutor.

One might have thought that all would now be well, but no sooner had Lagree been put to flight than our heroine was overwhelmed with hunger and thirst. She felt as though she should certainly expire, and it was with some difficulty that she dragged herself as far as a pretty little green and white house, which stood at no great distance. Here she was received by a beautiful lady dressed in green and white to match the house, which apparently belonged to her, and of which she seemed the only inhabitant.

She greeted the fainting Princess most kindly, gave her an excellent supper, and after a long night's rest in a delightful bed told her that after many troubles she should finally attain her desire.

As the green and white lady took leave of the Princess she gave her a nut, desiring her only to open it in the most urgent need.

After a long and tiring journey Fairer-than-a-Fairy was once more received in a house, and by a lady exactly like the one she had quitted. Here again she received a present with the same injunctions, but instead of a nut this lady gave her a golden pomegranate. The mournful Princess had to continue her weary way, and after many troubles and hardships she again found rest and shelter in a third house exactly similar to the two others.

These houses belonged to three sisters, all endowed with fairy gifts, and all so alike in mind and person that they wished their houses and garments to be equally alike. Their occupation consisted in helping those in misfortune, and they were as gentle and benevolent as Lagree had been cruel and spiteful.

The third Fairy comforted the poor traveller, begged her not to lose heart, and assured her that her troubles should be rewarded. She accompanied her advice by the gift of a crystal smelling bottle, with strict orders only to open it in case of urgent need. Fairer-than-a-Fairy thanked her warmly, and resumed her way cheered by pleasant thoughts.

After a time her road led through a wood, full of soft airs and sweet odours, and before she had gone a hundred yards she saw a wonderful silver Castle suspended by strong silver chains to four of the largest trees. It was so perfectly hung that a gentle breeze rocked it sufficiently to send you pleasantly to sleep.

Fairer-than-a-Fairy felt a strong desire to enter this Castle, but besides being hung a little above the ground there seemed to be neither doors nor windows. She had no doubt (though really I cannot think why) that the moment had come in which to use the nut which had been given her. She opened it, and out came a diminutive hall porter at whose belt hung a tiny chain, at the end of which was a golden key half as long as the smallest pin you ever saw.

The Princess climbed up one of the silver chains, holding in her hand the little porter who, in spite of his minute size, opened a secret door with his golden key and let her in. She entered a magnificent room which appeared to occupy the entire Castle, and which was lighted by gold and jewelled stars in the ceiling. In the midst of this room stood a couch, draped with curtains of all the colours of the rainbow, and suspended by golden cords so that it swayed with the Castle in a manner which rocked its occupant delightfully to sleep.

On this elegant couch lay Prince Rainbow, looking more beautiful than ever, and sunk in profound slumber, in which he had been held ever since his disappearance.

Fairer-than-a-Fairy, who now saw him for the first time in his real shape, hardly dared to gaze at him, fearing lest his appearance might not be in keeping with the voice and language which had won her heart. At the same time she could not help feeling rather hurt at the apparent indifference with which she was received.

She related all the dangers and difficulties she had gone through, and though she repeated the story twenty times in a loud clear voice, the Prince slept on and took no heed. She then had recourse to the golden pomegranate, and on opening it found that all the seeds were as many little violins which flew up in the vaulted roof and at once began playing melodiously.

The Prince was not completely roused, but he opened his eyes a little and looked all the handsomer.

Impatient at not being recognised, Fairer-than-a-Fairy now drew out her third present, and on opening the crystal scent-bottle a little siren flew out, who silenced the violins and then sang close to the Prince's ear the story of all his lady love had suffered in her search for him. She added some gentle reproaches to her tale, but before she had got far he was wide awake, and transported with joy threw himself at the Princess's feet. At the same moment the walls of the room expanded and opened out, revealing a golden throne covered with jewels. A magnificent Court now began to assemble, and at the same time several elegant carriages filled with ladies in magnificent dresses drove up. In the first and most splendid of these carriages sat Prince Rainbow's mother. She fondly embraced her son, after which she informed him that his father had been dead for some years, that the anger of the Fairies was at length appeased, and that he might return in peace to reign over his people, who were longing for his presence.

The Court received the new King with joyful acclamations which would have delighted him at any other time, but all his thoughts were full of Fairer-than-a-Fairy. He was just about to present her to his mother and the Court, feeling sure that her charms would win all hearts, when the three green and white sisters appeared.

They declared the secret of Fairer-than-a-Fairy's royal birth, and the Queen taking the two lovers in her carriage set off with them for the capital of the kingdom.

Here they were received with tumultuous joy. The wedding was celebrated without delay, and succeeding years diminished neither the virtues, beauty, nor the mutual affection of King Rainbow and his Queen, Fairer-than-a-Fairy.

THE THREE BROTHERS[17]

HERE WAS ONCE UPON A TIME A WITCH, WHO IN THE shape of a hawk used every night to break the windows of a certain village church. In the same village there lived three brothers, who were all determined to kill the mischievous hawk. But in vain did the two eldest mount guard in the church with their guns; as soon as the bird appeared high above their heads, sleep overpowered them, and they only awoke to hear the windows crashing in.

Then the youngest brother took his turn of guarding the windows, and to prevent his being overcome by sleep he placed a lot of thorns under his chin, so that if he felt drowsy and nodded his head, they would prick him and keep him awake.

The moon was already risen, and it was as light as day, when suddenly he heard a fearful noise, and at the same time a terrible desire to sleep overpowered him.

---

17   From the Polish. Kletke.

His eyelids closed, and his head sank on his shoulders, but the thorns ran into him and were so painful that he awoke at once. He saw the hawk swooping down upon the church, and in a moment he had seized his gun and shot at the bird. The hawk fell heavily under a big stone, severely wounded in its right wing. The youth ran to look at it, and saw that a huge abyss had opened below the stone. He went at once to fetch his brothers, and with their help dragged a lot of pine-wood and ropes to the spot. They fastened some of the burning pine-wood to the end of the rope, and let it slowly down to the bottom of the abyss. At first it was quite dark, and the flaming torch only lit up dirty grey stone walls. But the youngest brother determined to explore the abyss, and letting himself down by the rope he soon reached the bottom. Here he found a lovely meadow full of green trees and exquisite flowers.

In the middle of the meadow stood a huge stone castle, with an iron gate leading to it, which was wide open. Everything in the castle seemed to be made of copper, and the only inhabitant he could discover was a lovely girl, who was combing her golden hair; and he noticed that whenever one of her hairs fell on the ground it rang out like pure metal. The youth looked at her more closely, and saw that her skin was smooth and fair, her blue eyes bright and sparkling, and her hair as golden as the sun. He fell in love with her on the spot, and kneeling at her feet, he implored her to become his wife.

The lovely girl accepted his proposal gladly; but at the same time she warned him that she could never come up to the world above till her mother, the old witch, was dead. And she went on to tell him that the only way in which the old creature could be killed was with the sword that hung up in the castle; but the sword was so heavy that no one could lift it.

Then the youth went into a room in the castle where everything was made of silver, and here he found another beautiful girl, the sister of his bride. She was combing her silver hair, and every hair that fell on the ground rang out like pure metal. The second girl handed him the sword, but though he tried with all his strength he could not lift it. At last a third sister came to him and gave him a drop of something to drink, which she said would give him the needful strength. He drank one drop, but still he could not lift the sword; then he drank a second, and the sword began to move; but only after he had drunk a third drop was he able to swing the sword over his head.

Then he hid himself in the castle and awaited the old witch's arrival. At last as it was beginning to grow dark she appeared. She swooped down upon a big apple-tree, and after shaking some golden apples from it, she pounced down upon the earth. As soon as her feet touched the ground she became transformed from a hawk into a woman. This was the moment the youth was waiting for, and he swung his mighty sword in the air with all his strength and the witch's head fell off, and her blood spurted up on the walls.

Without fear of any further danger, he packed up all the treasures of the castle into great chests, and gave his brothers a signal to pull them up out of the abyss. First the treasures were attached to the rope and then the three love-ly girls. And now everything was up above and only he himself remained be-low. But as he was a little suspicious of his brothers, he fastened a heavy stone on to the rope and let them pull it up. At first they heaved with a will, but when the stone was half way up they let it drop suddenly, and it fell to the bottom broken into a hundred pieces.

"So that's what would have happened to my bones had I trusted myself to them," said the youth sadly; and he began to cry bitterly, not because of the treasures, but because of the lovely girl with her swanlike neck and golden hair.

For a long time he wandered sadly all through the beautiful underworld, and one day he met a magician who asked him the cause of his tears. The youth told him all that had befallen him, and the magician said:

"Do not grieve, young man! If you will guard the children who are hidden in the golden apple-tree, I will bring you at once up to the earth. Another magician who lives in this land always eats my children up. It is in vain that I

'THEN THE YOUTH SWUNG HIS MIGHTY SWORD IN THE AIR,
AND WITH ONE BLOW CUT OFF THE SERPENT'S HEAD.'

have hidden them under the earth and locked them into the castle. Now I have hidden them in the apple-tree; hide yourself there too, and at midnight you will see my enemy."

The youth climbed up the tree, and picked some of the beautiful golden apples, which he ate for his supper.

At midnight the wind began to rise, and a rustling sound was heard at the foot of the tree. The youth looked down and beheld a long thick serpent beginning to crawl up the tree. It wound itself round the stem and gradually got higher and higher. It stretched its huge head, in which the eyes glittered fiercely, among the branches, searching for the nest in which the little children lay. They trembled with terror when they saw the hideous creature, and hid themselves beneath the leaves.

Then the youth swung his mighty sword in the air, and with one blow cut off the serpent's head. He cut up the rest of the body into little bits and strewed them to the four winds.

The father of the rescued children was so delighted over the death of his enemy that he told the youth to get on his back, and in this way he carried him up to the world above.

With what joy did he hurry now to his brothers' house! He burst into a room where they were all assembled, but no one knew who he was. Only his bride, who was serving as cook to her sisters, recognised her lover at once.

His brothers, who had quite believed he was dead, yielded him up his treasures at once, and flew into the woods in terror. But the good youth forgave them all they had done, and divided his treasures with them. Then he built himself a big castle with golden windows, and there he lived happily with his golden-haired wife till the end of their lives.

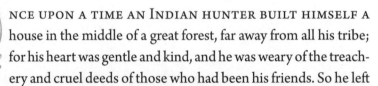

THE BOY AND THE WOLVES, OR THE BROKEN PROMISE[18]

ONCE UPON A TIME AN INDIAN HUNTER BUILT HIMSELF A house in the middle of a great forest, far away from all his tribe; for his heart was gentle and kind, and he was weary of the treachery and cruel deeds of those who had been his friends. So he left them, and took his wife and three children, and they journeyed on until they found a spot near to a clear stream, where they began to cut down trees, and to make ready their wigwam. For many years they lived peacefully and happily in this sheltered place, never leaving it except to hunt the wild animals, which served them both for food and clothes. At last, however, the strong man felt sick, and before long he knew he must die.

So he gathered his family round him, and said his last words to them. "You, my wife, the companion of my days, will follow me ere many moons have waned to the island of the blest. But for you, O my children, whose lives are but newly begun, the wickedness, unkindness, and ingratitude from which I fled are before you. Yet I shall go hence in peace, my children, if you will promise always to love each other, and never to forsake your youngest brother."

"Never!" they replied, holding out their hands. And the hunter died content.

Scarcely eight moons had passed when, just as he had said, the wife went forth, and followed her husband; but before leaving her children she bade the two elder ones think of their promise never to forsake the younger, for he was a child, and weak. And while the snow lay thick upon the ground, they tended him and cherished him; but when the earth showed green again, the heart of the young man stirred within him, and he longed to see the wigwams of the village where his father's youth was spent.

Therefore he opened all his heart to his sister, who answered: "My brother, I understand your longing for our fellow men, whom here we cannot see. But remember our father's words. Shall we not seek our own pleasures, and forget the little one?"

But he would not listen, and, making no reply, he took his bow and arrows and left the hut. The snows fell and melted, yet he never returned; and at last the heart of the girl grew cold and hard, and her little boy became a burden in her eyes, till one day she spoke thus to him: "See, there is food for many days to come. Stay here within the shelter of the hut. I go to seek our brother, and when I have found him I shall return hither."

But when, after hard journeying, she reached the village where her brother dwelt, and saw that he had a wife and was happy, and when she, too, was sought by a young brave, then she also forgot the boy alone in the forest, and thought only of her husband.

Now as soon as the little boy had eaten all the food which his sister had left him, he went out into the woods, and gathered berries and dug up roots, and

while the sun shone he was contented and had his fill. But when the snows began and the wind howled, then his stomach felt empty and his limbs cold, and he hid in trees all the night, and only crept out to eat what the wolves had left behind. And by-and-by, having no other friends, he sought their company, and sat by while they devoured their prey, and they grew to know him, and gave him food. And without them he would have died in the snow.

But at last the snows melted, and the ice upon the great lake, and as the wolves went down to the shore, the boy went after them. And it happened one day that his big brother was fishing in his canoe near the shore, and he heard the voice of a child singing in the Indian tone—

> *"My brother, my brother!*
> *I am becoming a wolf,*
> *I am becoming a wolf!"*

And when he had so sung he howled as wolves howl. Then the heart of the elder sunk, and he hastened toward him, crying, "Brother, little brother, come to me;" but he, being half a wolf, only continued his song. And the louder the elder called him, "Brother, little brother, come to me," the swifter he fled after his brothers the wolves, and the heavier grew his skin, till, with a long howl, he vanished into the depths of the forest.

So, with shame and anguish in his soul, the elder brother went back to his village, and, with his sister, mourned the little boy and the broken promise till the end of his life.

THE GLASS AXE[19]

HERE WAS ONCE UPON A TIME A KING AND QUEEN WHO had everything they could possibly wish for in this world except a child. At last, after twelve years, the Queen gave birth to a son; but she did not live long to enjoy her happiness, for on the following day she died. But before her death she called her husband to her and said, "Never let the child put his feet on the ground, for as soon as he does so he will fall into the power of a wicked Fairy, who will do him much harm." And these were the last words the poor Queen spoke.

The boy throve and grew big, and when he was too heavy for his nurse to carry, a chair was made for him on little wheels, in which he could wander through the palace gardens without help; at other times he was carried about on a litter, and he was always carefully watched and guarded for fear he should at any time put his feet to the ground.

But as this sort of life was bad for his health, the doctors ordered him horse exercise, and he soon became a first-rate rider, and used to go out for

19   From the Hungarian. Kletke.

long excursions on horseback, accompanied always by his father's stud groom and a numerous retinue.

Every day he rode through the neighbouring fields and woods, and always returned home in the evening safe and well. In this way many years passed, and the Prince grew to manhood, and hardly anyone remembered the Queen's warning, though precautions were still taken, more from use and wont than for any other reason.

One day the Prince and his suite went out for a ride in a wood where his father sometimes held a hunt. Their way led through a stream whose banks were overgrown with thick brushwood. Just as the horsemen were about to ford the river, a hare, startled by the sound of the horses' hoofs, started up from the grass and ran toward the thicket. The young Prince pursued the little creature, and had almost overtaken it, when the girth of his saddle suddenly broke in two and he fell heavily to the ground. No sooner had his foot touched the earth than he disappeared before the eyes of the horrified courtiers.

They sought for him far and near, but all in vain, and they were forced to recognise the power of the evil Fairy, against which the Queen had warned them on her death-bed. The old King was much grieved when they brought him the news of his son's disappearance, but as he could do nothing to free him from his fate, he gave himself up to an old age of grief and loneliness, cherishing at the same time the hope that some lucky chance might one day deliver the youth out of the hands of his enemy.

Hardly had the Prince touched the ground than he felt himself violently seized by an unseen power, and hurried away he knew not whither. A whole new world stretched out before him, quite unlike the one he had left. A splendid castle surrounded by a huge lake was the abode of the Fairy, and the only approach to it was over a bridge of clouds. On the other side of the lake high mountains rose up, and dark woods stretched along the banks; over all hung a thick mist, and deep silence reigned everywhere.

No sooner had the Fairy reached her own domain than she made herself visible, and turning to the Prince she told him that unless he obeyed all her commands down to the minutest detail he would be severely punished. Then she gave him an axe made of glass, and bade him cross the bridge of clouds and go into the wood beyond and cut down all the trees there before sunset. At the same time she cautioned him with many angry words against speaking to a girl he would most likely meet in the wood.

The Prince listened to her words meekly, and when she had finished took up the glass axe and set out for the forest. At every step he seemed to sink into the clouds, but fear gave wings to his feet, and he crossed the lake in safety and set to work at once.

But no sooner had he struck the first blow with his axe than it broke into a thousand pieces against the tree. The poor youth was so terrified he did not know what to do, for he was in mortal dread of the punishment the wicked old Fairy would inflict on him. He wandered to and fro in the wood, not knowing where he was going, and at last, worn out by fatigue and misery, he sank on the ground and fell fast asleep.

He did not know how long he had slept when a sudden sound awoke him, and opening his eyes he saw a girl standing beside him. Mindful of the Fairy's warning he did not dare to address her, but she on her part greeted him in the most friendly manner, and asked him at once if he were under the power of the wicked Fairy. The Prince nodded his head silently in answer.

Then the girl told him that she too was in the power of the Fairy, who had doomed her to wander about in her present guise until some youth should take pity on her and bear her in safety to the other side of the river which they saw in the distance, and on the other side of which the Fairy's domain and power ended.

The girl's words so inspired the Prince with confidence that he told her all his tale of woe, and ended up by asking her advice as to how he was to escape the punishment the Fairy would be sure to inflict on him when she discovered that he had not cut down the trees in the wood and that he had broken her axe.

"You must know," answered the girl, "that the Fairy in whose power we both are is my own mother, but you must not betray this secret, for it would cost me my life. If you will only promise to try and free me I will stand by you, and will accomplish for you all the tasks which my mother sets you."

The Prince promised joyfully all she asked; then having once more warned him not to betray her confidence, she handed him a draught to drink which very soon sunk his senses in a deep slumber.

His astonishment was great when he awoke to find the glass axe whole and unbroken at his side, and all the trees of the wood lying felled around him!

He made all haste across the bridge of clouds, and told the Fairy that her commands were obeyed. She was much amazed when she heard that all the wood was cut down, and saw the axe unbroken in his hand, and since she could not believe that he had done all this by himself, she questioned him narrowly if he had seen or spoken to the girl. But the Prince lied manfully, and swore he had never looked up from his work for a moment. Seeing she could get nothing more out of him, she gave him a little bread and water, and showing him to a small dark cupboard she told him he might sleep there.

Morning had hardly dawned when the Fairy awoke the Prince, and giving him the glass axe again she told him to cut up all the wood he had felled the day before, and to put it in bundles ready for firewood; at the same time she warned him once more against approaching or speaking a word to the girl if he met her in the wood.

Although his task was no easier than that of the day before, the youth set out much more cheerfully, because he knew he could count on the help of the girl. With quicker and lighter step he crossed the bridge of clouds, and hardly had he reached the other side than his friend stood before him and greeted him cheerfully. When she heard what the Fairy demanded this time, she answered smilingly, "Never fear," and handed him another draught, which very soon caused the Prince to sink into a deep sleep.

When he awoke everything was done. All the trees of the wood were cut up into firewood and arranged in bundles ready for use.

He returned to the castle as quickly as he could, and told the Fairy that her commands were obeyed. She was even more amazed than she had been before, and asked him again if he had either seen or spoken to the girl; but the Prince knew better than to betray his word, and once more lied freely.

On the following day the Fairy set him a third task to do, even harder than the other two. She told him he must build a castle on the other side of the lake, made of nothing but gold, silver, and precious stones, and unless he could accomplish this within an hour, the most frightful doom awaited him.

The Prince heard her words without anxiety, so entirely did he rely on the help of his friend. Full of hope he hurried across the bridge, and recognised at once the spot where the castle was to stand, for spades, hammers, axes, and every other building implement lay scattered on the ground ready for the workman's hand, but of gold, silver, and precious stones there was not a sign. But before the Prince had time to feel despondent the girl beckoned to him in the distance from behind a rock, where she had hidden herself for fear her mother should catch sight of her. Full of joy the youth hurried toward her, and begged her aid and counsel in the new piece of work he had been given to do.

But this time the Fairy had watched the Prince's movements from her window, and she saw him hiding himself behind the rock with her daughter. She uttered a piercing shriek so that the mountains re-echoed with the sound of it, and the terrified pair had hardly dared to look out from their hiding-place when the enraged woman, with her dress and hair flying in the wind, hurried over the bridge of clouds. The Prince at once gave himself

THE GIRL STOPS THE WITCH WITH A BIT OF THE ROCK

up for lost, but the girl told him to be of good courage and to follow her as quickly as he could. But before they left their shelter she broke off a little bit of the rock, spoke some magic words over it, and threw it in the direction her mother was coming from. In a moment a glittering palace arose before the eyes of the Fairy which blinded her with its dazzling splendour, and with its many doors and passages prevented her for some time from finding her way out of it.

In the meantime the girl hurried on with the Prince, hastening to reach the river, where once on the other side they would forever be out of the wicked Fairy's power. But before they had accomplished half the way they heard again the rustle of her garments and her muttered curses pursuing them closely.

The Prince was terrified; he dared not look back, and he felt his strength giving way. But before he had time to despair the girl uttered some more magic words, and immediately she herself was changed into a pond, and the Prince into a duck swimming on its surface.

When the Fairy saw this her rage knew no bounds, and she used all her magic wits to make the pond disappear; she caused a hill of sand to arise at her feet, meaning it to dry up the water at once. But the sand hill only drove the pond a little farther away, and its waters seemed to increase instead of diminishing. When the old woman saw that the powers of her magic were of so little avail, she had recourse to cunning. She threw a lot of gold nuts into the pond, hoping in this way to catch the duck, but all her efforts were fruitless, for the little creature refused to let itself be caught.

Then a new idea struck the wicked old woman, and hiding herself behind the rock which had sheltered the fugitives, she waited behind it, watching carefully for the moment when the Prince and her daughter should resume their natural forms and continue their journey.

She had not to wait long, for as soon as the girl thought her mother was safely out of the way, she changed herself and the Prince once more into their human shape, and set out cheerfully for the river.

But they had not gone many steps when the wicked Fairy hurried after them, a drawn dagger in her hand, and was close upon them, when suddenly, instead of the Prince and her daughter, she found herself in front of a great stone church, whose entrance was carefully guarded by a huge monk.

Breathless with rage and passion, she tried to plunge her dagger into the monk's heart, but it fell shattered in pieces at her feet. In her desperation she determined to pull down the church, and thus to destroy her two victims forever. She stamped three times on the ground, and the earth trembled, and both the church and the monk began to shake. As soon as the Fairy saw this she retreated to some distance from the building, so as not to be hurt herself by its fall. But once more her scheme was doomed to failure, for hardly had she gone a yard from the church than both it and the monk disappeared, and she found herself in a wood black as night, and full of wolves and bears and wild animals of all sorts and descriptions.

Then her wrath gave place to terror, for she feared every moment to be torn in pieces by the beasts who one and all seemed to defy her power. She thought it wisest to make her way as best she could out of the forest, and then to pursue the fugitives once more and accomplish their destruction either by force or cunning.

In the meantime the Prince and the girl had again assumed their natural forms, and were hurrying on as fast as they could to reach the river. But when they got there they found that there was no way in which they could cross it, and the girl's magic art seemed no longer to have any power. Then turning to the Prince she said, "The hour for my deliverance has not yet come, but as you promised to do all you could to free me, you must do exactly as I bid you now. Take this bow and arrow and kill every beast you see with them, and be sure you spare no living creature."

With these words she disappeared, and hardly had she done so than a huge wild boar started out of the thicket near and made straight for the Prince. But the youth did not lose his presence of mind, and drawing his bow he pierced the beast with his arrow right through the skull. The creature fell heavily on the ground, and out of its side sprang a little hare, which ran like the wind along the river bank. The Prince drew his bow once more, and the hare lay dead at his feet; but at the same moment a dove rose up in the air, and circled round the Prince's head in the most confiding manner. But mindful of the girl's commands, he dared not spare the little creature's life, and taking another arrow from his quiver he laid it as dead as the boar and the hare. But when he went to look at the body of the bird he found instead of the dove a round white egg lying on the ground.

While he was gazing on it and wondering what it could mean, he heard the sweeping of wings above him, and looking up he saw a huge vulture with open claws swooping down upon him. In a moment he seized the egg and flung it at the bird with all his might, and lo and behold! instead of the ugly monster the girl, now freed from her mother's realm, stood before the astonished Prince.

But while all this was going on the wicked old Fairy had managed to make her way out of the wood, and was now using the last resource in her power to overtake her daughter and the Prince. As soon as she was in the open again she mounted her chariot, which was drawn by a fiery dragon, and flew through the air in it. But just as she got to the river she saw the two lovers in each other's arms swimming through the water as easily as two fishes.

Quick as lightning, and forgetful of every danger, she flew down upon them. But the waters seized her chariot and sunk it in the lowest depths, and the waves bore the wicked old woman down the stream till she was caught in some thorn bushes, where she made a good meal for all the little fishes that were swimming about.

And so at last the Prince and his lovely Bride were free. They hurried as quickly as they could to the old King, who received them with joy and gladness. On the following day a most gorgeous wedding feast was held, and as far as we know the Prince and his Bride lived happily forever afterward.

THE DEAD WIFE[20]

NCE UPON A TIME THERE WERE A MAN AND HIS WIFE who lived in the forest, very far from the rest of the tribe. Very often they spent the day in hunting together, but after a while the wife found that she had so many things to do that she was obliged to stay at home; so he went alone, though he found that when his wife was not with him he never had any luck. One day, when he was away hunting, the woman fell ill, and in a few days she died. Her husband grieved bitterly, and buried her in the house where she had passed her life; but as the time went on he felt so lonely without her that he made a wooden doll about her height and size for company, and dressed it in her clothes. He seated it in front of the fire, and tried to think he had his wife back again. The next day he went out to hunt, and when he came home the first thing he did was to go up to the doll and brush off some of the ashes from the fire which had fallen on its face. But he was very busy now, for he had to cook and mend,

---

20 From the Iroquois.

besides getting food, for there was no one to help him. And so a whole year passed away.

At the end of that time he came back from hunting one night and found some wood by the door and a fire within. The next night there was not only wood and fire, but a piece of meat in the kettle, nearly ready for eating. He searched all about to see who could have done this, but could find no one. The next time he went to hunt he took care not to go far, and came in quite early. And while he was still a long way off he saw a woman going into the house with wood on her shoulders. So he made haste, and opened the door quickly, and instead of the wooden doll, his wife sat in front of the fire.

Then she spoke to him and said, "The Great Spirit felt sorry for you, because you would not be comforted, so he let me come back to you, but you must not stretch out your hand to touch me till we have seen the rest of our people. If you do, I shall die."

So the man listened to her words, and the woman dwelt there, and brought the wood and kindled the fire, till one day her husband said to her, "It is now two years since you died. Let us now go back to our tribe. Then you will be well, and I can touch you."

And with that he prepared food for the journey, a string of deer's flesh for her to carry, and one for himself; and so they started. Now the camp of the tribe was distant six days' journey, and when they were yet one day's journey off it began to snow, and they felt weary and longed for rest. Therefore they made a fire, cooked some food, and spread out their skins to sleep.

Then the heart of the man was greatly stirred, and he stretched out his arms to his wife, but she waved her hands and said, "We have seen no one yet; it is too soon."

But he would not listen to her, and caught her to him, and behold! he was clasping the wooden doll. And when he saw it was the doll he pushed it from him in his misery and rushed away to the camp, and told them all his story.

The Indian finds his wife sitting by the fire.

And some doubted, and they went back with him to the place where he and his wife had stopped to rest, and there lay the doll, and besides, they saw in the snow the steps of two people, and the foot of one was like the foot of the doll. And the man grieved sore, all the days of his life.

IN THE LAND OF SOULS[21]

AR AWAY, IN NORTH AMERICA, WHERE THE INDIANS dwell, there lived a long time ago a beautiful maiden, who was lovelier than any other girl in the whole tribe. Many of the young braves sought her in marriage, but she would listen to one only—a handsome chief, who had taken her fancy some years before. So they were to be married, and great rejoicings were made, and the two looked forward to a long life of happiness together, when the very night before the wedding feast a sudden illness seized the girl, and, without a word to her friends who were weeping round her, she passed silently away.

The heart of her lover had been set upon her, and the thought of her remained with him night and day. He put aside his bow, and went neither to fight nor to hunt, but from sunrise to sunset he sat by the place where she was laid, thinking of his happiness that was buried there. At last, after many days, a light seemed to come to him out of the darkness. He remembered having

---

21   From the American Indian.

heard from the old, old people of the tribe, that there was a path that led to the Land of Souls—that if you sought carefully you could find it.

So the next morning he got up early, and put some food in his pouch and slung an extra skin over his shoulders, for he knew not how long his journey would take, nor what sort of country he would have to go through. Only one thing he knew, that if the path was there, he would find it. At first he was puzzled, as there seemed no reason he should go in one direction more than another. Then all at once he thought he had heard one of the old men say that the Land of Souls lay to the south, and so, filled with new hope and courage, he set his face southwards. For many, many miles the country looked the same as it did round his own home. The forests, the hills, and the rivers all seemed exactly like the ones he had left. The only thing that was different was the snow, which had lain thick upon the hills and trees when he started, but grew less and less the farther he went south, till it disappeared altogether. Soon the trees put forth their buds, and flowers sprang up under his feet, and instead of thick clouds there was blue sky over his head, and everywhere the birds were singing. Then he knew that he was in the right road.

The thought that he should soon behold his lost bride made his heart beat for joy, and he sped along lightly and swiftly. Now his way led through a dark wood, and then over some steep cliffs, and on the top of these he found a hut or wigwam. An old man clothed in skins, and holding a staff in his hand, stood in the doorway; and he said to the young chief who was beginning to tell his story, "I was waiting for you, wherefore you have come I know. It is but a short while since she whom you seek was here. Rest in my hut, as she also rested, and I will tell you what you ask, and whither you should go."

On hearing these words, the young man entered the hut, but his heart was too eager within him to suffer him to rest, and when he arose, the old man rose too, and stood with him at the door. "Look," he said, "at the water which lies far out yonder, and the plains which stretch beyond. That is the Land of Souls, but no man enters it without leaving his body behind him. So, lay down your body here; your bow and arrows, your skin and your dog. They shall be kept for you safely."

Then he turned away, and the young chief, light as air, seemed hardly to touch the ground; and as he flew along the scents grew sweeter and the flowers more beautiful, while the animals rubbed their noses against him, instead of hiding as he approached, and birds circled round him, and fishes lifted up their heads and looked as he went by. Very soon he noticed with wonder, that neither rocks nor trees barred his path. He passed through them without knowing it, for indeed, they were not rocks and trees at all, but only the souls of them; for this was the Land of Shadows.

So he went on with winged feet till he came to the shores of a great lake, with a lovely island in the middle of it; while on the bank of the lake was a canoe of glittering stone, and in the canoe were two shining paddles.

The chief jumped straight into the canoe, and seizing the paddles pushed off from the shore, when to his joy and wonder he saw following him in another canoe exactly like his own the maiden for whose sake he had made this long journey. But they could not touch each other, for between them rolled great waves, which looked as if they would sink the boats, yet never did. And the young man and the maiden shrank with fear, for down in the depths of the water they saw the bones of those who had died before, and in the waves themselves men and women were struggling, and but few passed over. Only the children had no fear, and reached the other side in safety. Still, though the chief and the young girl quailed in terror at these horrible sights and sounds, no harm came to them, for their lives had been free from evil, and the Master of Life had said that no evil should happen unto them. So they reached unhurt the shore of the Happy Island, and wandered through the flowery fields and by the banks of rushing streams, and they knew not hunger nor thirst; neither cold nor heat. The air fed them and the sun warmed them, and they forgot the dead, for they saw no graves, and the young man's thoughts turned not to wars, neither to the hunting of animals. And gladly would these two have walked thus forever, but in the murmur of the wind he heard the Master of Life saying to him, "Return whither you came, for I have work for you to do, and your people need you, and for many years you shall rule over them. At the gate my messenger awaits you, and you shall take again your body which you left behind, and he will show you what you are to do. Listen to him, and have patience, and in time to come you shall rejoin her whom you must now leave, for she is accepted, and will remain ever young and beautiful, as when I called her hence from the Land of Snows."

THE WHITE DUCK

NCE UPON A TIME A GREAT AND POWERFUL KING married a lovely Princess. No couple were ever so happy; but before their honeymoon was over they were forced to part, for the King had to go on a warlike expedition to a far country, and leave his young wife alone at home. Bitter were the tears she shed, while her husband sought in vain to soothe her with words of comfort and counsel, warning her, above all things, never to leave the castle, to hold no intercourse with strangers, to beware of evil counsellors, and especially to be on her guard against strange women. And the Queen promised faithfully to obey her royal lord and master in these four matters.

So when the King set out on his expedition she shut herself up with her ladies in her own apartments, and spent her time in spinning and weaving, and in thinking of her royal husband. Often she was very sad and lonely, and it happened that one day while she was seated at the window, letting salt tears drop on her work, an old woman, a kind, homely-looking old body, stepped up to the window, and, leaning upon her crutch, addressed the Queen in friendly, flattering tones, saying:

"Why are you sad and cast down, fair Queen? You should not mope all day in your rooms, but should come out into the green garden, and hear the birds sing with joy among the trees, and see the butterflies fluttering above the flowers, and hear the bees and insects hum, and watch the sunbeams chase the dew-drops through the rose leaves and in the lily cups. All the brightness outside would help to drive away your cares, O Queen."

For long the Queen resisted her coaxing words, remembering the promise she had given the King, her husband; but at last she thought to herself: "After all, what harm would it do if I were to go into the garden for a short time and enjoy myself among the trees and flowers, and the singing birds and fluttering butterflies and humming insects, and look at the dew-drops hiding from the sunbeams in the hearts of the roses and lilies, and wander about in the sunshine, instead of remaining all day in this room?" For she had no idea that the kind-looking old woman leaning on her crutch was in reality a wicked witch, who envied the Queen her good fortune, and was determined to ruin her. And so, in all ignorance, the Queen followed her out into the garden and listened to her smooth, flattering words. Now, in the middle of the garden there was a pond of water, clear as crystal, and the old woman said to the Queen:

"The day is so warm, and the sun's rays so scorching, that the water in the pond looks very cool and inviting. Would you not like to bathe in it, fair Queen?"

"No, I think not," answered the Queen; but the next moment she regretted her words, and thought to herself: "Why shouldn't I bathe in that cool, fresh water? No harm could come of it." And, so saying, she slipped off her robes and stepped into the water. But scarcely had her tender feet touched the cool ripples when she felt a great shove on her shoulders, and the wicked witch had pushed her into the deep water, exclaiming:

"Swim henceforth, White Duck!"

And the witch herself assumed the form of the Queen, and decked herself out in the royal robes, and sat among the Court ladies, awaiting the King's

THE WITCH PERSUADES THE QUEEN TO BATHE

return. And suddenly the tramp of horses' hoofs was heard, and the barking of dogs, and the witch hastened forward to meet the royal carriages, and, throwing her arms round the King's neck, kissed him. And in his great joy the King did not know that the woman he held in his arms was not his own dear wife, but a wicked witch.

In the meantime, outside the palace walls, the poor White Duck swam up and down the pond; and near it laid three eggs, out of which there came one morning two little fluffy ducklings and a little ugly drake. And the White Duck brought the little creatures up, and they paddled after her in the pond, and caught goldfish, and hopped upon the bank and waddled about, ruffling their feathers and saying "Quack, quack" as they strutted about on the green banks of the pond. But their mother used to warn them not to stray too far, telling them that a wicked witch lived in the castle beyond the garden, adding, "She has ruined me, and she will do her best to ruin you." But the young ones did not listen to their mother, and, playing about the garden one day, they strayed close up to the castle windows. The witch at once recognised them by their smell, and ground her teeth with anger; but she hid her feelings, and, pretending to be very kind, she called them to her and joked with them, and led them into a beautiful room, where she gave them food to eat, and showed them a soft cushion on which they might sleep. Then she left them and went down into the palace kitchens, where she told the servants to sharpen the knives, and to make a great fire ready, and hang a large kettleful of water over it.

In the meantime the two little ducklings had fallen asleep, and the little drake lay between them, covered up by their wings, to be kept warm under their feathers. But the little drake could not go to sleep, and as he lay there wide awake in the night he heard the witch come to the door and say:

"Little ones, are you asleep?"

And the little drake answered for the other two:

"We cannot sleep, we wake and weep,
Sharp is the knife, to take our life;
The fire is hot, now boils the pot,
And so we wake, and lie and quake."

"They are not asleep yet," muttered the witch to herself; and she walked up and down in the passage, and then came back to the door, and said:

"Little ones, are you asleep?"

And again the little drake answered for his sisters:

"We cannot sleep, we wake and weep,
Sharp is the knife, to take our life;
The fire is hot, now boils the pot,
And so we wake, and lie and quake."

"Just the same answer," muttered the witch; "I think I'll go in and see." So she opened the door gently, and seeing the two little ducklings sound asleep, she there and then killed them.

The next morning the White Duck wandered round the pond in a distracted manner, looking for her little ones; she called and she searched, but could find no trace of them. And in her heart she had a foreboding that evil had befallen them, and she fluttered up out of the water and flew to the palace. And there, laid out on the marble floor of the court, dead and stone cold, were her three children. The White Duck threw herself upon them, and, covering up their little bodies with her wings, she cried:

"Quack, quack—my little loves!
Quack, quack—my turtle-doves!
I brought you up with grief and pain,

And now before my eyes you're slain.
I gave you always of the best;
I kept you warm in my soft nest.
I loved and watched you day and night—
You were my joy, my one delight."

The King heard the sad complaint of the White Duck, and called to the witch: "Wife, what a wonder is this? Listen to that White Duck."

But the witch answered, "My dear husband, what do you mean? There is nothing wonderful in a duck's quacking. Here, servants! Chase that duck out of the courtyard." But though the servants chased and chevied, they could not get rid of the duck; for she circled round and round, and always came back to the spot where her children lay, crying:

"Quack, quack—my little loves!
Quack, quack—my turtle-doves!
The wicked witch your lives did take—
The wicked witch, the cunning snake.
First she stole my King away,
Then my children did she slay.
Changed me, from a happy wife,
To a duck for all my life.
Would I were the Queen again;
Would that you had ne'er been slain."

And as the King heard her words he began to suspect that he had been deceived, and he called out to the servants, "Catch that duck, and bring it here." But, though they ran to and fro, the duck always fled past them, and would not let herself be caught. So the King himself stepped down amongst

THE KING CATCHES THE WHITE DUCK

them, and instantly the duck fluttered down into his hands. And as he stroked her wings she was changed into a beautiful woman, and he recognised his dear wife. And she told him that a bottle would be found in her nest in the garden, containing some drops from the spring of healing. And it was brought to her; and the ducklings and little drake were sprinkled with the water, and from the little dead bodies three lovely children arose. And the King and Queen were overjoyed when they saw their children, and they all lived happily together in the beautiful palace. But the wicked witch was taken by the King's command, and she came to no good end.

THE WITCH AND HER SERVANTS[22]

 LONG TIME AGO THERE LIVED A KING WHO HAD THREE sons; the eldest was called Szabo, the second Warza, and the youngest Iwanich.

One beautiful spring morning the King was walking through his gardens with these three sons, gazing with admiration at the various fruit trees, some of which were a mass of blossom, whilst others were bowed to the ground laden with rich fruit. During their wanderings they came unperceived on a piece of wasteland where three splendid trees grew. The King looked on them for a moment, and then, shaking his head sadly, he passed on in silence.

The sons, who could not understand why he did this, asked him the reason of his dejection, and the King told them as follows:

"These three trees, which I cannot see without sorrow, were planted by me on this spot when I was a youth of twenty. A celebrated magician, who

---

22   From the Russian. Kletke.

had given the seed to my father, promised him that they would grow into the three finest trees the world had ever seen. My father did not live to see his words come true; but on his death-bed he bade me transplant them here, and to look after them with the greatest care, which I accordingly did. At last, after the lapse of five long years, I noticed some blossoms on the branches, and a few days later the most exquisite fruit my eyes had ever seen.

"I gave my head-gardener the strictest orders to watch the trees carefully, for the magician had warned my father that if one unripe fruit were plucked from the tree, all the rest would become rotten at once. When it was quite ripe the fruit would become a golden yellow.

"Every day I gazed on the lovely fruit, which became gradually more and more tempting-looking, and it was all I could do not to break the magician's commands.

"One night I dreamt that the fruit was perfectly ripe; I ate some of it, and it was more delicious than anything I had ever tasted in real life. As soon as I awoke I sent for the gardener and asked him if the fruit on the three trees had not ripened in the night to perfection.

"But instead of replying, the gardener threw himself at my feet and swore that he was innocent. He said that he had watched by the trees all night, but in spite of it, and as if by magic, the beautiful trees had been robbed of all their fruit.

"Grieved as I was over the theft, I did not punish the gardener, of whose fidelity I was well assured, but I determined to pluck off all the fruit in the following year before it was ripe, as I had not much belief in the magician's warning.

"I carried out my intention, and had all the fruit picked off the tree, but when I tasted one of the apples it was bitter and unpleasant, and the next morning the rest of the fruit had all rotted away.

"After this I had the beautiful fruit of these trees carefully guarded by my most faithful servants; but every year, on this very night, the fruit was plucked and stolen by an invisible hand, and the next morning not a single apple remained on the trees. For some time past I have given up even having the trees watched."

When the King had finished his story, Szabo, his eldest son, said to him: "Forgive me, father, if I say I think you are mistaken. I am sure there are many men in your kingdom who could protect these trees from the cunning arts of a thieving magician; I myself, who as your eldest son claim the first right to do so, will mount guard over the fruit this very night."

The King consented, and as soon as evening drew on Szabo climbed up on to one of the trees, determined to protect the fruit even if it cost him his life. So he kept watch half the night; but a little after midnight he was overcome by an irresistible drowsiness, and fell fast asleep. He did not awake till it was bright daylight, and all the fruit on the trees had vanished.

The following year Warza, the second brother, tried his luck, but with the same result. Then it came to the turn of the third and youngest son.

Iwanich was not the least discouraged by the failure of his elder brothers, though they were both much older and stronger than he was, and when night came climbed up the tree as they had done. The moon had risen, and with her soft light lit up the whole neighbourhood, so that the observant Prince could distinguish the smallest object distinctly.

At midnight a gentle west wind shook the tree, and at the same moment a snow-white swanlike bird sank down gently on his breast. The Prince hastily seized the bird's wings in his hands, when, lo! to his astonishment he found he was holding in his arms not a bird but the most beautiful girl he had ever seen.

"You need not fear Militza," said the beautiful girl, looking at the Prince with friendly eyes. "An evil magician has not robbed you of your fruit, but he stole the seed from my mother, and thereby caused her death. When she was dying she bade me take the fruit, which you have no right to possess, from the

trees every year as soon as it was ripe. This I would have done to-night too, if you had not seized me with such force, and so broken the spell I was under."

Iwanich, who had been prepared to meet a terrible magician and not a lovely girl, fell desperately in love with her. They spent the rest of the night in pleasant conversation, and when Militza wished to go away he begged her not to leave him.

"I would gladly stay with you longer," said Militza, "but a wicked witch once cut off a lock of my hair when I was asleep, which has put me in her power, and if morning were still to find me here she would do me some harm, and you, too, perhaps."

Having said these words, she drew a sparkling diamond ring from her finger, which she handed to the Prince, saying: "Keep this ring in memory of Militza, and think of her sometimes if you never see her again. But if your love is really true, come and find me in my own kingdom. I may not show you the way there, but this ring will guide you.

"If you have love and courage enough to undertake this journey, whenever you come to a crossroad always look at this diamond before you settle which way you are going to take. If it sparkles as brightly as ever go straight on, but if its lustre is dimmed choose another path."

Then Militza bent over the Prince and kissed him on his forehead, and before he had time to say a word she vanished through the branches of the tree in a little white cloud.

Morning broke, and the Prince, still full of the wonderful apparition, left his perch and returned to the palace like one in a dream, without even knowing if the fruit had been taken or not; for his whole mind was absorbed by thoughts of Militza and how he was to find her.

As soon as the head-gardener saw the Prince going toward the palace he ran to the trees, and when he saw them laden with ripe fruit he hastened to tell the King the joyful news. The King was beside himself for joy, and hurried

MILITZA LEAVES IWANICH IN THE TREE

at once to the garden and made the gardener pick him some of the fruit. He tasted it, and found the apple quite as luscious as it had been in his dream. He went at once to his son Iwanich, and after embracing him tenderly and heaping praises on him, he asked him how he had succeeded in protecting the costly fruit from the power of the magician.

This question placed Iwanich in a dilemma. But as he did not want the real story to be known, he said that about midnight a huge wasp had flown through the branches, and buzzed incessantly round him. He had warded it off with his sword, and at dawn, when he was becoming quite worn out, the wasp had vanished as suddenly as it had appeared.

The King, who never doubted the truth of this tale, bade his son go to rest at once and recover from the fatigues of the night; but he himself went and ordered many feasts to be held in honour of the preservation of the wonderful fruit.

The whole capital was in a stir, and everyone shared in the King's joy; the Prince alone took no part in the festivities.

While the King was at a banquet, Iwanich took some purses of gold, and mounting the quickest horse in the royal stable, he sped off like the wind without a single soul being any the wiser.

It was only on the next day that they missed him; the King was very distressed at his disappearance, and sent search parties all over the kingdom to look for him, but in vain; and after six months they gave him up as dead, and in another six months they had forgotten all about him. But in the meantime the Prince, with the help of his ring, had had a most successful journey, and no evil had befallen him.

At the end of three months he came to the entrance of a huge forest, which looked as if it had never been trodden by human foot before, and which seemed to stretch out indefinitely. The Prince was about to enter the wood by a little path he had discovered, when he heard a voice shouting to him: "Hold, youth! Whither are you going?"

Iwanich turned round, and saw a tall, gaunt-looking man, clad in miserable rags, leaning on a crooked staff and seated at the foot of an oak-tree, which was so much the same colour as himself that it was little wonder the Prince had ridden past the tree without noticing him.

"Where else should I be going," he said, "than through the wood?"

"Through the wood?" said the old man in amazement. "It's easily seen that you have heard nothing of this forest, that you rush so blindly to meet your doom. Well, listen to me before you ride any further; let me tell you that this wood hides in its depths a countless number of the fiercest tigers, hyenas, wolves, bears, and snakes, and all sorts of other monsters. If I were to cut you and your horse up into tiny morsels and throw them to the beasts, there wouldn't be one bit for each hundred of them. Take my advice, therefore, and if you wish to save your life, follow some other path."

The Prince was rather taken aback by the old man's words, and considered for a minute what he should do; then looking at his ring, and perceiving that it sparkled as brightly as ever, he called out: "If this wood held even more terrible things than it does, I cannot help myself, for I must go through it."

Here he spurred his horse and rode on; but the old beggar screamed so loudly after him that the Prince turned round and rode back to the oak tree.

"I am really sorry for you," said the beggar, "but if you are quite determined to brave the dangers of the forest, let me at least give you a piece of advice which will help you against these monsters."

"Take this bagful of breadcrumbs and this live hare. I will make you a present of them both, as I am anxious to save your life; but you must leave your horse behind you, for it would stumble over the fallen trees or get entangled in the briers and thorns. When you have gone about a hundred yards into the wood the wild beasts will surround you. Then you must instantly seize your bag, and scatter the breadcrumbs among them. They will rush to eat them up greedily, and when you have scattered the last crumb you must lose no time in throwing the hare to them; as soon as the hare feels itself on the ground it will run away as quickly as possible, and the wild beasts will turn to pursue it. In this way you will be able to get through the wood unhurt."

Iwanich thanked the old man for his counsel, dismounted from his horse, and, taking the bag and the hare in his arms, he entered the forest. He had hardly lost sight of his gaunt grey friend when he heard growls and snarls in the thicket close to him, and before he had time to think he found himself surrounded by the most dreadful-looking creatures. On one side he saw the glittering eye of a cruel tiger, on the other the gleaming teeth of a great she-wolf;

THE PRICKLY MAN WITH HIS ATTENDANTS

here a huge bear growled fiercely, and there a horrible snake coiled itself in the grass at his feet.

But Iwanich did not forget the old man's advice, and quickly put his hand into the bag and took out as many breadcrumbs as he could hold in his hand at a time. He threw them to the beasts, but soon the bag grew lighter and lighter, and the Prince began to feel a little frightened. And now the last crumb was gone, and the hungry beasts thronged round him, greedy for fresh prey. Then he seized the hare and threw it to them.

No sooner did the little creature feel itself on the ground than it lay back its ears and flew through the wood like an arrow from a bow, closely pursued by the wild beasts, and the Prince was left alone. He looked at his ring, and when he saw that it sparkled as brightly as ever he went straight on through the forest.

He hadn't gone very far when he saw a most extraordinary looking man coming toward him. He was not more than three feet high, his legs were quite crooked, and all his body was covered with prickles like a hedgehog. Two lions walked with him, fastened to his side by the two ends of his long beard.

He stopped the Prince and asked him in a harsh voice: "Are you the man who has just fed my bodyguard?"

Iwanich was so startled that he could hardly reply, but the little man continued: "I am most grateful to you for your kindness; what can I give you as a reward?"

"All I ask," replied Iwanich, "is, that I should be allowed to go through this wood in safety."

"Most certainly," answered the little man; "and for greater security I will give you one of my lions as a protector. But when you leave this wood and come near a palace which does not belong to my domain, let the lion go, in order that he may not fall into the hands of an enemy and be killed."

With these words he loosened the lion from his beard and bade the beast guard the youth carefully.

With this new protector Iwanich wandered on through the forest, and though he came upon a great many more wolves, hyenas, leopards, and other wild beasts, they always kept at a respectful distance when they saw what sort of an escort the Prince had with him.

Iwanich hurried through the wood as quickly as his legs would carry him, but, nevertheless, hour after hour, went by and not a trace of a green field or a human habitation met his eyes. At length, toward evening, the mass of trees grew more transparent, and through the interlaced branches a wide plain was visible.

At the exit of the wood the lion stood still, and the Prince took leave of him, having first thanked him warmly for his kind protection. It had become

MILITZA AND HER MAIDENS IN THE GARDEN

quite dark, and Iwanich was forced to wait for daylight before continuing his journey.

He made himself a bed of grass and leaves, lit a fire of dry branches, and slept soundly till the next morning.

Then he got up and walked toward a beautiful white palace which he saw gleaming in the distance. In about an hour he reached the building, and opening the door he walked in.

After wandering through many marble halls, he came to a huge staircase made of porphyry, leading down to a lovely garden.

The Prince burst into a shout of joy when he suddenly perceived Militza in the centre of a group of girls who were weaving wreaths of flowers with which to deck their mistress.

As soon as Militza saw the Prince she ran up to him and embraced him tenderly; and after he had told her all his adventures, they went into the palace, where a sumptuous meal awaited them. Then the Princess called her court together, and introduced Iwanich to them as her future husband.

Preparations were at once made for the wedding, which was held soon after with great pomp and magnificence.

Three months of great happiness followed, when Militza received one day an invitation to visit her mother's sister.

Although the Princess was very unhappy at leaving her husband, she did not like to refuse the invitation, and, promising to return in seven days at the latest, she took a tender farewell of the Prince, and said: "Before I go I will hand you over all the keys of the castle. Go everywhere and do anything you like; only one thing I beg and beseech you, do not open the little iron door in the north tower, which is closed with seven locks and seven bolts; for if you do, we shall both suffer for it."

Iwanich promised what she asked, and Militza departed, repeating her promise to return in seven days.

When the Prince found himself alone he began to be tormented by pangs of curiosity as to what the room in the tower contained. For two days he resisted the temptation to go and look, but on the third he could stand it no longer, and taking a torch in his hand he hurried to the tower, and unfastened one lock after the other of the little iron door until it burst open.

What an unexpected sight met his gaze! The Prince perceived a small room black with smoke, lit up feebly by a fire from which issued long blue flames. Over the fire hung a huge cauldron full of boiling pitch, and fastened into the cauldron by iron chains stood a wretched man screaming with agony.

Iwanich was much horrified at the sight before him, and asked the man what terrible crime he had committed to be punished in this dreadful fashion.

"I will tell you everything," said the man in the cauldron; "but first relieve my torments a little, I implore you."

"And how can I do that?" asked the Prince.

"With a little water," replied the man; "only sprinkle a few drops over me and I shall feel better."

The Prince, moved by pity, without thinking what he was doing, ran to the courtyard of the castle, and filled a jug with water, which he poured over the man in the cauldron.

In a moment a most fearful crash was heard, as if all the pillars of the palace were giving way, and the palace itself, with towers and doors, windows and the cauldron, whirled round the bewildered Prince's head. This continued for a few minutes, and then everything vanished into thin air, and Iwanich found himself suddenly alone upon a desolate heath covered with rocks and stones.

The Prince, who now realised what his heedlessness had done, cursed too late his spirit of curiosity. In his despair he wandered on over the heath, never looking where he put his feet, and full of sorrowful thoughts. At last he saw a light in the distance, which came from a miserable-looking little hut.

The owner of it was none other than the kind-hearted gaunt grey beggar who had given the Prince the bag of breadcrumbs and the hare. Without recognising Iwanich, he opened the door when he knocked and gave him shelter for the night.

On the following morning the Prince asked his host if he could get him any work to do, as he was quite unknown in the neighbourhood, and had not enough money to take him home.

"My son," replied the old man, "all this country round here is uninhabited; I myself have to wander to distant villages for my living, and even then I do not very often find enough to satisfy my hunger. But if you would like to take service with the old witch Corva, go straight up the little stream which flows below my hut for about three hours, and you will come to a sand hill on the lefthand side; that is where she lives."

Iwanich thanked the gaunt grey beggar for his information, and went on his way.

After walking for about three hours the Prince came upon a dreary-looking grey stone wall; this was the back of the building and did not attract him; but when he came upon the front of the house he found it even less inviting, for the old witch had surrounded her dwelling with a fence of spikes, on every one of which a man's skull was stuck. In this horrible enclosure stood a small black house, which had only two grated windows, all covered with cobwebs, and a battered iron door.

The Prince knocked, and a rasping woman's voice told him to enter.

Iwanich opened the door, and found himself in a smoke-begrimed kitchen, in the presence of a hideous old woman who was warming her skinny hands at a fire. The Prince offered to become her servant, and the old hag told him she was badly in want of one, and he seemed to be just the person to suit her.

When Iwanich asked what his work, and how much his wages would be, the witch bade him follow her, and led the way through a narrow damp passage into a vault, which served as a stable. Here he perceived two pitch-black horses in a stall.

"You see before you," said the old woman, "a mare and her foal; you have nothing to do but to lead them out to the fields every day, and to see that neither of them runs away from you. If you look after them both for a whole year I will give you anything you like to ask; but if, on the other hand, you let either of the animals escape you, your last hour is come, and your head shall be stuck on the last spike of my fence. The other spikes, as you see, are already adorned, and the skulls are all those of different servants I have had who have failed to do what I demanded."

Iwanich, who thought he could not be much worse off than he was already, agreed to the witch's proposal.

At daybreak the next morning he drove his horses to the field, and brought them back in the evening without their ever having attempted to break away from him. The witch stood at her door and received him kindly, and set a good meal before him.

So it continued for some time, and all went well with the Prince. Early every morning he led the horses out to the fields, and brought them home safe and sound in the evening.

One day, while he was watching the horses, he came to the banks of a river, and saw a big fish, which through some mischance had been cast on the land, struggling hard to get back into the water.

Iwanich, who felt sorry for the poor creature, seized it in his arms and flung it into the stream. But no sooner did the fish find itself in the water again, than, to the Prince's amazement, it swam up to the bank and said:

"My kind benefactor, how can I reward you for your goodness?"

"I desire nothing," answered the Prince. "I am quite content to have been able to be of some service to you."

"You must do me the favour," replied the fish, "to take a scale from my body, and keep it carefully. If you should ever need my help, throw it into the river, and I will come to your aid at once."

IWANICH · CASTS · THE · FISH · INTO · THE · WATER

Iwanich bowed, loosened a scale from the body of the grateful beast, put it carefully away, and returned home.

A short time after this, when he was going early one morning to the usual grazing place with his horses, he noticed a flock of birds assembled together making a great noise and flying wildly backward and forward.

Full of curiosity, Iwanich hurried up to the spot, and saw that a large number of ravens had attacked an eagle, and although the eagle was big and powerful and was making a brave fight, it was overpowered at last by numbers, and had to give in.

But the Prince, who was sorry for the poor bird, seized the branch of a tree and hit out at the ravens with it; terrified at this unexpected onslaught they flew away, leaving many of their number dead or wounded on the battlefield.

As soon as the eagle saw itself free from its tormentors it plucked a feather from its wing, and, handing it to the Prince, said: "Here, my kind benefactor, take this feather as a proof of my gratitude; should you ever be in need of my help blow this feather into the air, and I will help you as much as is in my power."

Iwanich thanked the bird, and placing the feather beside the scale he drove the horses home.

Another day he had wandered farther than usual, and came close to a farmyard; the place pleased the Prince, and as there was plenty of good grass for the horses he determined to spend the day there. Just as he was sitting down under a tree he heard a cry close to him, and saw a fox which had been caught in a trap placed there by the farmer.

In vain did the poor beast try to free itself; then the good-natured Prince came once more to the rescue, and let the fox out of the trap.

The fox thanked him heartily, tore two hairs out of his bushy tail, and said: "Should you ever stand in need of my help throw these two hairs into the fire, and in a moment I shall be at your side ready to obey you."

Iwanich put the fox's hairs with the scale and the feather, and as it was getting dark he hastened home with his horses.

In the meantime his service was drawing near to an end, and in three more days the year was up, and he would be able to get his reward and leave the witch.

On the first evening of these last three days, when he came home and was eating his supper, he noticed the old woman stealing into the stables.

The Prince followed her secretly to see what she was going to do. He crouched down in the doorway and heard the wicked witch telling the horses to wait next morning till Iwanich was asleep, and then to go and hide themselves in the river, and to stay there till she told them to return; and if they didn't do as she told them the old woman threatened to beat them till they bled.

When Iwanich heard all this he went back to his room, determined that nothing should induce him to fall asleep the next day. On the following morning he led the mare and foal to the fields as usual, but bound a cord round them both which he kept in his hand.

But after a few hours, by the magic arts of the old witch, he was overpowered by sleep, and the mare and foal escaped and did as they had been told to do. The Prince did not awake till late in the evening; and when he did, he found, to his horror, that the horses had disappeared. Filled with despair, he cursed the moment when he had entered the service of the cruel witch, and already he saw his head sticking up on the sharp spike beside the others.

Then he suddenly remembered the fish's scale, which, with the eagle's feather and the fox's hairs, he always carried about with him. He drew the scale from his pocket, and hurrying to the river he threw it in. In a minute the grateful fish swam toward the bank on which Iwanich was standing, and said: "What do you command, my friend and benefactor?"

The Prince replied: "I had to look after a mare and foal, and they have run away from me and have hidden themselves in the river; if you wish to save my life drive them back to the land."

"Wait a moment," answered the fish, "and I and my friends will soon drive them out of the water." With these words the creature disappeared into the depths of the stream.

Almost immediately a rushing hissing sound was heard in the waters, the waves dashed against the banks, the foam was tossed into the air, and the two horses leapt suddenly on to the dry land, trembling and shaking with fear.

Iwanich sprang at once on to the mare's back, seized the foal by its bridle, and hastened home in the highest spirits.

When the witch saw the Prince bringing the horses home she could hardly conceal her wrath, and as soon as she had placed Iwanich's supper before him she stole away again to the stables. The Prince followed her, and heard her scolding the beasts harshly for not having hidden themselves better. She bade them wait next morning till Iwanich was asleep and then to hide themselves in the clouds, and to remain there till she called. If they did not do as she told them she would beat them till they bled.

The next morning, after Iwanich had led his horses to the fields, he fell once more into a magic sleep. The horses at once ran away and hid themselves in the clouds, which hung down from the mountains in soft billowy masses.

When the Prince awoke and found that both the mare and the foal had disappeared, he bethought him at once of the eagle, and taking the feather out of his pocket he blew it into the air.

In a moment the bird swooped down beside him and asked: "What do you wish me to do?"

"My mare and foal," replied the Prince, "have run away from me, and have hidden themselves in the clouds; if you wish to save my life, restore both animals to me."

"Wait a minute," answered the eagle; "with the help of my friends I will soon drive them back to you."

With these words the bird flew up into the air and disappeared among the clouds.

Almost directly Iwanich saw his two horses being driven toward him by a host of eagles of all sizes. He caught the mare and foal, and having thanked the eagle he drove them cheerfully home again.

The old witch was more disgusted than ever when she saw him appearing, and having set his supper before him she stole into the stables, and Iwanich heard her abusing the horses for not having hidden themselves better in the clouds. Then she bade them hide themselves the next morning, as soon as Iwanich was asleep, in the King's hen-house, which stood on a lonely part of the heath, and to remain there till she called. If they failed to do as she told them she would certainly beat them this time till they bled.

On the following morning the Prince drove his horses as usual to the fields. After he had been overpowered by sleep, as on the former days, the mare and foal ran away and hid themselves in the royal hen-house.

When the Prince awoke and found the horses gone he determined to appeal to the fox; so, lighting a fire, he threw the two hairs into it, and in a few moments the fox stood beside him and asked: "In what way can I serve you?"

"I wish to know," replied Iwanich, "where the King's hen-house is."

"Hardly an hour's walk from here," answered the fox, and offered to show the Prince the way to it.

While they were walking along the fox asked him what he wanted to do at the royal hen-house. The Prince told him of the misfortune that had befallen him, and of the necessity of recovering the mare and foal.

"That is no easy matter," replied the fox. "But wait a moment. I have an idea. Stand at the door of the hen-house, and wait there for your horses. In the meantime I will slip in among the hens through a hole in the wall and give them a good chase, so that the noise they make will arouse the royal henwives, and they will come to see what is the matter. When they see the horses they will at once imagine them to be the cause of the disturbance, and will drive them out. Then you must lay hands on the mare and foal and catch them.

All turned out exactly as the sly fox had foreseen. The Prince swung himself on the mare, seized the foal by its bridle, and hurried home.

While he was riding over the heath in the highest of spirits the mare suddenly said to her rider: "You are the first person who has ever succeeded in outwitting the old witch Corva, and now you may ask what reward you like for your service. If you promise never to betray me I will give you a piece of advice which you will do well to follow."

The Prince promised never to betray her confidence, and the mare continued: "Ask nothing else as a reward than my foal, for it has not its like in the world, and is not to be bought for love or money; for it can go from one end of the earth to another in a few minutes. Of course the cunning Corva will do her best to dissuade you from taking the foal, and will tell you that it is both idle and sickly; but do not believe her, and stick to your point."

Iwanich longed to possess such an animal, and promised the mare to follow her advice.

This time Corva received him in the most friendly manner, and set a sumptuous repast before him. As soon as he had finished she asked him what reward he demanded for his year's service.

"Nothing more nor less," replied the Prince, "than the foal of your mare."

The witch pretended to be much astonished at his request, and said that he deserved something much better than the foal, for the beast was lazy and nervous, blind in one eye, and, in short, was quite worthless.

But the Prince knew what he wanted, and when the old witch saw that he had made up his mind to have the foal, she said, "I am obliged to keep my promise and to hand you over the foal; and as I know who you are and what you want, I will tell you in what way the animal will be useful to you.

IWANICH SEIZES THE MAGICIAN BY THE BEARD AND DASHES HIM TO THE GROUND

The man in the cauldron of boiling pitch, whom you set free, is a mighty magician; through your curiosity and thoughtlessness, Militza came into his power, and he has transported her and her castle and belongings into a distant country.

"You are the only person who can kill him; and in consequence he fears you to such an extent that he has set spies to watch you, and they report your movements to him daily.

"When you have reached him, beware of speaking a single word to him, or you will fall into the power of his friends. Seize him at once by the beard and dash him to the ground."

Iwanich thanked the old witch, mounted his foal, put spurs to its sides, and they flew like lightning through the air.

Already it was growing dark, when Iwanich perceived some figures in the distance; they soon came up to them, and then the Prince saw that it was the magician and his friends who were driving through the air in a carriage drawn by owls.

When the magician found himself face to face with Iwanich, without hope of escape, he turned to him with false friendliness and said: "Thrice my kind benefactor!"

But the Prince, without saying a word, seized him at once by his beard and dashed him to the ground. At the same moment, the foal sprang on the top of the magician and kicked and stamped on him with his hoofs till he died.

Then Iwanich found himself once more in the palace of his bride, and Militza herself flew into his arms.

From this time forward they lived in undisturbed peace and happiness till the end of their lives.

THE MAGIC RING

NCE UPON A TIME THERE LIVED AN OLD COUPLE WHO had one son called Martin. Now when the old man's time had come, he stretched himself out on his bed and died. Though all his life long he had toiled and moiled, he only left his widow and son two hundred florins. The old woman determined to put by the money for a rainy day; but alas! the rainy day was close at hand, for their meal was all consumed, and who is prepared to face starvation with two hundred florins at their disposal? So the old woman counted out a hundred of her florins, and giving them to Martin, told him to go into the town and lay in a store of meal for a year.

So Martin started off for the town. When he reached the meat market he found the whole place in turmoil, and a great noise of angry voices and barking of dogs. Mixing in the crowd, he noticed a stag hound which the butchers had caught and tied to a post, and which was being flogged in a merciless manner. Overcome with pity, Martin spoke to the butchers, saying:

"Friends, why are you beating the poor dog so cruelly?"

"We have every right to beat him," they replied; "he has just devoured a newly-killed pig."

"Leave off beating him," said Martin, "and sell him to me instead."

"If you choose to buy him," answered the butchers derisively; "but for such a treasure we won't take a penny less than a hundred florins."

"A hundred!" exclaimed Martin. "Well, so be it, if you will not take less;" and, taking the money out of his pocket, he handed it over in exchange for the dog, whose name was Schurka.

When Martin got home, his mother met him with the question:

"Well, what have you bought?"

"Schurka, the dog," replied Martin, pointing to his new possession. Whereupon his mother became very angry, and abused him roundly. He ought to be ashamed of himself, when there was scarcely a handful of meal in the house, to have spent the money on a useless brute like that. On the following day she sent him back to the town, saying, "Here, take our last hundred florins, and buy provisions with them. I have just emptied the last grains of meal out of the chest, and baked a bannock; but it won't last over to-morrow."

Just as Martin was entering the town he met a rough-looking peasant who was dragging a cat after him by a string which was fastened round the poor beast's neck.

"Stop," cried Martin; "where are you dragging that poor cat?"

"I mean to drown him," was the answer.

"What harm has the poor beast done?" said Martin.

"It has just killed a goose," replied the peasant.

"Don't drown him, sell him to me instead," begged Martin.

"Not for a hundred florins," was the answer.

"Surely for a hundred florins you'll sell it?" said Martin. "See! here is the money;" and, so saying, he handed him the hundred florins, which the peasant pocketed, and Martin took possession of the cat, which was called Waska.

When he reached his home his mother greeted him with the question:

"Well, what have you brought back?"

"I have brought this cat, Waska," answered Martin.

"And what besides?"

"I had no money over to buy anything else with," replied Martin.

"You useless ne'er-do-well!" exclaimed his mother in a great passion. "Leave the house at once, and go and beg your bread among strangers;" and as Martin did not dare to contradict her, he called Schurka and Waska and started off with them to the nearest village in search of work. On the way he met a rich peasant, who asked him where he was going.

"I want to get work as a day labourer," he answered.

"Come along with me, then. But I must tell you I engage my labourers without wages. If you serve me faithfully for a year, I promise you it shall be for your advantage."

So Martin consented, and for a year he worked diligently, and served his master faithfully, not sparing himself in any way. When the day of reckoning had come the peasant led him into a barn, and pointing to two full sacks, said: "Take whichever of these you choose."

Martin examined the contents of the sacks, and seeing that one was full of silver and the other of sand, he said to himself:

"There must be some trick about this; I had better take the sand." And throwing the sack over his shoulders he started out into the world, in search of fresh work. On and on he walked, and at last he reached a great gloomy wood. In the middle of the wood he came upon a meadow, where a fire was burning, and in the midst of the fire, surrounded by flames, was a lovely damsel, more beautiful than anything that Martin had ever seen, and when she saw him she called to him:

"Martin, if you would win happiness, save my life. Extinguish the flames with the sand that you earned in payment of your faithful service."

"Truly," thought Martin to himself, "it would be more sensible to save a fellow being's life with this sand than to drag it about on one's back, seeing

MARTIN EXTINGUISHES THE FLAMES

what a weight it is." And forthwith he lowered the sack from his shoulders and emptied its contents on the flames, and instantly the fire was extinguished; but at the same moment lo! and behold the lovely damsel turned into a Serpent, and, darting upon him, coiled itself round his neck, and whispered lovingly in his ear:

"Do not be afraid of me, Martin; I love you, and will go with you through the world. But first you must follow me boldly into my Father's Kingdom, underneath the earth; and when we get there, remember this—he will offer you gold and silver, and dazzling gems, but do not touch them. Ask him, instead, for the ring which he wears on his little finger, for in that ring lies a magic power; you have only to throw it from one hand to the other, and at once twelve young men will appear, who will do your bidding, no matter how difficult, in a single night."

So they started on their way, and after much wandering they reached a spot where a great rock rose straight up in the middle of the road. Instantly the Serpent uncoiled itself from his neck, and, as it touched the damp earth, it resumed the shape of the lovely damsel. Pointing to the rock, she showed him an opening just big enough for a man to wriggle through. Passing into it, they entered a long underground passage, which led out on to a wide field, above which spread a blue sky. In the middle of the field stood a magnificent castle, built out of porphyry, with a roof of gold and with glittering battlements. And his beautiful guide told him that this was the palace in which her father lived and reigned over his kingdom in the Underworld.

Together they entered the palace, and were received by the King with great kindness. Turning to his daughter, he said:

"My child, I had almost given up the hope of ever seeing you again. Where have you been all these years?"

"My father," she replied, "I owe my life to this youth, who saved me from a terrible death."

Upon which the King turned to Martin with a gracious smile, saying: "I will reward your courage by granting you whatever your heart desires. Take as much gold, silver, and precious stones as you choose."

"I thank you, mighty King, for your gracious offer," answered Martin, "but I do not covet either gold, silver, or precious stones; yet if you will grant me a favour, give me, I beg, the ring from off the little finger of your royal hand. Every time my eye falls on it I shall think of your gracious Majesty, and when I marry I shall present it to my bride."

So the King took the ring from his finger and gave it to Martin, saying: "Take it, good youth; but with it I make one condition—you are never to confide to anyone that this is a magic ring. If you do, you will straightway bring misfortune on yourself."

Martin took the ring, and, having thanked the King, he set out on the same road by which he had come down into the Underworld. When he had regained the upper air he started for his old home, and having found his mother still living in the old house where he had left her, they settled down together very happily. So uneventful was their life that it almost seemed as if it would go on in this way always, without let or hindrance. But one day it suddenly came into his mind that he would like to get married, and, moreover, that he would choose a very grand wife—a King's daughter, in short. But as he did not trust himself as a wooer, he determined to send his old mother on the mission.

"You must go to the King," he said to her, "and demand the hand of his lovely daughter in marriage for me."

"What are you thinking of, my son?" answered the old woman, aghast at the idea. "Why cannot you marry someone in your own rank? That would be far more fitting than to send a poor old woman like me a-wooing to the King's Court for the hand of a Princess. Why, it is as much as our heads are worth. Neither my life nor yours would be worth anything if I went on such a fool's errand."

"Never fear, little mother," answered Martin. "Trust me; all will be well. But see that you do not come back without an answer of some kind."

And so, obedient to her son's behest, the old woman hobbled off to the palace, and, without being hindered, reached the courtyard, and began to mount the flight of steps leading to the royal presence chamber. At the head of the landing rows of courtiers were collected in magnificent attire, who stared at the queer old figure, and called to her, and explained to her, with every kind of sign, that it was strictly forbidden to mount those steps. But their stern words and forbidding gestures made no impression whatever on the old woman, and she resolutely continued to climb the stairs, bent on carrying out her son's orders. Upon this some of the courtiers seized her by the arms, and held her back by sheer force, at which she set up such a yell that the King himself heard it, and stepped out on to the balcony to see what was the matter. When he beheld the old woman flinging her arms wildly about, and heard her scream that she would not leave the place till she had laid her case before the King, he ordered that she should be brought into his presence. And forthwith she was conducted into the golden presence chamber, where, leaning back amongst cushions of royal purple, the King sat, surrounded by his counsellors and courtiers. Courtesying low, the old woman stood silent before him. "Well, my good old dame, what can I do for you?" asked the King.

"I have come," replied Martin's mother—"and your Majesty must not be angry with me—I have come a-wooing."

"Is the woman out of her mind?" said the King, with an angry frown.

But Martin's mother answered boldly: "If the King will only listen patiently to me, and give me a straightforward answer, he will see that I am not out of my mind. You, O King, have a lovely daughter to give in marriage. I have a son—a wooer—as clever a youth and as good a son-in-law as you will find in your whole kingdom. There is nothing that he cannot do. Now tell me, O King, plump and plain, will you give your daughter to my son as wife?" The King listened to the end of the old woman's strange request, but every moment his face grew darker, and his features sterner; till all at once he thought to himself, "Is it worthwhile that I, the King, should be angry with this poor old fool?" And all the courtiers and counsellors were amazed when they saw the hard lines round his mouth and the frown on his brow grow smooth, and heard the mild but mocking tones in which he answered the old woman, saying:

"If your son is as wonderfully clever as you say, and if there is nothing in the world that he cannot do, let him build a magnificent castle, just opposite my palace windows, in four-and-twenty hours. The palace must be joined together by a bridge of pure crystal. On each side of the bridge there must be growing trees, having golden and silver apples, and with birds of Paradise among the branches. At the right of the bridge there must be a church, with five golden cupolas; in this church your son shall be wedded to my daughter, and we will keep the wedding festivities in the new castle. But if he fails to execute this my royal command, then, as a just but mild monarch, I shall give orders that you and he are taken, and first dipped in tar and then in feathers, and you shall be executed in the market-place for the entertainment of my courtiers."

And a smile played round the King's lips as he finished speaking, and his courtiers and counsellors shook with laughter when they thought of the old woman's folly, and praised the King's wise device, and said to each other, "What a joke it will be when we see the pair of them tarred and feathered! The son is just as able to grow a beard on the palm of his hand as to execute such a task in twenty-four hours."

Now the poor old woman was mortally afraid and, in a trembling voice she asked:

"Is that really your royal will, O King? Must I take this order to my poor son?"

"Yes, old dame; such is my command. If your son carries out my order, he shall be rewarded with my daughter; but if he fails, away to the tar barrel and the stake with you both!"

On her way home the poor old woman shed bitter tears, and when she saw Martin she told him what the King had said, and sobbed out:

"Didn't I tell you, my son, that you should marry someone of your own rank? It would have been better for us this day if you had. As I told you, my going to Court has been as much as our lives are worth, and now we will both be tarred and feathered, and burnt in the public market-place. It is terrible!" and she moaned and cried.

"Never fear, little mother," answered Martin; "trust me, and you will see all will be well. You may go to sleep with a quiet mind."

And, stepping to the front of the hut, Martin threw his ring from the palm of one hand into the other, upon which twelve youths instantly appeared, and demanded what he wanted them to do. Then he told them the King's commands, and they answered that by the next morning all should be accomplished exactly as the King had ordered.

The next morning when the King awoke, and looked out of his window, to his amazement he beheld a magnificent castle, just opposite his own palace, and joined to it a bridge of pure crystal.

At each side of the bridge trees were growing, from whose branches hung golden and silver apples, among which birds of Paradise perched. At the right, gleaming in the sun, were the five golden cupolas of a splendid church, whose bells rang out, as if they would summon people from all corners of the earth to come and behold the wonder. Now, though the King would much rather have seen his future son-in-law tarred, feathered, and burnt at the stake, he remembered his royal oath, and had to make the best of a bad business. So he took heart of grace, and made Martin a Duke, and gave his daughter a rich dowry, and prepared the grandest wedding feast that had ever been seen, so that to this day the old people in the country still talk of it.

After the wedding Martin and his royal bride went to dwell in the magnificent new palace, and here Martin lived in the greatest comfort and luxury, such luxury as he had never imagined. But though he was as happy as the day was long, and as merry as a grig, the King's daughter fretted all day, thinking of the indignity that had been done her in making her marry Martin, the poor widow's son, instead of a rich young Prince from a foreign country. So unhappy was she that she spent all her time wondering how she should get rid of her undesirable husband. And first she determined to learn the secret of his power, and, with flattering, caressing words, she tried to coax him to tell her how he was so clever that there was nothing in the world that he could not do. At first he would tell her nothing; but once, when he was in a yielding mood, she approached him with a winning smile on her lovely face, and, speaking flattering words to him, she gave him a potion to drink, with a sweet, strong taste. And when he had drunk it Martin's lips were unsealed, and he told her that all his power lay in the magic ring that he wore on his finger, and he described to her how to use it, and, still speaking, he fell into a deep sleep. And when she saw that the potion had worked, and that he was sound asleep, the Princess took the magic ring from his finger, and, going into the courtyard, she threw it from the palm of one hand into the other. On the instant the twelve youths appeared, and asked her what she commanded them to do. Then she told them that by the next morning they were to do away with the castle, and the bridge, and the church, and put in their stead the humble hut in which Martin used to live with his mother, and that while he slept her husband was to be carried to his old lowly room; and that they were to bear her away to the utmost ends of the earth, where an old King lived who would make her welcome in his palace, and surround her with the state that befitted a royal Princess.

"You shall be obeyed," answered the twelve youths at the same moment. And lo and behold! the following morning, when the King awoke and looked out of his window he beheld to his amazement that the palace, bridge, church, and trees had all vanished, and there was nothing in their place but a bare, miserable-looking hut.

The Princess Summons the Twelve Youngmen.

Immediately the King sent for his son-in-law, and commanded him to explain what had happened. But Martin looked at his royal father-in-law, and answered never a word. Then the King was very angry, and, calling a council together, he charged Martin with having been guilty of witchcraft, and of having deceived the King, and having made away with the Princess; and he was condemned to imprisonment in a high stone tower, with neither meat nor drink, till he should die of starvation.

Then, in the hour of his dire necessity, his old friends Schurka (the dog) and Waska (the cat) remembered how Martin had once saved them from a cruel death; and they took counsel together as to how they should help him. And Schurka growled, and was of opinion that he would like to tear everyone in pieces; but Waska purred meditatively, and scratched the back of her ear with a velvet paw, and remained lost in thought. At the end of a few minutes she had made up her mind, and, turning to Schurka, said: "Let us go together into the town, and the moment we meet a baker you must make a rush between his legs and upset the tray from off his head; I will lay hold of the rolls, and will carry them off to our master." No sooner said than done. Together the

SCHURKA UPSETS THE BAKER

two faithful creatures trotted off into the town, and very soon they met a baker bearing a tray on his head, and looking round on all sides, while he cried:

> *"Fresh rolls, sweet cake,*
> *Fancy bread of every kind.*
> *Come and buy, come and take,*
> *Sure you'll find it to your mind."*

At that moment Schurka made a rush between his legs—the baker stumbled, the tray was upset, the rolls fell to the ground, and, while the man angrily pursued

Schurka, Waska managed to drag the rolls out of sight behind a bush. And when a moment later Schurka joined her, they set off at full tilt to the stone tower where Martin was a prisoner, taking the rolls with them. Waska, being very agile, climbed up by the outside to the grated window, and called in an anxious voice:

"Are you alive, master?"

"Scarcely alive—almost starved to death," answered Martin in a weak voice. "I little thought it would come to this, that I should die of hunger."

"Never fear, dear master. Schurka and I will look after you," said Waska. And in another moment she had climbed down and brought him back a roll, and then another, and another, till she had brought him the whole tray-load. Upon which she said: "Dear master, Schurka and I are going off to a distant kingdom at the utmost ends of the earth to fetch you back your magic ring. You must be careful that the rolls last till our return."

And Waska took leave of her beloved master, and set off with Schurka on their journey. On and on they travelled, looking always to right and left for traces of the Princess, following up every track, making inquiries of every cat and dog they met, listening to the talk of every wayfarer they passed; and at last they heard that the kingdom at the utmost ends of the earth where the twelve youths had borne the Princess was not very far off. And at last one day they reached that distant kingdom, and, going at once to the palace, they began to make friends with all the dogs and cats in the place, and to question them about the Princess and the magic ring; but no one could tell them much about either. Now one day it chanced that Waska had gone down to the palace cellar to hunt for mice and rats, and seeing an especially fat, well-fed mouse, she pounced upon it, buried her claws in its soft fur, and was just going to gobble it up, when she was stopped by the pleading tones of the little creature, saying, "If you will only spare my life I may be of great service to you. I will do everything in my power for you; for I am the King of the Mice, and if I perish the whole race will die out."

"So be it," said Waska. "I will spare your life; but in return you must do something for me. In this castle there lives a Princess, the wicked wife of my dear master. She has stolen away his magic ring. You must get it away from her at whatever cost; do you hear? Till you have done this I won't take my claws out of your fur."

"Good!" replied the mouse; "I will do what you ask." And, so saying, he summoned all the mice in his kingdom together. A countless number of mice, small and big, brown and grey, assembled, and formed a circle round their king, who was a prisoner under Waska's claws. Turning to them he said: "Dear and faithful subjects, who ever among you will steal the magic ring from the strange Princess will release me from a cruel death; and I shall honour him above all the other mice in the kingdom."

Instantly a tiny mouse stepped forward and said: "I often creep about the Princess's bedroom at night, and I have noticed that she has a ring which she treasures as the apple of her eye. All day she wears it on her finger, and at night she keeps it in her mouth. I will undertake, sire, to steal away the ring for you."

And the tiny mouse tripped away into the bedroom of the Princess, and waited for nightfall; then, when the Princess had fallen asleep, it crept up on to her bed, and gnawed a hole in the pillow, through which it dragged one by one little down feathers, and threw them under the Princess's nose. And the fluff flew into the Princess's nose, and into her mouth, and starting up she sneezed and coughed, and the ring fell out of her mouth on to the coverlet. In a flash the tiny mouse had seized it, and brought it to Waska as a ransom for the King of the Mice. Thereupon Waska and Schurka started off, and travelled night and day till they reached the stone tower where Martin was imprisoned; and the cat climbed up the window, and called out to him:

"Martin, dear master, are you still alive?"

"Ah! Waska, my faithful little cat, is that you?" replied a weak voice. "I am dying of hunger. For three days I have not tasted food."

"Be of good heart, dear master," replied Waska; "from this day forth you

will know nothing but happiness and prosperity. If this were a moment to trouble you with riddles, I would make you guess what Schurka and I have brought you back. Only think, we have got you your ring!"

At these words Martin's joy knew no bounds, and he stroked her fondly, and she rubbed up against him and purred happily, while below Schurka bounded in the air, and barked joyfully. Then Martin took the ring, and threw it from one hand into the other, and instantly the twelve youths appeared and asked what they were to do.

"Fetch me first something to eat and drink, as quickly as possible; and after that bring musicians hither, and let us have music all day long."

Now when the people in the town and palace heard music coming from the tower they were filled with amazement, and came to the King with the news that witchcraft must be going on in Martin's Tower, for, instead of dying of starvation, he was seemingly making merry to the sound of music, and to the clatter of plates, and glass, and knives and forks; and the music was so enchantingly sweet that all the passersby stood still to listen to it. On this the King sent at once a messenger to the Starvation Tower, and he was so astonished with what he saw that he remained rooted to the spot. Then the King sent his chief counsellors, and they too were transfixed with wonder. At last the King came himself, and he likewise was spellbound by the beauty of the music.

Then Martin summoned the twelve youths, spoke to them, saying, "Build up my castle again, and join it to the King's Palace with a crystal bridge; do not forget the trees with the golden and silver apples, and with the birds of Paradise in the branches; and put back the church with the five cupolas, and let the bells ring out, summoning the people from the four corners of the kingdom. And one thing more: bring back my faithless wife, and lead her into the women's chamber."

And it was all done as he commanded, and, leaving the Starvation Tower, he took the King, his father-in-law, by the arm, and led him into the new palace, where the Princess sat in fear and trembling, awaiting her death. And Martin spoke to the King, saying, "King and royal father, I have suffered much at the hands of your daughter. What punishment shall be dealt to her?"

Then the mild King answered: "Beloved Prince and son-in-law, if you love me, let your anger be turned to grace—forgive my daughter, and restore her to your heart and favour."

And Martin's heart was softened and he forgave his wife, and they lived happily together ever after. And his old mother came and lived with him, and he never parted with Schurka and Waska; and I need hardly tell you that he never again let the ring out of his possession.

THE FLOWER QUEEN'S
DAUGHTER[23]

 YOUNG PRINCE WAS RIDING ONE DAY THROUGH A MEAD-
ow that stretched for miles in front of him, when he came to a
deep open ditch. He was turning aside to avoid it, when he heard
the sound of someone crying in the ditch. He dismounted from
his horse, and stepped along in the direction the sound came from. To his
astonishment he found an old woman, who begged him to help her out of the
ditch. The Prince bent down and lifted her out of her living grave, asking her
at the same time how she had managed to get there.

"My son," answered the old woman, "I am a very poor woman, and soon
after midnight I set out for the neighbouring town in order to sell my eggs
in the market on the following morning; but I lost my way in the dark, and

---

23   From the *Bukowinaer*. Von Wliolocki.

fell into this deep ditch, where I might have remained forever but for your kindness."

Then the Prince said to her, "You can hardly walk; I will put you on my horse and lead you home. Where do you live?"

"Over there, at the edge of the forest in the little hut you see in the distance," replied the old woman.

The Prince lifted her on to his horse, and soon they reached the hut, where the old woman got down, and turning to the Prince said, "Just wait a moment, and I will give you something." And she disappeared into her hut, but returned very soon and said, "You are a mighty Prince, but at the same time you have a kind heart, which deserves to be rewarded. Would you like to have the most beautiful woman in the world for your wife?"

"Most certainly I would," replied the Prince.

So the old woman continued, "The most beautiful woman in the whole world is the daughter of the Queen of the Flowers, who has been captured by a dragon. If you wish to marry her, you must first set her free, and this I will help you to do. I will give you this little bell: if you ring it once, the King of the Eagles will appear; if you ring it twice, the King of the Foxes will come to you; and if you ring it three times, you will see the King of the Fishes by your side. These will help you if you are in any difficulty. Now farewell, and heaven prosper your undertaking." She handed him the little bell, and there disappeared hut and all, as though the earth had swallowed her up.

Then it dawned on the Prince that he had been speaking to a good fairy, and putting the little bell carefully in his pocket, he rode home and told his father that he meant to set the daughter of the Flower Queen free, and intended setting out on the following day into the wide world in search of the maid.

So the next morning the Prince mounted his fine horse and left his home. He had roamed round the world for a whole year, and his horse had died of exhaustion, while he himself had suffered much from want and misery, but still he had come on no trace of her he was in search of. At last one day he came to a hut, in front of which sat a very old man. The Prince asked him, "Do you not know where the Dragon lives who keeps the daughter of the Flower Queen prisoner?"

"No, I do not," answered the old man. "But if you go straight along this road for a year, you will reach a hut where my father lives, and possibly he may be able to tell you."

The Prince thanked him for his information, and continued his journey for a whole year along the same road, and at the end of it came to the little hut, where he found a very old man. He asked him the same question, and the old man answered, "No, I do not know where the Dragon lives. But go straight along this road for another year, and you will come to a hut in which my father lives. I know he can tell you."

And so the Prince wandered on for another year, always on the same road, and at last reached the hut where he found the third old man. He put the same question to him as he had put to his son and grandson; but this time the old man answered, "The Dragon lives up there on the mountain, and he has just begun his year of sleep. For one whole year he is always awake, and the next he sleeps. But if you wish to see the Flower Queen's daughter go up the second mountain: the Dragon's old mother lives there, and she has a ball every night, to which the Flower Queen's daughter goes regularly."

So the Prince went up the second mountain, where he found a castle all made of gold with diamond windows. He opened the big gate leading into the courtyard, and was just going to walk in, when seven dragons rushed on him and asked him what he wanted?

The Prince replied, "I have heard so much of the beauty and kindness of the Dragon's Mother, and would like to enter her service."

This flattering speech pleased the dragons, and the eldest of them said, "Well, you may come with me, and I will take you to the Mother Dragon."

They entered the castle and walked through twelve splendid halls, all made of gold and diamonds. In the twelfth room they found the Mother Dragon seated on a diamond throne. She was the ugliest woman under the sun, and, added to it all, she had three heads. Her appearance was a great shock to the Prince, and so was her voice, which was like the croaking of many ravens. She asked him, "Why have you come here?"

The Prince answered at once, "I have heard so much of your beauty and kindness, that I would very much like to enter your service."

"Very well," said the Mother Dragon; "but if you wish to enter my service, you must first lead my mare out to the meadow and look after her for three days; but if you don't bring her home safely every evening, we will eat you up."

The Prince undertook the task and led the mare out to the meadow. But no sooner had they reached the grass than she vanished. The Prince sought for her in vain, and at last in despair sat down on a big stone and contemplated his sad fate. As he sat thus lost in thought, he noticed an eagle flying over his head. Then he suddenly bethought him of his little bell, and taking it out of his pocket he rang it once. In a moment he heard a rustling sound in the air beside him, and the King of the Eagles sank at his feet.

"I know what you want of me," the bird said. "You are looking for the Mother Dragon's mare who is galloping about among the clouds. I will summon all the eagles of the air together, and order them to catch the mare and bring her to you." And with these words the King of the Eagles flew away. Toward evening the Prince heard a mighty rushing sound in the air, and when he looked up he saw thousands of eagles driving the mare before them. They sank at his feet on to the ground and gave the mare over to him. Then the Prince rode home to the old Mother Dragon, who was full of wonder when she saw him, and said, "You have succeeded to-day in looking after my mare, and as a reward you shall come to my ball to-night." She gave him at the same time a cloak made of copper, and led him to a big room where several young

The Dragons Dancing.

Drawn by
Henry Ford

he-dragons and she-dragons were dancing together. Here, too, was the Flower Queen's beautiful daughter. Her dress was woven out of the most lovely flowers in the world, and her complexion was like lilies and roses. As the Prince was dancing with her he managed to whisper in her ear, "I have come to set you free!"

Then the beautiful girl said to him, "If you succeed in bringing the mare back safely the third day, ask the Mother Dragon to give you a foal of the mare as a reward."

The ball came to an end at midnight, and early next morning the Prince again led the Mother Dragon's mare out into the meadow. But again she vanished before his eyes. Then he took out his little bell and rang it twice.

In a moment the King of the Foxes stood before him and said: "I know already what you want, and will summon all the foxes of the world together to find the mare who has hidden herself in a hill."

With these words the King of the Foxes disappeared, and in the evening many thousand foxes brought the mare to the Prince.

Then he rode home to the Mother Dragon, from whom he received this time a cloak made of silver, and again she led him to the ballroom.

The Flower Queen's daughter was delighted to see him safe and sound, and when they were dancing together she whispered in his ear: "If you succeed again to-morrow, wait for me with the foal in the meadow. After the ball we will fly away together."

On the third day the Prince led the mare to the meadow again; but once more she vanished before his eyes. Then the Prince took out his little bell and rang it three times.

In a moment the King of the Fishes appeared, and said to him: "I know quite well what you want me to do, and I will summon all the fishes of the sea together, and tell them to bring you back the mare, who is hiding herself in a river."

The Flower Queen's Daughter.

IN·WINTER·WHEN·EVERYTHING·IS·DEAD
SHE·MUST·COME·AND·LIVE·WITH·ME
IN·MY·PALACE·UNDERGROUND.

Toward evening the mare was returned to him, and when he led her home to the Mother Dragon she said to him:

"You are a brave youth, and I will make you my body-servant. But what shall I give you as a reward to begin with?"

The Prince begged for a foal of the mare, which the Mother Dragon at once gave him, and over and above, a cloak made of gold, for she had fallen in love with him because he had praised her beauty.

So in the evening he appeared at the ball in his golden cloak; but before the entertainment was over he slipped away, and went straight to the stables, where he mounted his foal and rode out into the meadow to wait for the Flower Queen's daughter. Toward midnight the beautiful girl appeared, and placing her in front of him on his horse, the Prince and she flew like the wind till they reached the Flower Queen's dwelling. But the dragons had noticed their flight, and woke their brother out of his year's sleep. He flew into a terrible rage when he heard what had happened, and determined to lay siege to the Flower Queen's palace; but the Queen caused a forest of flowers as high as the sky to grow up round her dwelling, through which no one could force a way.

When the Flower Queen heard that her daughter wanted to marry the Prince, she said to him: "I will give my consent to your marriage gladly, but my daughter can only stay with you in summer. In winter, when everything is dead and the ground covered with snow, she must come and live with me in my palace underground." The Prince consented to this, and led his beautiful bride home, where the wedding was held with great pomp and magnificence. The young couple lived happily together till winter came, when the Flower Queen's daughter departed and went home to her mother. In summer she returned to her husband, and their life of joy and happiness began again, and lasted till the approach of winter, when the Flower Queen's daughter went back again to her mother. This coming and going continued all her life long, and in spite of it they always lived happily together.

THE FLYING SHIP[24]

NCE UPON A TIME THERE LIVED AN OLD COUPLE WHO had three sons; the two elder were clever, but the third was a regular dunce. The clever sons were very fond of their mother, gave her good clothes, and always spoke pleasantly to her; but the youngest was always getting in her way, and she had no patience with him. Now, one day it was announced in the village that the King had issued a decree, offering his daughter, the Princess, in marriage to whoever should build a ship that could fly. Immediately the two elder brothers determined to try their luck, and asked their parents' blessing. So the old mother smartened up their clothes, and gave them a store of provisions for their journey, not forgetting to add a bottle of brandy. When they had gone the poor Simpleton began to tease his mother to smarten him up and let him start off.

"What would become of a dolt like you?" she answered. "Why, you would be eaten up by wolves."

But the foolish youth kept repeating, "I will go, I will go, I will go!"

<hr />

24   From the Russian.

Seeing that she could do nothing with him, the mother gave him a crust of bread and a bottle of water, and took no further heed of him.

So the Simpleton set off on his way. When he had gone a short distance he met a little old manikin. They greeted one another, and the manikin asked him where he was going.

"I am off to the King's Court," he answered. "He has promised to give his daughter to whoever can make a flying ship."

"And can you make such a ship?"

"Not I."

"Then why in the world are you going?"

"Can't tell," replied the Simpleton.

"Well, if that is the case," said the manikin, "sit down beside me; we can rest for a little and have something to eat. Give me what you have got in your satchel."

Now, the poor Simpleton was ashamed to show what was in it. However, he thought it best not to make a fuss, so he opened the satchel, and could scarcely believe his own eyes, for, instead of the hard crust, he saw two beautiful fresh rolls and some cold meat. He shared them with the manikin, who licked his lips and said:

"Now, go into that wood, and stop in front of the first tree, bow three times, and then strike the tree with your axe, fall on your knees on the ground, with your face on the earth, and remain there till you are raised up. You will then find a ship at your side, step into it and fly to the King's Palace. If you meet anyone on the way, take him with you."

The Simpleton thanked the manikin very kindly, bade him farewell, and went into the road. When he got to the first tree he stopped in front of it, did everything just as he had been told, and, kneeling on the ground with his face to the earth, fell asleep. After a little time he was aroused; he awoke and, rubbing his eyes, saw a ready-made ship at his side, and at once got into it. And the ship rose and rose, and in another minute was flying through the air, when the Simpleton,

who was on the look-out, cast his eyes down to the earth and saw a man beneath him on the road, who was kneeling with his ear upon the damp ground.

"Hallo!" he called out, "what are you doing down there?"

"I am listening to what is going on in the world," replied the man.

"Come with me in my ship," said the Simpleton.

So the man was only too glad, and got in beside him; and the ship flew, and flew, and flew through the air, till again from his outlook the Simpleton saw a man on the road below, who was hopping on one leg, while his other leg was tied up behind his ear. So he hailed him, calling out:

"Hallo! what are you doing, hopping on one leg?"

"I can't help it," replied the man. "I walk so fast that unless I tied up one leg I should be at the end of the earth in a bound."

"Come with us on my ship," he answered; and the man made no objections, but joined them; and the ship flew on, and on, and on, till suddenly the Simpleton, looking down on the road below, beheld a man aiming with a gun into the distance.

"Hallo!" he shouted to him, "what are you aiming at? As far as eye can see, there is no bird in sight."

"What would be the good of my taking a near shot?" replied the man; "I can hit beast or bird at a hundred miles' distance. That is the kind of shot I enjoy."

"Come into the ship with us," answered the Simpleton; and the man was only too glad to join them, and he got in; and the ship flew on, farther and farther, till again the Simpleton from his outlook saw a man on the road below, carrying on his back a basket full of bread. And he waved to him, calling out:

"Hallo! where are you going?"

"To fetch bread for my breakfast."

"Bread? Why, you have got a whole basket-load of it on your back."

"That's nothing," answered the man; "I should finish that in one mouthful."

"Come along with us in my ship, then."

And so the glutton joined the party, and the ship mounted again into the air, and flew up and onward, till the Simpleton from his outlook saw a man walking by the shore of a great lake, and evidently looking for something.

"Hallo!" he cried to him, "what are you seeking?"

"I want water to drink, I'm so thirsty," replied the man.

"Well, there's a whole lake in front of you; why don't you drink some of that?"

"Do you call that enough?" answered the other. "Why, I should drink it up in one gulp."

"Well, come with us in the ship."

And so the mighty drinker was added to the company; and the ship flew farther, and even farther, till again the Simpleton looked out, and this time he saw a man dragging a bundle of wood, walking through the forest beneath them.

THE COMRADES IN THE FLYING SHIP MEET THE DRINKER

"Hallo!" he shouted to him, "why are you carrying wood through a forest?"

"This is not common wood," answered the other.

"What sort of wood is it, then?" said the Simpleton.

"If you throw it upon the ground," said the man, "it will be changed into an army of soldiers."

"Come into the ship with us, then."

And so he too joined them; and away the ship flew on, and on, and on, and once more the Simpleton looked out, and this time he saw a man carrying straw upon his back.

"Hallo! Where are you carrying that straw to?"

"To the village," said the man.

"Do you mean to say there is no straw in the village?"

"Ah! but this is quite a peculiar straw. If you strew it about even in the hottest summer the air at once becomes cold, and snow falls, and the people freeze."

Then the Simpleton asked him also to join them.

At last the ship, with its strange crew, arrived at the King's Court. The King was having his dinner, but he at once despatched one of his courtiers to find out what the huge, strange new bird could be that had come flying through the air. The courtier peeped into the ship, and, seeing what it was, instantly went back to the King and told him that it was a flying ship, and that it was manned by a few peasants.

Then the King remembered his royal oath; but he made up his mind that he would never consent to let the Princess marry a poor peasant. So he thought and thought, and then said to himself:

"I will give him some impossible tasks to perform; that will be the best way of getting rid of him." And he there and then decided to despatch one of his courtiers to the Simpleton, with the command that he was to fetch the King the healing water from the world's end before he had finished his dinner.

But while the King was still instructing the courtier exactly what he was to say, the first man of the ship's company, the one with the miraculous power of hearing, had overheard the King's words, and hastily reported them to the poor Simpleton.

"Alas, alas!" he cried; "what am I to do now? It would take me quite a year, possibly my whole life, to find the water."

"Never fear," said his fleet-footed comrade, "I will fetch what the King wants."

Just then the courtier arrived, bearing the King's command.

"Tell his Majesty," said the Simpleton, "that his orders shall be obeyed;" and forthwith the swift runner unbound the foot that was strung up behind his ear and started off, and in less than no time had reached the world's end and drawn the healing water from the well.

"Dear me," he thought to himself, "that's rather tiring! I'll just rest for a

few minutes; it will be some little time yet before the King has got to dessert."
So he threw himself down on the grass, and, as the sun was very dazzling, he
closed his eyes, and in a few seconds had fallen sound asleep.

In the meantime all the ship's crew were anxiously awaiting him; the King's
dinner would soon be finished, and their comrade had not yet returned. So
the man with the marvellous quick hearing lay down, and, putting his ear to
the ground, listened.

"That's a nice sort of fellow!" he suddenly exclaimed. "He's lying on the
ground, snoring hard!"

At this the marksman seized his gun, took aim, and fired in the direction
of the world's end, in order to awaken the sluggard. And a moment later the
swift runner reappeared, and, stepping on board the ship, handed the healing
water to the Simpleton. So while the King was still sitting at table finishing his
dinner news was brought to him that his orders had been obeyed to the letter.

What was to be done now? The King determined to think of a still more impossible task. So he told another courtier to go to the Simpleton with the command that he and his comrades were instantly to eat up twelve oxen and twelve
tons of bread. Once more the sharp-eared comrade overheard the King's words
while he was still talking to the courtier, and reported them to the Simpleton.

"Alas, alas!" he sighed; "what in the world shall I do? Why, it would take us
a year, possibly our whole lives, to eat up twelve oxen and twelve tons of bread."

"Never fear," said the glutton. "It will scarcely be enough for me, I'm so hungry."

So when the courtier arrived with the royal message he was told to take
back word to the King that his orders should be obeyed. Then twelve roasted
oxen and twelve tons of bread were brought alongside of the ship, and at one
sitting the glutton had devoured it all.

"I call that a small meal," he said. "I wish they'd brought me some more."

Next, the King ordered that forty casks of wine, containing forty gallons
each, were to be drunk up on the spot by the Simpleton and his party. When

these words were overheard by the sharp-eared comrade and repeated to the Simpleton, he was in despair.

"Alas, alas!" he exclaimed; "what is to be done? It would take us a year, possibly our whole lives, to drink so much."

"Never fear," said his thirsty comrade. "I'll drink it all up at a gulp, see if I don't." And sure enough, when the forty casks of wine containing forty gallons each were brought alongside of the ship, they disappeared down the thirsty comrade's throat in no time; and when they were empty he remarked:

"Why, I'm still thirsty. I should have been glad of two more casks."

Then the King took counsel with himself and sent an order to the Simpleton that he was to have a bath, in a bath-room at the royal palace, and after that the betrothal should take place. Now the bath-room was built of iron, and the King gave orders that it was to be heated to such a pitch that it would suffocate the Simpleton. And so when the poor silly youth entered the room, he discovered that the iron walls were red hot. But, fortunately, his comrade with the straw on his back had entered behind him, and when the door was shut upon them he scattered the straw about, and suddenly the red-hot walls cooled down, and it became so very cold that the Simpleton could scarcely bear to take a bath, and all the water in the room froze. So the Simpleton climbed up upon the stove, and, wrapping himself up in the bath blankets, lay there the whole night. And in the morning when they opened the door there he lay sound and safe, singing cheerfully to himself.

Now when this strange tale was told to the King he became quite sad, not knowing what he should do to get rid of so undesirable a son-in-law, when suddenly a brilliant idea occurred to him.

"Tell the rascal to raise me an army, now at this instant!" he exclaimed to one of his courtiers. "Inform him at once of this, my royal will." And to himself he added, "I think I shall do for him this time."

As on former occasions, the quick-eared comrade had overheard the King's command and repeated it to the Simpleton.

SIMPLETON'S ARMY APPEARS BEFORE THE KING

"Alas, alas!" he groaned; "now I am quite done for."

"Not at all," replied one of his comrades (the one who had dragged the bundle of wood through the forest). "Have you quite forgotten me?"

In the meantime the courtier, who had run all the way from the palace, reached the ship panting and breathless, and delivered the King's message.

"Good!" remarked the Simpleton. "I will raise an army for the King," and he drew himself up. "But if, after that, the King refuses to accept me as his son-in-law, I will wage war against him, and carry the Princess off by force."

During the night the Simpleton and his comrade went together into a big field, not forgetting to take the bundle of wood with them, which the man spread out in all directions—and in a moment a mighty army stood upon the spot, regiment on regiment of foot and horse soldiers; the bugles sounded and the drums beat, the chargers neighed, and their riders put their lances in rest, and the soldiers presented arms.

In the morning when the King awoke he was startled by these warlike sounds, the bugles and the drums, and the clatter of the horses, and the shouts of the soldiers. And, stepping to the window, he saw the lances gleam in the sunlight and the armour and weapons glitter. And the proud monarch said to himself, "I am powerless in comparison with this man." So he sent him royal robes and costly jewels, and commanded him to come to the palace to be married to the Princess. And his son-in-law put on the royal robes, and he looked so grand and stately that it was impossible to recognise the poor Simpleton, so changed was he; and the Princess fell in love with him as soon as ever she saw him.

Never before had so grand a wedding been seen, and there was so much food and wine that even the glutton and the thirsty comrade had enough to eat and drink.

THE SNOW-DAUGHTER
AND THE FIRE-SON[25]

HERE WAS ONCE UPON A TIME A MAN AND HIS WIFE, and they had no children, which was a great grief to them. One winter's day, when the sun was shining brightly, the couple were standing outside their cottage, and the woman was looking at all the little icicles which hung from the roof. She sighed, and turning to her husband said, "I wish I had as many children as there are icicles hanging there." "Nothing would please me more either," replied her husband. Then a tiny icicle detached itself from the roof, and dropped into the woman's mouth, who swallowed it with a smile, and said, "Perhaps I shall give birth to a snow child now!" Her husband laughed at his wife's strange idea, and they went back into the house.

But after a short time the woman gave birth to a little girl, who was as white as snow and as cold as ice. If they brought the child anywhere near the

---

25   From the *Bukowinaer Tales and Legends.* Von Wliolocki.

fire, it screamed loudly till they put it back into some cool place. The little maid throve wonderfully, and in a few months she could run about and speak. But she was not altogether easy to bring up, and gave her parents much trouble and anxiety, for all summer she insisted on spending in the cellar, and in the winter she would sleep outside in the snow, and the colder it was the happier she seemed to be. Her father and mother called her simply "Our Snow-daughter," and this name stuck to her all her life.

One day her parents sat by the fire, talking over the extraordinary behaviour of their daughter, who was disporting herself in the snowstorm that raged outside. The woman sighed deeply and said, "I wish I had given birth to a Fire-son!" As she said these words, a spark from the big wood fire flew into the woman's lap, and she said with a laugh, "Now perhaps I shall give birth to a Fire-son!" The man laughed at his wife's words, and thought it was a good joke. But he ceased to think it a joke when his wife shortly afterward gave birth to a boy, who screamed lustily till he was put quite close to the fire, and who nearly yelled himself into a fit if the Snow-daughter came anywhere near him. The Snow-daughter herself avoided him as much as she could, and always crept into a corner as far away from him as possible. The parents called the boy simply "Our Fire-son," a name which stuck to him all his life. They had a great deal of trouble and worry with him too; but he throve and grew very quickly, and before he was a year old he could run about and talk. He was as red as fire, and as hot to touch, and he always sat on the hearth quite close to the fire, and complained of the cold; if his sister were in the room he almost crept into the flames, while the girl on her part always complained of the great heat if her brother were anywhere near. In summer the boy always lay out in the sun, while the girl hid herself in the cellar: so it happened that the brother and sister came very little into contact with each other—in fact, they carefully avoided it.

Just as the girl grew up into a beautiful woman, her father and mother both died one after the other. Then the Fire-son, who had grown up in the meantime into a fine, strong young man, said to his sister, "I am going out into the world, for what is the use of remaining on here?"

"I shall go with you," she answered, "for, except you, I have no one in the world, and I have a feeling that if we set out together we shall be lucky."

The Fire-son said, "I love you with all my heart, but at the same time I always freeze if you are near me, and you nearly die of heat if I approach you! How shall we travel about together without being odious the one to the other?"

"Don't worry about that," replied the girl, "for I've thought it all over, and have settled on a plan which will make us each able to bear with the other! See, I have had a fur cloak made for each of us, and if we put them on I shall not feel the heat so much nor you the cold." So they put on the fur cloaks, and set out cheerfully on their way, and for the first time in their lives quite happy in each other's company.

For a long time the Fire-son and the Snow-daughter wandered through the world, and when at the beginning of winter they came to a big wood they determined to stay there till spring. The Fire-son built himself a hut where he always kept up a huge fire, while his sister with very few clothes on stayed outside night and day. Now it happened one day that the King of the land held a hunt in this wood, and saw the Snow-daughter wandering about in the open air. He wondered very much who the beautiful girl clad in such garments could be, and he stopped and spoke to her. He soon learnt that she could not stand heat, and that her brother could not endure cold. The King was so charmed by the Snow-daughter, that he asked her to be his wife. The girl consented, and the wedding was held with much state. The King had a huge house of ice made for his wife underground, so that even in summer it did not melt. But for his brother-in-law he had a house built with huge ovens all round it, that were kept heated all day and night. The Fire-son was delighted, but the perpetual heat in which he lived made his body so hot, that it was dangerous to go too close to him.

One day the King gave a great feast, and asked his brother-in-law among the other guests. The Fire-son did not appear till everyone had assembled, and when he did, everyone fled outside to the open air, so intense was the heat he gave forth. Then the King was very angry and said, "If I had known what a lot of trouble you would have been, I would never have taken you into my house." Then the Fire-son replied with a laugh, "Don't be angry, dear brother! I love heat and my sister loves cold—come here and let me embrace you, and then I'll go home at once." And before the King had time to reply, the Fire-son seized him in a tight embrace. The King screamed aloud in agony, and when his wife, the Snow-daughter, who had taken refuge from her brother in the next room, hurried to him, the King lay dead on the ground burnt to a cinder. When the Snow-daughter saw this she turned on her brother and flew at him. Then a fight began, the like of which had never been seen on earth. When the people, attracted by the noise, hurried to the spot, they saw the Snow-daughter melting into water and the Fire-son burn to a cinder. And so ended the unhappy brother and sister.

THE STORY OF KING FROST[26]

HERE WAS ONCE UPON A TIME A PEASANT WOMAN WHO had a daughter and a step-daughter. The daughter had her own way in everything, and whatever she did was right in her mother's eyes; but the poor step-daughter had a hard time. Let her do what she would, she was always blamed, and got small thanks for all the trouble she took; nothing was right, everything wrong; and yet, if the truth were known, the girl was worth her weight in gold—she was so unselfish and good-hearted. But her step-mother did not like her, and the poor girl's days were spent in weeping; for it was impossible to live peacefully with the woman. The wicked shrew was determined to get rid of the girl by fair means or foul, and kept saying to her father: "Send her away, old man; send her away—anywhere so that my eyes shan't be plagued any longer by the sight of her, or my ears tormented by the sound of her voice. Send her out into the fields, and let the cutting frost do for her."

---

26 From the Russian.

In vain did the poor old father weep and implore her pity; she was firm, and he dared not gainsay her. So he placed his daughter in a sledge, not even daring to give her a horse cloth to keep herself warm with, and drove her out on to the bare, open fields, where he kissed her and left her, driving home as fast as he could, that he might not witness her miserable death.

Deserted by her father, the poor girl sat down under a fir-tree at the edge of the forest and began to weep silently. Suddenly she heard a faint sound: it was King Frost springing from tree to tree, and cracking his fingers as he went. At length he reached the fir-tree beneath which she was sitting, and with a crisp crackling sound he alighted beside her, and looked at her lovely face.

"Well, maiden," he snapped out, "do you know who I am? I am King Frost, king of the red noses."

"All hail to you, great King!" answered the girl, in a gentle, trembling voice. "Have you come to take me?"

"Are you warm, maiden?" he replied.

"Quite warm, King Frost," she answered, though she shivered as she spoke.

Then King Frost stooped down, and bent over the girl, and the crackling sound grew louder, and the air seemed to be full of knives and darts; and again he asked:

"Maiden, are you warm? Are you warm, you beautiful girl?"

And though her breath was almost frozen on her lips, she whispered gently, "Quite warm, King Frost."

Then King Frost gnashed his teeth, and cracked his fingers, and his eyes sparkled, and the crackling, crisp sound was louder than ever, and for the last time he asked her:

"Maiden, are you still warm? Are you still warm, little love?"

And the poor girl was so stiff and numb that she could just gasp, "Still warm, O King!"

Now her gentle, courteous words and her uncomplaining ways touched

King Frost, and he had pity on her, and he wrapped her up in furs, and covered her with blankets, and he fetched a great box, in which were beautiful jewels and a rich robe embroidered in gold and silver. And she put it on, and looked more lovely than ever, and King Frost stepped with her into his sledge, with six white horses.

In the meantime the wicked step-mother was waiting at home for news of the girl's death, and preparing pancakes for the funeral feast. And she said to her husband: "Old man, you had better go out into the fields and find your daughter's body and bury her." Just as the old man was leaving the house the little dog under the table began to bark, saying:

> "Your daughter shall live to be your delight;
> Her daughter shall die this very night."

"Hold your tongue, you foolish beast!" scolded the woman. "There's a pancake for you, but you must say:

> "Her daughter shall have much silver and gold;
> His daughter is frozen quite stiff and cold."

But the doggie ate up the pancake and barked, saying:

> "His daughter shall wear a crown on her head;
> Her daughter shall die unwooed, unwed."

Then the old woman tried to coax the doggie with more pancakes and to terrify it with blows, but he barked on, always repeating the same words. And suddenly the door creaked and flew open, and a great heavy chest was pushed in, and behind it came the step-daughter, radiant and beautiful, in a dress all

"MAIDEN ARE YOU WARM?"

glittering with silver and gold. For a moment the step-mother's eyes were dazzled. Then she called to her husband: "Old man, yoke the horses at once into the sledge, and take my daughter to the same field and leave her on the same spot exactly;" and so the old man took the girl and left her beneath the same tree where he had parted from his daughter. In a few minutes King Frost came past, and, looking at the girl, he said:

"Are you warm, maiden?"

"What a blind old fool you must be to ask such a question!" she answered angrily. "Can't you see that my hands and feet are nearly frozen?"

Then King Frost sprang to and fro in front of her, questioning her, and getting only rude, rough words in reply, till at last he got very angry, and cracked his fingers, and gnashed his teeth, and froze her to death.

But in the hut her mother was waiting for her return, and as she grew impatient she said to her husband: "Get out the horses, old man, to go and fetch her home; but see that you are careful not to upset the sledge and lose the chest."

But the doggie beneath the table began to bark, saying:

> "Your daughter is frozen quite stiff and cold,
> And shall never have a chest full of gold."

"Don't tell such wicked lies!" scolded the woman. "There's a cake for you; now say:

> "Her daughter shall marry a mighty King."

At that moment the door flew open, and she rushed out to meet her daughter, and as she took her frozen body in her arms she too was chilled to death.

THE DEATH OF
THE SUN-HERO[27]

ANY, MANY THOUSAND YEARS AGO THERE LIVED A mighty King whom heaven had blessed with a clever and beautiful son. When he was only ten years old the boy was cleverer than all the King's counsellors put together, and when he was twenty he was the greatest hero in the whole kingdom. His father could not make enough of his son, and always had him clothed in golden garments which shone and sparkled like the sun; and his mother gave him a white horse, which never slept, and which flew like the wind. All the people in the land loved him dearly, and called him the Sun-Hero, for they did not think his like existed under the sun. Now it happened one night that both his parents had the same extraordinary dream. They dreamt that a girl all dressed in red had come to them and said: "If you wish that your son should really

27   From the *Bukowinaer Tales and Legends*. Von Wliolocki.

become the Sun-Hero in deed and not only in name, let him go out into the world and search for the Tree of the Sun, and when he has found it, let him pluck a golden apple from it and bring it home."

When the King and Queen had each related their dreams to the other, they were much amazed that they should both have dreamt exactly the same about their son, and the King said to his wife, "This is clearly a sign from heaven that we should send our son out into the world in order that he may come home the great Sun-Hero, as the Red Girl said, not only in name but in deed."

The Queen consented with many tears, and the King at once bade his son set forth in search of the Tree of the Sun, from which he was to pluck a golden apple. The Prince was delighted at the prospect, and set out on his travels that very day.

For a long time he wandered all through the world, and it was not till the ninety-ninth day after he started that he found an old man who was able to tell him where the Tree of the Sun grew. He followed his directions, and rode on his way, and after another ninety-nine days he arrived at a golden castle, which stood in the middle of a vast wilderness. He knocked at the door, which was opened noiselessly and by invisible hands. Finding no one about, the Prince rode on, and came to a great meadow, where the Sun-Tree grew. When he reached the tree he put out his hand to pick a golden apple; but all of a sudden the tree grew higher, so that he could not reach its fruit. Then he heard someone behind him laughing. Turning round, he saw the girl in red walking toward him, who addressed him in these words:

"Do you really imagine, brave son of the earth, that you can pluck an apple so easily from the Tree of the Sun? Before you can do that, you have a difficult task before you. You must guard the tree for nine days and nine nights from the ravages of two wild black wolves, who will try to harm it. Do you think you can undertake this?"

"Yes," answered the Sun-Hero, "I will guard the Tree of the Sun nine days and nine nights."

The Sun-hero Guards The Apples of The Sun

Then the girl continued: "Remember, though, if you do not succeed the Sun will kill you. Now begin your watch."

With these words the Red Girl went back into the golden castle. She had hardly left him when the two black wolves appeared: but the Sun-Hero beat them off with his sword, and they retired, only, however, to reappear in a very short time. The Sun-Hero chased them away once more, but he had hardly sat down to rest when the two black wolves were on the scene again. This went on for seven days and nights, when the white horse, who had never done such a thing before, turned to the Sun-Hero and said in a human voice: "Listen to what I am going to say. A Fairy gave me to your mother in order that I might be of service to you; so let me tell you, that if you go to sleep and let the wolves harm the tree, the Sun will surely kill you. The Fairy, foreseeing this, put everyone in the world under a spell, which prevents their obeying the Sun's command to take your life. But all the same, she has forgotten one person, who will certainly kill you if you fall asleep and let the wolves damage the tree. So watch and keep the wolves away."

Then the Sun-Hero strove with all his might and kept the black wolves at bay, and conquered his desire to sleep; but on the eighth night his strength failed him, and he fell fast asleep. When he awoke a woman in black stood beside him, who said: "You have fulfilled your task very badly, for you have let the two black wolves damage the Tree of the Sun. I am the mother of the Sun, and I command you to ride away from here at once, and I pronounce sentence of death upon you, for you proudly let yourself be called the Sun-Hero without having done anything to deserve the name."

The youth mounted his horse sadly, and rode home. The people all thronged round him on his return, anxious to hear his adventures, but he told them nothing, and only to his mother did he confide what had befallen him. But the old Queen laughed, and said to her son: "Don't worry, my child; you see, the Fairy has protected you so far, and the Sun has found no one to kill you. So cheer up and be happy."

After a time the Prince forgot all about his adventure, and married a beautiful Princess, with whom he lived very happily for some time. But one day when he was out hunting he felt very thirsty, and coming to a stream he stooped down to drink from it, and this caused his death, for a crab came swimming up, and with its claws tore out his tongue. He was carried home in a dying condition, and as he lay on his death-bed the woman in black appeared and said: "So the Sun has, after all, found someone, who was not under the Fairy's spell, who has caused your death. And a similar fate will overtake everyone under the Sun who wrongfully assumes a title to which he has no right."

THE WITCH[28]

NCE UPON A TIME THERE WAS A PEASANT WHOSE WIFE died, leaving him with two children—twins—a boy and a girl. For some years the poor man lived on alone with the children, caring for them as best he could; but everything in the house seemed to go wrong without a woman to look after it, and at last he made up his mind to marry again, feeling that a wife would bring peace and order to his household and take care of his motherless children. So he married, and in the following years several children were born to him; but peace and order did not come to the household. For the step-mother was very cruel to the twins, and beat them, and half-starved them, and constantly drove them out of the house; for her one idea was to get them out of the way. All day she thought of nothing but how she should get rid of them; and at last an evil idea came into her head, and she determined to send them out into the great gloomy wood where a wicked witch lived. And so one morning she spoke to them, saying:

---

28   From the Russian.

"You have been such good children that I am going to send you to visit my granny, who lives in a dear little hut in the wood. You will have to wait upon her and serve her, but you will be well rewarded, for she will give you the best of everything."

So the children left the house together; and the little sister, who was very wise for her years, said to the brother:

"We will first go and see our own dear grandmother, and tell her where our step-mother is sending us."

And when the grandmother heard where they were going, she cried and said:

"You poor motherless children! How I pity you; and yet I can do nothing to help you! Your step-mother is not sending you to her granny, but to a wicked witch who lives in that great gloomy wood. Now listen to me, children. You must be civil and kind to everyone, and never say a cross word to anyone, and never touch a crumb belonging to anyone else. Who knows if, after all, help may not be sent to you?"

And she gave her grandchildren a bottle of milk and a piece of ham and a loaf of bread, and they set out for the great gloomy wood. When they reached it they saw in front of them, in the thickest of the trees, a queer little hut, and when they looked into it, there lay the witch, with her head on the threshold of the door, with one foot in one corner and the other in the other corner, and her knees cocked up, almost touching the ceiling.

"Who's there?" she snarled, in an awful voice, when she saw the children.

And they answered civilly, though they were so terrified that they hid behind one another, and said:

"Good-morning, granny; our step-mother has sent us to wait upon you, and serve you."

"See that you do it well, then," growled the witch. "If I am pleased with you, I'll reward you; but if I am not, I'll put you in a pan and fry you in the

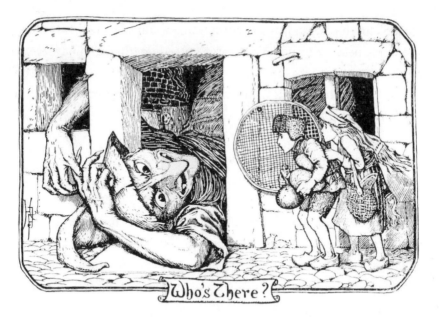

Who's There?

oven—that's what I'll do with you, my pretty dears! You have been gently reared, but you'll find my work hard enough. See if you don't."

And, so saying, she set the girl down to spin yarn, and she gave the boy a sieve in which to carry water from the well, and she herself went out into the wood. Now, as the girl was sitting at her distaff, weeping bitterly because she could not spin, she heard the sound of hundreds of little feet, and from every hole and corner in the hut mice came pattering along the floor, squeaking and saying:

"Little girl, why are your eyes so red?
If you want help, then give us some bread."

And the girl gave them the bread that her grandmother had given her. Then the mice told her that the witch had a cat, and the cat was very fond of ham; if she would give the cat her ham, it would show her the way out of the wood, and in the meantime they would spin the yarn for her. So the girl set out to look for the cat, and, as she was hunting about, she met her brother, in great trouble because he could not carry water from the well in a sieve, as it came pouring out as fast as he put it in. And as she was trying to comfort him they heard a rustling of wings, and a flight of wrens alighted on the ground beside them. And the wrens said:

> "Give us some crumbs, then you need not grieve.
> For you'll find that water will stay in the sieve."

Then the twins crumbled their bread on the ground, and the wrens pecked it, and chirruped and chirped. And when they had eaten the last crumb they told the boy to fill up the holes of the sieve with clay, and then to draw water from the well. So he did what they said, and carried the sieve full of water into the hut without spilling a drop. When they entered the hut the cat was curled up on the floor. So they stroked her, and fed her with ham, and said to her:

"Pussy, grey pussy, tell us how we are to get away from the witch?"

Then the cat thanked them for the ham, and gave them a pocket-handkerchief and a comb, and told them that when the witch pursued them, as she certainly would, all they had to do was to throw the handkerchief on the ground and run as fast as they could. As soon as the handkerchief touched the ground a deep, broad river would spring up, which would hinder the witch's progress. If she managed to get across it, they must throw the comb behind them and run for their lives, for where the comb fell a dense forest would start up, which would delay the witch so long that they would be able to get safely away.

The cat had scarcely finished speaking when the witch returned to see if the children had fulfilled their tasks.

"Well, you have done well enough for to-day," she grumbled; "but to-morrow you'll have something more difficult to do, and if you don't do it well, you pampered brats, straight into the oven you go."

Half-dead with fright, and trembling in every limb, the poor children lay down to sleep on a heap of straw in the corner of the hut; but they dared not close their eyes, and scarcely ventured to breathe. In the morning the witch gave the girl two pieces of linen to weave before night, and the boy a pile of wood to cut into chips. Then the witch left them to their tasks, and went out into the wood. As soon as she had gone out of sight the children took the comb and the handkerchief, and, taking one another by the hand, they started and ran, and ran, and ran. And first they met the watch-dog, who was going to leap on them and tear them to pieces; but they threw the remains of their bread to him, and he ate them and wagged his tail. Then they were hindered by the birch-trees, whose branches almost put their eyes out. But the little sister tied the twigs together with a piece of ribbon, and they got past safely, and, after running through the wood, came out on to the open fields.

In the meantime, in the hut the cat was busy weaving the linen and tangling the threads as it wove. And the witch returned to see how the children were getting on; and she crept up to the window, and whispered:

"Are you weaving, my little dear?"

"Yes, granny, I am weaving," answered the cat.

When the witch saw that the children had escaped her, she was furious, and, hitting the cat with a porringer, she said: "Why did you let the children leave the hut? Why did you not scratch their eyes out?"

But the cat curled up its tail and put its back up, and answered: "I have served you all these years and you never even threw me a bone, but the dear children gave me their own piece of ham."

Then the witch was furious with the watch-dog and with the birch-trees, because they had let the children pass. But the dog answered:

"I have served you all these years and you never gave me so much as a hard crust, but the dear children gave me their own loaf of bread."

And the birch rustled its leaves, and said: "I have served you longer than

THE COMB GROWS INTO A FOREST

I can say, and you never tied a bit of twine even round my branches; and the dear children bound them up with their brightest ribbons."

So the witch saw there was no help to be got from her old servants, and that the best thing she could do was to mount on her broom and set off in pursuit of the children. And as the children ran they heard the sound of the broom sweeping the ground close behind them, so instantly they threw the handkerchief down over their shoulder, and in a moment a deep, broad river flowed behind them.

When the witch came up to it, it took her a long time before she found a place which she could ford over on her broomstick; but at last she got across, and continued the chase faster than before. And as the children ran they heard a sound, and the little sister put her ear to the ground, and heard the broom sweeping the earth close behind them; so, quick as thought, she threw the comb down on the ground, and in an instant, as the cat had said, a dense forest sprung up, in which the roots and branches were so closely intertwined, that it was impossible to force a way through it. So when the witch came up to it on her broom she found that there was nothing for it but to turn round and go back to her hut.

But the twins ran straight on till they reached their own home. Then they told their father all that they had suffered, and he was so angry with their step-mother that he drove her out of the house, and never let her return; but he and the children lived happily together; and he took care of them himself, and never let a stranger come near them.

THE HAZEL-NUT CHILD[29]

HERE WAS ONCE UPON A TIME A COUPLE WHO HAD NO children, and they prayed to Heaven every day to send them a child, though it were no bigger than a hazel-nut. At last Heaven heard their prayer and sent them a child exactly the size of a hazel-nut, and it never grew an inch. The parents were very devoted to the little creature, and nursed and tended it carefully. Their tiny son too was as clever as he could be, and so sharp and sensible that all the neighbours marvelled over the wise things he said and did.

When the Hazel-nut child was fifteen years old, and was sitting one day in an egg-shell on the table beside his mother, she turned to him and said, "You are now fifteen years old, and nothing can be done with you. What do you intend to be?"

"A messenger," answered the Hazel-nut child.

Then his mother burst out laughing and said, "What an idea! You a messenger! Why, your little feet would take an hour to go the distance an ordinary person could do in a minute!"

---

29   From the *Bukowniaer*. Von Wliolocki.

But the Hazel-nut child replied, "Nevertheless I mean to be a messenger! Just send me a message and you'll see that I shall be back in next to no time."

So his mother said, "Very well, go to your aunt in the neighbouring village, and fetch me a comb." The Hazel-nut child jumped quickly out of the egg-shell and ran out into the street. Here he found a man on horseback who was just setting out for the neighbouring village. He crept up the horse's leg, sat down under the saddle, and then began to pinch the horse and to prick it with a pin. The horse plunged and reared and then set off at a hard gallop, which it continued in spite of its rider's efforts to stop it. When they reached the village, the Hazel-nut child left off pricking the horse, and the poor tired creature pursued its way at a snail's pace. The Hazel-nut child took advantage of this, and crept down the horse's leg; then he ran to his aunt and asked her for a comb. On the way home he met another rider, and did the return journey in exactly the same way. When he handed his mother the comb that his aunt had given him, she was much amazed and asked him, "But how did you manage to get back so quickly?"

"Ah! mother," he replied, "you see I was quite right when I said I knew a messenger was the profession for me."

His father too possessed a horse which he often used to take out into the fields to graze. One day he took the Hazel-nut child with him. At midday the father turned to his small son and said, "Stay here and look after the horse. I must go home and give your mother a message, but I shall be back soon."

When his father had gone, a robber passed by and saw the horse grazing without any one watching it, for of course he could not see the Hazel-nut child hidden in the grass. So he mounted the horse and rode away. But the Hazel-nut child, who was the most active little creature, climbed up the horse's tail and began to bite it on the back, enraging the creature to such an extent that it paid no attention to the direction the robber tried to make it go in, but galloped straight home. The father was much astonished when he saw a stranger riding his horse, but the Hazel-nut child climbed down quickly and told him all that had happened, and his father had the robber arrested at once and put into prison.

One autumn when the Hazel-nut child was twenty years old he said to his parents: "Farewell, my dear father and mother. I am going to set out into the world, and as soon as I have become rich I will return home to you."

The parents laughed at the little man's words, but did not believe him for a moment. In the evening the Hazel-nut child crept on to the roof, where some storks had built their nest. The storks were fast asleep, and he climbed on to the back of the father-stork and bound a silk cord round the joint of one of its wings, then he crept among its soft downy feathers and fell asleep.

The next morning the storks flew toward the south, for winter was approaching. The Hazel-nut child flew through the air on the stork's back, and when he wanted to rest he bound his silk cord on to the joint of the bird's other wing, so that it could not fly any farther. In this way he reached a country where the storks took up their abode close to the capital. When the people saw the Hazel-nut child they were much astonished, and took him with the stork to the King of the country. The King was delighted with the little creature and kept him always beside him, and he soon grew so fond of the little man that he gave him a diamond four times as big as himself. The Hazel-nut child fastened the diamond firmly under the stork's neck with a ribbon, and when he saw that the other storks were getting ready for their northern flight, he untied the silk cord from his stork's wings, and away they went, getting nearer home every minute. At length the Hazel-nut child came to his native village; then he undid the ribbon from the stork's neck and the diamond fell to the ground; he covered it first with sand and stones, and then ran to get his parents, so that they might carry the treasure home, for he himself was not able to lift the great diamond.

So the Hazel-nut child and his parents lived in happiness and prosperity after this till they died.

THE STORY OF BIG KLAUS
AND LITTLE KLAUS

N A CERTAIN VILLAGE THERE LIVED TWO PEOPLE WHO
had both the same name. Both were called Klaus, but one owned
four horses and the other only one. In order to distinguish the
one from the other, the one who had four horses was called Big
Klaus, and the one who had only one horse, Little Klaus. Now you shall hear
what befell them both, for this is a true story.

The whole week through, Little Klaus had to plough for Big Klaus, and
lend him his one horse; then Big Klaus lent him his four horses, but only once
a week, and that was on Sunday. Hurrah! how loudly Little Klaus cracked his
whip over all the five horses! for they were indeed as good as his on this one
day. The sun shone brightly, and all the bells in the church towers were peal-
ing; the people were dressed in their best clothes, and were going to church,
with their hymn-books under their arms, to hear the minister preach. They
saw Little Klaus ploughing with the five horses; but he was so happy that he
kept on cracking his whip, and calling out, "Gee-up, my five horses!"

"You mustn't say that," said Big Klaus. "Only one horse is yours."

But as soon as someone else was going by Little Klaus forgot that he must not say it, and called out, "Gee-up, my five horses!"

"Now you had better stop that," said Big Klaus, "for if you say it once more I will give your horse such a crack on the head that it will drop down dead on the spot!"

"I really won't say it again!" said Little Klaus. But as soon as more people passed by, and nodded him good-morning, he became so happy in thinking how well it looked to have five horses ploughing his field that, cracking his whip, he called out, "Gee-up, my five horses!"

"I'll see to your horses!" said Big Klaus; and, seizing an iron bar, he struck Little Klaus's one horse such a blow on the head that it fell down and died on the spot.

"Alas! Now I have no horse!" said Little Klaus, beginning to cry. Then he flayed the skin off his horse, dried it, and put it in a sack, which he threw over his shoulder, and went into the town to sell it. He had a long way to go, and had to pass through a great dark forest. A dreadful storm came on, in which he lost his way, and before he could get on to the right road night came on, and it was impossible to reach the town that evening.

Right in front of him was a large farmhouse. The window shutters were closed, but the light came through the chinks. "I should very much like to be allowed to spend the night there," thought Little Klaus; and he went and knocked at the door. The farmer's wife opened it, but when she heard what he wanted she told him to go away; her husband was not at home, and she took in no strangers.

"Well, I must lie down outside," said Little Klaus; and the farmer's wife shut the door in his face. Close by stood a large haystack, and between it and the house a little outhouse, covered with a flat thatched roof.

"I can lie down there," thought Little Klaus, looking at the roof; "it will make a splendid bed, if only the stork won't fly down and bite my legs." For a

"GEE·UP·MY·FIVE·HORSES!" ⚬ "I'LL·SEE·TO·YOUR·HORSES."

live stork was standing on the roof, where it had its nest. So Little Klaus crept up into the outhouse, where he lay down, and made himself comfortable for the night. The wooden shutters over the windows were not shut at the top, and he could just see into the room.

There stood a large table, spread with wine and roast meat and a beautiful fish. The farmer's wife and the sexton sat at the table, but there was no one else. She was filling up his glass, while he stuck his fork into the fish which was his favourite dish.

"If one could only get some of that!" thought Little Klaus, stretching his head toward the window. Ah, what delicious cakes he saw standing there! It *was* a feast!

Then he heard someone riding along the road toward the house. It was the farmer coming home. He was a very worthy man; but he had one great peculiarity—namely, that he could not bear to see a sexton. If he saw one he was made quite mad. That was why the sexton had gone to say good-day to the farmer's wife when he knew that her husband was not at home, and the good woman therefore put in front of him the best food she had. But when they heard the farmer coming they were frightened, and the farmer's wife begged the sexton to creep into a great empty chest. He did so, as he knew the poor man could not bear to see a sexton. The wife hastily hid all the beautiful food and the wine in her oven; for if her husband had seen it, he would have been sure to ask what it all meant.

"Oh, dear! oh, dear!" groaned Little Klaus up in the shed, when he saw the good food disappearing.

"Is anybody up there?" asked the farmer, catching sight of Little Klaus. "Why are you lying there? Come with me into the house."

Then Little Klaus told him how he had lost his way, and begged to be allowed to spend the night there.

"Yes, certainly," said the farmer; "but we must first have something to eat!"

The wife received them both very kindly, spread a long table, and gave them a large plate of porridge. The farmer was hungry, and ate with a good appetite; but Little Klaus could not help thinking of the delicious dishes of fish and roast meats and cakes which he knew were in the oven. Under the table at his feet he had laid the sack with the horse skin in it, for, as we know, he was going to the town to sell it. The porridge did not taste good to him, so he trod upon his sack, and the dry skin in the sack squeaked loudly.

"Hush!" said Little Klaus to his sack, at the same time treading on it again so that it squeaked even louder than before.

"Hullo! what have you got in your sack?" asked the farmer.

"Oh, it is a wizard!" said Little Klaus. "He says we should not eat porridge, for he has conjured the whole oven full of roast meats and fish and cakes."

"Goodness me!" said the farmer; and opening the oven he saw all the delicious, tempting dishes his wife had hidden there, but which he now believed the wizard in the sack had conjured up for them. The wife could say nothing, but she put the food at once on the table, and they ate the fish, the roast meat, and the cakes. Little Klaus now trod again on his sack, so that the skin squeaked.

"What does he say now?" asked the farmer.

"He says," replied Little Klaus, "that he has also conjured up for us three bottles of wine; they are standing in the corner by the oven!"

The wife had to fetch the wine which she had hidden, and the farmer drank and grew very merry. He would very much like to have had such a wizard as Little Klaus had in the sack.

"Can he conjure up the Devil?" asked the farmer. "I should like to see him very much, for I feel just now in very good spirits!"

"Yes," said Little Klaus; "my wizard can do everything that I ask. Isn't that true?" he asked, treading on the sack so that it squeaked. "Do you hear? He says 'Yes;' but that the Devil looks so ugly that we should not like to see him."

"Oh! I'm not at all afraid. What does he look like?"

"He will show himself in the shape of a sexton!"

"I say!" said the farmer, "he must be ugly! You must know that I can't bear to look at a sexton! But it doesn't matter. I know that it is the Devil, and I sha'n't mind! I feel up to it now. But he must not come too near me!"

"I must ask my wizard," said Little Klaus, treading on the sack and putting his ear to it.

"What does he say?"

"He says you can open the chest in the corner there, and you will see the Devil squatting inside it; but you must hold the lid so that he shall not escape."

"Will you help me to hold him?" begged the farmer, going toward the chest where his wife had hidden the real sexton, who was sitting inside in a terrible fright. The farmer opened the lid a little way, and saw him inside.

"Ugh!" he shrieked, springing back. "Yes, now I have seen him; he looked just like our sexton. Oh, it was horrid!"

So he had to drink again, and they drank till far on into the night.

THE·FARMER·THINKS·HE·SEES·THE·DEVIL
·IN·THE·CHEST

"You *must* sell me the wizard," said the farmer. "Ask anything you like! I will pay you down a bushelful of money on the spot."

"No, I really can't," said Little Klaus. "Just think how many things I can get from this wizard!"

"Ah! I should like to have him so much!" said the farmer, begging very hard.

"Well!" said Little Klaus at last, "as you have been so good as to give me shelter to-night, I will sell him. You shall have the wizard for a bushel of money, but I must have full measure."

"That you shall," said the farmer. "But you must take the chest with you. I won't keep it another hour in the house. Who knows that *he* isn't in there still?"

Little Klaus gave the farmer his sack with the dry skin, and got instead a good bushelful of money. The farmer also gave him a wheelbarrow to carry away his money and the chest. "Farewell," said Little Klaus; and away he went with his money and the big chest, wherein sat the sexton.

On the other side of the wood was a large deep river. The water flowed so rapidly that you could scarcely swim against the stream. A great new bridge had been built over it, on the middle of which Little Klaus stopped, and said aloud so that the sexton might hear:

"Now, what am I to do with this stupid chest? It is as heavy as if it were filled with stones! I shall only be tired, dragging it along; I will throw it into the river. If it swims home to me, well and good; and if it doesn't, it's no matter."

Then he took the chest with one hand and lifted it up a little, as if he were going to throw it into the water.

"No, don't do that!" called out the sexton in the chest. "Let me get out first!"

"Oh, oh!" said Little Klaus, pretending that he was afraid. "He is still in there! I must throw him quickly into the water to drown him!"

"Oh! no, no!" cried the sexton. "I will give you a whole bushelful of money if you will let me go!"

"Ah, that's quite another thing!" said Little Klaus, opening the chest. The sexton crept out very quickly, pushed the empty chest into the water and went to his house, where he gave Little Klaus a bushel of money. One he had had already from the farmer, and now he had his wheelbarrow full of money.

"Well, I have got a good price for the horse!" said he to himself when he shook all his money out in a heap in his room. "This will put Big Klaus in a rage when he hears how rich I have become through my one horse; but I won't tell him just yet!"

So he sent a boy to Big Klaus to borrow a bushel measure from him.

"Now what can he want with it?" thought Big Klaus; and he smeared some tar at the bottom, so that of whatever was measured a little should remain in it.

And this is just what happened; for when he got his measure back, three new silver five-shilling pieces were sticking to it.

"What does this mean?" said Big Klaus, and he ran off at once to Little Klaus.

"Where did you get so much money from?"

"Oh, that was from my horse-skin. I sold it yesterday evening."

"That's certainly a good price!" said Big Klaus; and running home in great haste, he took an axe, knocked all his four horses on the head, skinned them, and went into the town.

"Skins! skins! Who will buy skins?" he cried through the streets.

All the shoemakers and tanners came running to ask him what he wanted for them. "A bushel of money for each," said Big Klaus.

"Are you mad?" they all exclaimed. "Do you think we have money by the bushel?"

"Skins! skins! Who will buy skins?" he cried again, and to all who asked him what they cost, he answered, "A bushel of money."

"He is making game of us," they said; and the shoemakers seized their yard measures and the tanners their leathern aprons and they gave Big Klaus a good beating. "Skins! skins!" they cried mockingly; yes, we will tan *your* skin for you! Out of the town with him!" they shouted; and Big Klaus had to hurry off as quickly as he could, if he wanted to save his life.

"Aha!" said he when he came home, "Little Klaus shall pay dearly for this. I will kill him!"

Little Klaus's grandmother had just died. Though she had been very un-kind to him, he was very much distressed, and he took the dead woman and laid her in his warm bed to try if he could not bring her back to life. There she lay the whole night, while he sat in the corner and slept on a chair, which he had often done before. And in the night as he sat there the door opened, and Big Klaus came in with his axe. He knew quite well where Little Klaus's bed stood, and going up to it he struck the grandmother on the head just where he

THE SHOEMAKERS AND TANNERS DRIVE BIG KLAUS OUT OF THE TOWN

thought Little Klaus would be. "There!" said he. "Now you won't get the best of me again!" And he went home.

"What a very wicked man!" thought Little Klaus. "He was going to kill me! It was a good thing for my grandmother that she was dead already, or else he would have killed her!"

Then he dressed his grandmother in her Sunday clothes, borrowed a horse from his neighbour, harnessed the cart to it, sat his grandmother on the back seat so that she could not fall out when he drove, and away they went. When the sun rose they were in front of a large inn. Little Klaus got down, and went in to get something to drink. The host was very rich. He was a very worthy but hot-tempered man.

"Good morning!" said he to Little Klaus. "You are early on the road."

"Yes," said Little Klaus. "I am going to the town with my grandmother. She is sitting outside in the cart; I cannot bring her in. Will you not give her a glass of mead? But you will have to speak loud, for she is very hard of hearing."

"Oh yes, certainly I will!" said the host; and, pouring out a large glass of mead, he took it out to the dead grandmother, who was sitting upright in the cart.

"Here is a glass of mead from your son," said the host. But the dead woman did not answer a word, and sat still. "Don't you hear?" cried the host as loud as he could. "Here is a glass of mead from your son!"

Then he shouted the same thing again, and yet again, but she never moved in her place; and at last he grew angry, threw the glass in her face, so that she fell back into the cart, for she was not tied in her place.

"Hullo!" cried Little Klaus, running out of the door, and seizing the host by the throat. "You have killed my grandmother! Look! there is a great hole in her forehead!"

"Oh, what a misfortune!" cried the host, wringing his hands. "It all comes from my hot temper! Dear Little Klaus! I will give you a bushel of money, and will bury your grandmother as if she were my own; only don't tell about it, or I shall have my head cut off, and that would be very uncomfortable."

So Little Klaus got a bushel of money, and the host buried his grandmother as if she had been his own.

Now when Little Klaus again reached home with so much money he sent his boy to Big Klaus to borrow his bushel measure.

"What's this?" said Big Klaus. "Didn't I kill him? I must see to this myself!" So he went himself to Little Klaus with the measure.

"Well, now, where did you get all this money?" asked he, opening his eyes at the heap.

"You killed my grandmother—not me," said Little Klaus. "I sold her, and got a bushel of money for her."

"That is indeed a good price!" said Big Klaus; and, hurrying home, he took an axe and killed his grandmother, laid her in the cart, and drove off to the apothecary's, and asked whether he wanted to buy a dead body.

"Who is it, and how did you get it?" asked the apothecary.

"It is my grandmother," said Big Klaus. "I killed her in order to get a bushel of money."

"You are mad!" said the apothecary. "Don't mention such things, or you will lose your head!" And he began to tell him what a dreadful thing he had done, and what a wicked man he was, and that he ought to be punished; till Big Klaus was so frightened that he jumped into the cart and drove home as hard as he could. The apothecary and all the people thought he must be mad, so they let him go.

"You shall pay for this!" said Big Klaus as he drove home. "You shall pay for this dearly, Little Klaus!"

So as soon as he got home he took the largest sack he could find, and went to Little Klaus and said: "You have fooled me again! First I killed my horses, then my grandmother! It is all your fault; but you sha'n't do it again!" And he seized Little Klaus, pushed him in the sack, threw it over his shoulder, crying out, "Now I am going to drown you!"

He had to go a long way before he came to the river, and Little Klaus was not very light. The road passed by the church; the organ was sounding, and the people were singing most beautifully. Big Klaus put down the sack with Little Klaus in it by the church door, and thought that he might as well go in and hear a psalm before going on farther. Little Klaus could not get out, and everybody was in church; so he went in.

"Oh, dear! oh, dear!" groaned Little Klaus in the sack, twisting and turning himself. But he could not undo the string.

"Open the Sack" said Little Klaus.

There came by an old, old shepherd, with snow-white hair and a long staff in his hand. He was driving a herd of cows and oxen. These pushed against the sack so that it was overturned.

"Alas!" moaned Little Klaus, "I am so young and yet I must die!"

"And I, poor man," said the cattle-driver, "I am so old and yet I cannot die!"

"Open the sack," called out Little Klaus; "creep in here instead of me, and you will die in a moment!"

"I will gladly do that," said the cattle-driver; and he opened the sack, and Little Klaus struggled out at once.

"You will take care of the cattle, won't you?" asked the old man, creeping into the sack, which Little Klaus fastened up and then he went on with the cows and oxen. Soon after Big Klaus came out of the church, and taking up the sack on his shoulders it seemed to him as if it had become lighter; for the old cattle-driver was not half as heavy as Little Klaus.

"How easy he is to carry now! That must be because I heard part of the service."

So he went to the river, which was deep and broad, threw in the sack with the old driver, and called after it, for he thought Little Klaus was inside:

"Down you go! You won't mock me anymore now!"

Then he went home; but when he came to the crossroads, there he met Little Klaus, who was driving his cattle.

"What's this?" said Big Klaus. "Haven't I drowned you?"

"Yes," replied Little Klaus; "you threw me into the river a good half-hour ago!"

"But how did you get those splendid cattle?" asked Big Klaus.

"They are sea-cattle!" said Little Klaus. "I will tell you the whole story, and I thank you for having drowned me, because now I am on dry land and really rich! How frightened I was when I was in the sack! How the wind whistled in my ears as you threw me from the bridge into the cold water! I sank at once to the bottom; but I did not hurt myself, for underneath was growing the most beautiful soft grass. I fell on this, and immediately the sack opened; the loveliest maiden in snow-white garments, with a green garland round her wet hair, took me by the hand, and said, 'Are you Little Klaus? Here are some cattle for you to begin with, and a mile farther down the road there is another herd, which I will give you as a present!' Now I saw that the river was a great high-road for the sea-people. Along it they travel underneath from the sea to the land till the river ends. It was so beautiful, full of flowers and fresh grass; the fishes which were swimming in the water shot past my ears as the birds do here in the air. What lovely people there were, and what fine cattle were grazing in the ditches and dykes!"

"But why did you come up to us again?" asked Big Klaus. "I should not have done so, if it is so beautiful down below!"

"Oh!" said Little Klaus, "that was just so politic of me. You heard what I told you, that the sea-maiden said to me a mile farther along the road—and by the road she meant the river, for she can go by no other way—there was another herd of cattle waiting for me. But I know what windings the river makes, now here, now there, so that it is a long way round. Therefore it makes it much shorter if one comes on the land and drives across the field to the river. Thus I have spared myself quite half a mile, and have come much quicker to my sea-cattle!"

"Oh, you're a lucky fellow!" said Big Klaus. "Do you think I should also get some cattle if I went to the bottom of the river?"

"Oh, yes! I think so," said Little Klaus. "But I can't carry you in a sack to the river; you are too heavy for me! If you like to go there yourself and then creep into the sack, I will throw you in with the greatest of pleasure."

"Thank you," said Big Klaus; "but if I don't get any sea-cattle when I come there, you will have a good hiding, mind!"

"Oh, no! Don't be so hard on me!" Then they went to the river. When the cattle, which were thirsty, caught sight of the water, they ran as quickly as they could to drink.

"Look how they are running!" said Little Klaus. "They want to go to the bottom again!"

"Yes; but help me first," said Big Klaus, "or else you shall have a beating!"

And so he crept into the large sack, which was lying on the back of one of the oxen. "Put a stone in, for I am afraid I may not reach the bottom," said Big Klaus.

"It goes all right!" said Little Klaus; but still he laid a big stone in the sack, fastened it up tight, and then pushed it in. Plump! there was Big Klaus in the water, and he sank like lead to the bottom.

"I doubt if he will find any cattle!" said Little Klaus as he drove his own home.

PRINCE RING[30]

NCE UPON A TIME THERE WAS A KING AND HIS QUEEN IN their kingdom. They had one daughter, who was called Ingiborg, and one son, whose name was Ring. He was less fond of adventures than men of rank usually were in those days, and was not famous for strength or feats of arms. When he was twelve years old, one fine winter day he rode into the forest along with his men to enjoy himself. They went on a long way, until they caught sight of a hind with a gold ring on its horns. The Prince was eager to catch it, if possible, so they gave chase and rode on without stopping until all the horses began to founder beneath them. At last the Prince's horse gave way too, and then there came over them a darkness so black that they could no longer see the hind. By this time they were far away from any house, and thought it was high time to be making their way home again, but they found they had got lost now. At first they all kept together, but soon each began to think that he knew the right way best; so they separated, and all went in different directions.

---

30 From the Icelandic.

The Prince, too, had got lost like the rest, and wandered on for a time until he came to a little clearing in the forest not far from the sea, where he saw a woman sitting on a chair and a big cask standing beside her. The Prince went up to her and saluted her politely, and she received him very graciously. He looked down into the cask then, and saw lying at the bottom an unusually beautiful gold ring, which pleased him so much that he could not take his eyes off it. The woman saw this, and said that he might have it if he would take the trouble to get it; for which the Prince thanked her, and said it was at least worth trying. So he leaned over into the cask, which did not seem very deep, and thought he would easily reach the ring; but the more he stretched down after it the deeper grew the cask. As he was thus bending down into it the woman suddenly rose up and pushed him in head first, saying that now he could take up his quarters there. Then she fixed the top on the cask and threw it out into the sea.

The Prince thought himself in a bad plight now, as he felt the cask floating out from the land and tossing about on the waves. How many days he spent thus he could not tell, but at last he felt that the cask was knocking against rocks, at which he was a little cheered, thinking it was probably land and not merely a reef in the sea. Being something of a swimmer, he at last made up his mind to kick the bottom out of the cask, and having done so he was able to get on shore, for the rocks by the sea were smooth and level; but overhead there were high cliffs. It seemed difficult to get up these, but he went along the foot of them for a little, till at last he tried to climb up, which at last he did.

Having got to the top, he looked round about him and saw that he was on an island, which was covered with forest, with apples growing, and altogether pleasant as far as the land was concerned. After he had been there several days, he one day heard a great noise in the forest, which made him terribly afraid, so that he ran to hide himself among the trees. Then he saw a Giant approaching, dragging a sledge loaded with wood, and making straight for him, so that he

The Woman pushes Prince Ring into the Cask

could see nothing for it but to lie down just where he was. When the Giant came across him, he stood still and looked at the Prince for a little; then he took him up in his arms and carried him home to his house, and was exceedingly kind to him. He gave him to his wife, saying he had found this child in the wood, and she could have it to help her in the house. The old woman was greatly pleased, and began to fondle the Prince with the utmost delight. He stayed there with them, and was very willing and obedient to them in everything, while they grew kinder to him every day.

One day the Giant took him round and showed him all his rooms except the parlour; this made the Prince curious to have a look into it, thinking there must be some very rare treasure there. So one day, when the Giant had gone into the forest, he tried to get into the parlour, and managed to get the door open halfway. Then he saw that some living creature moved inside and ran along the floor toward him and said something, which made him so frightened that he sprang back from the door and shut it again. As soon as the fright began to pass off he tried it again, for he thought it would be interesting to hear what it said; but things went just as before with him. He then got angry with himself, and, summoning up all his courage, tried it a third time, and opened the door of the room and stood firm. Then he saw that it was a big Dog, which spoke to him and said:

"Choose me, Prince Ring."

The Prince went away rather afraid, thinking with himself that it was no great treasure after all; but all the same what it had said to him stuck in his mind.

It is not said how long the Prince stayed with the Giant, but one day the latter came to him and said he would now take him over to the mainland out of the island, for he himself had no long time to live. He also thanked him for his good service, and told him to choose someone of his possessions, for he would get whatever he wanted. Ring thanked him heartily, and said there was no need to pay him for his services, they were so little worth; but if he did wish to give him anything he would choose what was in the parlour. The Giant was taken by surprise, and said:

"There, you chose my old woman's right hand; but I must not break my word."

Upon this he went to get the Dog, which came running with signs of great delight; but the Prince was so much afraid of it that it was all he could do to keep from showing his alarm.

After this the Giant accompanied him down to the sea, where he saw a stone boat which was just big enough to hold the two of them and the Dog. On reaching the mainland the Giant took a friendly farewell of Ring, and told him he might take possession of all that was in the island after he and his wife died, which would happen within two weeks from that time. The Prince thanked him for this and for all his other kindnesses, and the Giant returned home, while Ring went up some distance from the sea; but he did not know what land he had come to, and was afraid to speak to the Dog. After he had walked on in silence for a time the Dog spoke to him and said:

"You don't seem to have much curiosity, seeing you never ask my name."

The Prince then forced himself to ask, "What is your name?"

"You had best call me Snati-Snati," said the Dog. "Now we are coming to a King's seat, and you must ask the King to keep us all winter, and to give you a little room for both of us."

The Prince now began to be less afraid of the Dog. They came to the King and asked him to keep them all the winter, to which he agreed. When the King's men saw the Dog they began to laugh at it, and make as if they would tease it; but when the Prince saw this he advised them not to do it, or they might have the worst of it. They replied that they didn't care a bit what he thought.

After Ring had been with the King for some days the latter began to think there was a great deal in him, and esteemed him more than the others. The King, however, had a counsellor called Red, who became very jealous when he saw how much the King esteemed Ring; and one day he talked to him, and said he could not understand why he had so good an opinion of this stranger, who had not yet shown himself superior to other men in anything. The King replied that it was only a short time since he had come there. Red then asked him to send them both to cut down wood the next morning, and see which of them could do most work. Snati-Snati heard this and told it to Ring, advising him to ask the King for two axes, so that he might have one in reserve if the first one got broken. The next morning the King asked Ring and Red to go and cut down trees for him, and both agreed. Ring got the two axes, and each went his own way; but when the Prince had got out into the wood Snati took one of the axes and began to hew along with him. In the evening the King came to look over their day's work, as Red had proposed, and found that Ring's wood-heap was more than twice as big.

"I suspected," said the King, "that Ring was not quite useless; never have I seen such a day's work."

Ring was now in far greater esteem with the King than before, and Red was all the more discontented. One day he came to the King and said, "If Ring is such a mighty man, I think you might ask him to kill the wild oxen in the wood here, and flay them the same day, and bring you the horns and the hides in the evening."

"Don't you think that a desperate errand?" said the King, "seeing they are so dangerous, and no one has ever yet ventured to go against them?"

Red answered that he had only one life to lose, and it would be interesting to see how brave he was; besides, the King would have good reason to ennoble him if he overcame them. The King at last allowed himself, though rather unwillingly, to be won over by Red's persistency, and one day asked Ring to go and kill the oxen that were in the wood for him, and bring their horns and hides to him in the evening. Not knowing how dangerous the oxen were, Ring was quite ready, and went off at once, to the great delight of Red, who was now sure of his death.

SNATI·AND·PRINCE·RING·FIGHT·WITH·THE·OXEN·

As soon as Ring came in sight of the oxen they came bellowing to meet him; one of them was tremendously big, the other rather less. Ring grew terribly afraid.

"How do you like them?" asked Snati.

"Not well at all," said the Prince.

"We can do nothing else," said Snati, "than attack them, if it is to go well; you will go against the little one, and I shall take the other."

With this Snati leapt at the big one, and was not long in bringing him down. Meanwhile the Prince went against the other with fear and trembling, and by the time Snati came to help him the ox had nearly got him under, but Snati was not slow in helping his master to kill it.

Each of them then began to flay their own ox, but Ring was only half through by the time Snati had finished his. In the evening, after they had finished this task, the Prince thought himself unfit to carry all the horns and both the hides, so Snati told him to lay them all on his back until they got to the Palace gate. The Prince agreed, and laid everything on the Dog except the skin of the smaller ox, which he staggered along with himself. At the Palace gate he left everything lying, went before the King, and asked him to come that length with him, and there handed over to him the hides and horns of the oxen. The King was greatly surprised at his valour, and said he knew no one like him, and thanked him heartily for what he had done.

After this the King set Ring next to himself, and all esteemed him highly, and held him to be a great hero; nor could Red any longer say anything against him, though he grew still more determined to destroy him. One day a good idea came into his head. He came to the King and said he had something to say to him.

"What is that?" said the King.

Red said that he had just remembered the gold cloak, gold chessboard, and bright gold piece that the King had lost about a year before.

"Don't remind me of them!" said the King.

Red, however, went on to say that, since Ring was such a mighty man that he could do everything, it had occurred to him to advise the King to ask him to search for these treasures, and come back with them before Christmas; in return the King should promise him his daughter.

The King replied that he thought it altogether unbecoming to propose such a thing to Ring, seeing that he could not tell him where the things were; but Red pretended not to hear the King's excuses, and went on talking about it until the King gave in to him. One day, a month or so before Christmas, the King spoke to Ring, saying that he wished to ask a great favour of him.

"What is that?" said Ring.

"It is this," said the King: "that you find for me my gold cloak, my gold chessboard, and my bright gold piece, that were stolen from me about a year ago. If you can bring them to me before Christmas I will give you my daughter in marriage."

"Where am I to look for them, then?" said Ring.

"That you must find out for yourself," said the King; "I don't know."

Ring now left the King, and was very silent, for he saw he was in a great difficulty: but, on the other hand, he thought it was excellent to have such a chance of winning the King's daughter. Snati noticed that his master was at a loss, and said to him that he should not disregard what the King had asked him to do; but he would have to act upon his advice, otherwise he would get into great difficulties. The Prince assented to this, and began to prepare for the journey.

After he had taken leave of the King, and was setting out on the search, Snati said to him, "Now you must first of all go about the neighbourhood, and gather as much salt as ever you can." The Prince did so, and gathered so much salt that he could hardly carry it; but Snati said, "Throw it on my back," which he accordingly did, and the Dog then ran on before the Prince, until they came to the foot of a steep cliff.

"We must go up here," said Snati.

"I don't think that will be child's play," said the Prince.

"Hold fast by my tail," said Snati; and in this way he pulled Ring up on the lowest shelf of the rock. The Prince began to get giddy, but up went Snati on to the second shelf. Ring was nearly swooning by this time, but Snati made a third effort and reached the top of the cliff, where the Prince fell down in a faint. After a little, however, he recovered again, and they went a short distance along a level plain, until they came to a cave. This was on Christmas Eve. They went up above the cave, and found a window in it, through which they looked, and saw four trolls lying asleep beside the fire, over which a large porridge-pot was hanging.

"Now you must empty all the salt into the porridge-pot," said Snati.

Ring did so, and soon the trolls wakened up. The old hag, who was the most frightful of them all, went first to taste the porridge.

"How comes this?" she said; "the porridge is salt! I got the milk by witchcraft yesterday out of four kingdoms, and now it is salt!"

All the others then came to taste the porridge, and thought it nice, but after they had finished it the old hag grew so thirsty that she could stand it no longer, and asked her daughter to go out and bring her some water from the river that ran near by.

"I won't go," said she, "unless you lend me your bright gold piece."

"Though I should die you shan't have that," said the hag.

"Die, then," said the girl.

"Well, then, take it, you brat," said the old hag, "and be off with you, and make haste with the water."

The girl took the gold and ran out with it, and it was so bright that it shone all over the plain. As soon as she came to the river she lay down to take a drink of the water, but meanwhile the two of them had got down off the roof and thrust her, head first, into the river.

The old hag began now to long for the water, and said that the girl would be running about with the gold piece all over the plain, so she asked her son to go and get her a drop of water.

"I won't go," said he, "unless I get the gold cloak."

"Though I should die you shan't have that," said the hag.

"Die, then," said the son.

"Well, then, take it," said the old hag, "and be off with you, but you must make haste with the water."

He put on the cloak, and when he came outside it shone so bright that he could see to go with it. On reaching the river he went to take a drink like his sister, but at that moment Ring and Snati sprang upon him, took the cloak from him, and threw him into the river.

The old hag could stand the thirst no longer, and asked her husband to go for a drink for her; the brats, she said, were of course running about and playing themselves, just as she had expected they would, little wretches that they were.

"I won't go," said the old troll, "unless you lend me the gold chessboard."

"Though I should die you shan't have that," said the hag.

"I think you may just as well do that," said he, "since you won't grant me such a little favour."

"Take it, then, you utter disgrace!" said the old hag, "since you are just like these two brats."

The old troll now went out with the gold chessboard, and down to the river, and was about to take a drink, when Ring and Snati came upon him, took the chessboard from him, and threw him into the river. Before they had got back again, however, and up on top of the cave, they saw the poor old fellow's ghost come marching up from the river. Snati immediately sprang upon him,

PRINCE·RING·&·SNATI·OVERTHROW·THE·TROLL'S·GHOST

and Ring assisted in the attack, and after a hard struggle they mastered him a second time. When they got back again to the window, they saw that the old hag was moving toward the door.

"Now we must go in at once," said Snati, "and try to master her there, for if she once gets out we shall have no chance with her. She is the worst witch that ever lived, and no iron can cut her. One of us must pour boiling porridge out of the pot on her, and the other punch her with red-hot iron."

In they went then, and no sooner did the hag see them than she said, "So you have come, Prince Ring; you must have seen to my husband and children."

Snati saw that she was about to attack them, and sprang at her with a red-hot iron from the fire, while Ring kept pouring boiling porridge on her without stopping, and in this way they at last got her killed. Then they burned the old troll and her to ashes, and explored the cave, where they found plenty of gold and treasures. The most valuable of these they carried with them as far as the cliff, and left them there. Then they hastened home to the King with his three treasures, where they arrived late on Christmas night, and Ring handed them over to him.

The King was beside himself with joy, and was astonished at how clever a man Ring was in all kinds of feats, so that he esteemed him still more highly than before, and betrothed his daughter to him; and the feast for this was to last all through Christmastide. Ring thanked the King courteously for this and all his other kindnesses, and as soon as he had finished eating and drinking in the hall went off to sleep in his own room. Snati, however, asked permission to sleep in the Prince's bed for that night, while the Prince should sleep where the Dog usually lay. Ring said he was welcome to do so, and that he deserved more from him than that came to. So Snati went up into the Prince's bed, but after a time he came back, and told Ring he could go there himself now, but to take care not to meddle with anything that was in the bed.

Now the story comes back to Red, who came into the hall and showed the King his right arm wanting the hand, and said that now he could see what kind of a man his intended son-in-law was, for he had done this to him without any cause whatever. The King became very angry, and said he would soon find out the truth about it, and if Ring had cut off his hand without good cause he should be hanged; but if it was otherwise, then Red should die. So the King sent for

Ring and asked him for what reason he had done this. Snati, however, had just told Ring what had happened during the night, and in reply he asked the King to go with him and he would show him something. The King went with him to his sleeping-room, and saw lying on the bed a man's hand holding a sword.

"This hand," said Ring, "came over the partition during the night, and was about to run me through in my bed, if I had not defended myself."

The King answered that in that case he could not blame him for protecting his own life, and that Red was well worthy of death. So Red was hanged, and Ring married the King's daughter.

The first night that they went to bed together Snati asked Ring to allow him to lie at their feet, and this Ring allowed him to do. During the night he heard a howling and outcry beside them, struck a light in a hurry and saw an ugly dog's skin lying near him, and a beautiful Prince in the bed. Ring instantly took the skin and burned it, and then shook the Prince, who was lying unconscious, until he woke up. The bridegroom then asked his name; he replied that he was called Ring, and was a King's son. In his youth he had lost his mother, and in her place his father had married a witch, who had laid a spell on him that he should turn into a dog, and never be released from the spell unless a Prince of the same name as himself allowed him to sleep at his feet the first night after his marriage. He added further, "As soon as she knew that you were my namesake she tried to get you destroyed, so that you might not free me from the spell. She was the hind that you and your companions chased; she was the woman that you found in the clearing with the cask, and the old hag that we just now killed in the cave."

After the feasting was over the two namesakes, along with other men, went to the cliff and brought all the treasure home to the Palace. Then they went to the island and removed all that was valuable from it. Ring gave to his namesake, whom he had freed from the spell, his sister Ingiborg and his father's kingdom to look after, but he himself stayed with his father-in-law the King, and had half the kingdom while he lived and the whole of it after his death.

THE SWINEHERD

HERE WAS ONCE A POOR PRINCE. HE POSSESSED A KING-
dom which, though small, was yet large enough for him to
marry on, and married he wished to be.

Now it was certainly a little audacious of him to venture to
say to the Emperor's daughter, "Will you marry me?" But he did venture to say
so, for his name was known far and wide. There were hundreds of princesses
who would gladly have said "Yes," but would she say the same?

Well, we shall see.

On the grave of the Prince's father grew a rose-tree, a very beautiful rose-
tree. It only bloomed every five years, and then bore but a single rose, but oh,
such a rose! Its scent was so sweet that when you smelt it you forgot all your
cares and troubles. And he had also a nightingale which could sing as if all the
beautiful melodies in the world were shut up in its little throat. This rose and
this nightingale the Princess was to have, and so they were both put into silver
caskets and sent to her.

The Emperor had them brought to him in the great hall, where the Princess was playing "Here comes a duke a-riding" with her ladies-in-waiting. And

when she caught sight of the big caskets which contained the presents, she clapped her hands for joy.

"If only it were a little pussycat!" she said. But the rose-tree with the beautiful rose came out.

"But how prettily it is made!" said all the ladies-in-waiting.

"It is more than pretty," said the Emperor, "it is charming!"

But the Princess felt it, and then she almost began to cry.

"Ugh! Papa," she said, "it is not artificial, it is *real*!"

"Ugh!" said all the ladies-in-waiting, "it is real!"

"Let us see first what is in the other casket before we begin to be angry," thought the Emperor, and there came out the nightingale. It sang so beautifully that one could scarcely utter a cross word against it.

"*Superbe! charmant!*" said the ladies-in-waiting, for they all chattered French, each one worse than the other.

"How much the bird reminds me of the musical snuff-box of the late Empress!" said an old courtier. "Ah, yes, it is the same tone, the same execution!"

"Yes," said the Emperor; and then he wept like a little child.

"I hope that this, at least, is not real?" asked the Princess.

"Yes, it is a real bird," said those who had brought it.

"Then let the bird fly away," said the Princess; and she would not on any account allow the Prince to come.

But he was nothing daunted. He dirtied his face, drew his cap well over his face, and knocked at the door. "Good-day, Emperor," he said. "Can I get a place here as servant in the castle?"

"Yes," said the Emperor, "but there are so many who ask for a place that I don't know whether there will be one for you; but, still, I will think of you. Stay, it has just occurred to me that I want someone to look after the swine, for I have so very many of them."

And the Prince got the situation of Imperial Swineherd. He had a wretched little room close to the pigsties; here he had to stay, but the whole day he sat working, and when evening was come he had made a pretty little pot. All round it were little bells, and when the pot boiled they jingled most beautifully and played the old tune—

> *"Where is Augustus dear?*
> *Alas! he's not here, here, here!"*

But the most wonderful thing was, that when one held one's finger in the steam of the pot, then at once one could smell what dinner was ready in any fire-place in the town. That was indeed something quite different from the rose.

Now the Princess came walking past with all her ladies-in-waiting, and when she heard the tune she stood still and her face beamed with joy, for she also could play "Where is Augustus dear?"

It was the only tune she knew, but that she could play with one finger.

"Why, that is what I play!" she said. "He must be a most accomplished Swineherd! Listen! Go down and ask him what the instrument costs."

And one of the ladies-in-waiting had to go down; but she put on wooden clogs. "What will you take for the pot?" asked the lady-in-waiting.

"I will have ten kisses from the Princess," answered the Swineherd.

"Heaven forbid!" said the lady-in-waiting.

"Yes, I will sell it for nothing less," replied the Swineherd.

"Well, what does he say?" asked the Princess.

"I really hardly like to tell you," answered the lady-in-waiting.

"Oh, then you can whisper it to me."

"He is disobliging!" said the Princess, and went away. But she had only gone a few steps when the bells rang out so prettily—

"Where is Augustus dear?
Alas! he's not here, here, here."

"Listen!" said the Princess. "Ask him whether he will take ten kisses from my ladies-in-waiting."

"No, thank you," said the Swineherd. "Ten kisses from the Princess, or else I keep my pot."

"That is very tiresome!" said the Princess. "But you must put yourselves in front of me, so that no one can see."

And the ladies-in-waiting placed themselves in front and then spread out their dresses; so the Swineherd got his ten kisses, and she got the pot.

What happiness that was! The whole night and the whole day the pot was made to boil; there was not a fire-place in the whole town where they did not know what was being cooked, whether it was at the chancellor's or at the shoemaker's.

The ladies-in-waiting danced and clapped their hands.

"We know who is going to have soup and pancakes; we know who is going to have porridge and sausages—isn't it interesting?"

"Yes, very interesting!" said the first lady-in-waiting.

"But don't say anything about it, for I am the Emperor's daughter."

"Oh, no, of course we won't!" said everyone.

The Swineherd—that is to say, the Prince (though they did not know he was anything but a true Swineherd)—let no day pass without making something, and one day he made a rattle which, when it was turned round, played all the waltzes, galops, and polkas which had ever been known since the world began.

"But that is *superbe!*" said the Princess as she passed by. "I have never heard a more beautiful composition. Listen! Go down and ask him what this instrument costs; but I won't kiss him again."

THE SWINEHERD TAKES THE TEN KISSES

"He wants a hundred kisses from the Princess," said the lady-in-waiting who had gone down to ask him.

"I believe he is mad!" said the Princess, and then she went on; but she had only gone a few steps when she stopped.

"One ought to encourage art," she said. "I am the Emperor's daughter! Tell him he shall have, as before, ten kisses; the rest he can take from my ladies-in-waiting."

"But we don't at all like being kissed by him," said the ladies-in-waiting.

"That's nonsense," said the Princess; "and if I can kiss him, you can too. Besides, remember that I give you board and lodging."

So the ladies-in-waiting had to go down to him again.

"A hundred kisses from the Princess," said he, "or each keeps his own."

"Put yourselves in front of us," she said then; and so all the ladies-in-waiting put themselves in front, and he began to kiss the Princess.

"What can that commotion be by the pigsties?" asked the Emperor, who was standing on the balcony. He rubbed his eyes and put on his spectacles. "Why those are the ladies-in-waiting playing their games; I must go down to them."

So he took off his shoes, which were shoes though he had trodden them down into slippers. What a hurry he was in, to be sure!

As soon as he came into the yard he walked very softly, and the ladies-in-waiting were so busy counting the kisses and seeing fair play that they never noticed the Emperor. He stood on tip-toe.

"What is that?" he said, when he saw the kissing; and then he threw one of his slippers at their heads just as the Swineherd was taking his eighty-sixth kiss.

"Be off with you!" said the Emperor, for he was very angry. And the Princess and the Swineherd were driven out of the empire.

Then she stood still and wept; the Swineherd was scolding, and the rain was streaming down.

"Alas, what an unhappy creature I am!" sobbed the Princess. "If only I had taken the beautiful Prince! Alas, how unfortunate I am!"

And the Swineherd went behind a tree, washed the dirt from his face, threw away his old clothes, and then stepped forward in his splendid dress, looking so beautiful that the Princess was obliged to courtesy.

"I now come to this. I despise you!" he said. "You would have nothing to do with a noble Prince; you did not understand the rose or the nightingale, but you could kiss the Swineherd for the sake of a toy. This is what you get for it!" And he went into his kingdom and shut the door in her face, and she had to stay outside singing—

> "Where's my Augustus dear?
> Alas! he's not here, here, here!"

HOW TO TELL
A TRUE PRINCESS

HERE WAS ONCE UPON A TIME A PRINCE WHO WANTED to marry a Princess, but she must be a true Princess. So he travelled through the whole world to find one, but there was always something against each. There were plenty of Princesses, but he could not find out if they were true Princesses. In every case there was some little defect, which showed the genuine article was not yet found. So he came home again in very low spirits, for he had wanted very much to have a true Princess. One night there was a dreadful storm; it thundered and lightened and the rain streamed down in torrents. It was fearful! There was a knocking heard at the Palace gate, and the old King went to open it.

There stood a Princess outside the gate; but oh, in what a sad plight she was from the rain and the storm! The water was running down from her hair and her dress into the points of her shoes and out at the heels again. And yet she said she was a true Princess!

"Well, we shall soon find that!" thought the old Queen. But she said nothing, and went into the sleeping-room, took off all the bedclothes, and laid a

A TRUE PRINCESS

pea on the bottom of the bed. Then she put twenty mattresses on top of the pea, and twenty eider-down quilts on the top of the mattresses. And this was the bed in which the Princess was to sleep.

The next morning she was asked how she had slept.

"Oh, very badly!" said the Princess. "I scarcely closed my eyes all night! I am sure I don't know what was in the bed. I laid on something so hard that my whole body is black and blue. It is dreadful!"

Now they perceived that she was a true Princess, because she had felt the pea through the twenty mattresses and the twenty eider-down quilts.

No one but a true Princess could be so sensitive.

So the Prince married her, for now he knew that at last he had got hold of a true Princess. And the pea was put into the Royal Museum, where it is still to be seen if no one has stolen it. Now this is a true story.

THE BLUE MOUNTAINS

HERE WERE ONCE A SCOTSMAN AND AN ENGLISHMAN and an Irishman serving in the army together, who took it into their heads to run away on the first opportunity they could get. The chance came and they took it. They went on travelling for two days through a great forest, without food or drink, and without coming across a single house, and every night they had to climb up into the trees through fear of the wild beasts that were in the wood. On the second morning the Scotsman saw from the top of his tree a great castle far away. He said to himself that he would certainly die if he stayed in the forest without anything to eat but the roots of grass, which would not keep him alive very long. As soon, then, as he got down out of the tree he set off toward the castle, without so much as telling his companions that he had seen it at all; perhaps the hunger and want they had suffered had changed their nature so much that the one did not care what became of the other if he could save himself. He travelled on most of the day, so that it was quite late when he reached the castle, and to his great disappointment found nothing but closed doors and no smoke rising from the chimneys. He thought there was nothing for it but to die after

all, and had lain down beside the wall, when he heard a window being opened high above him. At this he looked up, and saw the most beautiful woman he had ever set eyes on.

"Oh, it is Fortune that has sent you to me," he said.

"It is indeed," said she. "What are you in need of, or what has sent you here?"

"Necessity," said he. "I am dying for want of food and drink."

"Come inside, then," she said; "there is plenty of both here."

Accordingly he went in to where she was, and she opened a large room for him, where he saw a number of men lying asleep. She then set food before him, and after that showed him to the room where the others were. He lay down on one of the beds and fell sound asleep. And now we must go back to the two that he left behind him in the wood.

When nightfall and the time of the wild beasts came upon these, the Englishman happened to climb up into the very same tree on which the Scotsman was when he got a sight of the castle; and as soon as the day began to dawn and the Englishman looked to the four quarters of heaven, what did he see but the castle too! Off he went without saying a word to the Irishman, and everything happened to him just as it had done to the Scotsman.

The poor Irishman was now left all alone, and did not know where the others had gone to, so he just stayed where he was, very sad and miserable. When night came he climbed up into the same tree as the Englishman had been on the night before. As soon as day came he also saw the castle, and set out toward it; but when he reached it he could see no signs of fire or living being about it. Before long, however, he heard the window opened above his head, looked up, and beheld the most beautiful woman he had ever seen. He asked if she would give him food and drink, and she answered kindly and heartily that she would, if he would only come inside. This he did very willingly, and she set before him food and drink that he had never seen the like of

The Princess Revives The Irishman

before. In the room there was a bed, with diamond rings hanging at every loop of the curtains, and everything that was in the room besides astonished him so much that he actually forgot that he was hungry. When she saw that he was not eating at all, she asked him what he wanted yet, to which he replied that he would neither eat nor drink until he knew who she was, or where she came from, or who had put her there.

"I shall tell you that," said she. "I am an enchanted Princess, and my father has promised that the man who releases me from the spell shall have the third of his kingdom while he is alive, and the whole of it after he is dead, and marry me as well. If ever I saw a man who looked likely to do this, you are the one. I have been here for sixteen years now, and no one who ever came to the castle has asked me who I was, except yourself. Every other man that has come, so long as I have been here, lies asleep in the big room down there."

"Tell me, then," said the Irishman, "what is the spell that has been laid on you, and how you can be freed from it."

"There is a little room there," said the Princess, "and if I could get a man to stay in it from ten o'clock till midnight for three nights on end I should be freed from the spell."

"I am the man for you, then," said he; "I will take on hand to do it."

Thereupon she brought him a pipe and tobacco, and he went into the room; but before long he heard a hammering and knocking on the outside of the door, and was told to open it.

"I won't," he said.

The next moment the door came flying in, and those outside along with it. They knocked him down, and kicked him, and knelt on his body till it came to midnight; but as soon as the cock crowed they all disappeared. The Irishman was little more than alive by this time. As soon as daylight appeared the Princess came, and found him lying full length on the floor, unable to speak a word. She took a bottle, rubbed him from head to foot with something from it, and thereupon he was as sound as ever; but after what he had got that night he was very unwilling to try it a second time. The Princess, however, entreated him to stay, saying that the next night would not be so bad, and in the end he gave in and stayed.

When it was getting near midnight he heard them ordering him to open the door, and there were three of them for every one that there had been the previous evening. He did not make the slightest movement to go out to them or to open the door, but before long they broke it up, and were in on top of him. They laid hold of him, and kept throwing him between them up to the ceiling, or jumping above him, until the cock crowed, when they all disappeared. When day came the Princess went to the room to see if he was still alive, and taking the bottle put it to his nostrils, which soon brought him to himself. The first thing he said then was that he was a fool to go on getting himself killed for anyone he ever saw, and was determined to be off and stay there no longer. When the Princess learned his intention she entreated him to stay, reminding him that another night would free her from the spell. "Besides," she said, "if there is a single spark of life in you when the day comes, the stuff that is in this bottle will make you as sound as ever you were."

With all this the Irishman decided to stay; but that night there were three at him for every one that was there the two nights before, and it looked very unlikely that he would be alive in the morning after all that he got. When morning dawned, and the Princess came to see if he was still alive, she found him lying on the floor as if dead. She tried to see if there was breath in him, but could not quite make it out. Then she put her hand on his pulse, and found a faint movement in it. Accordingly, she poured what was in the bottle on him, and before long he rose up on his feet, and was as well as ever he was. So that business was finished, and the Princess was freed from the spell.

The Princess then told the Irishman that she must go away for the present, but would return for him in a few days in a carriage drawn by four grey horses. He told her to "be aisy," and not speak like that to him. "I have paid dear for you for the last three nights," he said, "if I have to part with you now;" but in the twinkling of an eye she had disappeared. He did not know what to do with himself when he saw that she was gone, but before she went she had given him a little rod, with which he could, when he pleased, waken the men who had been sleeping there, some of them for sixteen years.

After being thus left alone, he went in and stretched himself on three chairs that were in the room, when what does he see coming in at the door but a little fair-haired lad.

"Where did you come from, my lad?" said the Irishman.

"I came to make ready your food for you," said he.

"Who told you to do that?" said the Irishman.

"My mistress," answered the lad—"the Princess that was under the spell and is now free."

By this the Irishman knew that she had sent the lad to wait on him. The lad also told him that his mistress wished him to be ready the next morning at nine o'clock, when she would come for him with the carriage, as she had promised. He was greatly pleased at this, and the next morning, when the time was drawing near, went out into the garden; but the little fair-haired lad took a big pin out of his pocket, and stuck it into the back of the Irishman's coat without his noticing it, whereupon he fell sound asleep.

Before long the Princess came with the carriage and four horses, and asked the lad whether his master was awake. He said that he wasn't. "It is bad for him," said she, "when the night is not long enough for him to sleep. Tell him that if he doesn't meet me at this time to-morrow it is not likely that he will ever see me again all his life."

As soon as she was gone the fair-haired lad took the pin out of his master's coat, who instantly awoke. The first word he said to the lad was, "Have you seen her?"

"Yes," said he, "and she bade me tell you that if you don't meet her at nine o'clock to-morrow you will never see her again."

He was very sorry when he heard this, and could not understand why the sleep should have fallen upon him just when she was coming. He decided, however, to go early to bed that night, in order to rise in time the next morn-ing, and so he did. When it was getting near nine o'clock he went out to the garden to wait till she came, and the fair-haired lad along with him; but as soon as the lad got the chance he stuck the pin into his master's coat again and he fell asleep as before. Precisely at nine o'clock came the Princess in the carriage with four horses, and asked the lad if his master had got up yet; but he said "No, he was asleep, just as he was the day before."

"Dear! dear!" said the Princess, "I am sorry for him. Was the sleep he had last night not enough for him? Tell him that he will never see me here again; and here is a sword that you will give him in my name, and my blessing along with it."

With this she went off, and as soon as she had gone the lad took the pin out of his master's coat. He awoke instantly, and the first word he said was, "Have you seen her?" The lad said that he had, and there was the sword she had left for him. The Irishman was ready to kill the lad out of sheer vexation, but when he gave a glance over his shoulder not a trace of the fair-haired lad was left.

Being thus left all alone, he thought of going into the room where all the men were lying asleep, and there among the rest he found his two comrades who had deserted along with him. Then he remembered what the Princess had told him—that he had only to touch them with the rod she had given him and they would all awake; and the first he touched were his own comrades. They started to their feet at once, and he gave them as much silver and gold as they could carry when they went away. There was plenty to do before he got all the others wakened, for the two doors of the castle were crowded with them all the day long.

The loss of the Princess, however, kept rankling in his mind day and night, till finally he thought he would go about the world to see if he could find anyone to give him news of her. So he took the best horse in the stable and set out. Three years he spent travelling through forests and wildernesses, but could find no one able to tell him anything of the Princess. At last he fell into so great despair that he thought he would put an end to his own life, and for this purpose laid hold of the sword that she had given him by the hands of the fair-haired lad; but on drawing it from its sheath he noticed that there was some writing on one side of the blade. He looked at this, and read there, "You will find me in the Blue Mountains." This made him take heart again, and he gave up the idea of killing himself, thinking that he would go on in hope of meeting someone who could tell him where the Blue Mountains were. After he had gone a long way without thinking where he was going, he saw at last a light far away, and made straight for it. On reaching it he found it came from a little house, and as soon as the man inside heard the noise of the horse's feet he came out to see who was there. Seeing a stranger on horseback, he asked what brought him there and where he was going.

"I have lived here," said he, "for three hundred years, and all that time I have not seen a single human being but yourself."

"I have been going about for the last three years," said the Irishman, "to see if I could find anyone who can tell me where the Blue Mountains are."

"Come in," said the old man, "and stay with me all night. I have a book which contains the history of the world, which I shall go through to-night, and if there is such a place as the Blue Mountains in it we shall find it out."

The Irishman stayed there all night, and as soon as morning came rose to go. The old man said he had not gone to sleep all night for going through the book, but there was not a word about the Blue Mountains in it. "But I'll tell you what," he said, "if there is such a place on earth at all, I have a brother who lives nine hundred miles from here, and he is sure to know where they are, if anyone in this world does." The Irishman answered that he could never go these nine hundred miles, for his horse was giving in already. "That doesn't matter," said the old man; "I can do better than that. I have only to blow my whistle and you will be at my brother's house before nightfall."

So he blew the whistle, and the Irishman did not know where on earth he was until he found himself at the other old man's door, who also told him that it was three hundred years since he had seen anyone, and asked him where he was going.

"I am going to see if I can find anyone that can tell me where the Blue Mountains are," he said.

"If you will stay with me to-night," said the old man, "I have a book of the history of the world, and I shall know where they are before daylight, if there is such a place in it at all."

He stayed there all night, but there was not a word in the book about the Blue Mountains. Seeing that he was rather cast down, the old man told him that he had a brother nine hundred miles away, and that if information could be got about them from anyone it would be from him; "and I will enable you," he said, "to reach the place where he lives before night." So he blew his whistle, and the Irishman landed at the brother's house before nightfall. When the old man saw him he said he had not seen a single man for three hundred years, and was very much surprised to see anyone come to him now.

"Where are you going to?" he said.

"I am going about asking for the Blue Mountains," said the Irishman.

"The Blue Mountains?" said the old man.

"Yes," said the Irishman.

"I never heard the name before; but if they do exist I shall find them out. I am master of all the birds in the world, and have only to blow my whistle and every one will come to me. I shall then ask each of them to tell where it came from, and if there is any way of finding out the Blue Mountains that is it."

So he blew his whistle, and when he blew it then all the birds of the world began to gather. The old man questioned each of them as to where they had come from, but there was not one of them that had come from the Blue Mountains. After he had run over them all, however, he missed a big Eagle that was wanting, and wondered that it had not come. Soon afterward he saw something big coming toward him, darkening the sky. It kept coming nearer and growing bigger, and what was this after all but the Eagle? When she arrived the old man scolded her, and asked what had kept her so long behind.

"I couldn't help it," she said; "I had more than twenty times further to come than any bird that has come here to-day."

"Where have you come from, then?" said the old man.

"From the Blue Mountains," said she.

"Indeed!" said the old man; "and what are they doing there?"

"They are making ready this very day," said the Eagle, "for the marriage of the daughter of the King of the Blue Mountains. For three years now she has refused to marry anyone whatsoever, until she should give up all hope of the coming of the man who released her from the spell. Now she can wait no longer, for three years is the time that she agreed with her father to remain without marrying."

The Irishman knew that it was for himself she had been waiting so long, but he was unable to make any better of it, for he had no hope of reaching the Blue Mountains all his life. The old man noticed how sad he grew, and asked the Eagle what she would take for carrying this man on her back to the Blue Mountains.

"I must have threescore cattle killed," said she, "and cut up into quarters, and every time I look over my shoulder he must throw one of them into my mouth."

As soon as the Irishman and the old man heard her demand they went out hunting, and before evening they had killed threescore cattle. They made quarters of them, as the Eagle told them, and then the old man asked her to lie down, till they would get it all heaped up on her back. First of all, though, they had to get a ladder of fourteen steps, to enable them to get on to the Eagle's back, and there they piled up the meat as well as they could. Then the old man told the Irishman to mount, and to remember to throw a quarter of beef to her every time she looked round. He went up, and the old man gave the Eagle

The Irishman arrives at the Blue Mountains

the word to be off, which she instantly obeyed; and every time she turned her head the Irishman threw a quarter of beef into her mouth.

As they came near the borders of the kingdom of the Blue Mountains, however, the beef was done, and, when the Eagle looked over her shoulder, what was the Irishman at but throwing the stone between her tail and her neck! At this she turned a complete somersault, and threw the Irishman off into the sea, where he fell into the bay that was right in front of the King's Palace. Fortunately the points of his toes just touched the bottom, and he managed to get ashore.

When he went up into the town all the streets were gleaming with light, and the wedding of the Princess was just about to begin. He went into the first house he came to, and this happened to be the house of the King's henwife. He asked the old woman what was causing all the noise and light in the town.

"The Princess," said she, "is going to be married to-night against her will, for she has been expecting every day that the man who freed her from the spell would come."

"There is a guinea for you," said he; "go and bring her here."

The old woman went, and soon returned along with the Princess. She and the Irishman recognised each other, and were married, and had a great wedding that lasted for a year and a day.

THE TINDER-BOX

 SOLDIER CAME MARCHING ALONG THE HIGH ROAD— left, right! left, right! He had his knapsack on his back and a sword by his side, for he had been to the wars and was now returning home.

An old Witch met him on the road. She was very ugly to look at: her underlip hung down to her breast.

"Good evening, Soldier!" she said. "What a fine sword and knapsack you have! You are something like a soldier! You ought to have as much money as you would like to carry!"

"Thank you, old Witch," said the Soldier.

"Do you see that great tree there?" said the Witch, pointing to a tree beside them. "It is hollow within. You must climb up to the top, and then you will see a hole through which you can let yourself down into the tree. I will tie a rope round your waist, so that I may be able to pull you up again when you call."

"What shall I do down there?" asked the Soldier.

"Get money!" answered the Witch. "Listen! When you reach the bottom of the tree you will find yourself in a large hall; it is light there, for there are more than three hundred lamps burning. Then you will see three doors, which you can open—the keys are in the locks. If you go into the first room, you will see a great chest in the middle of the floor with a dog sitting upon it; he has eyes as large as saucers, but you needn't trouble about him. I will give you my blue-check apron, which you must spread out on the floor, and then go back quickly and fetch the dog and set him upon it; open the chest and take as much money as you like. It is copper there. If you would rather have silver, you must go into the next room, where there is a dog with eyes as large as mill-wheels. But don't take any notice of him; just set him upon my apron, and help yourself to the money. If you prefer gold, you can get that too, if you go into the third room, and as much as you like to carry. But the dog that guards the chest there has eyes as large as the Round Tower at Copenhagen! He is a savage dog, I can tell you; but you needn't be afraid of him either. Only, put him on my apron and he won't touch you, and you can take out of the chest as much gold as you like!"

"Come, this is not bad!" said the Soldier. "But what am I to give you, old Witch; for surely you are not going to do this for nothing?"

"Yes, I am!" replied the Witch. "Not a single farthing will I take! For me you shall bring nothing but an old tinder-box which my grandmother forgot last time she was down there."

"Well, tie the rope round my waist!" said the Soldier.

"Here it is," said the Witch, "and here is my blue-check apron."

Then the Soldier climbed up the tree, let himself down through the hole, and found himself standing, as the Witch had said, underground in the large hall, where the three hundred lamps were burning.

Well, he opened the first door. Ugh! there sat the dog with eyes as big as saucers glaring at him.

"You are a fine fellow!" said the Soldier, and put him on the Witch's apron, took as much copper as his pockets could hold; then he shut the chest, put the dog on it again, and went into the second room. Sure enough there sat the dog with eyes as large as mill-wheels.

"You had better not look at me so hard!" said the Soldier. "Your eyes will come out of their sockets!"

And then he set the dog on the apron. When he saw all the silver in the chest, he threw away the copper he had taken, and filled his pockets and knapsack with nothing but silver.

Then he went into the third room. Horrors! the dog there had two eyes, each as large as the Round Tower at Copenhagen, spinning round in his head like wheels.

"Good evening!" said the Soldier and saluted, for he had never seen a dog like this before. But when he had examined him more closely, he thought to himself: "Now then, I've had enough of this!" and put him down on the floor, and opened the chest. Heavens! what a heap of gold there was! With all that he could buy up the whole town, and all the sugar pigs, all the tin soldiers, whips and rocking horses in the whole world. Now he threw away all the silver with which he had filled his pockets and knapsack, and filled them with gold instead—yes, all his pockets, his knapsack, cap, and boots even, so that he could hardly walk. Now he was rich indeed. He put the dog back upon the chest, shut the door, and then called up through the tree:

"Now pull me up again, old Witch!"

"Have you got the tinder-box also?" asked the Witch.

"Botheration!" said the Soldier, "I had clean forgotten it!" And then he went back and fetched it.

The Witch pulled him up, and there he stood again on the high road, with pockets, knapsack, cap, and boots filled with gold.

"What do you want to do with the tinder-box?" asked the Soldier.

"That doesn't matter to you," replied the Witch. "You have got your money, give me my tinder-box."

THE SOLDIER FILLS HIS KNAPSACK WITH MONEY

"We'll see!" said the Soldier. "Tell me at once what you want to do with it, or I will draw my sword, and cut off your head!"

"No!" screamed the Witch.

The Soldier immediately cut off her head. That was the end of her! But he tied up all his gold in her apron, slung it like a bundle over his shoulder, put the tinder-box in his pocket, and set out toward the town.

It was a splendid town! He turned into the finest inn, ordered the best chamber and his favourite dinner; for now that he had so much money he was really rich.

It certainly occurred to the servant who had to clean his boots that they were astonishingly old boots for such a rich lord. But that was because he had not yet bought new ones; the next day he appeared in respectable boots and fine clothes. Now, instead of a common soldier he had become a noble lord, and the people told him about all the grand doings of the town and the King, and what a beautiful Princess his daughter was.

"How can one get to see her?" asked the Soldier.

"She is never to be seen at all!" they told him; "she lives in a great copper castle, surrounded by many walls and towers! No one except the King may go in or out, for it is prophesied that she will marry a common soldier, and the King cannot submit to that."

"I should very much like to see her," thought the Soldier; but he could not get permission.

Now he lived very gaily, went to the theatre, drove in the King's garden, and gave the poor a great deal of money, which was very nice of him; he had experienced in former times how hard it is not to have a farthing in the world. Now he was rich, wore fine clothes, and made many friends, who all said that he was an excellent man, a real nobleman. And the Soldier liked that. But as he was always spending money, and never made any more, at last the day came when he had nothing left but two shillings, and he had to leave the beautiful rooms in which he had been living, and go into a little attic under the roof, and clean his own boots, and mend them with a darning-needle. None of his friends came to visit him there, for there were too many stairs to climb.

It was a dark evening, and he could not even buy a light. But all at once it flashed across him that there was a little end of tinder in the tinder-box, which he had taken from the hollow tree into which the Witch had helped him down. He found the box with the tinder in it; but just as he was kindling a light, and had struck a spark out of the tinder-box, the door burst open, and the dog with eyes as large as saucers, which he had seen down in the tree, stood before him and said:

"What does my lord command?"

"What's the meaning of this?" exclaimed the Soldier. "This is a pretty kind of tinder-box, if I can get whatever I want like this. Get me money!" he cried to the dog, and hey, presto! he was off and back again, holding a great purse full of money in his mouth.

Now the Soldier knew what a capital tinder-box this was. If he rubbed once, the dog that sat on the chest of copper appeared; if he rubbed twice, there came the dog that watched over the silver chest; and if he rubbed three times, the one that guarded the gold appeared. Now, the Soldier went down again to his beautiful rooms, and appeared once more in splendid clothes. All his friends immediately recognised him again, and paid him great court.

One day he thought to himself: "It is very strange that no one can get to see the Princess. They all say she is very pretty, but what's the use of that if she has to sit forever in the great copper castle with all the towers? Can I not manage to see her somehow? Where is my tinder-box?" and so he struck a spark, and, presto! there came the dog with eyes as large as saucers.

"It is the middle of the night, I know," said the Soldier; "but I should very much like to see the Princess for a moment."

The dog was already outside the door, and before the Soldier could look round, in he came with the Princess. She was lying asleep on the dog's back, and was so beautiful that anyone could see she was a real Princess. The Soldier really could not refrain from kissing her—he was such a thorough Soldier. Then the dog ran back with the Princess. But when it was morning, and the King and Queen were drinking tea, the Princess said that the night before she had had such a strange dream about a dog and a Soldier: she had ridden on the dog's back, and the Soldier had kissed her.

"That is certainly a fine story," said the Queen. But the next night one of the ladies-in-waiting was to watch at the Princess's bed, to see if it was only a dream, or if it had actually happened.

The Soldier had an overpowering longing to see the Princess again, and so the dog came in the middle of the night and fetched her, running as fast as he could. But the lady-in-waiting slipped on india-rubber shoes and followed

The DOG BRings in The Princess

them. When she saw them disappear into a large house, she thought to herself: "Now I know where it is;" and made a great cross on the door with a piece of chalk. Then she went home and lay down, and the dog came back also, with the Princess. But when he saw that a cross had been made on the door of the house where the Soldier lived, he took a piece of chalk also, and made crosses on all the doors in the town; and that was very clever, for now the lady-in-waiting could not find the right house, as there were crosses on all the doors.

Early the next morning the King, Queen, ladies-in-waiting, and officers came out to see where the Princess had been.

"There it is!" said the King, when he saw the first door with a cross on it.

"No, there it is, my dear!" said the Queen, when she likewise saw a door with a cross.

"But here is one, and there is another!" they all exclaimed; wherever they looked there was a cross on the door. Then they realised that the sign would not help them at all.

But the Queen was an extremely clever woman, who could do a great deal more than just drive in a coach. She took her great golden scissors, cut up a piece of silk, and made a pretty little bag of it. This she filled with the finest buckwheat grains, and tied it round the Princess's neck; this done, she cut a little hole in the bag, so that the grains would strew the whole road wherever the Princess went.

In the night the dog came again, took the Princess on his back and ran away with her to the Soldier, who was very much in love with her, and would have liked to have been a Prince, so that he might have had her for his wife.

The dog did not notice how the grains were strewn right from the castle to the Soldier's window, where he ran up the wall with the Princess.

In the morning the King and the Queen saw plainly where their daughter had been, and they took the Soldier and put him into prison.

There he sat. Oh, how dark and dull it was there! And they told him: "To-morrow you are to be hanged." Hearing that did not exactly cheer him, and he had left his tinder-box in the inn.

The next morning he could see through the iron grating in front of his little window how the people were hurrying out of the town to see him hanged. He heard the drums and saw the soldiers marching; all the people were running to and fro. Just below his window was a shoemaker's apprentice, with leather apron and shoes; he was skipping along so merrily that one of his shoes flew off and fell against the wall, just where the Soldier was sitting peeping through the iron grating.

"Oh, shoemaker's boy, you needn't be in such a hurry!" said the Soldier to him. "There's nothing going on till I arrive. But if you will run back to the house where I lived, and fetch me my tinder-box, I will give you four shillings. But you must put your best foot foremost."

"SKIPPING ALONG SO MERRILY"

The shoemaker's boy was very willing to earn four shillings, and fetched the tinder-box, gave it to the Soldier, and—yes—now you shall hear.

Outside the town a great scaffold had been erected, and all round were standing the soldiers, and hundreds of thousands of people. The King and Queen were sitting on a magnificent throne opposite the judges and the whole council.

The Soldier was already standing on the top of the ladder; but when they wanted to put the rope round his neck, he said that the fulfilment of one innocent request was always granted to a poor criminal before he underwent his punishment. He would so much like to smoke a small pipe of tobacco; it would be his last pipe in this world.

The King could not refuse him this, and so he took out his tinder-box, and rubbed it once, twice, three times. And lo, and behold! there stood all three dogs—the one with eyes as large as saucers, the second with eyes as large as mill-wheels, and the third with eyes each as large as the Round Tower of Copenhagen.

"Help me now, so that I may not be hanged!" cried the Soldier. And thereupon the dogs fell upon the judges and the whole council, seized some by the legs, others by the nose, and threw them so high into the air that they fell and were smashed into pieces.

"I won't stand this!" said the King; but the largest dog seized him too, and the Queen as well, and threw them up after the others. This frightened the soldiers, and all the people cried: "Good Soldier, you shall be our King, and marry the beautiful Princess!"

Then they put the Soldier into the King's coach, and the three dogs danced in front, crying "Hurrah!" And the boys whistled and the soldiers presented arms.

The Princess came out of the copper castle, and became Queen; and that pleased her very much.

The wedding festivities lasted for eight days, and the dogs sat at table and made eyes at everyone.

THE WITCH IN
THE STONE BOAT[31]

 HERE WERE ONCE A KING AND A QUEEN, AND THEY had a son called Sigurd, who was very strong and active, and good-looking. When the King came to be bowed down with the weight of years he spoke to his son, and said that now it was time for him to look out for a fitting match for himself, for he did not know how long he might last now, and he would like to see him married before he died.

Sigurd was not averse to this, and asked his father where he thought it best to look for a wife. The King answered that in a certain country there was a King who had a beautiful daughter, and he thought it would be most desirable if Sigurd could get her. So the two parted, and Sigurd prepared for the journey, and went to where his father had directed him.

He came to the King and asked his daughter's hand, which he readily granted him, but only on the condition that he should remain there as long as he could, for the King himself was not strong and not very able to govern his kingdom. Sigurd accepted this condition, but added that he would have to get leave to go home again to his own country when he heard news of his father's death. After that Sigurd married the Princess, and helped his father-in-law to govern the kingdom. He and the Princess loved each other dearly, and after a year a son came to them, who was two years old when word came to Sigurd that his father was dead. Sigurd now prepared to return home with his wife and child, and went on board ship to go by sea.

They had sailed for several days, when the breeze suddenly fell, and there came a dead calm, at a time when they needed only one day's voyage to reach home. Sigurd and his Queen were one day on deck, when most of the others on the ship had fallen asleep. There they sat and talked for a while, and had their little son along with them. After a time Sigurd became so heavy with sleep that he could no longer keep awake, so he went below and lay down, leaving the Queen alone on the deck, playing with her son.

A good while after Sigurd had gone below the Queen saw something black on the sea, which seemed to be coming nearer. As it approached she could make out that it was a boat, and could see the figure of someone sitting in it and rowing it. At last the boat came alongside the ship, and now the Queen saw that it was a stone boat, out of which there came up on board the ship a fearfully ugly Witch. The Queen was more frightened than words can describe, and could neither speak a word nor move from the place so as to awaken the King or the sailors. The Witch came right up to the Queen, took the child from her and laid it on the deck; then she took the Queen, and stripped her of all her fine clothes, which she proceeded to put on herself, and looked then like a human being. Last of all she took the Queen, put her into the boat, and said—

The Witch comes On board

"This spell I lay upon you, that you slacken not your course until you come to my brother in the Underworld."

The Queen sat stunned and motionless, but the boat at once shot away from the ship with her, and before long she was out of sight.

When the boat could no longer be seen the child began to cry, and though the Witch tried to quiet it she could not manage it; so she went below to where the King was sleeping with the child on her arm, and awakened him, scolding him for leaving them alone on deck, while he and all the crew were asleep. It was great carelessness of him, she said, to leave no one to watch the ship with her.

Sigurd was greatly surprised to hear his Queen scold him so much, for she had never said an angry word to him before; but he thought it was quite excusable in this case, and tried to quiet the child along with her, but it was no use. Then he went and wakened the sailors, and bade them hoist the sails, for a breeze had sprung up and was blowing straight toward the harbour.

They soon reached the land which Sigurd was to rule over, and found all the people sorrowful for the old King's death, but they became glad when they got Sigurd back to the Court, and made him King over them.

The King's son, however, hardly ever stopped crying from the time he had been taken from his mother on the deck of the ship, although he had always been such a good child before, so that at last the King had to get a nurse for him—one of the maids of the Court. As soon as the child got into her charge he stopped crying, and behaved well as before.

After the sea voyage it seemed to the King that the Queen had altered very much in many ways, and not for the better. He thought her much more haughty and stubborn and difficult to deal with than she used to be. Before long others began to notice this as well as the King. In the Court there were two young fellows, one of eighteen years old, the other of nineteen, who were very fond of playing chess, and often sat long inside playing at it. Their room was next the Queen's, and often during the day they heard the Queen talking.

One day they paid more attention than usual when they heard her talk, and put their ears close to a crack in the wall between the rooms, and heard the Queen say quite plainly, "When I yawn a little, then I am a nice little maiden; when I yawn halfway, then I am half a troll; and when I yawn fully, then I am a troll altogether."

As she said this she yawned tremendously, and in a moment had put on the appearance of a fearfully ugly troll. Then there came up through the floor of the room a three-headed Giant with a trough full of meat, who saluted her as his sister and set down the trough before her. She began to eat out of it, and never stopped till she had finished it. The young fellows saw all this going on, but did not hear the two of them say anything to each other. They were astonished though at how greedily the Queen devoured the meat, and how much she ate of it, and were no longer surprised that she took so little when she sat at table with the King. As soon as she had finished it the Giant disappeared with the trough by the same way as he had come, and the Queen returned to her human shape.

Now we must go back to the King's son after he had been put in charge of the nurse. One evening, after she had lit a candle and was holding the child, several planks sprang up in the floor of the room, and out at the opening came a beautiful woman dressed in white, with an iron belt round her waist, to which was fastened an iron chain that went down into the ground. The woman came up to the nurse, took the child from her, and pressed it to her breast; then she gave it back to the nurse and returned by the same way as she had come, and the floor closed over her again. Although the woman had not spoken a single word to her, the nurse was very much frightened, but told no one about it.

The next evening the same thing happened again, just as before, but as the woman was going away she said in a sad tone, "Two are gone, and one only is left," and then disappeared as before. The nurse was still more frightened when she heard the woman say this, and thought that perhaps some danger was hanging over the child, though she had no ill-opinion of the unknown woman, who, indeed, had behaved toward the child as if it were her own. The most mysterious thing was the woman saying "and only one is left;" but the nurse guessed that this must mean that only one day was left, since she had come for two days already.

At last the nurse made up her mind to go to the King, and told him the whole story, and asked him to be present in person the next day about the time when the woman usually came. The King promised to do so, and came to the nurse's room a little before the time, and sat down on a chair with his drawn sword in his hand. Soon after the planks in the floor sprang up as before, and the woman came up, dressed in white, with the iron belt and chain. The King saw at once that it was his own Queen, and immediately hewed asunder the iron chain that was fastened to the belt. This was followed by such noises and crashings down in the earth that all the King's Palace shook, so that no one expected anything else than to see every bit of it shaken to pieces. At last, however, the noises and shaking stopped, and they began to come to themselves again.

The King and Queen embraced each other, and she told him the whole story—how the Witch came to the ship when they were all asleep and sent her off in the boat. After she had gone so far that she could not see the ship, she sailed on through darkness until she landed beside a three-headed Giant. The Giant wished her to marry him, but she refused; whereupon he shut her up by herself, and told her she would never get free until she consented. After a time she began to plan how to get her freedom, and at last told him that she would consent if he would allow her to visit her son on earth three days on end. This he agreed to, but put on her this iron belt and chain, the other end of which he fastened round his own waist, and the great noises that were heard when the King cut the chain must have been caused by the Giant's falling down the underground passage when the chain gave way so suddenly. The Giant's

Sigurd hews the chain asunder.

dwelling, indeed, was right under the Palace, and the terrible shakings must have been caused by him in his death-throes.

The King now understood why the Queen he had had for some time past had been so ill-tempered. He at once had a sack drawn over her head and made her be stoned to death, and after that torn in pieces by untamed horses. The two young fellows also told now what they had heard and seen in the Queen's room, for before this they had been afraid to say anything about it, on account of the Queen's power.

The real Queen was now restored to all her dignity, and was beloved by all. The nurse was married to a nobleman, and the King and Queen gave her splendid presents.

THUMBELINA

HERE WAS ONCE A WOMAN WHO WANTED TO HAVE quite a tiny, little child, but she did not know where to get one from. So one day she went to an old Witch and said to her: "I should so much like to have a tiny, little child; can you tell me where I can get one?"

"Oh, we have just got one ready!" said the Witch. "Here is a barley-corn for you, but it's not the kind the farmer sows in his field, or feeds the cocks and hens with, I can tell you. Put it in a flowerpot, and then you will see something happen."

"Oh, thank you!" said the woman, and gave the Witch a shilling, for that was what it cost. Then she went home and planted the barley-corn; immediately there grew out of it a large and beautiful flower, which looked like a tulip, but the petals were tightly closed as if it were still only a bud.

"What a beautiful flower!" exclaimed the woman, and she kissed the red and yellow petals; but as she kissed them the flower burst open. It was a real tulip, such as one can see any day; but in the middle of the blossom, on the green velvety petals, sat a little girl, quite tiny, trim, and pretty. She was scarcely half a thumb in height; so they called her Thumbelina. An elegant polished walnut shell served Thumbelina as a cradle, the blue petals of a violet were her mattress, and a rose-leaf her coverlid. There she lay at night, but in the day-time she used to play about on the table; here the woman had put a bowl, surrounded by a ring of flowers, with their stalks in water, in the middle of which floated a great tulip petal, and on this Thumbelina sat, and sailed from one side of the bowl to the other, rowing herself with two white horsehairs for oars. It was such a pretty sight! She could sing, too, with a voice more soft and sweet than had ever been heard before.

One night, when she was lying in her pretty little bed, an old toad crept in through a broken pane in the window. She was very ugly, clumsy, and clammy; she hopped on to the table where Thumbelina lay asleep under the red rose-leaf.

"This would make a beautiful wife for my son," said the toad, taking up the walnut shell, with Thumbelina inside, and hopping with it through the window into the garden.

There flowed a great wide stream, with slippery and marshy banks; here the toad lived with her son. Ugh! how ugly and clammy he was, just like his mother! "Croak, croak, croak!" was all he could say when he saw the pretty little girl in the walnut shell.

"Don't talk so loud, or you'll wake her," said the old toad. "She might escape us even now; she is as light as a feather. We will put her at once on a broad water-lily leaf in the stream. That will be quite an island for her; she is so small and light. She can't run away from us there, whilst we are preparing the guest chamber under the marsh where she shall live."

Outside in the brook grew many water lilies, with broad green leaves, which looked as if they were swimming about on the water. The leaf farthest away was the largest, and to this the old toad swam with Thumbelina in her walnut shell.

CROAK CROAK CROAK was all he could say.

The tiny Thumbelina woke up very early in the morning, and when she saw where she was she began to cry bitterly; for on every side of the great green leaf was water, and she could not get to the land.

The old toad was down under the marsh, decorating her room with rushes and yellow marigold leaves, to make it very grand for her new daughter-in-law; then she swam out with her ugly son to the leaf where Thumbelina lay. She wanted to fetch the pretty cradle to put it into her room before Thumbelina herself came there. The old toad bowed low in the water before her, and said: "Here is my son; you shall marry him, and live in great magnificence down under the marsh."

Thumbelina rides on the waterlily-leaf

"Croak, croak, croak!" was all that the son could say. Then they took the neat little cradle and swam away with it; but Thumbelina sat alone on the great green leaf and wept, for she did not want to live with the clammy toad, or marry her ugly son. The little fishes swimming about under the water had seen the toad quite plainly, and heard what she had said; so they put up their heads to see the little girl. When they saw her, they thought her so pretty that they were very sorry she should go down with the ugly toad to live. No; that must not happen. They assembled in the water round the green stalk which supported the leaf on which she was sitting and nibbled the stem in two. Away floated the leaf down the stream, bearing Thumbelina far beyond the reach of the toad.

On she sailed past several towns, and the little birds sitting in the bushes saw her, and sang, "What a pretty little girl!" The leaf floated farther and farther away; thus Thumbelina left her native land.

A beautiful little white butterfly fluttered above her, and at last settled on the leaf. Thumbelina pleased him, and she, too, was delighted, for now the toads could not reach her, and it was so beautiful where she was travelling; the sun shone on the water and made it sparkle like the brightest silver. She took off her sash, and tied one end round the butterfly; the other end she fastened to the leaf, so that now it glided along with her faster than ever.

A great cockchafer came flying past; he caught sight of Thumbelina, and in a moment had put his arms round her slender waist, and had flown off with her to a tree. The green leaf floated away down the stream, and the butterfly with it, for he was fastened to the leaf and could not get loose from it. Oh, dear! how terrified poor little Thumbelina was when the cockchafer flew off with her to the tree! But she was especially distressed on the beautiful white butterfly's account, as she had tied him fast, so that if he could not get away he must starve to death. But the cockchafer did not trouble himself about that; he sat down with her on a large green leaf, gave her the honey out of the flowers to eat, and told her that she was very pretty, although she wasn't in the least like a cockchafer. Later on, all the other cockchafers who lived in the same tree came to pay calls; they examined Thumbelina closely, and remarked, "Why, she has only two legs! How very miserable!"

"She has no feelers!" cried another.

"How ugly she is!" said all the lady chafers—and yet Thumbelina was really very pretty.

The cockchafer who had stolen her knew this very well; but when he heard all the ladies saying she was ugly, he began to think so too, and would not keep her; she might go wherever she liked. So he flew down from the tree with her and put her on a daisy. There she sat and wept, because she was so ugly that the cockchafer would have nothing to do with her; and yet she was the most beautiful creature imaginable, so soft and delicate, like the loveliest rose-leaf.

The whole summer poor little Thumbelina lived alone in the great wood. She plaited a bed for herself of blades of grass, and hung it up under a clover-leaf, so that she was protected from the rain; she gathered honey from the flowers for food, and drank the dew on the leaves every morning. Thus the summer and autumn passed, but then came winter—the long, cold winter. All the birds who had sung so sweetly about her had flown away; the trees shed their leaves, the flowers died; the great clover-leaf under which she had lived curled up, and nothing remained of it but the withered stalk. She was terribly cold, for her clothes were ragged, and she herself was so small and thin. Poor little Thumbelina! she would surely be frozen to death. It began to snow, and every snowflake that fell on her was to her as a whole shovelful thrown on one of us, for we are so big, and she was only an inch high. She wrapt herself round in a dead leaf, but it was torn in the middle and gave her no warmth; she was trembling with cold.

Just outside the wood where she was now living lay a great cornfield. But the corn had been gone a long time; only the dry, bare stubble was left standing in the frozen ground. This made a forest for her to wander about in. All at once she came across the door of a field-mouse, who had a little hole under a corn-stalk. There the mouse lived warm and snug, with a storeroom full of corn, a splendid kitchen and dining room. Poor little Thumbelina went up to the door and begged for a little piece of barley, for she had not had anything to eat for the last two days.

"Poor little creature!" said the field-mouse, for she was a kind-hearted old thing at the bottom. "Come into my warm room and have some dinner with me."

As Thumbelina pleased her, she said: "As far as I am concerned you may spend the winter with me; but you must keep my room clean and tidy, and tell me stories, for I like that very much."

And Thumbelina did all that the kind old field-mouse asked, and did it remarkably well too.

"Now I am expecting a visitor," said the field-mouse; "my neighbour comes to call on me once a week. He is in better circumstances than I am, has great, big rooms, and wears a fine black-velvet coat. If you could only marry him, you would be well provided for. But he is blind. You must tell him all the prettiest stories you know."

But Thumbelina did not trouble her head about him, for he was only a mole. He came and paid them a visit in his black-velvet coat.

"He is so rich and so accomplished," the field-mouse told her. "His house is twenty times larger than mine; he possesses great knowledge, but he cannot bear the sun and the beautiful flowers, and speaks slightingly of them, for he has never seen them."

Thumbelina had to sing to him, so she sang "Lady-bird, lady-bird, fly away home!" and other songs so prettily that the mole fell in love with her; but he did not say anything, he was a very cautious man. A short time before he had dug a long passage through the ground from his own house to that of his neighbour; in this he gave the field-mouse and Thumbelina permission to walk as often as they liked. But he begged them not to be afraid of the dead bird that lay in the passage: it was a real bird with beak and feathers, and must have died a little time ago, and now laid buried just where he had made his tunnel. The mole took a piece of rotten wood in his mouth, for that glows like fire in the dark, and went in front, lighting them through the long dark passage. When they came to the place where the dead bird lay, the mole put his broad nose against the ceiling and pushed a hole through, so that the daylight could shine down. In the middle of the path lay a dead swallow, his pretty wings pressed close to his sides, his claws and head drawn under his feathers; the poor bird had evidently died of cold. Thumbelina was very sorry, for she was very fond of all little birds; they had sung and twittered so beautifully to her all through the summer. But the mole kicked him with his bandy legs and said:

"Now he can't sing anymore! It must be very miserable to be a little bird! I'm thankful that none of my little children are; birds always starve in winter."

Thumbelina brings thistledown for the Swallow

"Yes, you speak like a sensible man," said the field-mouse. "What has a bird, in spite of all his singing, in the wintertime? He must starve and freeze, and that must be very pleasant for him, I must say!"

Thumbelina did not say anything; but when the other two had passed on she bent down to the bird, brushed aside the feathers from his head, and kissed his closed eyes gently. "Perhaps it was he that sang to me so prettily in the summer," she thought. "How much pleasure he did give me, dear little bird!"

The mole closed up the hole again which let in the light, and then escorted the ladies home. But Thumbelina could not sleep that night; so she got out of bed, and plaited a great big blanket of straw, and carried it off, and spread it over the dead bird, and piled upon it thistledown as soft as cotton wool, which she had found in the field-mouse's room, so that the poor little thing should lie warmly buried.

"Farewell, pretty little bird!" she said. "Farewell, and thank you for your beautiful songs in the summer, when the trees were green, and the sun shone down warmly on us!" Then she laid her head against the bird's heart. But the bird was not dead: he had been frozen, but now that she had warmed him, he was coming to life again.

In autumn, the swallows fly away to foreign lands; but there are some who are late in starting, and then they get so cold that they drop down as if dead, and the snow comes and covers them over.

Thumbelina trembled, she was so frightened; for the bird was very large in comparison with herself—only an inch high. But she took courage, piled up the down more closely over the poor swallow, fetched her own coverlid and laid it over his head.

The next night she crept out again to him. There he was alive, but very weak; he could only open his eyes for a moment and look at Thumbelina, who was standing in front of him with a piece of rotten wood in her hand, for she had no other lantern.

"Thank you, pretty little child!" said the swallow to her. "I am so beautifully warm! Soon I shall regain my strength, and then I shall be able to fly out again into the warm sunshine."

"Oh!" she said, "it is very cold outside; it is snowing and freezing! stay in your warm bed; I will take care of you!"

Then she brought him water in a petal, which he drank, after which he related to her how he had torn one of his wings on a bramble, so that he could not fly as fast as the other swallows, who had flown far away to warmer lands. So at last he had dropped down exhausted, and then he could remember no more. The whole winter he remained down there, and Thumbelina looked after him and nursed him tenderly. Neither the mole nor the field-mouse learnt anything of this, for they could not bear the poor swallow.

When the spring came, and the sun warmed the earth again, the swallow said farewell to Thumbelina, who opened the hole in the roof for him which the mole had made. The sun shone brightly down upon her, and the swallow

Thumbelina has to spin

asked her if she would go with him; she could sit upon his back. Thumbelina wanted very much to fly far away into the green wood, but she knew that the old field-mouse would be sad if she ran away. "No, I mustn't come!" she said.

"Farewell, dear good little girl!" said the swallow, and flew off into the sunshine. Thumbelina gazed after him with the tears standing in her eyes, for she was very fond of the swallow.

"Tweet, tweet!" sang the bird, and flew into the green wood. Thumbelina was very unhappy. She was not allowed to go out into the warm sunshine. The corn which had been sowed in the field over the field-mouse's home grew up high into the air, and made a thick forest for the poor little girl, who was only an inch high.

"Now you are to be a bride, Thumbelina!" said the field-mouse, "for our neighbour has proposed for you! What a piece of fortune for a poor child like you! Now you must set to work at your linen for your dowry, for nothing must be lacking if you are to become the wife of our neighbour, the mole!"

Thumbelina had to spin all day long, and every evening the mole visited her, and told her that when the summer was over the sun would not shine so hot; now it was burning the earth as hard as a stone. Yes, when the summer had passed, they would keep the wedding.

But she was not at all pleased about it, for she did not like the stupid mole. Every morning when the sun was rising, and every evening when it was setting, she would steal out of the housedoor, and when the breeze parted the ears of corn so that she could see the blue sky through them, she thought how bright and beautiful it must be outside, and longed to see her dear swallow again. But he never came; no doubt he had flown away far into the great green wood.

By the autumn, Thumbelina had finished the dowry.

"In four weeks you will be married!" said the field-mouse; "don't be obstinate, or I shall bite you with my sharp white teeth! You will get a fine husband! The King himself has not such a velvet coat. His storeroom and cellar are full, and you should be thankful for that."

Well, the wedding day arrived. The mole had come to fetch Thumbelina to live with him deep down under the ground, never to come out into the warm sun again, for that was what he didn't like. The poor little girl was very sad; for now she must say good-bye to the beautiful sun.

"Farewell, bright sun!" she cried, stretching out her arms toward it, and taking another step outside the house; for now the corn had been reaped, and only the dry stubble was left standing. "Farewell, farewell!" she said, and put her arms round a little red flower that grew there. "Give my love to the dear swallow when you see him!"

"Tweet, tweet!" sounded in her ear all at once. She looked up. There was the swallow flying past! As soon as he saw Thumbelina, he was very glad. She told him how unwilling she was to marry the ugly mole, as then she had to live underground where the sun never shone, and she could not help bursting into tears.

"The cold winter is coming now," said the swallow. "I must fly away to warmer lands: will you come with me? You can sit on my back, and we will fly far away from the ugly mole and his dark house, over the mountains, to the warm countries where the sun shines more brightly than here, where it is always summer, and there are always beautiful flowers. Do come with me, dear little Thumbelina, who saved my life when I lay frozen in the dark tunnel!"

"Yes, I will go with you," said Thumbelina, and got on the swallow's back, with her feet on one of his outstretched wings. Up he flew into the air, over woods and seas, over the great mountains where the snow is always lying. And if she was cold she crept under his warm feathers, only keeping her little head out to admire all the beautiful things in the world beneath. At last they came to warm lands; there the sun was brighter, the sky seemed twice as high, and in the hedges hung the finest green and purple grapes; in the woods grew oranges and lemons: the air was scented with myrtle and mint, and on the roads were pretty little children running about and playing with great gorgeous butterflies. But the swallow flew on farther, and it became more and more beautiful. Under the most splendid green trees, beside a blue lake, stood a glittering white marble castle. Vines hung about the high pillars; there were many swallows' nests, and in one of these lived the swallow who was carrying Thumbelina.

"Here is my house!" said he. "But it won't do for you to live with me; I am not tidy enough to please you. Find a home for yourself in one of the lovely flowers that grow down there; now I will set you down, and you can do whatever you like."

"That will be splendid!" said she, clapping her little hands.

There lay a great white marble column which had fallen to the ground and broken into three pieces, but between these grew the most beautiful white

WE WILL CALL YOU
MAYBLOSSOM

flowers. The swallow flew down with Thumbelina, and set her upon one of the broad leaves. But there, to her astonishment, she found a tiny little man sitting in the middle of the flower, as white and transparent as if he were made of glass; he had the prettiest golden crown on his head, and the most beautiful wings on his shoulders; he himself was no bigger than Thumbelina. He was the spirit of the flower. In each blossom there dwelt a tiny man or woman; but this one was the King over the others.

"How handsome he is!" whispered Thumbelina to the swallow.

The little Prince was very much frightened at the swallow, for in comparison with one so tiny as himself he seemed a giant. But when he saw Thumbelina, he was delighted, for she was the most beautiful girl he had ever seen. So he took his golden crown from off his head and put it on hers, asking her her name, and if she would be his wife, and then she would be Queen of all the flowers. Yes! he was a different kind of husband to the son of the toad and the mole with the black-velvet coat. So she said "Yes" to the noble Prince. And out of each flower came a lady and gentleman, each so tiny and pretty that it was a pleasure to see them. Each brought Thumbelina a present, but the best of all was a beautiful pair of wings which were fastened on to her back, and now she too could fly from flower to flower. They all wished her joy, and the swallow sat above in his nest and sang the wedding march, and that he did as well as he could; but he was sad, because he was very fond of Thumbelina and did not want to be separated from her.

"You shall not be called Thumbelina!" said the spirit of the flower to her; "that is an ugly name, and you are much too pretty for that. We will call you May Blossom."

"Farewell, farewell!" said the little swallow with a heavy heart, and flew away to farther lands, far, far away, right back to Denmark. There he had a little nest above a window, where his wife lived, who can tell fairy stories. "Tweet, tweet!" he sang to her. And that is the way we learnt the whole story.

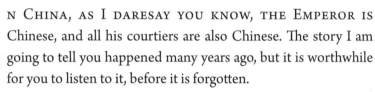

THE NIGHTINGALE

I n China, as I daresay you know, the Emperor is Chinese, and all his courtiers are also Chinese. The story I am going to tell you happened many years ago, but it is worthwhile for you to listen to it, before it is forgotten.

The Emperor's Palace was the most splendid in the world, all made of priceless porcelain, but so brittle and delicate that you had to take great care how you touched it. In the garden were the most beautiful flowers, and on the loveliest of them were tied silver bells which tinkled, so that if you passed you could not help looking at the flowers. Everything in the Emperor's garden was admirably arranged with a view to effect; and the garden was so large that even the gardener himself did not know where it ended. If you ever got beyond it, you came to a stately forest with great trees and deep lakes in it. The forest sloped down to the sea, which was a clear blue. Large ships could sail under the boughs of the trees, and in these trees there lived a Nightingale. She sang so beautifully that even the poor fisherman who had so much to do stood and listened when he came at night to cast his nets. "How beautiful it is!" he said; but he had to attend to his work, and forgot about the bird. But when she sang the next night and the fisherman came there again, he said the same thing, "How beautiful it is!"

From all the countries round came travellers to the Emperor's town, who were astonished at the Palace and the garden. But when they heard the Nightingale they all said, "This is the finest thing after all!"

The travellers told all about it when they went home, and learned scholars wrote many books upon the town, the Palace, and the garden. But they did not forget the Nightingale; she was praised the most, and all the poets composed splendid verses on the Nightingale in the forest by the deep sea.

The books were circulated throughout the world, and some of them reached the Emperor. He sat in his golden chair, and read and read. He nodded his head every moment, for he liked reading the brilliant accounts of the town, the Palace, and the garden. "But the Nightingale is better than all," he saw written.

"What is that?" said the Emperor. "I don't know anything about the Nightingale! Is there such a bird in my empire, and so near as in my garden? I have never heard it! Fancy reading for the first time about it in a book!"

And he called his First Lord to him. He was so proud that if anyone of lower rank than his own ventured to speak to him or ask him anything, he would say nothing but "P!" and that does not mean anything.

"Here is a most remarkable bird which is called a Nightingale!" said the Emperor. "They say it is the most glorious thing in my kingdom. Why has no one ever said anything to me about it?"

"I have never before heard it mentioned!" said the First Lord. "I will look for it and find it!"

But where was it to be found? The First Lord ran up and down stairs, through the halls and corridors; but none of those he met had ever heard of the Nightingale. And the First Lord ran again to the Emperor, and told him that it must be an invention on the part of those who had written the books.

"Your Imperial Majesty cannot really believe all that is written! There are some inventions called the Black Art!"

"But the book in which I read this," said the Emperor, "is sent me by His Great Majesty the Emperor of Japan; so it cannot be untrue, and I will hear the Nightingale! She must be here this evening! She has my gracious permission to appear, and if she does not, the whole Court shall be trampled under foot after supper!"

"Tsing pe!" said the First Lord; and he ran up and down stairs, through the halls and corridors, and half the Court ran with him, for they did not want to be trampled under foot. Everyone was asking after the wonderful Nightingale which all the world knew of, except those at Court.

At last they met a poor little girl in the kitchen, who said, "Oh! I know the Nightingale well. How she sings! I have permission to carry the scraps over from the Court meals to my poor sick mother, and when I am going home at night, tired and weary, and rest for a little in the wood, then I hear the Nightingale singing! It brings tears to my eyes, and I feel as if my mother were kissing me!"

"Little kitchenmaid!" said the First Lord, "I will give you a place in the kitchen, and you shall have leave to see the Emperor at dinner, if you can lead us to the Nightingale, for she is invited to come to Court this evening."

And so they all went into the wood where the Nightingale was wont to sing, and half the Court went too.

When they were on the way there they heard a cow mooing.

"Oh!" said the Courtiers, "now we have found her! What a wonderful power for such a small beast to have! I am sure we have heard her before!"

"No; that is a cow mooing!" said the little kitchenmaid. "We are still a long way off!"

Then the frogs began to croak in the marsh. "Splendid!" said the Chinese chaplain. "Now we hear her; it sounds like a little church bell!"

THE KITCHENMAID LISTENS TO THE NIGHTINGALE

"No, no; those are frogs!" said the little kitchenmaid. "But I think we shall soon hear her now!"

Then the Nightingale began to sing.

"There she is!" cried the little girl. "Listen! She is sitting there!" And she pointed to a little dark-grey bird up in the branches.

"Is it possible!" said the First Lord. "I should never have thought it! How ordinary she looks! She must surely have lost her feathers because she sees so many distinguished men round her!"

"Little Nightingale," called out the little kitchenmaid, "our Gracious Emperor wants you to sing before him!"

"With the greatest of pleasure!" said the Nightingale; and she sang so gloriously that it was a pleasure to listen.

"It sounds like glass bells!" said the First Lord. "And look how her little throat works! It is wonderful that we have never heard her before! She will be a great success at Court."

"Shall I sing once more for the Emperor?" asked the Nightingale, thinking that the Emperor was there.

"My esteemed little Nightingale," said the First Lord, "I have the great pleasure to invite you to Court this evening, where His Gracious Imperial Highness will be enchanted with your charming song!"

"It sounds best in the green wood," said the Nightingale; but still, she came gladly when she heard that the Emperor wished it. At the Palace everything was splendidly prepared. The porcelain walls and floors glittered in the light of many thousand gold lamps; the most gorgeous flowers which tinkled out well were placed in the corridors. There was such a hurrying and draft that all the bells jingled so much that one could not hear oneself speak. In the centre of the great hall where the Emperor sat was a golden perch, on which the Nightingale sat. The whole Court was there, and the little kitchenmaid was allowed to stand behind the door, now that she was a Court cook. Everyone was dressed in his best, and everyone was looking toward the little grey bird to whom the Emperor nodded.

The Nightingale sang so gloriously that the tears came into the Emperor's eyes and ran down his cheeks. Then the Nightingale sang even more beautifully; it went straight to all hearts. The Emperor was so delighted that he said she should wear his gold slipper round her neck. But the Nightingale thanked him, and said she had had enough reward already. "I have seen tears in the

Emperor's eyes—that is a great reward. An Emperor's tears have such power!" Then she sang again with her gloriously sweet voice.

"That is the most charming coquetry I have ever seen!" said all the ladies round. And they all took to holding water in their mouths that they might gurgle whenever anyone spoke to them. Then they thought themselves nightingales. Yes, the lackeys and chambermaids announced that they were pleased; which means a great deal, for they are the most difficult people of all to satisfy. In short, the Nightingale was a real success.

She had to stay at Court now; she had her own cage, and permission to walk out twice in the day and once at night.

She was given twelve servants, who each held a silken string which was fastened round her leg. There was little pleasure in flying about like this.

The whole town was talking about the wonderful bird, and when two people met each other one would say "Nightin," and the other "Gale," and then they would both sigh and understand one another. Yes, and eleven grocer's children were called after her, but not one of them could sing a note.

One day the Emperor received a large parcel on which was written "The Nightingale."

"Here is another new book about our famous bird!" said the Emperor.

But it was not a book, but a little mechanical toy, which lay in a box—an artificial nightingale which was like the real one, only that it was set all over with diamonds, rubies, and sapphires. When it was wound up, it could sing the piece the real bird sang, and moved its tail up and down, and glittered with silver and gold. Round its neck was a little collar on which was written, "The Nightingale of the Emperor of Japan is nothing compared to that of the Emperor of China."

"This is magnificent!" they all said, and the man who had brought the clockwork bird received on the spot the title of "Bringer of the Imperial First Nightingale."

"Now they must sing together; what a duet we shall have!"

THE PRESENT FROM THE EMPEROR OF JAPAN

And so they sang together, but their voices did not blend, for the real Nightingale sang in her way and the clockwork bird sang waltzes.

"It is not its fault!" said the bandmaster; "it keeps very good time and is quite after my style!"

Then the artificial bird had to sing alone. It gave just as much pleasure as the real one, and then it was so much prettier to look at; it sparkled like bracelets and necklaces. Three-and-thirty times it sang the same piece without being tired. People would like to have heard it again, but the Emperor thought that the living Nightingale should sing now—but where was she? No one had noticed that she had flown out of the open window away to her green woods.

"What *shall* we do!" said the Emperor.

And all the Court scolded, and said that the Nightingale was very ungrateful. "But we have still the best bird!" they said and the artificial bird had to sing again, and that was the thirty-fourth time they had heard the same piece. But they did not yet know it by heart; it was much too difficult. And the bandmaster praised the bird tremendously; yes, he assured them it was better than a real nightingale, not only because of its beautiful plumage and diamonds, but inside as well. "For see, my Lords and Ladies and your Imperial Majesty, with the real Nightingale one can never tell what will come out, but all is known about the artificial bird! You can explain it, you can open it and show people where the waltzes lie, how they go, and how one follows the other!"

"That's just what we think!" said everyone; and the bandmaster received permission to show the bird to the people the next Sunday. They should hear it sing, commanded the Emperor. And they heard it, and they were as pleased as if they had been intoxicated with tea, after the Chinese fashion, and they all said "Oh!" and held up their forefingers and nodded time. But the poor fishermen who had heard the real Nightingale said: "This one sings well enough, the tunes glide out; but there is something wanting—I don't know what!"

The real Nightingale was banished from the kingdom.

The artificial bird was put on silken cushions by the Emperor's bed, all the presents which it received, gold and precious stones, lay round it, and it was given the title of Imperial Night Singer, First from the left. For the Emperor counted that side as the more distinguished, being the side on which the heart is; the Emperor's heart is also on the left.

And the bandmaster wrote a work of twenty-five volumes about the artificial bird. It was so learned, long, and so full of the hardest Chinese words that everyone said they had read it and understood it; for once they had been very stupid about a book, and had been trampled under foot in consequence. So a whole year passed. The Emperor, the Court, and all the Chinese knew every note of the artificial bird's song by heart. But they liked it all the better for this; they could even sing with it, and they did. The street boys sang "Tra-la-la-la-la," and the Emperor sang too sometimes. It was indeed delightful.

But one evening, when the artificial bird was singing its best, and the Emperor lay in bed listening to it, something in the bird went crack. Something snapped! Whir-r-r! all the wheels ran down and then the music ceased. The Emperor sprang up, and had his physician summoned, but what could *he* do! Then the clockmaker came, and, after a great deal of talking and examining, he put the bird somewhat in order, but he said that it must be very seldom used as the works were nearly worn out, and it was impossible to put in new ones. Here was a calamity! Only once a year was the artificial bird allowed to sing, and even that was almost too much for it. But then the bandmaster made a little speech full of hard words, saying that it was just as good as before. And so, of course, it *was* just as good as before. So five years passed, and then a great sorrow came to the nation. The Chinese look upon their Emperor as everything, and now he was ill, and not likely to live it was said.

Already a new Emperor had been chosen, and the people stood outside in the street and asked the First Lord how the old Emperor was. "P!" said he, and shook his head.

Cold and pale lay the Emperor in his splendid great bed; the whole Court believed him dead, and one after the other left him to pay their respects to the new Emperor. Everywhere in the halls and corridors cloth was laid down so that no footstep could be heard, and everything was still—very, very still. And nothing came to break the silence.

The Emperor longed for something to come and relieve the monotony of this deathlike stillness. If only someone would speak to him! If only someone would sing to him. Music would carry his thoughts away, and would break the spell lying on him. The moon was streaming in at the open window; but that, too, was silent, quite silent.

"Music! music!" cried the Emperor. "You little bright golden bird, sing! do sing! I gave you gold and jewels; I have hung my gold slipper round your neck with my own hand—sing! do sing!" But the bird was silent. There was no one to wind it up, and so it could not sing. And all was silent, so terribly silent!

All at once there came in at the window the most glorious burst of song. It was the little living Nightingale, who, sitting outside on a bough, had heard the need of her Emperor and had come to sing to him of comfort and hope. And as she sang the blood flowed quicker and quicker in the Emperor's weak limbs, and life began to return.

"Thank you, thank you!" said the Emperor. "You divine little bird! I know you. I chased you from my kingdom, and you have given me life again! How can I reward you?"

"You have done that already!" said the Nightingale. "I brought tears to your eyes the first time I sang. I shall never forget that. They are jewels that rejoice a singer's heart. But now sleep and get strong again; I will sing you a lullaby." And the Emperor fell into a deep, calm sleep as she sang.

The sun was shining through the window when he awoke, strong and well. None of his servants had come back yet, for they thought he was dead. But the Nightingale sat and sang to him.

"You must always stay with me!" said the Emperor. "You shall sing whenever you like, and I will break the artificial bird into a thousand pieces."

"Don't do that!" said the Nightingale. "He did his work as long as he could. Keep him as you have done! I cannot build my nest in the Palace and live here; but let me come whenever I like. I will sit in the evening on the bough outside the window, and I will sing you something that will make you feel happy and grateful. I will sing of joy, and of sorrow; I will sing of the evil and the good

THE TRUE NIGHTINGALE SINGS TO THE EMPEROR

which lies hidden from you. The little songbird flies all around, to the poor fisherman's hut, to the farmer's cottage, to all those who are far away from you and your Court. I love your heart more than your crown, though that has about it a brightness as of something holy. Now I will sing to you again; but you must promise me one thing—"

"Anything!" said the Emperor, standing up in his Imperial robes, which he had himself put on, and fastening on his sword richly embossed with gold.

"One thing I beg of you! Don't tell anyone that you have a little bird who tells you everything. It will be much better not to!" Then the Nightingale flew away.

The servants came in to look at their dead Emperor.

The Emperor said, "Good-morning!"

HERMOD AND HADVOR[32]

NCE UPON A TIME THERE WERE A KING AND A QUEEN who had an only daughter, called Hadvor, who was fair and beautiful, and being an only child, was heir to the kingdom. The King and Queen had also a foster son, named Hermod, who was just about the same age as Hadvor, and was good-looking, as well as clever at most things. Hermod and Hadvor often played together while they were children, and liked each other so much that while they were still young they secretly pledged to someday marry to each other.

As time went on the Queen fell sick, and suspecting that it was her last illness, sent for the King to come to her. When he came she told him that she had not long to live, and therefore wished to ask one thing of him, which was, that if he married another wife he should promise to take no other one than the Queen of Hetland the Good. The King gave the promise, and thereafter the Queen died.

---

32 From the Icelandic.

Time went past, and the King, growing tired of living alone, fitted out his ship and sailed out to sea. As he sailed there came upon him so thick a mist that he altogether lost his bearings, but after long trouble he found land. There he laid his ship to, and went on shore all alone. After walking for some time he came to a forest, into which he went a little way and stopped. Then he heard sweet music from a harp, and went in the direction of the sound until he came to a clearing, and there he saw three women, one of whom sat on a golden chair, and was beautifully and grandly dressed; she held a harp in her hands, and was very sorrowful. The second was also finely dressed, but younger in appearance, and also sat on a chair, but it was not so grand as the first one's. The third stood beside them, and was very pretty to look at; she had a green cloak over her other clothes, and it was easy to see that she was maid to the other two.

After the King had looked at them for a little he went forward and saluted them. The one that sat on the golden chair asked him who he was and where he was going; and he told her all the story—how he was a king, and had lost his queen, and was now on his way to Hetland the Good, to ask the Queen of that country in marriage. She answered that fortune had contrived this wonderfully, for pirates had plundered Hetland and killed the King, and she had fled from the land in terror, and had come hither after great trouble, and she was the very person he was looking for, and the others were her daughter and maid. The King immediately asked her hand; she gladly received his proposal and accepted him at once. Thereafter they all set out, and made their way to the ship; and after that nothing is told of their voyage until the King reached his own country. There he made a great feast, and celebrated his marriage with this woman; and after that things are quiet for a time.

Hermod and Hadvor took but little notice of the Queen and her daughter, but, on the other hand, Hadvor and the Queen's maid, whose name was Olof, were very friendly, and Olof came often to visit Hadvor in her castle. Before long the King went out to war, and no sooner was he away than the Queen

The King finds the Queen of Hetland

came to talk with Hermod, and said that she wanted him to marry her daughter. Hermod told her straight and plain that he would not do so, at which the Queen grew terribly angry, and said that in that case neither should he have Hadvor, for she would now lay this spell on him, that he should go to a desert island and there be a lion by day and a man by night. He should also think always of Hadvor, which would cause him all the more sorrow, and from this spell he should never be freed until Hadvor burned the lion's skin, and that would not happen very soon.

As soon as the Queen had finished her speech Hermod replied that he also laid a spell on her, and that was, that as soon as he was freed from her enchantments she should become a rat and her daughter a mouse, and fight with each other in the hall until he killed them with his sword.

After this Hermod disappeared, and no one knew what had become of him; the Queen caused search to be made for him, but he could nowhere be found. One time, when Olof was in the castle beside Hadvor, she asked the Princess if she knew where Hermod had gone to. At this Hadvor became very sad, and said that she did not.

"I shall tell you then," said Olof, "for I know all about it.

"Hermod has disappeared through the wicked devices of the Queen, for she is a witch, and so is her daughter, though they have put on these beautiful forms. Because Hermod would not fall in with the Queen's plans, and marry her daughter, she has laid a spell on him, to go on an island and be a lion by day and a man by night, and never be freed from this until you burn the lion's skin. Besides," said Olof, "she has looked out a match for you; she has a brother in the Underworld, a three-headed Giant, whom she means to turn into a beautiful prince and get him married to you. This is no new thing for the Queen; she took me away from my parents' house and compelled me to serve her; but she has never done me any harm, for the green cloak I wear protects me against all mischief."

Hadvor now became still sadder than before at the thought of the marriage destined for her, and entreated Olof to think of some plan to save her.

"I think," said Olof, "that your wooer will come up through the floor of the castle to you, and so you must be prepared when you hear the noise of his coming and the floor begins to open, and have at hand blazing pitch, and pour plenty of it into the opening. That will prove too much for him."

About this time the King came home from his expedition, and thought it a great blow that no one knew what had become of Hermod; but the Queen consoled him as best she could, and after a time the King thought less about his disappearance.

Hadvor remained in her castle, and had made preparations to receive her wooer when he came. One night, not long after, a loud noise and rumbling was heard under the castle. Hadvor at once guessed what it was, and told her maids to be ready to help her. The noise and thundering grew louder and louder, until the floor began to open, whereupon Hadvor made them take the cauldron of pitch and pour plenty of it into the opening. With that the noises grew fainter and fainter, till at last they ceased altogether.

The next morning the Queen rose early, and went out to the Palace gate, and there she found her brother the Giant lying dead. She went up to him and said, "I pronounce this spell, that you become a beautiful prince, and that Hadvor shall be unable to say anything against the charges that I shall bring against her."

The body of the dead Giant now became that of a beautiful prince, and the Queen went in again.

"I don't think," said she to the King, "that your daughter is as good as she is said to be. My brother came and asked her hand, and she has had him put to death. I have just found his dead body lying at the Palace gate."

The King went along with the Queen to see the body, and thought it all very strange; so beautiful a youth, he said, would have been a worthy match for Hadvor, and he would readily have agreed to their marriage. The Queen asked leave to decide what Hadvor's punishment should be, which the King was very willing to allow, so as to escape from punishing his own daughter. The Queen's decision was that the King should make a big grave mound for her brother, and put Hadvor into it beside him.

Olof knew all the plans of the Queen, and went to tell the Princess what had been done, whereupon Hadvor earnestly entreated her to tell her what to do.

"First and foremost," said Olof, "you must get a wide cloak to wear over your other clothes, when you are put into the mound. The Giant's ghost will walk after you are both left together in there, and he will have two dogs along with him. He will ask you to cut pieces out of his legs to give to the dogs, but that you must not promise to do unless he tells you where Hermod has gone to, and tells you how to find him. He will then let you stand on his shoulders, so as to get out of the mound; but he means to cheat you all the same, and will catch you by the cloak to pull you back again; but you must take care to have the cloak loose on your shoulders, so that he will only get hold of that."

The mound was all ready now, and the Giant laid in it, and into it Hadvor also had to go without being allowed to make any defence. After they were both left there everything happened just as Olof had said. The prince became a Giant again, and asked Hadvor to cut the pieces out of his legs for the dogs; but she refused until he told her that Hermod was in a desert island, which she could not reach unless she took the skin off the soles of his feet and made shoes out of that; with these shoes she could travel both on land and sea. This Hadvor now did, and the Giant then let her get up on his shoulders to get out of the mound. As she sprang out he caught hold of her cloak; but she had taken care to let it lie loose on her shoulders, and so escaped.

She now made her way down to the sea, to where she knew there was the shortest distance over to the island in which Hermod was. This strait she easily crossed, for the shoes kept her up. On reaching the island she found a sandy beach all along by the sea, and high cliffs above. Nor could she see any way to get up these, and so, being both sad at heart and tired with the long journey, she lay down and fell asleep. As she slept she dreamed that a tall woman came to her and said, "I know that you are Princess Hadvor, and are searching for Hermod. He is on this island; but it will be hard for you to get to him if you have no one to help you, for you cannot climb the cliffs by your own strength. I have therefore let down a rope, by which you will be able to climb up; and as the island is so large that you might not find Hermod's dwelling place so easily, I lay down this clew beside you. You need only hold the end of the thread, and the clew will run on before and show you the way. I also lay this belt beside you, to put on when you awaken; it will keep you from growing faint with hunger."

The woman now disappeared, and Hadvor woke, and saw that all her dream had been true. The rope hung down from the cliff, and the clew and belt lay beside her. The belt she put on, the rope enabled her to climb up the cliff, and the clew led her on till she came to the mouth of a cave, which was not very big. She went into the cave, and saw there a low couch, under which she crept and lay down.

When evening came she heard the noise of footsteps outside, and became aware that the lion had come to the mouth of the cave, and shook itself there, after which she heard a man coming toward the couch. She was sure this was Hermod, because she heard him speaking to himself about his own condition, and calling to mind Hadvor and other things in the old days. Hadvor made no sign, but waited till he had fallen asleep, and then crept out and burned the lion's skin, which he had left outside. Then she went back into the cave and wakened Hermod, and they had a most joyful meeting.

In the morning they talked over their plans, and were most at a loss to know how to get out of the island. Hadvor told Hermod her dream, and said

Hadvor burns the Lion's Skin.

she suspected there was someone in the island who would be able to help them. Hermod said he knew of a Witch there, who was very ready to help anyone, and that the only plan was to go to her. So they went to the Witch's cave, and found her there with her fifteen young sons, and asked her to help them to get to the mainland.

"There are other things easier than that," said she, "for the Giant that was buried will be waiting for you, and will attack you on the way, as he has turned himself into a big whale. I shall lend you a boat, however, and if you meet the whale and think your lives are in danger, then you can name me by name."

They thanked her greatly for her help and advice, and set out from the island, but on the way they saw a huge fish coming toward them, with great splashing and dashing of waves. They were sure of what it was, and thought they had as good reason as ever they would have to call on the Witch, and so they did. The next minute they saw coming after them another huge whale, followed by fifteen smaller ones. All of these swam past the boat and went on to meet the whale. There was a fierce battle then, and the sea became so stormy that it was not very easy to keep the boat from being filled by the waves. After this fight had gone on for some time, they saw that the sea was dyed with blood; the big whale and the fifteen smaller ones disappeared, and they got to land safe and sound.

Now the story goes back to the King's hall, where strange things had happened in the meantime. The Queen and her daughter had disappeared, but a rat and a mouse were always fighting with each other there. Ever so many people had tried to drive them away, but no one could manage it. Thus some time went on, while the King was almost beside himself with sorrow and care for the loss of his Queen, and because these monsters destroyed all mirth in the hall.

One evening, however, while they all sat dull and down-hearted, in came Hermod with a sword by his side, and saluted the King, who received him with the greatest joy, as if he had come back from the dead. Before Hermod sat down, however, he went to where the rat and the mouse were fighting, and cut them in two with his sword. All were astonished then by seeing two witches lying dead on the floor of the hall.

Hermod now told the whole story to the King, who was very glad to be rid of such vile creatures. Next he asked for the hand of Hadvor, which the King readily gave him, and being now an old man, gave the kingdom to him as well; and so Hermod became King.

Olof married a good-looking nobleman, and that is the end of the story.

THE STEADFAST TIN-SOLDIER

HERE WERE ONCE UPON A TIME FIVE-AND-TWENTY tin-soldiers—all brothers, as they were made out of the same old tin spoon. Their uniform was red and blue, and they shouldered their guns and looked straight in front of them. The first words that they heard in this world, when the lid of the box in which they lay was taken off, were: "Hurrah, tin-soldiers!" This was exclaimed by a little boy, clapping his hands; they had been given to him because it was his birthday, and now he began setting them out on the table. Each soldier was exactly like the other in shape, except just one, who had been made last when the tin had run short; but there he stood as firmly on his one leg as the others did on two, and he is the one that became famous.

There were many other playthings on the table on which they were being set out, but the nicest of all was a pretty little castle made of cardboard, with windows through which you could see into the rooms. In front of the castle stood some little trees surrounding a tiny mirror which looked like a lake. Wax swans were floating about and reflecting themselves in it. That was all very pretty; but the most beautiful thing was a little lady, who stood in the open doorway. She was cut out of paper, but she had on a dress of the finest muslin, with a scarf of narrow blue ribbon round her shoulders, fastened in the middle with a glittering rose made of gold paper, which was as large as her head. The little lady was stretching out both her arms, for she was a Dancer, and was lifting up one leg so high in the air that the Tin-soldier couldn't find it anywhere, and thought that she, too, had only one leg.

"That's the wife for me!" he thought; "but she is so grand, and lives in a castle, whilst I have only a box with four-and-twenty others. This is no place for her! But I must make her acquaintance." Then he stretched himself out behind a snuff-box that lay on the table; from thence he could watch the dainty little lady, who continued to stand on one leg without losing her balance.

When the night came all the other tin-soldiers went into their box, and the people of the house went to bed. Then the toys began to play at visiting, dancing, and fighting. The tin-soldiers rattled in their box, for they wanted to be out too, but they could not raise the lid. The nutcrackers played at leap-frog, and the slate pencil ran about the slate; there was such a noise that the canary woke up and began to talk to them, in poetry too! The only two who did not stir from their places were the Tin-soldier and the little Dancer. She remained on tip-toe, with both arms outstretched; he stood steadfastly on his one leg, never moving his eyes from her face.

The clock struck twelve, and crack! off flew the lid of the snuff-box; but there was no snuff inside, only a little black imp—that was the beauty of it.

"Hullo, Tin-soldier!" said the imp. "Don't look at things that aren't intended for the likes of you!"

But the Tin-soldier took no notice, and seemed not to hear.

"Very well, wait till to-morrow!" said the imp.

When it was morning, and the children had got up, the Tin-soldier was put in the window; and whether it was the wind or the little black imp, I don't know, but all at once the window flew open and out fell the little Tin-soldier,

DON'T LOOK
AT THINGS THAT AREN'T
INTENDED FOR THE LIKES
OF YOU!

across

head over heels, from the third-story window! That was a terrible fall, I can tell you! He landed on his head with his leg in the air, his gun being wedged between two paving stones.

The nursery maid and the little boy came down at once to look for him, but, though they were so near him that they almost trod on him, they did not notice him. If the Tin-soldier had only called out "Here I am!" they must have found him; but he did not think it fitting for him to cry out, because he had on his uniform.

Soon it began to drizzle; then the drops came faster, and there was a regular downpour. When it was over, two little street boys came along.

"Just look!" cried one. "Here is a Tin-soldier! He shall sail up and down in a boat!"

·DOWN · THE · DRAIN·

So they made a little boat out of newspaper, put the Tin-soldier in it, and made him sail up and down the gutter; both the boys ran along beside him, clapping their hands. What great waves there were in the gutter, and what a swift current! The paper boat tossed up and down, and in the middle of the stream it went so quick that the Tin-soldier trembled; but he remained steadfast, showed no emotion, looked straight in front of him, shouldering his gun. All at once the boat passed under a long tunnel that was as dark as his box had been.

"Where can I be coming now?" he wondered. "Oh, dear! This is the black imp's fault! Ah, if only the little lady were sitting beside me in the boat, it might be twice as dark for all I should care!"

Suddenly there came along a great water rat that lived in the tunnel.

"Have you a passport?" asked the rat. "Out with your passport!"

But the Tin-soldier was silent, and grasped his gun more firmly.

The boat sped on, and the rat behind it. Ugh! how he showed his teeth, as he cried to the chips of wood and straw: "Hold him, hold him! he has not paid the toll! He has not shown his passport!"

But the current became swifter and stronger. The Tin-soldier could already see daylight where the tunnel ended; but in his ears there sounded a roaring enough to frighten any brave man. Only think! at the end of the tunnel the gutter discharged itself into a great canal; that would be just as dangerous for him as it would be for us to go down a waterfall.

Now he was so near to it that he could not hold on any longer. On went the boat, the poor Tin-soldier keeping himself as stiff as he could: no one should say of him afterward that he had flinched. The boat whirled three, four times round, and became filled to the brim with water: it began to sink! The Tin-soldier was standing up to his neck in water, and deeper and deeper sank the boat, and softer and softer grew the paper; now the water was over his head. He was thinking of the pretty little Dancer, whose face he should never see again, and there sounded in his ears, over and over again:

> "Forward, forward, soldier bold!
> Death's before thee, grim and cold!"

The paper came in two, and the soldier fell—but at that moment he was swallowed by a great fish.

Oh! how dark it was inside, even darker than in the tunnel, and it was really very close quarters! But there the steadfast little Tin-soldier lay full length, shouldering his gun.

Up and down swam the fish, then he made the most dreadful contortions, and became suddenly quite still. Then it was as if a flash of lightning had passed through him; the daylight streamed in, and a voice exclaimed, "Why, here is the little Tin-soldier!" The fish had been caught, taken to market, sold, and brought into the kitchen, where the cook had cut it open with a great knife. She took up the soldier between her finger and thumb, and carried him into the room, where everyone wanted to see the hero who had been found inside a fish; but the Tin-soldier was not at all proud. They put him on the table, and—no, but what strange things do happen in this world!—the Tin-soldier was in the same room

in which he had been before! He saw the
same children, and the same toys on the
table; and there was the same grand castle with the pretty little Dancer. She was
still standing on one leg with the other
high in the air; she too was steadfast.
That touched the Tin-soldier, he was
nearly going to shed tin-tears; but that
would not have been fitting for a soldier.
He looked at her, but she said nothing.

All at once one of the little boys
took up the Tin-soldier, and threw him
into the stove, giving no reasons; but
doubtless the little black imp in the
snuff-box was at the bottom of this too.

There the Tin-soldier lay, and felt a
heat that was truly terrible; but whether he was suffering from actual fire, or
from the ardour of his passion, he did
not know. All his colour had disappeared; whether this had happened on

his travels or whether it was the result of trouble, who can say? He looked at
the little lady, she looked at him, and he felt that he was melting; but he remained steadfast, with his gun at his shoulder. Suddenly a door opened, the
draft caught up the little Dancer, and off she flew like a sylph to the Tin-soldier
in the stove, burst into flames—and that was the end of her! Then the Tin-soldier melted down into a little lump, and when next morning the maid was
taking out the ashes, she found him in the shape of a heart. There was nothing
left of the little Dancer but her gilt rose, burnt as black as a cinder.

BLOCKHEAD-HANS

AR AWAY IN THE COUNTRY LAY AN OLD MANOR HOUSE where lived an old squire who had two sons. They thought themselves so clever, that if they had known only half of what they did know, it would have been quite enough. They both wanted to marry the King's daughter, for she had proclaimed that she would have for her husband the man who knew best how to choose his words.

Both prepared for the wooing a whole week, which was the longest time allowed them; but, after all, it was quite long enough, for they both had preparatory knowledge, and everyone knows how useful that is. One knew the whole Latin dictionary and also three years' issue of the daily paper of the town off by heart, so that he could repeat it all backward or forward as you pleased. The other had worked at the laws of corporation, and knew by heart what every member of the corporation ought to know, so that he thought he could quite well speak on State matters and give his opinion. He understood, besides this, how to embroider braces with roses and other flowers, and scrolls, for he was very ready with his fingers.

"I shall win the king's daughter!" they both cried.

·then·they·oiled·
the·corners·of·their·mouths

Their old father gave each of them a fine horse; the one who knew the
dictionary and the daily paper by heart had a black horse, while the other who
was so clever at corporation law had a milk-white one. Then they oiled the
corners of their mouths so that they might be able to speak more fluently. All
the servants stood in the courtyard and saw them mount their steeds, and
here by chance came the third brother; for the squire had three sons, but nobody counted him with his brothers, for he was not so learned as they were,
and he was generally called "Blockhead-Hans."

"Oh, oh!" said Blockhead-Hans. "Where are you off to? You are in your
Sunday-best clothes!"

"We are going to Court, to woo the Princess! Don't you know what is
known throughout all the country side?" And they told him all about it.

"Hurrah! I'll go too!" cried Blockhead-Hans; and the brothers laughed at him and rode off.

"Dear father!" cried Blockhead-Hans, "I must have a horse too. What a desire for marriage has seized me! If she will have me, she *will* have me, and if she won't have me, I will have her."

"Stop that nonsense!" said the old man. "I will not give you a horse. *You* can't speak; *you* don't know how to choose your words. Your brothers! Ah! they are very different lads!"

"Well," said Blockhead-Hans, "if I can't have a horse, I will take the goat which is mine; he can carry me!"

And he did so. He sat astride on the goat, struck his heels into its side, and went rattling down the high-road like a hurricane.

Hoppetty hop! what a ride! "Here I come!" shouted Blockhead-Hans, singing so that the echoes were roused far and near. But his brothers were riding slowly in front. They were not speaking, but they were thinking over all the good things they were going to say, for everything had to be thought out.

"Hullo!" bawled Blockhead-Hans, "here I am! Just look what I found on the road!'—and he showed them a dead crow which he had picked up.

"Blockhead!" said his brothers, "what are you going to do with it?"

"With the crow? I shall give it to the Princess!"

"Do so, certainly!" they said, laughing loudly and riding on.

"Slap! bang! here I am again! Look what I have just found! You don't find such things every day on the road!"

And the brothers turned round to see what in the world he could have found.

"Blockhead!" said they, "that is an old wooden shoe without the top! Are you going to send that, too, to the Princess?"

"Of course I shall!" returned Blockhead-Hans; and the brothers laughed and rode on a good way.

"Slap! bang! here I am!" cried Blockhead-Hans; "better and better—it is really famous!"

"What have you found now?" asked the brothers. "Oh," said Blockhead-Hans, "it is really too good! How pleased the Princess will be!"

"Why!" said the brothers, "this is pure mud, straight from the ditch."

"Of course it is!" said Blockhead-Hans, "and it is the best kind! Look how it runs through one's fingers!" and, so saying, he filled his pocket with the mud.

But the brothers rode on so fast that dust and sparks flew all around, and they reached the gate of the town a good hour before Blockhead-Hans. Here came the suitors numbered according to their arrival, and they were ranged in rows, six in each row, and they were so tightly packed that they could not move their arms. This was a very good thing, for otherwise they would have torn each other in pieces, merely because the one was in front of the other.

All the country people were standing round the King's throne, and were crowded together in thick masses almost out of the windows to see the Princess receive the suitors; and as each one came into the room all his fine phrases went out like a candle!

"It doesn't matter!" said the Princess. "Away! out with him!"

At last she came to the row in which the brother who knew the dictionary by heart was, but he did not know it any longer; he had quite forgotten it in the rank and file. And the floor creaked, and the ceiling was all made of glass mirrors, so that he saw himself standing on his head, and by each window were standing three reporters and an editor; and each of them was writing down what was said, to publish it in the paper that came out and was sold at the street corners for a penny. It was fearful, and they had made up the fire so hot that it was grilling.

"It is hot in here, isn't it!" said the suitor.

"Of course it is!" My father is roasting young chickens to-day!" said the Princess.

"Ahem!" There he stood like an idiot. He was not prepared for such a speech; he did not know what to say, although he wanted to say something witty. "Ahem!"

"It doesn't matter!" said the Princess. "Take him out!" and out he had to go.

Now the other brother entered.

"How hot it is!" he said.

"Of course! We are roasting young chickens to-day!" remarked the Princess.

"How do you—um!" he said, and the reporters wrote down. "How do you—um."

"It doesn't matter!" said the Princess. "Take him out!"

Now Blockhead-Hans came in; he rode his goat right into the hall.

"I say! How roasting hot it is here!" said he.

"Of course! I am roasting young chickens to-day!" said the Princess.

"That's good!" replied Blockhead-Hans; "then can I roast a crow with them?"

"With the greatest of pleasure!" said the Princess; "but have you anything you can roast them in? for I have neither pot nor saucepan."

"Oh, rather!" said Blockhead-Hans. "Here is a cooking implement with tin rings," and he drew out the old wooden shoe, and laid the crow in it.

"That is quite a meal!" said the Princess; "but where shall we get the soup from?"

"I've got that in my pocket!" said Blockhead-Hans. "I have so much that I can quite well throw some away!" and he poured some mud out of his pocket.

"I like you!" said the Princess. "You can answer, and you can speak, and I will marry you; but do you know that every word which we are saying and have said has been taken down and will be in the paper to-morrow? By each window do you see there are standing three reporters and an old editor, and this old editor is the worst, for he doesn't understand anything!" but she only said this to tease Blockhead-Hans. And the reporters giggled, and each dropped a blot of ink on the floor.

"Ah! are those the great people?" said Blockhead-Hans. "Then I will give the editor the best!" So saying, he turned his pockets inside out, and threw the mud right in his face.

"That was neatly done!" said the Princess. "I couldn't have done it; but I will soon learn how to!"

Blockhead-Hans became King, got a wife and a crown, and sat on the throne; and this we have still damp from the newspaper of the editor and the reporters—and they are not to be believed for a moment.

A STORY ABOUT
A DARNING-NEEDLE

HERE WAS ONCE A DARNING-NEEDLE WHO THOUGHT
herself so fine that she believed she was an embroidery-needle.
"Take great care to hold me tight!" said the Darning-needle to
the Fingers who were holding her. "Don't let me fall! If I once
fall on the ground I shall never be found again, I am so fine!"

"It is all right!" said the Fingers, seizing her round the waist.

"Look, I am coming with my train!" said the Darning-needle as she drew a
long thread after her; but there was no knot at the end of the thread.

The Fingers were using the needle on the cook's shoe. The upper leather
was unstitched and had to be sewn together.

"This is common work!" said the Darning-needle. "I shall never get
through it. I am breaking! I am breaking!" And in fact she did break. "Didn't I
tell you so!" said the Darning-needle. "I am too fine!"

"Now she is good for nothing!" said the Fingers; but they had to hold her tight while the cook dropped some sealing-wax on the needle and stack it in the front of her dress.

"Now I am a breast-pin!" said the Darning-needle. "I always knew I should be promoted. When one is something, one will become something!" And she laughed to herself; you can never see when a Darning-needle is laughing. Then she sat up as proudly as if she were in a State coach, and looked all round her.

"May I be allowed to ask if you are gold?" she said to her neighbour, the Pin. "You have a very nice appearance, and a peculiar head; but it is too small! You must take pains to make it grow, for it is not everyone who has a head of sealing-wax." And so saying the Darning-needle raised herself up so proudly that she fell out of the dress, right into the sink which the cook was rinsing out.

"Now I am off on my travels!" said the Darning-needle. "I do hope I sha'n't get lost!" She did indeed get lost.

"I am too fine for this world!" said she as she lay in the gutter; "but I know who I am, and that is always a little satisfaction!"

"And the Darning-needle kept her proud bearing and did not lose her good-temper.

All kinds of things swam over her—shavings, bits of straw, and scraps of old newspapers.

"Just look how they sail along!" said the Darning-needle. "They don't know what is underneath them! Here I am sticking fast! There goes a shaving thinking of nothing in the world but of itself, a mere chip! There goes a straw—well, how it does twist and twirl, to be sure! Don't think so much about yourself, or you will be knocked against a stone. There floats a bit of newspaper. What is written on it is long ago forgotten, and yet how proud it is! I am sitting patient and quiet. I know who I am, and that is enough for me!"

One day something thick lay near her which glittered so brightly that the Darning-needle thought it must be a diamond. But it was a bit of bottle-glass, and because it sparkled the Darning-needle spoke to it, and gave herself out as a breast-pin.

"No doubt you are a diamond?"

"Yes, something of that kind!" And each believed that the other was something very costly; and they both said how very proud the world must be of them.

"I have come from a lady's work-box," said Darning-needle, "and this lady was a cook; she had five fingers on each hand; anything so proud as these fingers I have never seen! And yet they were only there to take me out of the work-box and to put me back again!"

"Were they of noble birth, then?" asked the bit of bottle-glass.

"Of noble birth!" said the Darning-needle; "no indeed, but proud! They were five brothers, all called "Fingers." They held themselves proudly one against the other, although they were of different sizes. The outside one, the Thumb, was short and fat; he was outside the rank, and had only one bend in his back, and could only make one bow; but he said that if he were cut off from a man that he was no longer any use as a soldier. Dip-into-Everything, the second finger, dipped into sweet things as well as sour things, pointed to the sun and the moon, and guided the pen when they wrote. Longman, the third, looked at the others over his shoulder. Goldband, the fourth, had a gold sash round his waist; and little Playman did nothing at all, and was the more proud. There was too much ostentation, and so I came away."

"And now we are sitting and shining here!" said the bit of bottle-glass.

At that moment more water came into the gutter; it streamed over the edges and washed the bit of bottle-glass away.

"Ah! now he has been promoted!" said the Darning-needle. "I remain here; I am too fine. But that is my pride, which is a sign of respectability!" And she sat there very proudly, thinking lofty thoughts.

"I really believe I must have been born a sunbeam, I am so fine! It seems to me as if the sunbeams were always looking under the water for me. Ah, I am so fine that my own mother cannot find me! If I had my old eye which broke off, I believe I could weep; but I can't—it is not fine to weep!"

One day two street urchins were playing and wading in the gutter, picking up old nails, pennies, and such things. It was rather dirty work, but it was a great delight to them.

"Oh, oh!" cried out one, as he pricked himself with the Darning-needle; "he is a fine fellow though!"

"I am not a fellow; I am a young lady!" said the Darning-needle; but no one heard. The sealing-wax had gone, and she had become quite black; but black makes one look very slim, and so she thought she was even finer than before.

"Here comes an egg-shell sailing along!" said the boys, and they stuck the Darning-needle into the egg-shell.

"The walls white and I black—what a pretty contrast it makes!" said the Darning-needle. "Now I can be seen to advantage! If only I am not seasick! I should give myself up for lost!"

But she was not seasick, and did not give herself up.

"It is a good thing to be steeled against seasickness; here one has indeed an advantage over man! Now my qualms are over. The finer one is the more one can bear."

"Crack!" said the egg-shell as a wagon-wheel went over it.

"Oh! how it presses!" said the Darning-needle. "I shall indeed be seasick now. I am breaking!" But she did not break, although the wagon-wheel went over her; she lay there at full length, and there she may lie.